THE MASTER'S APPRENTICE

A Retelling of the Faust Legend

OTHER TITLES BY OLIVER PÖTZSCH

The Hangman's Daughter Series

The Hangman's Daughter

The Dark Monk

The Beggar King

The Poisoned Pilgrim

The Werewolf of Bamberg

The Play of Death

The Council of Twelve

The Black Musketeers Series

Book of the Night

Sword of Power

Knight Kyle and the Magic Silver Lance

Holy Rage

THE MASTER'S APPRENTICE

Translated by Lisa Reinhardt

Oliver Pötzsch

AMAZON **CROSSING**

Text copyright © 2018 by Oliver Pötzsch and Ullstein Buchverlage GmbH

Translation copyright © 2020 by Lisa Reinhardt

Previously published as *Der Spielmann: Die Geschichte des Johann Georg Faustus 1* by Ullstein Buchverlage GmbH in Germany in 2018. Translated from German by Lisa Reinhardt. First published in English by Amazon Crossing in 2020.

Published by Amazon Crossing, Seattle

www.apub.com

ISBN-13: 9781542009980

ISBN-10: 1542009987

Cover design by M. S. Corley

Printed in the United States of America

For Aliahmad Alizade:
as clever and ambitious as Faust, and as lovable and
buoyant as Margarethe.
On winding roads to the finish line.

These people never smell the old rat, e'en when he has them by the collar.

—Johann Wolfgang von Goethe,
Faust, Part I (translated by Charles T. Brooks)

HISTORICAL NOTE

AROUND THE YEAR 1500, A MAN WE KNOW VERY LITTLE ABOUT traveled the German empire; the few sources and countless myths surrounding this man have led historians to believe that he really existed. He was the greatest magician of his time, and a con artist, astrologer, and charlatan. He was as clever and learned as a dozen scholars and as cunning as the Borgias. Not long after his violent death, a book was written about him, which many consider the first German bestseller. Playwrights including Christopher Marlowe and Johann Wolfgang von Goethe wrote dramas about him, and he became a popular character in puppet shows. To this day he is the symbol of the ambitious, restless individual who is prepared to make a deal with the devil to gain fame and fortune—but ultimately pays with his soul.

His name was Johann Georg Faustus.

This is his true story.

Prologue

IN THE FALL THAT THE CHILDREN DISAPPEARED, THE JUG-glers came to town.

From an alcove in the upper city gate, little Johann stood with his mouth open, watching the boisterous, dancing, singing train of colorful people. Like a small army, they crossed the drawbridge spanning the boggy moat, marched through the wide-open gate, and filled Knittlingen with life. At the front of the train, two dark-skinned men were doing cartwheels, followed by a handful of musicians with tabor pipes, bagpipes, and tambourines. Next came masked acrobats, a hunchbacked dwarf in a fool's costume, sword-wielding show fighters, and a real-life shaggy bear, which a giant was leading by a chain. Johann had never seen such splendor! Almost as if the emperor himself had traveled to the small town in the Palatinate. The huddled stone houses suddenly seemed to glow in a strange light, and Johann smelled something new and tantalizing—the scent of the wide world.

One after another the jugglers moved past him, followed by a crowd of laughing children who had been longing for this day as much as Johann had. One of the acrobats winked at him; someone laughed and gave him a nudge that almost tripped him. Johann realized he'd been so busy gaping at the jugglers that he hadn't noticed he was stepping out onto the road. Wagon wheels rolled past him within a hair's breadth, leaving deep furrows in the ground, which was still wet from the last rain. Cold autumn fog crept down from the wooded hills surrounding the town, but Johann didn't feel it. He couldn't take his eyes off the noisy, never-ending caravan of people, carts, horses, and oxen pouring into town.

Where do they all come from? he wondered. *From faraway Nuremberg? From foreign lands beyond the Alps—or even beyond the ocean? Where sea serpents, lions, and dragons live . . .*

Johann's world didn't extend beyond the hills of the Kraichgau. Behind those hills began the world of myths, fairy tales, and legends. Whenever his mother found the strength, she told him stories: stories of the sleeping emperor Barbarossa; of knights, gnomes, and fairy queens; of the boogeyman in the woods; of imperial diets in Augsburg and Regensburg; and of grand feasts. Johann would sit in her lap and listen, entranced by her soft voice.

After the jugglers came the itinerant merchants, some pulling carts while others carried their goods bundled on their backs. Every year, on the day of Saints Simon and Jude, the merchants set up their stalls along Market Street, which led from the upper city gate to Saint Leonhard's Church. The autumn market was Knittlingen's biggest fair—even bigger than the Cantate market in spring. Peddlers came from Bretten, Pforzheim, and even Heidelberg to sell their wares.

Johann had been looking forward to this day for weeks. He was eight years old, and last year's autumn market was nothing but a faint memory. He'd taken up position at the city gate early this morning so he wouldn't miss the arrival of any artists or merchants, but only now, as lunchtime neared, was the town truly starting to get busy. When the last peddler had passed through the gate, Johann followed the caravan into town. Hawkers fought over the best spots near the church; a bearded, already-drunken itinerant preacher announced the imminent end of the world from atop a wine barrel; musicians played dancing tunes; the first cask was tapped with loud hammering outside the Lion Inn. The air smelled of beer mash, cider, horse dung, smoke, and delicious cooking smells from the many street kitchens. And under all that lay the first hint of snow. Peasants said that on Saints Simon and Jude Day, winter knocked at the door.

The whole of Knittlingen had spruced up for this day. The wealthier residents wore their best Sunday frock coats and fustian shirts; the women covered their hair with skillfully tied scarves. Johann struggled to make his way through the crowd of bickering, laughing, and bartering grown-ups. Every now and then he passed other children he knew: the baker's red-haired twins, Josef and Max;

the blacksmith's broad-shouldered son, who was as strong as an ox at twelve years of age; and short, skinny Hans from the Lion Inn. But as usual, they avoided Johann or whispered behind his back as soon as he'd walked past them. Johann was so used to it that he hardly noticed. Only sometimes, when he roamed the woods around Knittlingen alone with his dreams, would he feel sad.

His mother told him not to mind the other children. He was different— smarter, brighter than them. Of noble blood, she'd once told him, though Johann didn't understand what she meant.

Johann had quickly grown bored at the German school he attended over at the hostel. While the rest of the students struggled with math, German, and the few scraps of Latin from the catechism, learning came easily to Johann. Sometimes he even corrected the teacher, a bitter old man who doubled as Knittlingen's sacristan. Johann often wanted to dig deeper, asking about foreign countries, the phases of the moon, the force of water—but no matter what he asked, the old man never had an answer. And when the other boys beat up Johann, the teacher just stood by, trying to suppress a grin.

"Watch where you're going, midget! If you step on my toes again, I'll turn your smart-aleck face to mush."

Ludwig, who was two years older and almost two heads taller than Johann, and the son of the Knittlingen prefect, punched him in the stomach. Johann gasped and held his belly but, thinking of his mother's words, didn't fight back. If he was truly of noble blood, then why had God made him so darn scrawny? He would gladly give some of his brains for more muscles—the only currency that counted for anything among children.

"Piss off!" Ludwig snarled and picked a piece of smoked sausage from between his teeth. Fat was running down his chin. "Go wipe your ass with books instead of standing around in people's way!"

Johann said nothing and took to his heels before Ludwig could punch him again.

At last he'd elbowed his way to the small square in front of the church, where the jugglers had set up their stage using wooden planks and four barrels and had begun performing their tricks. One musician started a drumroll while another struck a cymbal to announce the next act. Jugglers threw colorful wooden balls and burning torches through the air, catching them at the very last moment— much to the pleasant horror of the Knittlingers.

Johann applauded the jugglers eagerly, as well as the following act, a hunch-backed dwarf performing raunchy poems about wine, women, and song until a giant dipped him into a tankard as big as a barrel. The audience hooted with laughter, and Johann didn't hear the soft voice beside him. Then someone pulled on his ear, and he started with fright. He thought it was Ludwig, ready for another round.

"Hey, are you deaf? Did one of the jugglers cast a spell on you and turn you to stone?"

Johann spun around and smiled with relief. Standing in front of him was Margarethe, Ludwig's younger sister. She wore a gray dress with a white apron, its hem already spattered with dung. Her flaxen hair looked wild and windswept, as usual. Margarethe was one of the few children in Knittlingen who liked Johann and spent time with him. Twice already she'd saved him from the other boys by threatening to tell her father. Even Ludwig listened to her. Johann had to pay for her kindness with double beatings afterward, but it didn't hurt as much as it normally did. He'd simply close his eyes and think of Margarethe's hair glowing like wheat in the summer sun. However, there was one problem: whenever Margarethe spoke to him, his mouth appeared to be sealed—it was jinxed! Now, too, he couldn't get out a single word.

"You like the jugglers, don't you?" Margarethe asked and bit into a juicy red apple.

Johann nodded silently, and Margarethe continued as she chewed: "Did you know that jugglers and musicians are children of the devil?" She gave a shudder. "That's what the church says. Whoever dances to their music they lead straight to hell." She lowered her voice and made the sign of the cross. "Perhaps they took the children, too. I wouldn't be surprised."

"Don't talk nonsense," said Johann. "The wolves took them, even the hunts-men say so. And they must know!"

Despite the cheering and laughter, a chill suddenly ran down his spine as though he were standing alone in the forest. Four children had gone missing in recent weeks: seven-year-old Fritz from Knittlingen, his five-year-old brother, and two girls from neighboring Bretten. The two Bretten girls had been playing in the woods; Fritz, the butcher's boy, had disappeared from Marktgasse Lane, and his brother, little Peter, had been herding a pig in nearby Eichenloh Forest. The sow had arrived home alone. Some folks said wild beasts had killed the children. Others said there were hungry and ruthless outlaws living in the woods who preferred the tender flesh of children to that of poached deer. Someone had seen smoke rise up from the edge of the distant forest on the hills; apparently, a whiff of burning meat had been in the air.

Johann clenched his teeth and silently stared at the jugglers on stage. Suddenly the smell from the street kitchens made him feel sick.

Burning meat . . .

A murmur went through the crowd, rousing him from his thoughts. Margarethe squeezed his hand, and he gave another start. He shuddered and couldn't tell whether it was because of Margarethe's touch or because of the missing children.

Or because of *him*.

"Didn't I tell you?" whispered Margarethe. "Just look at him! He must be straight from hell."

The man stepping onto the stage indeed looked like a demon incarnate. He was tall and haggard and wore a black-and-red-striped coat billowing behind him like the wings of a bat. His face was as pale as though there was no blood in him, his nose sharp like the beak of a bird of prey. He wore a wide black felt hat with a red feather, like those of traveling scholars.

Most frightening of all were his eyes, gleaming black and deep like pools in a swamp. To Johann they seemed like the eyes of a man much older than their owner seemed to be. When those eyes moved across the crowd, everyone fell silent. For a brief moment, Johann thought he could feel the man's gaze like fingers reaching out to touch him. Then the strange man slowly and ceremoniously raised his head and looked up at the cloudy sky. A light drizzle set in.

"The stars," he began in a voice that was at once quiet and penetrating, audible across the whole church square. His accent was slightly foreign, soft, like that of travelers from beyond the Rhine.

"The stars don't lie! They're invisible during the day, and yet they are there. They shine above us, guide our path—a path that has been predestined for each one of us." He paused dramatically, his eyes moving across the crowd again. "*Ah oui, c'est vrai!* I can read those paths for you. I am a master of the seven arts and keeper of the seven times seven seals! I'm a doctor of the university of black magic in Krakow."

"A sorcerer," Margarethe whispered. "I knew it!"

Johann said nothing and waited for the mysterious stranger to continue. The man now addressed his audience with his arms outstretched, like a priest.

"Is there anyone who would like to know their future?" he asked loudly. "One kreuzer per question." He gave a thin smile. "If I foretell your imminent death, the answer is free."

A few people laughed, but it sounded hollow and nervous. A tense silence had descended upon the square. Finally a young, sturdy farmer's son raised his arm, and the foreigner asked him up on stage.

"What would you like to know?" asked the magician as the trembling young man handed over a coin.

"I, well . . . ," the peasant said awkwardly. "My Elsbeth and me, we've been together for over a year. But the dear Lord still hasn't granted us a child. I'd like to know if fate will smile upon us."

The foreigner took the man's hand, which was calloused from laboring in the fields, and bent over it. Johann thought it looked as though he sniffed the hand, even licked and tasted it like an animal would a salty rock. A considerable amount of time passed as the magician ran his fingers across the young man's palm, murmuring almost inaudibly. Finally he straightened back up.

"Your wife is going to carry your child before next spring. And it will be a boy! He'll be healthy and strong, born under the constellation of Pisces. The stars have spoken!"

The strange man raised his hands and—seemingly out of nowhere—a black raven flew up into the sky. The crowd gasped with surprise, and somewhere at the back, an elderly maidservant fainted.

Bowing and scraping, the farmer's son left the stage, and another nervous client took his place. Johann watched with excitement as the creepy stranger foretold a good harvest, a successful house build, the best day for sowing, and three more healthy sons and daughters for Knittlingen. Two crows flew up from his previously empty hand, playing cards with mysterious blood-red symbols tumbled to the ground out of nowhere, and he pulled a real black cat out of his hat. Johann was so captivated that he almost forgot to breathe. He'd never seen anything like it. This man was a real magician! He'd cast a spell on all of them.

At last the show was over. The foreigner took a bow and strode gracefully off the stage. The acrobats took his place and started to perform their tricks. But no matter how high they leaped, no matter how many somersaults they tumbled,

Johann now found their show dull. He had seen true magic, had caught a glimpse of another world beyond the earthly world he knew! And now it was already over? Johann trembled with disappointment. Not even Margarethe's presence cheered him up. She was still beside him, holding his hand. The funny harlequins and jugglers seemed to appeal to her much more than the scary magician had.

"How did he do it?" muttered Johann again and again, mostly to himself. "How did he do it? How did he make the raven and crows fly up, and where did the cat come from? What's his secret?"

"Ravens, crows, black cats—I told you he's in league with the devil," groused Margarethe without taking her eyes off the jugglers. "And now hush or I'll have nightmares about that man. Brr! I only hope he leaves town today."

Johann was shocked by the thought. If the mysterious stranger left town today, Johann would never find out what lay behind his tricks! He looked around. Where had the man gone? Johann couldn't see him next to the stage, where the other jugglers waited for their turn. Had he already left?

Johann let go of Margarethe's hand and made his way toward the stage. Margarethe was focused on the acrobats and didn't even notice him leaving. He turned left and walked around the church. It was much quieter away from Market Street. A blind beggar tapped his stick along the dirty cobblestones; a drunken man vomited in a corner. No one else was in sight. Gray autumn fog seeped through the lanes. It almost seemed to Johann it was thicker here than on the other, busier side of the church. Viscous.

Then he saw the wagon.

It stood a little off to the side, next to the empty town hall, and was covered with a dirty canvas embroidered with strange symbols and runes Johann couldn't read. A tired-looking old horse was munching on barley from a bucket tied around its neck. On the wagon's outside wall above the box seat hung a large, rusty cage that held two crows and a raven. The cage creaked and swayed when the birds moved.

How did he do it? How did he make the raven appear?

Entranced, Johann walked toward the birds as they flapped their wings restlessly. What if they were enchanted? He tiptoed quietly toward the cage, reached out his hand—

"If you're hungry, let me warn you: those birds are tough. And they dissolve in your stomach and return to me, their creator. You wouldn't find them very satisfying."

Johann spun around and looked into the face of the pale magician, who was standing right behind him, looking down at him. How could he not have noticed the man approaching? Was that another spell?

The man frowned at first, then his lips twisted into a smile. Johann saw small, sharp teeth, like those of a predator.

"Oh, it's the boy from the front row." The man's eyes twinkled with amusement. "I could have fitted a barn inside your gaping mouth." He leaned down to Johann, who thought he could smell a faint waft of sulfur. "How old are you, boy?"

"I . . . I'm eight," Johann said hoarsely, feeling very uncomfortable. He thought the air suddenly grew much colder; it felt like the middle of winter. The music and noise from the fair seemed to come from far away, as if from the other side of a heavy door.

"Hmm . . ." The man tilted his head to one side, just like the birds in the cage beside him. Then, after what felt like an eternity, he straightened up to his full height.

"And what's your name?" he asked abruptly.

"I . . . My name is Johann Georg, son of Jörg Gerlach, the farmer," replied Johann. "But my mother calls me Faustus."

"Faustus, I see . . . What a beautiful yet strange name." The man gave a quick smile. For a moment Johann thought the stranger's black eyes flashed, like sheet lightning behind storm clouds. "Then I'm sure you know the meaning of this Latin word?"

"It means 'the lucky one,'" Johann replied eagerly. "Or 'the bearer of luck,' 'the blessed one.' My mother always says I was born under a lucky star. She believes fate has great plans for me." He shrugged. "Though I don't really know what she means by that. She says I'm of noble blood."

"Of noble blood? That's a good one! You'd have to wash more often to pass as a nobleman." The man laughed. "In any case, your mother seems to be a wise and ambitious woman. Our names can shape our destinies."

He suddenly grabbed Johann by his arm and pulled him very close. He opened Johann's fist and studied his palm. Something about it seemed to irritate him. He brought his face even closer to Johann's hand. As before onstage, he sniffed it, and for a brief moment Johann thought he felt a rough tongue on his skin, like that of a billy goat.

"Those lines . . . those lines," he whispered, as if muttering an ancient incantation. "Indeed . . ." He stared at Johann. "Do you know when you were born, boy?"

Johann hesitated. He'd always wondered why his mother remembered the exact day of his birth. Most children knew only their saint's day. "April twenty-three in the year of our Lord 1478—on Saint George's Day," he said eventually. "My mother told me to remember the date well."

The man tilted his head to the side once more. "The day of the prophet. Hmm . . ." His fingers dug into Johann's shoulder, stinging like long, sharp talons. "Maybe I should—"

Right then Johann heard a high-pitched wail that frightened him to the core. It sounded like someone was being strangled to death. He spun around in panic. At first he thought it had been the crows or the raven, but then he realized it had come from inside the wagon. Now he heard soft whimpering and whining from the same direction. The stranger heard it, too.

"Cats," he said with a smile. "My old Selena just had a litter of five. I'll have to drown them all if they keep up the noise."

The whining stopped abruptly.

"Forget what you heard! Trust me—it's better for you."

The magician let go of Johann. He took the cage off its hook, turned, and climbed onto the box seat. He set down the cage beside him and picked up the reins. The black birds watched Johann from small, evil-looking eyes.

"I must be off," the magician said impatiently. "I want to be in Bruchsal by sundown. Work to do. So much work, and I'm not getting any younger!" He gave a cackling laugh, then turned serious.

"Those lines," he muttered again. "Born on the day of the prophet . . ." He shook his head in disbelief. "Well, young Faustus, we might meet again one day. The stars don't lie!"

He cracked his reins, and the wagon jerked forward.

As the carriage slowly rolled toward the lower gate and into the late autumn fog, Johann heard the high-pitched wailing sound once more. Just before the wagon disappeared behind one of the last houses, the canopy suddenly trembled, then stretched and bulged as if someone was desperately pushing against it from the inside. Then the fog closed in like a white curtain.

Johann remained standing in the middle of the lane, unable to move. He thought he was in a dream. What was magic, what was real? At last he shook himself and walked back around the church with trembling knees, back to the noisy fair, where the masses soon swallowed him up. The musicians played, jugs were handed around, and as the sun slowly disappeared behind the city wall, the Knittlingers celebrated the day of Saints Simon and Jude, on what might have been the last warm day of the season. One thing Johann knew for certain: no matter how many years went by, he'd never forget the magician.

Act I

The Man from the West

1

THE SUN BLAZED AS IF IT WANTED TO SET FIRE TO THE world.

Johann lay on his back with his eyes closed, feeling the warmth bake into his body. The last winter had been long and was replaced by a wet, cold spring. The first sowing had been washed away during a massive thunderstorm, like so often in recent years here in the Kraichgau region, north of the Black Forest. It wasn't until now, in July, that summer seemed to have fully arrived. The grain on the fields around Knittlingen stood tall and offered the ideal hiding place for snoozing, daydreaming, and avoiding work.

Or for a first stealthy kiss.

Johann squinted, turned his head almost imperceptibly, and saw that Margarethe was lying just as still as he was, soaking up the warmth. They'd been lying next to each other in silence for a while now, listening to the wind and the chirping of the swallows. It was the Lord's day, and most Knittlingen farmers stayed at home or frequented one of the many taverns; hardly anyone worked the fields. An ancient, weathered stone cross in the middle of a rye field formed the center of their hiding place. Johann had flattened the stalks with his feet. As long as they were close to the ground, nobody could see them.

It was the perfect love nest.

It had taken all of Johann's courage to ask Margarethe to meet him here. For days he'd hung around her, unable to open his mouth. In the end he wrote her an encrypted letter. They'd had their secret code for a few years now: with a needle Johann pierced tiny holes in individual letters, and put together, those letters spelled a message.

This time the message had read that he wanted her to meet him here and that he would show her a new trick. He hadn't said what kind of trick.

Johann had often visited Margarethe at the Knittlingen prefecture in recent years. It was only a stone's throw away from his parents' house. For as long as he could remember, he'd made Margarethe laugh with his tricks and entertained her with Aesop's animal stories or one of the funny Greek comedies he'd found at the library of the Maulbronn monastery. When they'd been younger, they used to play in the hay or hide in the prefecture's huge storehouse. But they were no longer children. A fuzz of black hair was sprouting on Johann's face. He'd turned sixteen a few months ago, just like Margarethe. The Knittlingen lads had been making eyes at her for a while now.

The unkempt, sassy, flaxen-haired girl with the dirty dress had grown into a bright young woman. Her skin wasn't tanned from the sun like that of the other girls her age but was almost as white as marble, like the skin of a highborn princess, and covered with freckles. She had also been graced with an ample bosom. Most importantly, Margarethe was the daughter of the Knittlingen prefect and was the best catch in town. And he, Johann Georg Gerlach, second-youngest son of farmer Jörg Gerlach, had managed to meet her in the fields.

Only question was, What next?

Johann stretched awkwardly and gave a loud yawn. Margarethe turned to look at him. Her eyes were as blue as the cornflowers growing in the rye field. She also stretched and sat up.

"Didn't you say you were going to show me a new trick?" she said, giving him a half-curious, half-challenging look. "That's why we came here. Or did you have other plans for a poor, innocent girl like me, Herr Johann Georg Faustus?" Like so many others in town, she used his nickname with a mocking undertone. But he didn't mind.

"No, no." Johann sat up hastily and fished a tattered pack of cards from under his jerkin. "This is . . ." He faltered when he saw the disappointment in Margarethe's face.

"You asked me here because you want to play cards? That's for the boys at the tavern." She wagged one finger. "If they don't arrest you first!" The game with cards was still relatively new and frowned upon by the authorities. The church called playing cards "the devil's prayer book."

"Wait and see!" Johann fanned out the cards in his hand. "Here, pick one card. Any card. And think about your sweetheart."

"How dare you, you cocky devil!" Margarethe giggled and reached for a card. She passed it to Johann, who flipped it over with a dramatic gesture.

It was the jack of hearts with a rose in his hand.

Johann returned the card to the deck with a triumphant smile. "So you did think of your sweetheart after all."

"Pure coincidence. Let me try again." Margarethe picked out another card, and it was the jack of hearts once more. When the trick worked a third time, she clapped her hands excitedly, like she used to as a child. "How did you do it?" she demanded impatiently. "Go on, tell me!"

Johann grinned. It was this innocence and her readiness to be amazed that had always fascinated him about Margarethe. She never seemed sad, never brooded like he did. Her laugh was high and clear, and when he heard it ringing out across the church square, the gloomy thoughts that often buzzed around him like fat moths dispersed.

"It is magic," he declared theatrically.

"Magic? Bah! You're nothing but a charlatan. Just you wait!"

Margarethe jerked the cards from his hand and sent them flying through the air. Shrieking with laughter, she threw herself on him, and soon they tussled like a pair of young dogs. A pleasant shiver ran down Johann's spine. They had scuffled in play many times before, but the sensation he experienced now with Margarethe's thighs pressing against his was new.

New and very, very nice.

"What is this?" asked Margarethe with a chuckle, placing her hand on his crotch. "Another deck of cards?"

Johann had been in love with Margarethe for as long as he could remember. There were a few girls in Knittlingen who gave him suggestive looks, but she was the only one who interested him. Still, he struggled to show it. Usually, he was considered quick-witted and scathingly sarcastic, and many Knittlingers called him insolent or a know-it-all. But with Margarethe he found himself tongue-tied, just like when he was a little boy. He couldn't come up with a reply to her coquettish question.

"It's . . . it's nothing," he replied lamely.

"Nothing? Let me see if there's nothing in the pants of Herr Faustus, Knittlingen's greatest trickster and braggart!"

Margarethe tried to pin him to the ground, but Johann was quicker and rolled on top of her.

"Braggart," she gasped, her eyes blazing with a mix of fear and desire. "You're nothing but a braggart. Admit it!"

Johann had hoped the card trick would impress her. Ever since seeing the eerie magician at the fair eight years ago, he'd been fascinated by conjuring tricks—much to the dismay of his father, who considered such things heretical nonsense. Johann made coins appear from ears; put live mice in his pockets, whereupon they reappeared from beneath Margarethe's skirts, accompanied by her screams; juggled with balls, knives, and torches; and turned sour wine into sweet wine just by blowing across the cup. Every time jugglers and magicians came through town, Johann studied their tricks. Sometimes they'd explain one to him, and he'd practice secretly in the stable behind the house. Rehearsing magic tricks hadn't helped his reputation among the Knittlingers. Folks believed sleight of hand to be the work of the devil—as much as they enjoyed watching the traveling artists in their bright garments.

As he and Margarethe chased each other across the field, Johann felt the small leather satchel he'd put in his trouser pocket that morning. It contained a strange powder he'd bought off a traveling juggler for a slice of ham and two eggs the week before. When lit with a flame, the powder smoked, flashed, and cracked loudly. Johann had hoped to impress Margarethe with the show.

But perhaps he no longer needed the powder.

"Ha! Got you!"

Shrieking, Margarethe hurled herself at him again. She pinned Johann's arms to the ground, which he didn't mind at all. Her face was so close to his that he could smell her warm breath and her hair, which carried a wonderful scent of honey, hay, and sunshine. They pressed their hips against one another, and Johann felt Margarethe's hot, damp skin beneath her thin dress. He'd waited for this moment for so long.

His whole life, really.

"You . . . you charlatan," Margarethe gasped. "Johann Georg Gerlach, you're nothing but a charlatan. But a very likable charlatan, admittedly."

A dreamy look entered her eyes and she brought her face even closer, until their lips almost touched.

"You're special," she whispered and brushed a strand of his raven-black hair from his forehead. "So different from the other boys. What's your secret, Johann Faustus? Tell me, what's your secret?"

Johann was sweating. It was as hot as a baker's oven, and his mouth felt completely dry.

"Margarethe, I—" he whispered.

Fingers dug into his upper arm and yanked him to his feet. Margarethe cried out with surprise when she was also pulled up by a hand. Between them stood Johann's father, a burly, bullnecked man with a sunburned face. He shook the young lovers like a pair of kittens. Then he let go of Margarethe and slapped Johann across the face so hard that he fell backward into the rye.

"What do you think you're doing, God damn it?" shouted Jörg Gerlach. "The prefect's daughter! Are you insane? Pray that her father doesn't hear of this, or he'll thrash you from one end of town to the other."

"But we didn't do anything!" protested Margarethe.

Gerlach raised his finger, trembling with fury. "I ain't stupid, girl! I know what I saw. You're not children anymore. Don't try to fool me!" He shot a look of disgust at his son, who was still lying amid the stalks and wiping a trickle of blood from his chin. Then he turned back to Margarethe. "I've put up with my son making eyes at you for too long. He's put a spell on you with his accursed tricks, and you fall for them like a silly goose!"

"But, Father," Johann said, holding his burning cheek. He tried to curb his anger. If he provoked his father even more, he'd be forbidden from seeing Margarethe again. "Nothing happened—honestly."

"Nothing happened?" Gerlach spun around. "Don't you see what damage you're causing with your wanton behavior? Margarethe is promised to a merchant's son from Bretten! He won't marry a girl who's been touched by another. And then the prefect will raise my interest out of spite. I'm already the town's laughingstock, thanks to you. You won't ruin my reputation any longer. Not you!" He stamped on the playing cards. The jack with the rose in his hand was lying under the farmer's heel, smeared with muck and dirt.

"Stuff of the devil," he snarled.

Johann moved backward. Until now, Margarethe being promised to a merchant's son had been nothing but idle gossip. Margarethe had never mentioned anything. But his father's words had turned rumor to reality—and Johann's dream of a future with Margarethe burst like a bubble. This blow hurt so much more than his father's slap.

"Stuff of the devil!" shouted Jörg Gerlach again and ripped the jack of hearts into small shreds. "Accursed, heretic stuff of the devil! Made for jugglers, scoundrels, and fraudsters!"

Johann had never seen his father this angry before. His face was scarlet with rage. It seemed like he was letting out everything that had long been stewing in him. They had never been close, but lately they'd grown even further apart. Johann's elder brothers, Karl and Lothar, were his father's favorites. He took them out on the horse, asked them along on trips to neighboring markets—and Karl, the eldest, was even allowed to join their father at the tavern and drink wine at the same table. The Gerlachs were a respected family with a large farm. Their house was right by the Knittlingen church. Everyone knew that Karl would inherit the farm, and Lothar, who was apprenticed to the blacksmith, would take over the smithy one day. The two youngest sons, Johann and seven-year-old Martin, would go empty handed.

"I don't want that pimply Bretten boy for a husband," said Margarethe angrily. She had jumped to her feet and stood with her hands on her hips. "I've only seen him twice, but that was enough. Adalbert Schmeltzle is as dumb as an ox, with teeth like a horse. I'd rather enter a nunnery!"

Jörg Gerlach's face twisted into a sneer. "You've got no say in the matter, girl. That's between fathers. Now run along before word gets out that you're rolling in the field with my son. And you . . ." He turned back to Johann. "Go home as fast as you can. Mother is worse, and she's been calling for you." He shook his head. "Aren't you ashamed? While you're out playing silly games in the field, your mother is coughing her lungs out! You promised to look after her—seeing as you're no good for anything else."

Johann, back on his feet, doubled up as if he'd been struck. His father knew he'd hit a sore point, and dealt the next blow.

"The priest said after mass that he'd soon have to administer the last rites. Who knows how many days she's got left." He nodded grimly. "Perhaps it's better for everyone if she leaves us sooner rather than later."

"How can you speak about Mother that way? You . . . you . . ."

Johann raised his arm, caught himself, and lowered it again. He spun around and started to run. He raced through the tall stalks of grain toward town, almost blind and deaf with grief. He didn't hear Margarethe's desperate cries and stumbled toward the city gate, his eyes swimming with tears of anger and despair. While he realized that his father just wanted to hurt him, he also knew in his heart that he was right.

His mother was dying.

With clenched teeth, Johann kept running, through the open gate, past the dozing guard. It was noon, and the lanes of Knittlingen lay deserted. It was unbearably hot, even in the shade, and it hadn't rained more than a few drops for weeks. Regardless of the heat, Johann ran up toward the church, which was situated atop a low, slanting ridge. Laughter could be heard from the taverns and inns, where farmers and tradesmen had gathered for their traditional pint following Sunday mass. Someone called out to Johann but he didn't stop. He could still hear his father's cruel words in his head.

Who knows how many days she's got left . . .

He shouldn't have left his mother's side—not for this long. His father always knew where it hurt the most. His mother had been sickly for years, but for the last few months, she hadn't been able to leave her bed at all. Johann would sit with her for long hours, reading from books he'd borrowed from the Maulbronn monastery or telling her stories he'd picked up from travelers at the taverns. Today had been the first day in a long time he hadn't sat by her bedside.

Instead he'd gone into the fields to meet a girl for a first kiss. A girl who was promised to another.

His mother's cough had been bad this morning, her phlegm streaked with red. Johann couldn't remember a time when his mother hadn't been ill. And his father had always treated his mother's illness with a cold indifference that frightened Johann. Sometimes he thought his father would be glad if she died. If she were an old horse, he'd probably put her down and look for a younger horse. But as it was, he left the task of caring for his sick wife to Johann.

Over the years, Johann had learned much from his frequent visits to the Knittlingen barber-surgeon and to the nearby monastery library, where he'd read countless books about healing—though he'd found many of the books rather strange. A lot of them spoke of the breath of hell, witches' brimstone, and pious invocations, but there weren't many useful recipes. Books were often like that: whenever he reached a point where he wanted to know more, they called upon God or blamed the devil.

Running out of breath, Johann climbed the last few steps to his home. The house of the Gerlach family sat on the hillside between Saint Leonhard's Church and the prefecture, which served as an administrative center and housed the town's wine and fruit presses. Johann's house was large, several stories high and with an attached barn and several stables for cows, horses, and smaller livestock. Jörg Gerlach owned more than sixty acres of land around Knittlingen, making him one of the wealthiest farmers in town. He employed a dozen maids and farmhands.

Johann rushed through the doors and past the hunchbacked old maidservant who was lighting the stove in the hallway. His two older brothers, Karl and Lothar, were there, sitting at the large table in the kitchen, shoveling stew into their mouths. Johann guessed they'd just arrived back from the fields. The strong young men had to work even on a Sunday. Johann was still short and slight and hardly any use in the fields. The two brothers looked up angrily when they heard Johann arrive.

"So Father finally found you, you slug," grumbled Karl, the eldest brother. "If you don't help in the fields, you could at least look after Mother." He gestured at the door to her chamber. "Hurry up and go inside before she soils her bed again."

Johann bit his lip. Neither Karl nor Lothar had ever cared for their mother. They'd lost interest in her the day she could no longer breastfeed them. They had literally sucked her dry. The older brothers considered the weak, sickly woman in the back room a burden.

"Go on!" growled Lothar. "Get a move on, midget! We worked our asses off while you were probably lying in the sunshine."

The smoke of the open fire didn't vent well through the opening in the ceiling, and Johann's eyes stung as he walked down the low hallway braced by sooty beams. He knocked softy at his mother's door but got no reply. He entered.

The chamber smelled of herbs, vomit, and moldy rushes. It was dark because the shutters were closed. The barber-surgeon was of the opinion that sunlight was bad for his mother, that even plain daylight could kill her in the long run. A sliver of fatwood was burning on the table in the middle of the chamber. There were a crude chest, a cross on the wall, and a bed, where his mother lay under a thin woolen blanket, pale and with her eyes closed. For a brief moment Johann thought she had died. But then her eyelids fluttered and she smiled.

"Ah, my Faustus," she said hoarsely. "Are you back from your walk?"

Johann hadn't told her that he was going to meet Margarethe, but she might have guessed something. He merely nodded and brushed her sweat-dampened hair from her forehead.

His mother's face was small and wrinkly, like that of a baby bird fallen from its nest. Her hair was thin and gray. Once upon a time she'd been a stunning beauty with blonde curls, but giving birth to four children, suffering several stillbirths, and being struck by disease had turned her into an old woman before she'd seen forty summers. Only her eyes still burned with a fire that must have bewitched Jörg Gerlach all those years ago. That and the large dowry. Johann's mother came from a wealthy family. Her grandfather used to be a goldsmith in Mainz.

"Please, do me a favor and open the shutters," she asked Johann. "I want to see the sunshine."

"But the barber—" Johann started.

"He is a miserable quack," said his mother with a cough. "Please open them before I wither like a flower in the dark."

Johann pushed open the shutters, and light flooded into the room. Dust shimmered in the rays of sunshine, and the fresh air smelled of summer and hay.

"That's better. Come, sit with me." She patted her mattress. Johann sat down beside her and let his mother stroke his hair. "Your hair is as beautiful and black as the feathers of a young raven," she whispered.

"F . . . Father said you were feeling worse," Johann said softly.

Instead of a reply, his mother started to cough again. Johann handed her a filthy old rag. She spat into it and then dropped it, her hand limp. Johann noticed with a fright that there was blood on the rag again. But he didn't say anything, not least to keep his own fear at bay.

"Tell me what you've heard from travelers in the taverns," his mother asked eventually.

Johann hesitated briefly. Then he began to talk, his voice growing steadier. When he was a child, she used to tell him stories about the big, wide world, and now he was her window to the outside. He had been for years now.

"They broke a robber on the wheel in Speyer—he'd been operating on the imperial road with his gang," he said. "Allegedly, he cut the throats of five merchants. Hans Harschauber from the Lion Inn was at the execution. He said it was a huge spectacle with hundreds of people watching."

"What else?" asked his mother with her eyes closed, breathing calmly now.

"The farmers in Württemberg are unhappy because of the cold spring, the poor harvest, and the high taxes. Many starved to death last winter or went into the woods. Apparently, Count Eberhard is a harsh ruler. Oh, and near Venice, a huge fish washed ashore. It's supposed to be as big as the Cologne Cathedral!"

His mother laughed, triggering another coughing fit. "Sounds like a fairy tale to me," she said, gasping for breath. "Do you believe it?"

"I heard it from a Venetian merchant staying at the Lion."

For a few years now, a new post road that led from the Netherlands to Tirol and from there across the Alps had run right past Knittlingen. Many travelers came to town along with the mounted messengers. Whenever he got a chance, Johann sat in a hiding place at the Lion Inn and listened to their tales. His mother used to do the same before she got too ill. The strangers told stories about a world so much bigger, more colorful and beautiful than Johann ever dared to dream.

"Give me your hand, my boy," his mother suddenly demanded.

Johann moved closer and held out his arm. She squeezed his hand so hard that it almost hurt. Johann hadn't known his mother still possessed such strength.

"My little Johann," she whispered. "My Faustus, my lucky child."

She called him that only when they were alone. One time his older brothers had heard the nickname and teased him with it for weeks. They knew their mother indulged him, and they were jealous.

"Why do you call me your lucky child when I'm not lucky at all?" he asked. "No one likes me, and Father calls me lazybones and a weakling. He says I've nothing but nonsense in my head."

"Oh, your father. Just let him talk. Who cares?" She smiled, and for an instant Johann saw in her eyes the lively girl with blonde curls from long ago. Young and beautiful like Margarethe, and her laughter just as clear and cheerful.

"I know there's more in you," she said, patting his hand. "You ask too many questions, and people don't like that. They only believe what they see, and they don't want anything to change. But you look further and dig deeper. You always have, even as a small boy." She raised her head a bit. "How is school going for you?"

"Good. Very good, even." Johann nodded. The thought of school brightened his mood a little.

A few months ago, his mother had asserted her wish that he be allowed to attend the higher Latin School, even though he'd completed his time at school. His father had been against it, especially because Latin School was expensive and usually reserved for the sons of wealthy patricians. But Jörg Gerlach had soon realized that this was very important to his wife and she'd never leave him in peace until he agreed. Since then, Johann had been learning Latin, grammar, arithmetic, and even a little astronomy. Along with his trips to the nearby Maulbronn monastery, his hours at Latin School were Johann's small escapes from the bleakness of everyday life in town. Sometimes he dreamed of studying at a university, like the one in Heidelberg, or even farther away. But he knew his father would never let him.

"Father Bernhard taught us about the heavenly bodies and star constellations," he continued. "He said there are scholars who claim that the sun, not the Earth, is the center of the universe."

"Heresy!" His mother smiled. "Don't let the priest hear you say that."

"Next Sunday night, the father wants to show us the stars from the steeple. He even has an astrolabe! He'll use it to show us the constellations the seafaring folk use to find their way on their journeys. Cassiopeia, the Great Bear, Pisces, Scorpius . . ." Johann hesitated.

"What is it?" asked his mother.

"You've often said that I was born under a lucky star. That's why I know the date of my birth. But what star was it?"

"Well, which one do you think, silly?" His mother winked at him, and he caught yet another glimpse of the young girl from long ago. "Jupiter, of course, the lucky planet! God has great plans for anyone born under Jupiter. He who is born under the lucky star is possessed by a deep longing for freedom and knowledge. He is never content but forever trying to get to the bottom of things. He is a prospector in the mine of knowledge, always searching for the truth. And he is someone who can lead people."

"How do you know all that?"

She paused. "A . . . a wise man once told me. A very wise and widely traveled man. He was a sage despite his young age. He told me fate would smile especially upon you. That's why I named you Faustus. It was his idea. Born on the day of the prophet, he said."

Johann frowned. His mother had never spoken to him like this before. He vaguely remembered someone else talking about a prophet—the magician he'd met on that memorable day at the fair years ago.

"Who was that man?" he demanded.

His mother hesitated. "He went away long ago. He . . . he came from the west . . ." Another coughing fit gripped her. It got so bad that Johann feared she'd suffocate. When she handed him the dirty cloth with a weak gesture, he saw that it was saturated with blood. Johann sprang to his feet.

"You need medicine," he said. "I'll go to the barber-surgeon right away."

His mother closed her eyes and breathed heavily. "Forget the barber. I've told you many times he's a quack. No better than all those charlatans at the fairs. All I need is rest. Rest and the stories you tell me."

The Knittlingen barber-surgeon was a drunkard who firmly believed he could heal any disease with bloodletting and purging. He thought any new findings in the art of healing were nonsense, just like the ancient knowledge of the monks and Arabic scholars. But there was no doctor in Knittlingen, and the physician in nearby Bretten was much too expensive.

"Then . . . then I'll go to the Maulbronn monastery," Johann said. "Father Antonius will know a remedy. He's helped us before."

But his mother didn't reply; she seemed to have fallen asleep. Her breathing was shallow but calm. Johann squeezed her hand.

"I'm going to see Father Antonius at Maulbronn," he whispered. "I'll be back in a few hours. Promise."

He stroked her cheek one last time. Then, quietly, he left her chamber.

~

His mother gazed after him for a long while. Her eyes rested on the worm-eaten, knotty pinewood door her son had closed behind him. As a child, Elisabeth Gerlach had always dreamed of a prince, a man who would carry her to faraway lands on his white steed. But all she'd gotten was a drunk Knittlingen farmer.

The other girls had said Jörg Gerlach was a good catch, a bear of a man and rich to boot. But his mind was narrow and his soul didn't want to soar; to him happiness was a steaming field, a good harvest, a folk dance on the fiddle, and a mug full of brown ale or wine.

Elisabeth had known soon after their wedding that she'd never be happy with Jörg Gerlach. But who cared? No one ever said joy and happiness played a role in marriage. People married to have children and to share the workload of the house and the fields. So every time Jörg had climbed atop Elisabeth and heaved and groaned, she'd closed her eyes and dreamed of distant lands and her prince on his white horse.

She gave birth to four live sons and became ill and weak. Two were like their thick father and one, the youngest, was a lovable cripple who'd always be dependent on others.

Only Johann was different.

She had sensed it when he lay in her arms as a newborn. Those alert eyes that seemed to take in everything, absorbing the world like a sponge. She had always known that fate had great plans for him.

And the man from the west had said it, too, and smiled strangely. The beautiful young man with raven-black hair as soft as silk.

Her prince.

Elisabeth closed her eyes and dreamed the man would return and take her away on his white horse, far away to a land with no disease and no pain.

Born on the day of the prophet . . .

"My Faustus," she whispered. She coughed again and spat blood into the rushes on the floor. Then she drifted off to sleep, a small, frail body, withered by the little bit of life she had been granted.

~

Outside the house, Johann ran into his little brother, Martin. The younger boy seemed to have been waiting for him and broke into a happy smile when Johann came out the door.

"H . . . h . . . here you are!" he called out. "Margarethe told me I'd find you at home." Johann just kept walking, and Martin struggled to keep up with his older brother. He jogged alongside Johann in his crudely carved clogs. Martin was small and scrawny, with a crooked back, and he stuttered—especially when he was excited. Sometimes, when Johann wasn't around, the other children called him a dimwit or a dwarf.

"Wh . . . wh . . . what's the matter?" asked Martin. "Wh . . . wh . . . where are you going?" He gave him a conspiratorial wink. "Are you going to make m . . . m . . . magic again? I won't tell!"

Johann sighed. Seven-year-old Martin stuck to him like a burr. Karl and Lothar were too old to play with their pitiful little brother, and they were ashamed of him. Martin often followed along when Johann wanted to practice his tricks alone in the woods. The younger boy would jump up and down like an eager puppy, would climb trees by the wayside, would pester Johann with questions, and wouldn't be persuaded to turn back. Nonetheless, Johann loved his little brother very much. Martin was so much more like him than like Karl and Lothar. Despite the stammer and the hunchback, Martin was smart and thirsty for knowledge, and just like Johann, he was closer to their mother than to their father, who didn't have much attention for the small latecomer.

"I don't have time for you right now," Johann said, rushing ahead with long strides. "Mother is very ill. I'm on my way to the monastery to get some medicine."

"B . . . bring me with you!"

"It'll take too long," Johann replied with a shake of his head. "I want to return to Mother as fast as I can." He stopped, leaned down to Martin, and gave him a serious look. "But I have an important task for you, do you hear me? Stay with Mother and look after her. Wipe the sweat from her forehead, fetch hot water for her, and sweep up the old rushes. They smell like death. If she gets worse, run and get the barber, all right?"

Martin nodded. He could tell by his brother's eyes that he was serious.

"And you'll c . . . c . . . come back soon?" asked Martin anxiously.

Johann patted his shoulder. "That's why I want to go on my own, so I can come back as fast as possible. Now go to Mother. She needs you."

Martin obeyed, and Johann went on his way. He hurried along Market Street toward the upper city gate, which he passed a short while later. Knittlingen was a small town of about two thousand souls. Its walls were surrounded by a foul-smelling moat fed by a handful of brooks. The church and the prefecture formed the center of town. For as long as anyone could remember, Knittlingen had been in the tenure of the Maulbronn monastery, which also appointed the prefect. The monastery itself was about an hour's walk from town.

Johann left the city and turned right, where the old imperial road led south. The path was dry and dusty, and hardly anyone was traveling this Sunday. Johann could make out a cart in the distance, and one lone horseman cantered past him; other than that, the road was quiet.

He'd walked this road many times before, knew every step, every tree, every field along the path. The track wound its way through cornfields and past gently sloping vineyards before climbing steeply toward the forest. Johann gazed at the fields and vineyards, spreading like a chessboard to his left and right. Everything around Knittlingen was well ordered, everything had its proper place—farmers, monks, the mighty Kraichgau houses of knights, the count palatine in Heidelberg, and above him, the king and the pope. Sometimes Johann felt he was the only one who didn't fit into the fabric of the world.

He thought about the argument with his father. He'd often wondered why they always clashed. He guessed it was because they were so different. His father was a strong man with a bushy brown beard and a broad back, while Johann was delicate and sinewy, with raven-black hair, and he was much too short for his age. They were also worlds apart in their opinions, their desires, and what made them happy.

Johann wasn't entirely sure yet what he considered happiness.

On the hilltop, he passed the ancient Knittlingen execution site, a square of mortared stones with old gallows. No one hung there today, but on many other occasions Johann had walked past the gently swaying remains of a convict. The German king himself afforded protection on all imperial roads, and to preserve safety, robbers and thieves were always hanged in elevated places by the roadside—a warning to other scoundrels near and far. To Johann, the stinking corpses were a reminder of the transitory nature of life.

He'd slowed down for the last steep part, but now, atop the hill, he ran until his heart raced. His thoughts were a jumble. Worry for his mother, anger about his father, and his feelings for Margarethe whirled through his mind like a storm. He passed an oxcart on its slow and steady way to the monastery. The driver was almost asleep from the heat. Then the forest ended and the road wound its way down into a lovely valley fringed by vineyards. On the left lay the well-known monastery.

It was an imposing complex made of sandstone with a wall, a church, and several other buildings. Eight fortified towers and a round walk showed that the monks were willing to defend their property. But they hadn't needed to in a long time. Maulbronn grew and prospered, like so many monasteries in the German empire.

Johann entered the abbey through a huge gate into a courtyard that was bordered by another wall at the back. Here, in the front part, the worldly facilities were situated, like the bakery with the granary, the smithy, a mill, and accommodation for pilgrims and travelers. The narrow lanes between the sandstone buildings were as busy as ever. Two lay brothers in brown robes rolled an empty wine barrel toward the building housing the wine press; a shaggy dog lifted his leg at the trough outside the inn and got booted by the innkeeper; a group of pilgrims in dusty traveling frocks searched for their quarters. A broad-shouldered, bearded monk in the smithy slammed a piece of iron with his hammer. Pacing through the lanes in silent prayer were choir monks, who, in contrast to the lay brothers, were shaved and wore white robes with black scapulars. Many of them were noblemen who were in search of a simple life—or who, as second- or third-born sons, were excluded as heirs.

Johann loved the monastery's aura of scholarship and eternity. Time seemed to stand still here. The sandstone walls were hundreds of years old, and the knowledge hoarded behind them was legendary. Johann visited the abbey as often as he could and occasionally ran small errands for the brothers. Sometimes he was even allowed to visit the library—always a very special occasion. So many books, so many answers to his questions! Normally, outsiders weren't allowed to set foot in the famous library—let alone a sixteen-year-old boy. But Johann enjoyed the friendship of a powerful benefactor at Maulbronn, someone who even permitted him to take home a book every now and then. And Johann wanted to see this man today.

He approached a lay brother who was driving a squeaking pig toward the butchery. "God be with you, Brother," he said in greeting. "Do you know where I might find Father Antonius?"

"Where do you think, boy?" The monk grinned and pointed at the tall monastery church. "At the infirmary, of course. Both the cellarer and the prior have been struck down by a nasty summer fever, and so have a number of brothers. He's got his hands full."

Johann nodded gratefully and went on his way to the church behind the next wall. This was where the spiritual, quiet part of the monastery began. The porter knew the boy and merely grunted as Johann passed. The Maulbronn librarian was a good friend of Father Bernhard, Johann's teacher at Latin School. But Father Antonius wasn't just the librarian. His medical skills were known far beyond the walls of Maulbronn. Johann felt certain the man would have a remedy that would help his mother.

Johann reverently entered the church, whose sandstone blocks were painted in blue and red. The tall windows allowed slanted sunlight to illuminate the altar and the adjoining choir, with its elaborately carved stalls. In a side chapel, a monk was quietly reading a mass. Johann had heard that the Cistercians used to work their fields themselves once upon a time, but now they were too busy managing a fortune that grew with each generation. The monastery called more than a dozen villages in the surrounding area its own. The farmers paid their duties more or less willingly. That was how it had been since time immemorial: knights fought, monks prayed, and farmers toiled.

And what am I going to do? Johann asked himself as he walked past the tall cross above the altar. *What plans does God have for me?*

He left the church through the silent cloister and followed the corridor that led to the infirmary. Rows of beds stood to his left and right, most of them holding coughing monks under thin blankets. A younger monk was scattering fresh rushes while an old, gray-haired brother poured steaming water into a bowl with herbs. A pleasant fragrance spread through the long, high-ceilinged room. When the old man heard Johann's hurried footsteps, he looked up. A tired smile spread on his face.

"Johann!" he exclaimed. "I should have known you'd come today. It's your day off." His expression turned serious. "But I'm afraid I must disappoint you. I'm too busy to visit the library with you." He gestured toward the full beds. More coughing and sniffling could be heard. "We've got our hands full with a nasty fever. Dear Father Jeremias died of it just yesterday, though he was very old, too. God rest his soul." He sighed deeply and made the sign of the cross. "How is my dear friend Father Bernhard? I hope he's doing well?"

"Father Bernhard is well and sends his greetings," Johann replied. "But my mother is very ill."

The other monk, a clean-shaven young man in a white robe, looked up and frowned at them. The Cistercians followed the rule of silence closely, and often they communicated merely with hand signals. The rule wasn't always enforced in the infirmary, but one was still expected to keep a low voice.

Father Antonius waved Johann to an alcove off to the side and listened to the boy's report. Then he nodded gravely. "She's coughing blood, you say? I don't want to jump to conclusions, but . . ."

"What is it?" Johann said, giving the monk a pleading look. "Please, tell me!"

Father Antonius sighed. "You know your mother hasn't been well for a long time. When a body is weakened thus, diseases find an easy target. Nasty diseases like the white plague."

Johann closed his eyes to hide his fear. He'd heard about the white plague. Travelers often brought it from Venice, Geneva, or Rome. Those who caught it grew increasingly weak, slept more and more, and coughed. The disease seemed to consume them from the inside—which was why it was also known as consumption. It wasn't quite as bad as the black plague, but eventually they both resulted in death.

"And there is no remedy?" said Johann. "You know so much about healing, Father. Please!" He felt a thick lump in his throat. If Father Antonius didn't know of any medicine, only the dear Lord could help his mother.

"Hmm, there might be a remedy." Father Antonius moved his head from side to side, considering. "But I don't keep it here. It's down in the store." He hesitated briefly, then he patted Johann on the shoulder. "I'm sure they can cope without me here for a short while. Come, there's something else I want to show you. It might just cheer you up."

Father Antonius gently pushed the boy ahead of him. They walked to the cloister, where a group of monks stood by a bubbling fountain, talking in hushed voices. They faltered when they saw Johann, but the father paid them no heed. Together they entered a small room. A set of stairs led to a lower chamber illuminated by narrow windows high against the ceiling.

This was the store, and it smelled musty and fragrant at the same time, mixed with a slightly metallic, caustic smell Johann couldn't place. Barrels and crates were stacked against the walls alongside many shelves; salted legs of ham hung from the ceiling together with sausages and bundles of dried herbs. On the far side of the room stood a table with a strange apparatus that reminded Johann vaguely of a fruit press. In front of it stood several open crates, and on the floor, glinting in the light of the afternoon, sticks of iron were scattered about, like the broken teeth of some kind of mythical creature. The metallic smell seemed to come from the apparatus.

"What is that?" asked Johann, puzzled.

"That's just what I was going to show you. Ha, I knew you'd be interested! It is a printing press." Father Antonius winked mischievously and walked to the press. "The prior and I managed to convince the abbot to buy one for the monastery. We got it quite cheaply from a monastery near Worms, along with some boxes of Latin and Greek books for the library. Once we start using the press, things will change around here. And not only here." The father made a sweeping gesture with both arms. "A new age is dawning, I'm sure! So many new insights and discoveries reach us—not only from Italy but also from the Spanish moors and faraway Constantinople. Old Latin, Greek, and even Jewish manuscripts are being rediscovered, and now we can print and duplicate them all! Just imagine, everything humanity has ever thought up can be put down with letters—and will still be legible centuries down the line. Knowledge will become immortal! I'm so grateful for the privilege of witnessing such exciting times at my old age."

Johann's eyes grew big. He'd heard about printing presses but never seen one before. Every now and then, a printed leaflet found its way to Knittlingen, usually bearing religious content. The playing cards Johann had bought from his savings and that his father trampled into the dirt had also been printed.

The pages of printed books were made with paper instead of the blotchy parchment used in most old books at the Maulbronn library. In the past, monks had copied each book by hand using iron gall ink to duplicate it, but now presses increasingly took over this task. The letters were cast from lead and tin. A job that used to take months or even years could now be done within days. Johann struggled to imagine how many books could be produced thus in a short space of time. Hundreds? Thousands? Already there were more books than he could ever read!

As he slowly walked around the printing press and touched the metallic, ink-stained shafts with the back-to-front letters, Father Antonius lifted a small clay bottle from one of the shelves.

"I made this medicine last week with a recipe from an old monastic book," he explained. "The book was in one of the boxes from Worms." The father smiled. "It's mainly made of . . . well, cheese mold."

Johann looked at him with surprise. "Cheese mold?"

"And a little sheep dung and honey." Father Antonius raised his hand. "I know, it sounds a bit strange. But it's an old recipe and supposed to help with the white plague. You don't have to tell your mother exactly what it contains." He handed Johann the corked bottle. "Give her one sip today and then one sip morning and night every day for the next week. Praying won't hurt, either."

"Thank you, Father." Johann was about to leave when one of the books in the crates by the printing press caught his eye. A few months at Latin School had improved Johann's Latin greatly, and so he stared with surprise at the title and author of the book on top of the pile.

Speculum Astronomiae.

"Mirror of Astronomy," he muttered. "By Albertus Magnus, venerable brother of the Dominicans and bishop of Regensburg."

Astronomy, Johann knew from Father Bernhard's class, was the knowledge of the stars, just like astrology. He recalled his mother mentioning the stars and the day of his birth yet again earlier this day. But he hadn't realized men of the church also took an interest in the stars.

"Does the church believe in the power of the stars?" he asked Father Antonius.

"Well, it's a thin line between what the church believes and what it condemns as heresy," the monk replied. "The stars are an expression of God's will, says the pope, and so does the great Albertus Magnus, who wrote this book more than two hundred years ago. Even bishops occasionally have their horoscopes cast." Father Antonius gave a small grin. "Although personally, I don't really believe in it. Albertus Magnus also wrote about alchemy and magic. Some say he was a sorcerer himself. But where does black magic begin? And what is God's will?" He smiled. "Why do you ask?"

"It's . . . it's just . . ." Johann was about to tell the father about his conversation with his mother when he realized how long he'd already been at the monastery. He had to return to Knittlingen! His mother needed the medicine as soon as possible.

"I'm afraid I don't have any money on me," Johann said hesitantly. "But I'm sure my father will reimburse you." Deep down, he doubted it. His father was a miser who considered the monks a bunch of quacks.

"No need to trouble your father." Father Antonius waved his hand dismissively. "It's a gift of the church. If you ask me, the farmers of Knittlingen have paid us more than enough. May God protect your mother and may the medicine bring her relief."

"Thank you so much, Father!" Johann briefly squeezed the father's hand before rushing outside and stuffing the precious bottle under his shirt. During his conversation with Father Antonius he'd almost forgotten how ill his mother was, and now he'd have to hurry if he wanted to make it home before nightfall.

Johann left the church and ran past the smithy and the inn, through the monastery gate, and toward the hill that separated Maulbronn from Knittlingen. The sun was low on the horizon, and the trees cast long shadows. The small bottle pressing against his chest, Johann ran up the steep path until he reached the dense beech forest. There was a spring in his step now that his worries weren't weighing him down as much. He felt certain the medicine would help his mother—Father Antonius had always been right. All would be well! And next time he visited Maulbronn, the father might tell him more about this Albertus Magnus who might have been a sorcerer.

Soon Johann had reached Gallows Hill. The place appeared much gloomier now that it was getting dark. The branches of an elm tree near the gallows groaned in the wind like a hanged man drawing his last breath.

And someone was awaiting Johann there.

Three figures were sitting on the stone platform. When Johann came closer, they jumped off the wall and walked toward him.

Johann started with fright. At first he thought they were highway robbers out to get him, but then he recognized them as three boys from town. They were a little older than him, and he knew them well. Two of them used to beat him up occasionally at his old school when he asked too many questions in class. But the third one was the most dangerous: Ludwig, Margarethe's older brother.

Ludwig was nearly eighteen now, a whole head taller than Johann, with a pockmarked face and shifty eyes. He often knocked about with Johann's elder brothers, drinking and fighting with the boys from neighboring villages. Ludwig had bullied Johann for as long as the younger boy could remember. The prefect's son had never liked the fact that his sister was meeting up with the village misfit and know-it-all. Ludwig had no time for Johann's magic tricks. Sometimes he even seemed envious when Johann enchanted Margarethe and her friends with chicken eggs and scarves.

Now Ludwig's vigorous and triumphant demeanor told Johann that this time he wouldn't get away with a joke and a few smart lines.

"Look at that, your tiny cripple of a brother was right," Ludwig scoffed. "We only had to give the dwarf a little shake and he spilled. You were over at Maulbronn with those Bible thumpers again. I bet you wiped their asses with parchment." Ludwig had always hated books at school; evidently his attitude hadn't changed.

"I went to get medicine for my mother," Johann replied firmly and felt for the small bottle under his shirt. "She is very ill."

"When is your mother ever not ill?" Ludwig jeered and looked around at his younger friends for approval. "Do you know what folks are saying? The say Elisabeth the harlot caught the French disease. She went to bed with some foreign mercenary, and God is punishing her for it."

"What did you call my mother? Say it again and I'll . . . I'll . . ." Johann took one step toward Ludwig. His anger was greater than his fear now, his voice trembling. It wasn't the first time boys from town had teased him with the fact that his mother had been seen with other men in the past. They were careful never to do so while Johann's father was around, though, as he'd respond with brutal violence. Still, Johann's mother had a certain reputation in Knittlingen.

"You'll what?" asked Ludwig. When Johann didn't reply, the older boy continued. "Your mother is a whore. Do you hear me? A dirty whore! And I won't stand by and watch my sister become one, too."

It was too much for Johann. Shaking with anger, he raised his fist—when it suddenly dawned on him why Ludwig and the two others had ambushed him here: someone must have seen him and Margarethe in the field! And now Ludwig felt compelled to defend his little sister's honor. Even if he fought with Ludwig now, the rumor was out, and it was more damaging to Margarethe than to him, especially since her father wanted to marry her off to a merchant's son from Bretten. He had to pull himself together, for Margarethe's sake.

"Listen," Johann said in a conciliatory tone. "I don't know what you've heard, but there's nothing going on between Margarethe and me—"

"It's too late for excuses," Ludwig shouted angrily. "You need a good tanning. Grab him!"

The two other boys stepped toward Johann at Ludwig's command. Instinctively, Johann reached into his pocket where he'd put the powder earlier that day. It had a strong, pungent smell and was supposed to explode amid loud hissing and popping—but even unlit, Johann thought, it might serve him well. With one swift movement he hurled the powder into the face of one of the boys, who dropped to his knees almost instantly, rubbing his eyes and crying.

"He blinded me!" he whimpered. "The bastard blinded me! Help!"

"You'll pay for this!" screamed Ludwig, lunging at Johann, who tried to escape. But Ludwig, strong as an ox, grabbed him. Johann didn't stand the faintest chance.

While the boy with the powder in his eyes still rolled on the ground crying, Ludwig and the third boy started in on Johann. He thrashed as much as he could, but it was no use. They had brought a strong length of rope, and they tied his hands and feet until he lay before them as a twitching bundle.

Ludwig looked down at him and grinned. "Well, how do you like it now, smart-ass? Your tricks can't help you now." He turned to his friend. "Let's carry him behind the gallows, like the mangy crook he is."

The two of them grabbed Johann and lugged him over to the crumbling platform where the gallows rose into the night sky like a warning finger. When they came to the other side of the platform, Johann realized what they had planned for him.

Behind the execution site lay a huge anthill. It was almost up to Ludwig's hips.

Johann screamed and squirmed, but the boys paid him no heed. The hill was a bustling scurry of tiny red insects busy carting pine needles and small twigs. Not far from it, half covered by dirt, lay a human skull and bones, presumably belonging to a hanged man. The wood ants had carefully cleaned the bones of any remaining sinews and flesh.

The lads pulled down Johann's pants and whipped his naked buttocks with pine branches until blood ran down his legs. He raged and screamed with pain and anger at this humiliation—but no one heard him way up here, far from

Knittlingen. The bottle of medicine he'd been clutching in his fingers fell to the ground, and Ludwig kicked it away like trash.

Then, still using a branch, he pummeled Johann like a madman. "You think you're better than the rest of us, do you?" shouted Ludwig, panting. "Ha, how's your learning helping you now, and all your smart comments? What's the use of your heretic tricks now?"

Breathing heavily, Ludwig finally let go of the blood-smeared branch. Beads of sweat stood on his forehead.

"Now, in he goes!" he shouted. "This'll be a lesson to the filthy bastard—he won't roll around in the fields with my sister again."

The third boy staggered toward them with half-closed eyes, his swollen face twisted into a grimace of hate. "One, two, three!" shouted Ludwig. "Enjoy your meal, you little beasts."

The three boys hurled Johann right into the anthill.

The insects started to attack him instantly. They crawled over Johann's naked, bleeding haunches, biting by the hundreds and spraying their acid, which burned like fire in his open sores. Johann screamed. The pain almost took his breath away. He tossed his body back and forth, yanked on his fetters, but the ants were everywhere—in his hair, his ears, his eyes, his mouth, on his skin. A murderous army of tiny soldiers, out to destroy him. There was no escape.

Laughing, the three boys turned to leave.

"Oh, and your medicine," Ludwig said and turned one last time to Johann, who tossed and squirmed like a hare in a trap. Margarethe's brother picked up the small corked bottle from the ground beside the anthill.

"If those white monks gave it to you, it'll only be water and vinegar or whatever else they sell people," Ludwig said. "Your father agrees. He won't mind if we use it to feed the ants. I'm sure the little beasts will love it."

He pulled the cork out of the bottle and slowly poured out its contents, creating a small puddle among the pine needles that soon seeped into the ground. Ludwig wrinkled his nose in disgust.

"Yuck! I told you, nothing but expensive hocus-pocus. Your mother should consider herself lucky she doesn't have to drink this." He signaled for his friends to follow him. "Come on, let's go. If he really knows how to do magic, he can free himself."

With one last smirk in Johann's direction, the three went on their way, leaving the groaning and whimpering boy in the anthill. The insects' bites felt like needles. Johann thought of the pale bones nearby and screamed loudly again as he tossed back and forth. After a while he managed to crawl a little way away from the hill and into a muddy, damp wallow, which had probably been used by wild boars the night before. The cool mud eased the worst of his pain. The ants gradually dispersed until there were just a few left on his scalp and in his pubic hair, searching for an invisible adversary.

Johann didn't manage to undo his ties until it was fully dark. With his last remaining strength he limped through the night toward Knittlingen, bleeding and filthy.

When he reached home, his mother was dead.

2

THE FOLLOWING DAYS AND WEEKS SEEMED LIKE A NEVER-ending nightmare to Johann.

He'd only seen his mother one last time before she'd been carried to her grave, looking almost unreal—like a small, dried-up doll. In the middle of summer, dead bodies decayed very fast, so the funeral took place the day after her death, at the cemetery of Saint Leonhard's Church. Almost all the burghers of Knittlingen had come, as well as the day laborers, maidservants, and other workers. They shook the quiet widower's hand and patted Johann's and Martin's heads, while Lothar and Karl stood around listlessly, showing little emotion—as if it had been some distant relative who'd passed away. Margarethe and her father had also attended but remained at the back. Johann was relieved that Ludwig hadn't come. He thought he might have struck down Margarethe's brother with a stone right there at the cemetery.

The priest said a brief prayer as the casket was lowered into the grave. Then Johann's mother was nothing but a memory.

The end had come fast. Apparently his mother had called for Johann in her last few hours and coughed up much blood. She'd wanted to tell him something important, it seemed. When little Martin had left to fetch the barber, she'd died, all alone. In the grief-stricken commotion, no one had asked why Johann had returned from the monastery with torn, bloody trousers, his body covered in welts. His father had merely given him an angry look.

He gave him the same look now at the funeral. "Why weren't you by her side?" he whispered at Johann. "*You* were supposed to look after her, not that stupid cripple brother of yours. Instead you're God knows where, getting into fights. This is your fault alone!"

Johann said nothing. His face was puffy and red from all the tears he'd cried the night before. He knew his father was being unfair, but he felt guilty nonetheless. If he'd only returned sooner from the monastery! Father Antonius's medicine might have saved his mother's life. He didn't tell his father what happened at Gallows Hill; the farmer probably wouldn't have believed Johann, anyhow. Instead, when he wasn't at Latin School with Father Bernhard, which brought him some distraction, he spent the following days roaming the woods, vineyards, and hills around Knittlingen on his own. He barely saw Margarethe during that time, and if he did, Ludwig was always nearby, casting dark glances at him and quickly pulling his sister along. Johann wrote letters to her in their secret code, but she didn't reply.

As days became weeks his wounds healed, but the pain inside remained. The pain and a quiet longing for revenge. He would never forget what happened at Gallows Hill. His mother was gone, forever! He felt terribly alone in the world. Little Martin clung to him more than ever, as if afraid his beloved brother would leave him just like their mother had.

Every night Johann stood by the small, crooked cross in the graveyard. He prayed to and railed against God at the same time, asking countless questions without ever receiving an answer.

Summer came to an end and fall arrived with fog, wind, and rain. The grain harvest was in, and next up was the grape harvest. People began to look forward to the next Saints Simon and Jude Fair—the highlight of their year. The wheel of life kept turning.

Every hand was needed for the grape harvest, so there was no school. Day after day, rain or shine, Johann stood side by side with the other Knittlingen boys and girls on the slopes of the vineyards, picking grapes, throwing them into the basket strapped to his back, and carrying his load to one of the three *Keltern*—the buildings housing the wine presses—at the prefecture. It was hard work, and Johann's back ached as if he'd been whipped, but he still went to his mother's grave every evening with a fresh bundle of flowers.

When he arrived home one particularly foggy evening, his father was sitting at the kitchen table, a half-empty mug of wine in front of him. Jörg Gerlach's red face told Johann that his father had had a fair bit to drink, like so often in recent weeks. People were saying it was because he grieved for his beloved (if somewhat strange) wife, but Johann knew better. His father was a drunkard,

always had been. And now that his mother was no more, there was no one left
to restrain him.

"I told the father that you won't return to Latin School after the grape
harvest," Gerlach said to his son. His eyes looked glassy and red; his face was
doughy like a dumpling.

Johann staggered backward as if he'd walked into a wall. "But—why?"

"What they teach you there is useless. And the school's far too expensive.
Why d'you need to learn all that nonsense when all you're going to do in life is
muck out stables?"

"So that's what you've got planned for me, is it?" Johann glowered at his
father, his voice shaking. It was the first time his father had spoken to him in
a long while—and now this. No sympathy, no kind words, just the end of his
dreams. "You want me to be a stable boy?"

Jörg Gerlach shrugged his shoulders. "I need neither a priest nor a scholar.
What did you expect? I've got four sons, but only Karl can inherit the farm.
And you're no good for anything other than picking grapes or mucking out—
or can you conjure up roast pigeons and make milk and honey flow in the
Knittlingen moat? Do your oh-so-clever books teach you anything useful like
that?" He laughed and took a long sip of his wine. His tongue sounded heavier
when he continued to speak. "What did your mother use to call you? Faustus
the lucky one? She spoiled you for far too long! Better get used to the fact that
this is the start of different, less lucky years for you. It's time you got to know
real life, Johann, and stopped reading and dreaming all day long. You'll thank
me one day! Oh yes, you'll thank me. Did you hear me, you . . . you juggler!
Good-for-nothing!"

But Johann didn't hear the last words. He'd turned away and stormed out
of the house. What did he ever do to his father that the man had to torture him
at every turn? Latin School had been the last ray of light in his life, now that
Mother was dead and Margarethe couldn't or wouldn't see him anymore. Secretly
he'd hoped that he might enter the monastery as a lay brother following Latin
School, as a kind of assistant to Father Antonius. But that wouldn't happen if
he didn't learn Latin!

He hadn't seen Father Antonius in a long time. The old monk had been
made prior a few weeks earlier, after the previous prior died of that accursed

summer fever. Since then, the father had been too busy with administrative tasks to have time for Johann's worries and dreams.

Johann walked aimlessly through the lanes and alleyways of Knittlingen in the dim light of dusk, until he suddenly found himself on Market Street outside the Lion Inn. It seemed to him like a stroke of fate. This was where his mother used to sit as a girl, secretly listening to the stories of travelers. And Johann used to love being here, too. But since his mother's death he'd avoided the place; the memories were just too painful.

At that moment he saw the wagon.

It stood next to the inn, tied to the hitching rail where usually the post riders' horses received their hay. Even though it had been eight years, Johann recognized the wagon instantly: it belonged to the magician Johann had met during the Knittlingen fair. The dirty canvas showed the same strange runes, and even the old horse munching on his feed seemed to be the same. Johann felt oddly restless, and his depressing thoughts drifted into the background. His curiosity aroused, he opened the door to the inn and looked inside.

Since the post road led past Knittlingen, the Lion was always busy. All sorts of strangers chose to spend the night. Now, too, several travelers sat beside numerous locals at the scratched tables, sharing jugs of wine. Something was going on toward the back of the room. A whole throng of Knittlingers—Margarethe's father, the prefect, among them—were standing together, so that Johann couldn't see the table behind them. Some of them whispered to each other, while others led loud discussions. Hans Harschauber, the innkeeper, walked toward Johann with a mug of beer. He smiled and patted Johann's shoulder.

"Well, Johann," he said in greeting. Harschauber was one of the few people in Knittlingen who always treated him kindly. "Are you fetching a keg for your father? It's good to see you here. Too much moping about the house isn't healthy."

Johann didn't reply. He scanned the room but didn't see the one he was looking for. Harschauber followed his gaze. He winked and nodded toward the group of men in front of the table.

"A traveling astrologer is lodging here," he explained quietly. "Apparently he's staying for the fair. But he's already relieving our Herr Prefect of his money!" Harschauber laughed. "He's having his horoscope cast as we speak. He's probably just been told that he'll make it to emperor one day."

"A . . . an astrologer?" Johann's heart beat faster. He walked toward the noisy crowd until he finally caught a glimpse of the man at the table.

It was the magician.

Just like his wagon, he was unchanged. He wore the same felt hat with the red feather he had worn eight years ago, and the same black-and-red-striped coat, which made his lean body look even more gaunt than it already was. His eyes gleamed like old copper buttons in his extremely pale face, his nose protruding sharply. Johann guessed the magician was somewhere between forty and fifty years old. But on second look, he wasn't so sure. The man might just as well have been much younger or much older. On the table in front of him lay blotchy scrolls of parchment with confusing charts and drawings, similar to those depicted on the wagon canvas. The prefect stood beside him and listened intently.

"Fourteen hundred ninety-four is a good year for you," the magician was saying, running his long, skinny fingers across the parchment. His voice still had the soft, exotic sound of the west. Johann thought the man probably came from the Alsace or even France. "*Oui*, 1494 is good. But 1495 is going to be better yet, for you and for your town! The sun will be in Leo and the moon in Saturn, and a hot summer and a good harvest await. Hmm, however . . ." He paused dramatically.

"What is it?" asked the prefect, and the men around him fell silent with anticipation.

"*Mon Dieu!* I see bad weather in April, with lots of storms and hail. Hold back some of your seed, because you're going to need it."

A murmur went through the crowd, and the prefect kneaded his hat, which he'd been clutching tightly the whole time. "Thank you, Magister," he said quietly, placing a few coins on the table.

The foreigner wrinkled his nose in distaste. "Who do you think I am?" he growled, and his voice was suddenly as rough as the bark of an angry dog. "A charlatan or a swindler? That is not enough! A few kreuzers might buy you a line from some little old herb woman, but not a decent horoscope. I've studied at Avignon, Krakow, and even Paris!"

"And if I refuse to pay more?" asked the prefect briskly. "What are you going to do? The horoscope's already cast."

The foreigner flashed a smile, and then his lips turned into two thin lines. He glared at the prefect with eyes that were no longer gleaming but dark and cold like the blackness behind the moon.

"Pay me. Only the stars and I know what happens if you don't."

The foreigner had spoken quietly, yet everyone in the room seemed to have heard him. For a few moments, the barroom grew strangely silent. Then the prefect placed two silver coins on the table, put his hat on, and walked out. The others followed him, glancing back at the stranger with fear in their eyes. In the end, only Johann was left.

"Dumb peasants," the magician muttered, and Johann wasn't sure if he'd spoken to him or just to himself. The sinister man rolled up his parchment scrolls and pocketed the coins. At some point he looked up and saw Johann standing there.

"What do you want?" he asked. "Question time is over, boy. Go home like the rest of the numbskulls."

"I . . . I . . . ," Johann stammered. He wasn't sure what he was doing here. But, just like last time, he felt a strange fascination radiating from the foreigner—and also something frightening.

Suddenly the man's expression changed and he frowned. "Hang on—I know you! You're the boy I met before in this town, aren't you? Let me see your hand." His arm darted forward like a snake, grabbing Johann's hand, and he began to read his palm. Then he smiled. "Indeed, it's you! Johann Georg Faustus, right? The lucky one."

Johann straightened up with surprise. "You . . . you still know my name? After all these years?"

The foreigner laughed and let go of Johann's hand. "Name is but sound and smoke, but those lines don't lie. I can recognize anyone by their palm. How is your mother?"

"She . . . she died a few weeks ago," Johann replied softly. "The white plague, most likely."

"I'm sorry." The stranger nodded. "I would have liked to speak with her again. Well . . ." He gathered his scrolls and stood up. "I must go look after the horse and birds. Come back tomorrow if you like—I'll be offering my services here at the Lion again, and I'll be in the area until the fair."

"What services do you offer?"

"Oh, the usual." The foreigner shrugged. "I cast horoscopes, read palms, and sometimes dabble in a bit of hydromancy or pyromancy—whatever people desire."

"Pyro . . . what?" Johann was puzzled. "Is that magic? Are you a magician?"

The man laughed again. "Ha, don't call me a magician! I don't want to end up at the stake. The church doesn't particularly like wizards and magicians." He raised a finger. "No, I'm not a magician but an astrologer. A traveling magister, versed in the arts of alchemy and"—he winked at Johann—"yes, admittedly, also a little in the art of magic, such as it is taught at the University of Krakow. White magic, that is, not black. And now, if you'll excuse me."

He left Johann where he was, crossed the barroom, and climbed the stairs. Johann's head was full of words. White and black magic, alchemy, astrology, hydromancy . . . clearly, this man was far more than just a traveling juggler.

Johann was about to turn away when he noticed something glinting under the table. He leaned down and saw a small knife, about as long as his hand. The handle appeared to be worked from some kind of bone and was adorned with black patterns and lines. The surprisingly heavy blade was wide with a narrow point and sharp as a razor. There was a small hole in the end of the handle.

Johann ran his thumb along the blade thoughtfully. The knife must have belonged to the foreigner. He'd have to give it back—he was no thief, after all. And Johann had a feeling it wasn't a good idea to steal the blade of a magician. Surely that would bring bad luck. But it was such a nice knife! Why couldn't he just keep it overnight, or for a few days? The magician would be in town until the fair. Johann could always return the knife to him then and say he found it in the streets.

He weighed the knife in his hand, glanced around furtively, then slid it into the pocket of his jerkin. The weapon felt cool and hot at the same time against his skin, like a burning stone.

Still deep in thought, Johann walked out onto the dark street, and immediately his gloomy thoughts returned. Inside the warm, brightly lit inn, he'd forgotten all about his father and Latin School. Maybe Johann could talk to him again, promise to work harder? School was all he had left!

Johann was about to head for home when he heard a low whistle from a small alleyway. He spun around and his heart leaped with joy. Margarethe! He realized now just how much he had missed her.

"Margarethe!" he called out and ran toward her. "I thought you didn't want to see me anymore. Didn't you read the letters I wrote you?"

She held a finger to her lips. "My brother can't catch us," she whispered. "Or he'll tell Father. And he already knows too much about us! They're trying to keep me away from you because they're worried about the wedding. Ludwig says if he catches me with you one more time, Father will send me to a nunnery."

"Your brother can go to hell!" replied Johann grimly.

"Johann, don't you understand?" Margarethe gave him a pleading look. "I'm supposed to marry! It's a done deal between my father and the Schmeltzle family. They shook hands on it just a few days ago—as if I were a horse at market." She paused. "We'll celebrate my engagement next spring, when I'm seventeen. Old enough, my father says."

"Then let's go away from here," Johann said. "There's nothing to keep me in Knittlingen."

"Go away?" Margarethe gave a sad laugh. "And live off what? Your tricks, perhaps?"

"I'll think of something!"

"Oh Johann, my Faustus," sighed Margarethe. "I'd love to. Believe me. But there's no way out."

He took her hand and felt her shudder. He thought about their time together in the field, only a few weeks ago, how they had almost kissed, and the salty sweat on her skin. "You'll never find happiness with that man!"

"Happiness?" Margarethe laughed again, but this time tears twinkled in the corners of her eyes. "Who said I'm supposed to find happiness? I must bear his children and be a good wife. His family will elevate ours. The dear Lord never said happiness was part of married life."

"Margarethe, you don't believe that. Let's go away from here. We could—"

Johann noticed Margarethe's frozen expression and spun around. Ludwig was standing behind him with a whole gang, all of them eyeing him with loathing. In his excitement at seeing Margarethe again, Johann hadn't even heard them approach.

"Ludwig, don't!" pleaded Margarethe.

But her brother ignored her. He shoved Johann deeper into the alleyway. "Didn't I tell you to stay away from my sister?" he snarled. "Haven't you had enough? You just wait. When I'm finished with you this time, you won't be able to sit down until Christmas. You'll wish you'd never been born!" He leaned down and grabbed a nail-studded length of timber from a pile of rotten boards.

Johann clenched his fists. There were too many of them to fight back. Should he run? Call for help? But who would help *him*—the village smart aleck and good-for-nothing? People would say he had it coming.

Then Johann remembered the knife.

His fingers went to his pocket. The handle felt cool and pleasant. But he hesitated. If he stabbed Ludwig now, he'd be a murderer and branded forever. He couldn't do it! The price was too high. So he merely stood as still as a rabbit that smells the hunter but doesn't flee.

"Leave him!" shouted Margarethe, trying to run up to him. "Johann!" But two of the young men held her.

"Pull down his pants!" snarled Ludwig. "I'm going to teach him a lesson he won't forget for the rest of his life."

Johann thought of the knife again. It throbbed in his pocket like a small, breathing animal. How he'd enjoy cutting Ludwig's plump cheek open!

Ludwig raised the plank and was about to strike when a voice rang out from the street.

"There you are, you lazy layabout! Have you forgotten? You were supposed to take care of my horse! What did I give you a kreuzer for?"

Johann started. The foreigner stood in the alley and waved at him as if they'd known each other for a long time. In the dim light of night, only his outline with the wide coat was visible, resembling a scarecrow in the fields.

"Is that your new friend?" jeered Ludwig. "A skinny, dishonorable juggler? Ha! He can't help you now."

He raised his length of timber once more when the stranger spoke again.

"If you don't come right now, boy, I see great misfortune. Very great misfortune, for everyone here. The stars don't lie, and they shine wanly upon you boys. *Do you understand me?*"

It was the same voice the stranger had used earlier to threaten Ludwig's father inside the Lion. Low and cold, like a wind from the far north sweeping through the lanes. His last words had been clipped and as sharp as the blade of a butcher's knife. Ludwig lowered his arm slowly, as though someone were forcing it down.

"Damn it . . . All right, I'll let you get away this time," he said uncertainly to Johann. "But next time, you're done. I will get you—if not today, then tomorrow or next week. You mangy bastard! That's what you are. A bastard!"

He turned around and signaled for his friends to follow. Margarethe managed to break away and rushed over to Johann. "Tomorrow morning by the Trottenkelter press at the prefecture!" she whispered. "When the bells chime six o'clock, before morning mass. I—"

Ludwig dragged her away before she could finish.

"Your mother is a dead whore!" he shouted at Johann as he walked away. "D'you hear me? A dead whore!" Then the gang disappeared around a corner, Margarethe in tow.

Torn between fear, anger, and the hope of seeing Margarethe again the next day, Johann staggered into the street, where the magician waited for him with a smile.

"I believe you owe me a favor," he said when Johann stood in front of him. "It looks like I just saved you from a good beating. The least you can do is tell me what those boys wanted from you." He grinned a wolfish grin. "Let me guess: something to do with that freckled girl."

"One . . . one of them is her brother," Johann replied haltingly. He was still shaking. "He doesn't want us to see each other. He beat me up before and threw me into an anthill with my hands and feet tied."

"Into an anthill? Wow, that's nasty."

For a few moments neither of them spoke, and Johann's breathing gradually slowed. They could hear music and the laughter of men coming from the inn. Then Johann remembered the knife in his pocket. The cold metal he'd admired earlier suddenly repulsed him. He pulled the weapon from his jerkin and held it out to the stranger.

"You must have lost this under the table earlier. I picked it up for you."

"Yes, that's my knife." The foreigner raised an eyebrow in surprise. "Well, thank you." He took the knife and weighed it in his hand, thinking. Then he gave Johann an appraising look.

"Hmm, did I just hear that boy call your mother a dead whore?"

Johann nodded.

"And you just put up with it? If someone threw *me* into an anthill and called my mother a dead whore, do you know what I would do to him?"

Johann looked at the magician expectantly.

"I would wait until he sleeps, then I would bash his skull in with a cudgel. And once the blood ran from his nose and eyes, I would use this knife to cut off his lips. His lips and his goddamned tongue. So he would never say such filth about my mother again."

Johann waited for the man to laugh at his joke. But he didn't laugh; his pale face remained completely unmoved.

"Why do you put up with it, boy?" the man asked eventually, running his finger along the blade. "Are you always going to put up with it? Have you never thought of revenge?"

Revenge . . .

Johann closed his eyes for a moment. Oh yes, he had! In his many sleepless nights over the last few weeks he'd seen the same image over and over in his head: himself, lying bound and naked in an anthill, while Ludwig poured out the medicine with an evil smile on his lips. The same medicine that might have saved his mother's life. Oh yes, Johann had thought about revenge. He'd fantasized about wringing Ludwig's neck as if he were a chicken, and about slitting open his fat guts with a knife. The thought had entered his mind and burrowed its way into his brain like a tick he couldn't shake.

"Ahhh, you feel it, don't you?" The stranger's lips twisted into a triumphant smile. "Don't be afraid to admit it. I can see it in your eyes. Hatred burns inside you, and that is nothing to be ashamed of. Hatred can be very healing, purging the soul like fire. But it needs a direction, and it needs closure. You do want that boy to be dead, don't you? Dead like your mother?"

Johann said nothing, but then he nodded slowly.

"Then say it," the man urged. "It'll make you feel better! Just like sweet medicine."

"I . . . I want Ludwig to be dead," Johann said hoarsely before he knew what he was doing.

The man nodded and gave him a pat on the back. "There you go. You'll see, you'll feel much better." He gave a wide grin and bared his teeth, which gleamed unnaturally white in the light of the moon. Then he held the knife out to Johann.

"I'm giving this to you. You found it, so it shall be yours. I get the impression you could use a knife. It's a throwing knife and very old. I just sharpened it. It cuts skin and sinews like butter."

Johann hesitated, but the foreigner placed the weapon in his hand. "Take it, you silly boy. If you don't know what else to do with it, use it to peel turnips."

"Thank you," Johann said and put the knife back in his pocket. It felt much heavier than before.

"Oh, how terribly rude of me—I haven't even introduced myself." The stranger held out his hand to Johann. "My name is Tonio. Tonio del Moravia. Krakow magister of the seven arts and keeper of the seven times seven seals. Tonio to my friends. Shake hands."

Johann took Tonio's hand; it felt cold and damp, like the scaly skin of a fish.

"It was a pleasure to meet you," Tonio said and patted Johann's shoulder. "Now keep your eyes open on your way home. I can't bail you out every time."

Whistling, he untied his horse and walked away. A cool breeze suddenly swept the fallen leaves through the dark lanes, and a chill ran down Johann's spine.

Summer in Knittlingen was truly over.

~

The man who called himself Tonio led his horse into the stable and tied it to the wagon, which the lads working for the innkeeper had pushed in there. Above the box seat dangled the cage holding the raven and two crows. The birds screeched and flapped their wings when they recognized their master.

"So, what do you think?" asked the man with a wink. He stood below the cage, speaking to his birds as though they could understand him. "The boy strikes me as promising. Reminds me of you, Baphomet." The man laughed and gave the cage a nudge, making it swing from side to side with a squeaking sound. The raven fluttered wildly with his wings, struggling to stay on his perch, and stared at his master from mean yellow eyes.

"*Kraa,*" the bird called and it sounded almost like a human word. "*Kraa!*"

"Shh!" said the man. "Don't worry, Baphomet, you're still my favorite. At least until we find the right one and all this searching can come to an end." He uttered a sudden curse and gave the cage another push, causing the raven to scream like an angry child.

"Damn it, Baphomet, and I was so certain about you! I truly thought the day had come. Well, perhaps I'm mistaken yet again. It's been a while . . ." The stranger looked pensive, then he shook his head. "I must be mistaken. It can't be. Not yet—it's too soon. But it's worth a try, I think. Don't you?"

The birds fluttered and screeched.

"Easy, easy, you little beasts," the man said. "You had your time. Don't complain. Here, take this and be quiet."

He fished a few chunks of dried meat from a pouch and threw them into the cage. The birds pounced and devoured the chunks.

"And remember," the man said with a smile. "If he isn't the one, you get his liver. Promise."

He turned around and walked out of the stable, humming softly.

~

The next morning, Johann rose before sunrise.

He and Martin shared the attic room, where rats and martens scurried among the shingles. He dressed as quietly as he could, hoping his brother wouldn't wake. He'd hidden the knife Tonio had given him in his straw-filled pillow. If his father found it, he'd almost certainly accuse him of stealing it. He took out the knife and studied it in the sparse light. It looked valuable. The black inlay on the bone handle gleamed like gemstones. He noticed only now that three letters had been carved into the handle:

G d R.

What was their meaning? Could they be the initials of a name? The magician was Tonio del Moravia, so they couldn't be his. Perhaps he had stolen the knife from someone or bought it off its previous owner? But maybe the letters stood for something entirely different.

Johann weighed the knife in his hand, feeling its heaviness. He guessed he could always sell it if he found he had no use for it. Quietly he lifted the end of one of the floorboards and hid the knife underneath. It was better if Martin didn't see the knife; the young boy wasn't good at keeping secrets.

After hesitating for another moment, Johann replaced the floorboard and sneaked downstairs. Outside the house, he scooped a few handfuls of water from a bucket, washed his face, and combed his hair with his fingers. Then he hurried toward the prefecture, which lay behind the church.

The prefecture was surrounded by a high wall, like a town inside the town. Behind the walls were the wine presses, the tithe barn, the prefect's quarters, stables, more barns, and the jail, as well as a torture chamber. The inner part was protected by an additional moat and drawbridge. During times of war, the prefecture acted almost as a castle. But now, during grape-harvest season, the bridge was down and the gates wide open. The sun hadn't fully risen; a rooster crowed somewhere, but other than that, all was quiet. Not even the servants were out yet.

Johann entered the first courtyard and turned left toward the Trottenkelter, the building housing the oldest type of press at the prefecture. For decades people here had been pressing grapes to extract the juice with their feet. Three huge tubs that were almost as tall as a man stood inside the cool stone building, and barrels were stacked along the walls. The smell of mashed grapes was so overwhelming that Johann grew dizzy for a moment.

He and Margarethe had met up secretly here before. From the ground, no one could see a person hiding inside the tubs. And at the moment, most of the work took place at the large screw presses in the buildings on the opposite side of the courtyard. Therefore, this high-ceilinged, drafty building served as an ideal hiding place.

Johann climbed the ladder leaning against the left-hand tub. Soon he saw Margarethe's flaxen hair gleaming below. He jumped down into the tub and almost slipped and fell on a bit of old mash. Margarethe giggled.

"Don't fall," she said. "Or everyone will smell where you've been hiding."

"Where *we've* been hiding, you mean." Johann smiled. He'd missed Margarethe's chuckle so much. Her chuckle and her full red lips, which he'd almost kissed once.

Margarethe grew serious. "I'm sorry about what happened yesterday," she said. "I should have known my brother would follow me. At least I know for certain that he isn't after me now—Father is making him clean the big presses over at the Grosse Kelter before breakfast, as punishment for loitering about town last night instead of helping at work."

Johann nodded grimly. "Your father is a fair man. My father lets Karl and Lothar get away with murder while I have to do the dirty work. And he doesn't give a damn about Martin." His expression darkened even more. "Especially now that Mother is no longer with us. He even wants to take me out of Latin School."

"Oh God, Johann, I'm so sorry!" Margarethe gave him a hug.

It felt good to be so close to her. He'd never told her what had happened at Gallows Hill that night. There hadn't been an opportunity, but he was also too ashamed. He felt safe now in Margarethe's arms, almost as if he were in the arms of his mother. But then he remembered that he'd soon lose Margarethe, too.

"You can't go to Bretten," he whispered.

Margarethe stiffened and pushed him away. "I . . . I don't want to talk about it. Not today. Let's not think about next year for now." She closed her eyes. "I often think about that day in the field. You and me together by the old stone cross. Your kiss . . ."

"I . . . I wasn't going to kiss you!"

"Really? I remember it differently. See, our lips were this close." She pulled him close to her again. "This close . . ."

Johann stroked her hair. It smelled sweet and alluring, of grapes, milk, and cider . . .

Margarethe suddenly loosened her embrace. "What was that?" she asked quietly. "Do you hear that?"

Johann listened, and after a few moments he heard it, too.

It sounded like a soft whining. Desolate and cold, like wind pushing through cracks in a wall, but definitely human. For a second, Johann even thought he could hear words, but before he could make anything out, the sound stopped.

"It's nothing," he said with a shrug. "A crying child, perhaps."

"I don't know." Margarethe shivered. "What if it's something else?"

"What do you mean?" asked Johann.

"You haven't heard?" Margarethe lowered her voice. "Three children disappeared from the Schillingswald Forest in the last few days. The first one was a four-year-old boy who must have gotten lost. His siblings went out looking for him and didn't come back. People are whispering that the kobolds snatched the children and took them to their underground realm."

Johann realized he'd been too preoccupied with his own worries recently to listen to any news. He shuddered when he thought about how many times he'd roamed through Schillingswald Forest by himself since the death of his mother. The forest stretched from the city's southern boundary for many miles toward Pforzheim. It would be easy for someone who didn't know the forest well to get lost.

"And do you believe it was the kobolds, too?" asked Johann mockingly. He didn't want her to see that he was also a little frightened.

"Of course not!" Margarethe shook her head vehemently. "They could have been taken by robbers or wild animals—wolves or bears, perhaps. Maybe they simply got lost. Remember? Two years ago, little Liesl Müller went missing for more than a week, and then a hunter found her, almost starved to death."

Johann nodded, thinking back on the incident. He remembered the mother's wailing and then the cries of joy all over town when Liesl was found. Since that time, the girl had been strangely quiet and withdrawn.

And then Johann remembered the other missing children.

They had disappeared eight years ago, around the time Johann had first seen Tonio the magician. Johann had always remembered the magician's face as clearly as if he'd seen him just the day before, but he'd forgotten about the missing children. Suddenly he recalled something else, like from a dream.

The magician's wagon driving away behind the church, the canvas bulging briefly as if from a gust of wind, and a soft wailing sound. Of baby chickens or kittens.

Or of children . . .

But the image disappeared as fast as it had arrived. Johann couldn't tell if the memory had been real or if it had been the imaginative mind of an eight-year-old.

"What is it?" asked Margarethe, concerned. "Is it because of your mother?"

Johann shook himself. "It's nothing." He attempted a smile. "Nothing to do with us, anyhow."

"Well, in any case, Father doesn't want me to go beyond the city walls until they know why the children have disappeared." Margarethe rolled her eyes. "As if I was a little child who couldn't look after herself. I'm sixteen! It's ridiculous. He's probably just using the excuse to prevent us from meeting in the fields again."

"Then we just meet here," Johann replied.

"And why should I do that again?" Margarethe winked at him. "You were rather naughty last time, throwing an innocent girl to the ground and—"

She broke off when they heard the whining once more. But this time it was louder, much louder, and it turned into wailing and crying. Then someone screamed as though they were terrified. The screams came from somewhere across the courtyard. Doors and shutters were thrown open; hurried footsteps crossed the yard.

"Something must have happened!" said Johann, unwilling to let go of Margarethe. "Fire, maybe?"

"Let's go see." Margarethe climbed to the top of the tub. Johann followed her and, in his haste, splattered red grape mash on his pants. They jumped off the edge of the tub and ran out into the courtyard. Several workers and maids were running toward the open gate of the Grosse Kelter, the building housing the biggest presses, where the screams were coming from.

And also a piercing wail that sounded like a large dying bird.

"That's Mother!" shouted Margarethe. "Oh God, something terrible must have happened!"

Together they ran to the Grosse Kelter. Inside stood four presses far larger than those in the Trottenkelter. Heavy beams made of entire trees provided the necessary weight to squash the grapes. A crowd of people had gathered around the second press, staring at something in horror.

Underneath the press lay Ludwig.

Johann almost didn't recognize him. The pressing plate must have come down on him while he was cleaning the basket underneath. Blood and mash were mixed in a red mass and covered Ludwig's face and hands. His rib cage was pushed in like a large rotten apple, and his arms were dangling lifelessly over the rim of the basket. When one of the workers poured a bucket of water over the dead body, they could see Ludwig's face. Bulging, empty eyes stared up at the ceiling. His lips were twisted into a grimace of pain and terror, and a thin stream of blood ran from the corner of his mouth and into the vat.

"Oh God, my son, my son!" Ludwig's mother cried over and over, like a madwoman. "My poor son!"

She knelt beside Ludwig and held his limp, lifeless hand. Her cries gradually grew quieter and eventually turned into a mournful lament. Johann watched her dress become soaked with blood and grape mash. The prefect stood stone still among his workers, seeming unable to grasp what had happened.

"The beam must've come loose when he was cleaning the basket," whispered a broad-shouldered day laborer next to Johann. "I bet the mounting was rotten. I told the old man a long time ago he needs to replace the press—but he didn't want to hear! And now he's lost his only son."

Margarethe stared at the horrific scene in silence. Johann knew she'd never liked her older brother very much—but he still was her brother. He thought of the sounds they'd heard from their hiding place earlier. Had it been Ludwig's soft whimpering as he lay dying under the wine press, drowning in his own blood? Johann thought he wouldn't wish this kind of death upon his worst enemy.

Then he flinched.

My worst enemy . . .

Hadn't he wished Ludwig dead the night before? Tonio the magician had encouraged him to say it out loud. And now Ludwig was dead! How was this possible? It must have been a terrible coincidence, because anything else would be too awful to even think about. He looked at Ludwig's twisted face, contorted in horror. What was it Tonio had said?

Hatred can be very healing . . . But it needs a direction . . . and closure . . .

This here was the closure.

Johann suddenly felt sick to his stomach. He started to gag and turned away so he wouldn't have to see Ludwig anymore. When he looked down, he saw his own slimy red trouser legs. He hadn't eaten anything yet, and his mouth filled with sour bile.

This is the taste of revenge, he thought. *Not sweet, but sour.*

Johann sank to his knees and spat out thick green mucus while the lamenting of Ludwig's mother rose and fell like a never-ending chorale. When he had no more left to vomit, Johann looked down at himself, his lips trembling.

His fingers, pants, and shirt were red with grape mash, but it could also have been blood.

Ludwig's blood.

3

JOHANN HARDLY SAW MARGARETHE IN THE FOLLOWING days. The prefect's family was busy with the funeral preparations. It pained Johann to see how much effort was put into Ludwig's last journey. Johann's mother had deserved as much.

They washed Ludwig and dressed him in his best shirt. His casket wasn't a rough-and-ready box but crafted from heavy beechwood, and the funeral feast took place at the house of the prefect, with ham, sausages, and fragrant loaves of wheat bread. Ludwig had been the family's only son; all the other children except Margarethe had died in infancy. He was supposed to be the heir, and now there was only Margarethe. Johann's father told him and his brothers about the large crowd of mourners and rambled on about Ludwig—what a great fellow he'd been, strong as an ox, hardworking, and loyal to his father, just like his own eldest sons.

"Oh Lord, protect us from misfortune!" he prayed and threw his arms around Karl and Lothar. "I don't know how I'd carry on without you two."

Johann knew: if he should die before his father, the man wouldn't shed a tear for him.

Johann gave the Lion Inn a wide berth during those days. He couldn't stop thinking about how Tonio had encouraged him to say the death wish out loud. At night he tossed and turned for hours while rats scurried across the floorboards. He thought about how he'd shaken Tonio's hand after he'd voiced his desire for revenge, almost as if they'd sealed a pact. Johann had longed for Ludwig's death and then it had arrived. If this was indeed a pact, then what would he have to pay? Or had he unwittingly given something already? He hadn't gone near the knife under the floorboard again since, as if it were cursed.

But then Johann called himself a fool. Tonio might be an astrologer, a juggler, and a creepy magician, but surely he couldn't kill anyone just by wishing them dead. It was nothing but an unfortunate coincidence. A sad coincidence, nothing more.

Johann had heard from workers at the prefecture that the mounting holding the tree trunk above the press basket had indeed been rotten. Still, an uneasy feeling remained, along with a fear that Johann didn't understand. During one of his sleepless nights, he remembered some of the protective signs his mother had once taught him. He wrote them on a scrap of parchment, put the parchment inside a small leather satchel, and pushed it into a knothole in the threshold to his and Martin's room. People had shielded themselves from evil for centuries this way, and Johann immediately felt a little better—although he had an inkling that those words and symbols were just make-believe.

To take his mind off his fears and gloomy thoughts, he worked even harder in the vineyards, where the harvest was slowly drawing to a close. He carried almost two dozen loads each day, filled to the brim with the best grapes. But his father wouldn't change his mind. His decision stood firm: Johann wasn't allowed to return to Latin School.

His father hadn't visited his mother's grave in days. In fact, he seemed to be looking for a new, younger wife already. Only Johann and little Martin walked to the cemetery every day, bringing a fresh bunch of flowers. Summer blooms had turned to autumn flowers, and now that it was almost November, some days the only blossoms they could find came from the monk's pepper in the Maulbronn monastery garden. Johann knew his mother had particularly liked this inconspicuous plant.

All of Knittlingen was excited about the Saints Simon and Jude Fair. When the day finally arrived, Johann stood by the upper city gate like he'd done so many times over the years, watching the merchants and jugglers parade into town. But unlike in the past, he wasn't feeling excited. He and little Martin drifted with the crowd, snacking on something here and watching the jugglers for a while there, but the magic of the past had gone. And Johann heard people talk about the missing children. The number had gone up to seven, and all of them came from in and around Knittlingen.

But the children weren't the only topic of conversation at the fair. In the summer of 1493, the wise old emperor Friedrich, who had ruled the country for half a century, had died after a prolonged battle with a gangrenous leg. His son Maximilian, an adventurous knight who loved jousting, was now the sole German king. Word from faraway Granada was that the heathen Moors had finally been banished from Spain for good. And a Genoese man supposedly had found a new sea route to India and China via the Atlantic, although most people doubted it. Why should this nobody of a man succeed where the Portuguese had been trying and failing for many years? Although they had been following the coastline of Africa to the south—a lost cause. News from the Alsace was more reliable: another peasant uprising had been crushed swiftly; the leaders, as usual, had been drawn and quartered as a warning to others.

These days, messengers on horseback spread such stories faster than wildfire. The old folks shook their heads, reminiscing over a cup of mulled wine about the good old days when politics ended behind the next hill and God alone steered history.

Johann looked around and noticed some whispering girls glancing in his direction. He guessed they were gossiping about him and Margarethe. He'd spoken with her only a handful of times since her brother's accident. Every time he asked her about the impending marriage, she avoided his question. It was as if she had closed her eyes to what awaited her. Johann hoped to run into her at the fair soon. He might even snatch a few moments alone with her, like in the old days.

There was no sign of the magician on the square or in the lanes around Saint Leonhard's Church. Had he left town already? Surely the fair meant lucrative business for him. But deep down, Johann was glad he didn't have to see the eerie foreigner again. The man reminded him too much of Ludwig's cruel death. Still, he couldn't get the magician out of his head, like a melody that had etched itself into his memory.

"Will th . . . the devil get me, too, if I'm n . . . naughty?" said a familiar voice beside him.

Johann looked down and sighed. He thought he'd shaken his little brother, but now Martin had found him again. The boy clung to the tail of his shirt, afraid of losing his big brother in the crowd once more. Spellbound, Martin watched the puppets in a theater show moving back and forth in the window of a shabby box with filthy curtains and a painted background. Just then the devil himself appeared, dragging a poor sinner in the shape of a monk into the abyss. Johann couldn't help but smile.

"No, Martin, he won't," he said. "The devil only takes bad children."

"Did he also take the seven children that have gone missing?"

"You're talking nonsense. Satan has better things to do than take a bunch of brats to hell. But if you keep clinging to me like a burr, he just might."

He tried to walk away, but Martin followed him like a puppy. Annoyed, Johann spun around.

"I'm looking for Margarethe, and you're slowing me down."

"I know wh . . . where she is," Martin said proudly. "I saw her not long ago. If . . . if you take me with you, I can show you."

Johann rolled his eyes and took Martin by the hand. "You win. Take me to her."

Margarethe was sitting on the edge of a fountain a little way off the market square. She seemed deep in thought. Her brother's death had hit her quite hard, considering she'd feared Ludwig more than she'd loved him. Unlike her mother, though, she no longer wore black. It had been a terrible accident, but now life went on.

"May I?" Johann sat down beside her, and she smiled.

"I've got a stomachache from all the sweets," she said. "I think that's one thing about the fair that never changes. Not as far as I can think back, anyhow."

Johann laughed. "Do you remember the time we ate so much candy that I spewed on your lovely white dress? Your father gave me a good belting. And Ludwig—" He broke off. "I'm sorry," he said softly. "I wasn't thinking."

Margarethe shrugged. "It's all right. He was a monster, even though he was my brother. We both know it. Maybe he had some good inside him, but if he did, he never showed us. To him, I was a possession, not a sister."

They sat in silence as little Martin balanced along the edge of the fountain like the tightrope walkers performing in the square. It was afternoon by now, and the first drunken figures staggered through the lanes. Soon the musicians would play dancing tunes—much to the dislike of the church, which considered dancing to be the devil's wanton temptation. The air smelled of wine and rotten pomace, reminding Johann of Ludwig lying in the press basket like a squashed grape.

"Do you feel like going down to the Weissach River with me?" suggested Margarethe abruptly. "We can go back to the fair later."

Johann frowned. It was typical of Margarethe to come out with such a spontaneous idea; she was like a leaf in the wind, moved by her whims. Maybe she just wanted to get away for a while because Knittlingen and the fair reminded her of her brother and his horrible death.

"Didn't your father forbid you to leave the city?" he asked cautiously.

Margarethe waved her hand dismissively. "I'm nothing but thin air to him since Ludwig's death. He spends his days staring at the ceiling, just like Mother. Ludwig was the apple of their eyes. I'm just a girl who'll be married soon and out of the house."

"B . . . but what about the m . . . missing children?" stammered Martin, squeezing Johann's hand. "Our father also said not to l . . . leave town."

Indeed, just before the fair, Jörg Gerlach had told Johann explicitly not to go out into the fields with Martin. It had almost sounded as if the old farmer remembered his fatherly duties for once, but Johann suspected he was just trying to prevent him from meeting up with Margarethe.

"Do you know what I think?" said Margarethe. "I think those children have just gotten lost. Schillingswald Forest is huge—they could be in Pforzheim by now for all anyone knows."

"And what if it was the k . . . kobolds or the b . . . boogeyman?" asked Martin anxiously.

"Oh, Martin, you're such a scaredy-cat!" Margarethe laughed. "They only exist in your imagination!" She stood up. "I tell you what. We're going to Schillingswald Forest to look for the children. Imagine if we find them! They'd celebrate us in the whole of the Kraichgau!"

"You're not serious, are you?" asked Johann.

But Margarethe crossed her arms on her chest defiantly. "You're just shitting your pants like everyone else here! If you don't come, I'll go by myself."

Johann gave a sigh. He knew that when Margarethe made up her mind to do something, nothing would stop her. And of course he wouldn't let her go into the woods by herself. At least it was a way to be alone with her.

"All right," he said with a shrug. "But only until it starts to get dark. We must be back before the city gates close." He turned to Martin. "You better go home now. This isn't for little children."

"B . . . but I want to come!" said Martin in protest. "If you d . . . don't take me, I'll tell F . . . Father where you've gone and w . . . with whom," he added angrily.

Johann was about to make a harsh reply, but Margarethe cut him off: "Let him come. At least this way people can't gossip if anyone sees us."

Johann nodded reluctantly. "All right, then." He turned to Martin again. "But don't wet your pants if we do see a kobold after all."

Cursing under his breath, Johann walked ahead. He'd been thrilled at the thought of being alone with Margarethe, and now he'd have to put up with Martin! Would it never end?

Together they left the church and the fair behind and hurried toward the lower city gate. The shouts of the drunks and the noise of the fair faded away. All of Knittlingen seemed to be on Market Street and in the square, and the lanes on the far side of the church lay deserted. Finally they arrived at the gate, which was still open at this time of day. The only remaining guard had dozed off over a jug of wine presumably brought to him by a sympathetic colleague. The three explorers sneaked past him without problems.

Beyond the moat lay a few fields with a meandering stream, and behind the fields the forest began.

Even though the sun was still high in the sky, Johann thought the trees looked sinister and menacing, like an impregnable black wall rising up in front of them. He'd been here many times before, but today the edge of the forest seemed like the boundary to a foreign, evil land. They ran across a stubble field and soon reached the blackberry and hawthorn bushes at the forest edge. A jay screeched somewhere, and something big, probably a deer, disappeared rustling into the bushes.

"And now?" asked Johann, who was considering Margarethe's idea increasingly stupid. "What do we do now?"

Margarethe pointed at the stream entering the woods. "A path begins there. I know it from when I used to go into the forest with my father. If we follow the stream, we can't lose the path. It leads to a clearing with some large rocks and a cave. Maybe the children are hiding there."

"And you think no one else has thought to look there?" asked Johann mockingly.

"I don't know." Margarethe walked ahead. "But I do know one thing: if we stand around here for much longer, we might as well turn back around and let the others search."

Johann gave a shrug and followed her into the forest. Underneath the trees, it looked like dusk had already fallen. Many of the beech and oak trees hadn't lost all their foliage yet. Patches of thick undergrowth made it hard to see the path. The stream gurgled along peacefully, and it was as though a large bell hung over the woods, muffling every sound within.

They followed the stream in silence, as if they feared waking sleeping beasts. Johann knew the area. He used to bring the pigs here to fill their bellies on acorns, although he never went deeper than a few hundred steps into the woods. Beyond lay the unknown, inaccessible territory of hunters, forest workers, and outlaws.

The deeper they walked into the forest, the darker it got. Fir trees took the place of beeches and oaks, barely allowing any light to reach the forest floor. Thickets of thorny bushes slowed their progress even more, as well as fallen trees overgrown with moss and fungi. Several times they had to take a detour around obstacles and struggled to find the stream again. They reluctantly called out for the children, but it seemed to Johann their voices were instantly swallowed up by the trees.

"I . . . I'm scared!" whined Martin. His small, hunched body was trembling, and his stammer had grown worse, which always happened when he was afraid. "Wh . . . what if the b . . . b . . . boogeyman finds us a . . . and eats us?"

"I told you not to come, damn it!" swore Johann.

"Don't be afraid, Martin," Margarethe said soothingly. "The boogeyman would spit someone like you right back out." Her face was smeared with dirt and sweat, making her look like an angry forest sprite.

Johann knew the tales of the boogeyman and the kobolds. The stories were as old as time. But while he thought kobolds were just a myth, he wasn't so sure about the boogeyman. Every now and then, travelers told stories about dirty, ragged figures hanging about the woods; outcasts, the insane, wanted criminals—the forest was their home, and Johann, Martin, and Margarethe shouldn't have been there.

"I think we should turn back. It's late," he said to Margarethe. "We can come again tomorrow."

"Just to the clearing," Margarethe replied. "I'm sure we're nearly there. I came here with Father once."

Indeed, a short while after, they arrived at a small clearing drenched in afternoon sun. A handful of ducks fluttered into the air, quacking loudly, from a pond the stream flowed into; a pile of large, moss-covered boulders stood in the center of the clearing, forming a small cave at their base.

"Ha, I told you!" exclaimed Margarethe triumphantly.

Johann looked around the clearing. He'd never been here before. It was a quiet, peaceful spot, and he could indeed imagine that lost children might seek shelter here. They fanned out and searched the cracks in the boulders and the cave. But they found nothing, apart from old bear droppings and animal bones. Johann found a symbol scratched into one of the boulders: a bearded head with horns.

"What is that?" he asked, running his fingers along the moss-covered lines. "It looks very old."

"I bet the boogeyman drew this," Margarethe said with a wink. "That's just what he looks like—same as you if you don't wash your face."

Laughing, she ran down to the pond and washed her own face, arms, and legs, lifting up her dress high enough for Johann to see her marble-white thighs. He followed and washed himself, too, casting furtive glances at her. The water was surprisingly warm for the end of October. The sun shone onto the surface, and the two of them looked at their reflections in the water: Margarethe's freckled face with her flaxen curls, and Johann's narrow, pale face with the dreamy expression in his eyes and the raven-black hair his mother had loved so much.

Meanwhile, Martin had climbed atop one of the biggest boulders and waved from up high. His fears seemed forgotten.

"I can see the city from up here!" He laughed, clearly feeling at ease; even his stammer had vanished for the moment. "Let's stay a little longer, please?" he begged. "It's so nice here!"

Margarethe looked at Johann, and eventually he nodded. He also enjoyed the tranquil atmosphere of this place. "All right!" he called up to Martin. "But you stay in the clearing, understood?"

Martin threw his arms in the air and whooped—this hunchbacked little person reminding Johann of one of those mythical kobolds. He loved his brother more than anything in that moment. After his mother's death, Martin was the only one in the family he felt he belonged to. How could he ever have considered leaving Knittlingen? He had to stay for Martin. Martin needed him, and he needed Martin.

"He looks so happy up there," Margarethe said with a smile, watching Martin's little dance of joy.

"I think he likes being with us," Johann replied. "We're his family."

Margarethe laughed. "You mean like father, mother, child?" She started pulling him toward the cave. "Then quick, let's go into our house and cook a sorrel soup, like we used to when we were children, my dear husband." She sounded playful, yet there was an undertone of desire.

Johann was glad to let Margarethe lead him away.

~

Martin stood atop the boulders as if he were the king of the world.

He'd never been so happy in his life! He had been shunned and despised for as long as he could remember. People called him a cripple and a fool. But he didn't care, because all that mattered to him was his brother Johann. Especially now that Mother was dead. Johann protected him, played with him, and, most important, explained the world to him. Martin had so many questions. Why did the sun rise and set again? Where did lightning and thunder come from? Who made plants grow in the fields and calves in the stables? Why had the dear Lord given him, little Martin, a hunched back and a stammering tongue?

Johann didn't always know the answer, but he always went searching for an explanation. And now his big brother had taken him into the woods with beautiful Margarethe. They had brought him, the little cripple, along with them. Johann, Margarethe, and Martin. They'd always be together, for certain! His brother would never forsake him.

Martin climbed down from the boulder and walked toward the pond. He knew Johann and Margarethe were doing naughty things inside the cave. Earlier, Johann had made him promise to leave him and Margarethe alone for a little while. So he played among the reeds and made small boats from tree bark, letting them float on the pond. Then he tried to hit them with pebbles and watched them go under. One of the little rafts sank right in front of him. He leaned forward and thought he saw a black shadow in the depths, like a monstrous, slimy fish. Frightened, he shot up and stepped back.

There was a gurgling sound, and a bubble rose to the pond's surface. A slight smell of sulfur wafted across the clearing.

Martin thought of all the scary stories people told about the Schillingswald Forest. He thought about the kobolds and the boogeyman, who snatched little children. Suddenly the old rhyme the other children sang when they played no longer sounded funny, out here in the woods.

Who's afraid of the boogeyman? No one! And if he comes? Then we run!

But then he heard Margarethe giggle in the cave, the afternoon sun shone brightly, and the shadow in the water had disappeared as quickly as it had come. The smell of sulfur also faded. Martin breathed a sigh of relief.

Still, the pond now seemed unappealing. He stood up and went looking for a nice stick he could practice using his little knife on. Maybe he'd carve a heart on it and give it to Johann or Margarethe.

Martin knew the best sticks wouldn't be in the middle of the clearing but near the edge, where the forest began. He was walking toward a gnarly old oak when he heard an unusual sound. He paused and listened.

It was the sound of a willow whistle.

Martin knew willow whistles because he'd once made one with Johann. But he'd never extracted such heavenly tunes from it. The whistle he was hearing now played a soft melody, cheerful and sad at the same time.

It came from somewhere in the forest, not far from him.

Martin hesitated for a moment, then he entered the woods and immediately noticed how much darker it was than in the clearing. Again he heard the melody, but this time it seemed to come from another direction.

Martin was afraid, but at the same time he wanted to find out where the melody came from and who played it. With grim determination he clutched his little knife tightly and walked deeper into the forest. He didn't dare to call out. A strange magic lay in the air; the trees seemed to bend down to him like friendly, curious giants.

The whistle sounded very near now.

Martin closed his eyes for a moment. What a wonderful melody! It almost sounded as if his mother were singing by his bed. He hoped the song would never end.

Susie, dear Susie, what's rustling in the straw?

'Tis the little goslings, they don't have any shoes.
Susie, dear Susie, what's rustling—

There was a cracking sound and the melody broke off.
"What—?" he just managed to say.
Then Martin knew that the boogeyman was real.
And it was much worse than in his nightmares.

~

Johann and Margarethe were lying in the cave, where it was dark and cozy. The moss-covered ground made for a soft bed. They lay close together and Johann trembled all over, although he hoped Margarethe wouldn't notice.

"Now I can tell you," Margarethe whispered and leaned over him. Her hair tickled his nose. There was so little space in the cave that her breasts were pressed against his chest. "I didn't want to come here because of the missing children, but because of you."

"B . . . because of me?"

Margarethe chuckled. "You stammer like your little brother. Don't act more foolish than you really are! Didn't you notice the girls' looks at the fair? I think it's time we gave them something to gossip about." She brought her lips close to his. "You've tried to kiss me twice before. It's now or never."

Johann turned crimson with embarrassment and didn't know what to say. But he didn't need to say anything. Margarethe kissed his lips. She tasted so sweet, sweeter than honey or apples. They embraced tightly while she continued to kiss and caress him. Margarethe took his hand and placed it on her bosom, which had grown considerably in the last year.

"Touch me here," she breathed.

Johann didn't need to be told twice. At first he stroked her very gently, but then he pushed his hand under her bodice. He touched her nipples, which were hard with excitement. A shiver went through Margarethe's body.

"That's good," she whispered. "You're the first to touch me like that, you know. I've always loved you, Johann. From the moment I first saw you. You're so . . . so different. There's something great inside you—I can feel it." Then she chuckled again and her hand traveled to his codpiece. "I wasn't talking about *that*."

Johann tried to turn away in embarrassment, but she held him. "It's all right, Johann. It's all right."

They stroked and kissed each other, and Margarethe proved to be the more adventurous one. "If I must be engaged soon, at least I want to know what to do," she said softly. "It's my gift to you. But I must remain a virgin—we have to be careful."

Johann closed his eyes and let it happen. His fingers moved instinctively, sliding under her skirt and between her legs. She opened her thighs with a soft moan.

"My Johann," she whispered. "My Faustus . . ."

All his dreams seemed to come true at once. He loved Margarethe and she loved him back! What could keep them apart now? Perhaps they'd convince her father to break off the engagement, or perhaps he'd simply run away with Margarethe and Martin. Anything was possible!

They kissed, licked, and tasted each other in the most intimate, forbidden places. While Margarethe stroked him, he let his fingers circle, playfully at first, then more and more urging, until Margarethe's excitement erupted with a cry she struggled to suppress. They were so engrossed in their lovemaking that they didn't notice how fast the sun went down outside.

When Johann finally stumbled back into the darkening clearing, Martin had gone.

"Martin, where are you? Martin! Martin!"

Johann had climbed atop the highest boulder, where his little brother had stood and waved to them not long ago. With growing despair he scanned the clearing below, which was steadily being swallowed up by long shadows. At first he'd thought Martin was playing tricks on them. He and Margarethe had searched every crack in the boulders, hoping Martin would jump out of one at any moment. But his brother wasn't by the rocks or anywhere else in the clearing. How was this possible? Why would Martin go into the woods by himself? Unless . . . Ice-cold fear shot through Johann.

The pond!

He jumped off the boulder and ran toward the water.

"Wait!" called Margarethe after him. Her hair was full of bits of bark and moss from the cave, her face filled with anguish. All the feelings of happiness they'd shared a few moments before had vanished. "Where are you going? Don't leave me alone!"

But Johann didn't listen. He ran to the pond and jumped into the murky water, which didn't feel nearly as warm as an hour or two ago. Martin couldn't swim. The water wasn't more than waist deep, but Johann knew that was enough for someone to drown in. Just the year before, the smith's three-year-old son had drowned like a rat in the shallow city moat. His older sister had taken her eyes off him for only an instant.

"Martin! Martin!"

Panicked, Johann trudged through the pond, waving his arms back and forth in the water and hitting countless sticks with his feet on the slimy bottom. But he couldn't see Martin anywhere. Margarethe arrived at the pond, panting.

"Do you think he might have gone home without us?" she asked.

"Never! He was much too frightened. You heard what he said about the boogeyman!"

Suddenly Johann remembered the drawing on the rock—a bearded man with horns like a billy goat.

Horns of the devil.

Fear gnawed at Johann's stomach like a small animal.

"We have to search for him!" he shouted. "He . . . he must be somewhere in the woods!"

Again he rushed off without waiting for Margarethe. The entire clearing lay in the shade now; only the tip of the highest boulder still bore a patch of sunlight. The place Johann had found so peaceful earlier now seemed gloomy and menacing.

When Johann entered the forest, he realized how late it had become. Here, among the fir trees, night had already fallen. The trunks were black lines and the space in between was foggy gray twilight, and Johann could barely make out the ground. He stumbled and fell over roots and shrubs several times but got back to his feet and pressed on every time. He had promised to look after his little brother, and now Martin had disappeared. Swallowed up by this forest!

Or by something unspeakably evil.

"Johann! Johann! Wait for me!"

Margarethe's voice rang out behind him, sounding scared and quite far away now. Johann stopped, gasping for breath. It was completely pointless! The forest was huge. He'd never find his brother this way.

"Martin!" he shouted into the twilight. "Martin, can you hear me? Where are you?"

But he received no reply.

Instead, he heard something else.

It was a soft whimpering, a plaintive moaning that seemed to come from the trees themselves, or the fog surrounding them. Johann froze.

"Martin?" he croaked. His voice almost failed him. "Martin, is . . . is that you?"

It was impossible to tell where the sound was coming from; it seemed to come from all directions at the same time. Johann knew it could be difficult to rely on one's hearing for orientation in the forest. The Knittlingen prefect sometimes held hunts in Schillingswald Forest, and Johann had helped as a beater before. The beaters flushed small game out of their hiding places by swinging sticks and shouting, but they always stayed within sight of each other. They knew how quickly the woods could play tricks on you.

Johann held his breath and listened intently. He felt certain now. What he was hearing was the whimpering of a child.

"Martin!" he shouted into the darkness. "I can hear you! Where are you?"

Suddenly there was a piercing scream somewhere behind him. Johann thought it was Martin. But then he heard Margarethe's voice. She sounded frightened.

"Oh my God, go away, *go away!*" Her voice became more and more shrill, and she sounded scared to death. Johann had never heard Margarethe scream like this before.

"Margarethe!" he called out. "What is it?"

"Away, away, away!" she screamed again, high pitched, almost like an animal. And the forest echoed Margarethe's screams tenfold.

Away . . . away . . . away . . .

Johann spun around in panic. What was going on? Who or what else was in the forest with them?

"Margarethe?" he shouted again, and the trees seemed to swallow his calls. "Margarethe! Where are you?"

The screams had come from the clearing, he thought. Johann decided to look for her there. She was in danger! He picked up a solid branch and headed back. It seemed to be getting darker by the moment. Trees and background blended to a blackish gray. Johann kept running. Where was the damned clearing? There! He could see a spot that seemed a little lighter than the rest. Holding the cudgel tightly, Johann sped up and soon found the clearing.

But there was no sign of Margarethe or the mysterious attacker.

The screams and the whimpering had stopped. It was utterly still; even the birds had stopped singing, as if they waited for a signal.

"Margarethe!" shouted Johann. "Martin!" And he kept shouting, more and more desperate: "Margarethe, Martin! Margarethe, Martin!"

Ducks quacked by the pond and flapped their wings. Apart from that, Johann heard only his own voice as a jarring echo, as if an insane doppelgänger mocked him.

Margarethe . . . Martin . . . Margarethe . . . Martin . . . Margarethe . . . Martin . . .

The boulders were completely black now, like ink or blood seeping into the clearing.

Johann was gripped by an unspeakable fear.

He turned around and ran like never before in his life, racing along the stream. He stumbled and fell, got back to his feet, fell again, and kept running, out of breath, unable to form a single clear thought. All he heard were the thuds of his feet on the forest floor, the wind in the treetops above him, and the echo of his own voice inside him.

Margarethe . . . Martin . . . Margarethe . . . Martin . . . Margarethe . . . Martin . . .

Then suddenly there was more light and he staggered out into the fields. The lights of Knittlingen glowed warmly on the far side of the fields, and he could hear cheerful music coming from the fair.

Johann broke down crying.

He had made it out of the woods. But the only two people in the world he loved and whom he'd sworn to protect hadn't. Something evil lurking in the depths of the forest had taken them.

4

JOHANN SAT AT THE TABLE IN THE PREFECT'S HOUSE AND felt the eyes of the people in the room on him like daggers. They all glowered at him in silence, except Margarethe's mother, who was crying softly in the background.

"So you ran away," said Jörg Gerlach angrily, repeating what Johann had just told them in a trembling voice outside at the fair. "You left your little brother and Margarethe alone in the forest and ran away like a frightened rabbit. Not only did you disregard my order to stay inside the city walls, but you also acted cowardly! You . . . you . . ." Trembling with rage, he raised his hand to strike Johann, but the prefect stopped him.

"Leave it, Jörg," he said. "It's important that we find out what exactly happened."

Unlike Johann's father, the prefect was a level-headed man. Grief for his son had painted dark rings around his eyes. The news that now his daughter—his only remaining child—had gone missing had turned his face even more gray and wrinkled. He looked more dead than alive. Johann had found him and his own father at the fair and told them in brief, broken words what had happened. Jörg Gerlach had grabbed his son by the arm, and together with a handful of other men, including the priest and the bailiff, they'd gone to the prefect's house to question Johann.

"You're saying there was someone else in the forest with you?" asked the prefect.

Johann nodded uncertainly. "At least, I . . . I think so."

"What do you mean, you *think* so?" snarled his father. "Speak plainly!"

"Margarethe kept shouting 'Go away!' and I heard a whimpering."

"A whimpering? The boy's out of his mind!" said the bailiff.

As the head of the city watch, the serious old man was in charge of the questioning. They were sitting around the table in the living room. No one touched the full jugs of wine in front of them.

"It could be robbers living in the woods," the blacksmith suggested. "I heard them talking about a band of highwaymen in Tiefenbach waylaying carriages. Not even the imperial road is safe any longer!"

"Let us send out men with torches immediately!" said the prefect. "We have to find our children—now, before it's too late!"

"And what about the boy?" asked the priest, studying Johann, who was shivering all over. "He still seems to be out of his senses."

"Put him in the hole!" ordered Gerlach. "Maybe it'll help him remember what really happened—it has worked for others. And it's still a mild punishment for what he's done."

The bailiff hesitated at first but then nodded. "You're right, Jörg. Perhaps he'll come to his senses and then he can tell us the truth."

They took Johann, who was unsteady on his feet, by the arms and walked him to the prefecture's tower, which stood at the far end of the courtyard. The prison room was a dark, musty chamber with one tiny, barred window and a heavy, iron-studded door, which crashed shut behind him. Johann was alone. Soon he could hear the shouts of men outside and dogs barking—the search had begun. They would comb the forest the same way they did during a hunt, including the clearing Johann had described to them. He hoped and prayed they would find Margarethe and Martin. But deep down inside he felt that the two had gone forever, like the other children before them.

Johann's knees buckled.

Racked by silent fits of crying, he sank onto the dirt floor. Until then, a shell of fear and shock had enclosed him. He'd replied to the men's questions like a puppet, but now an icy wave of reality came crashing over him. He had sinned gravely, and prison really did seem like a mild punishment for his crimes. How could he have run away and left Margarethe and Martin behind? What had possessed him to do such a thing? No one had attacked him or pursued him. Everything that had seemed like the most wonderful thing in the world before— Margarethe's kiss, touching her body all over, their whispers and moans—all that seemed dirty and bad to him now. Perhaps the church was right to condemn lust as the tool of the devil, because the two of them seemed to have called upon the devil, upon pure evil, with their doings.

He had been punished by God.

Johann desperately tried to figure out what had happened in the forest. Had there been outlaws about, like the blacksmith suspected? The whimpering could have come from Martin with someone holding a hand over his mouth. Margarethe fought back and shouted, "Go away," so it would seem there was only one assailant, not several. He would have stood a chance against one man! He should have at least tried, instead of running like a chicken. The devil's face etched into the rock, Margarethe's screams, the twilight, the whimpering— everything had frightened him so much that he'd panicked.

The whimpering . . .

An old memory rose to the surface.

The wagon . . . The cage with the raven and the crows . . . The canvas billowing in the wind . . .

He'd heard a similar kind of whimpering before, eight years ago, when the magician was leaving town with his wagon. Could Tonio be behind all this? One misfortune after the other had occurred since the man had returned to Knittlingen. First he had made Johann wish for Ludwig's death, where-upon it became reality. And now Martin and Margarethe had gone missing in Schillingswald Forest. Johann realized he hadn't seen Tonio at the fair.

Because he was in the forest?

Of course Johann knew that children and youths were abducted from time to time. There were horror stories of hungry outcasts, of lunatics and wild men who caught little children and ate them. But Johann didn't really believe that part. The poor souls were probably sold to the highest bidder and spent the rest of their days as mine workers below ground, as slaves in faraway countries, or as child harlots. But the suspects were always gangs of robbers—a single man with a child would be too conspicuous. Tonio's presence in town and the terrible events could only be a stupid coincidence.

Johann huddled down in a corner of the prison chamber and thought about his life. Faustus, his mother had called him, the lucky one. The name had never seemed more wrong to him as in this dark hour. All his cleverness, his wit, his thirst for knowledge had led him not to the top, but into this abyss with no way out.

Time passed very slowly. Every now and then he could hear shouts and the barking of dogs in the distance. Half of Knittlingen was probably out in the forest, while he, the coward, the loser, was sitting in the hole.

When the first twilight broke through the dark of night, the shouts and barking suddenly became louder. The men were coming back. Soon afterward, heavy footsteps approached the door to his cell, then the bolt was pushed back and the door opened. The gray rectangle was filled by the bailiff, his coat ripped and muddy at the hem, his face damp with sweat and dew. But the man smiled as he lifted a lantern to illuminate Johann's face.

"Good news, boy," he said. "At least the prefect won't bite off your head now. They found Margarethe."

It would be a whole week before Johann was allowed to see Margarethe.

During that time, the people of Knittlingen—adults as well as children—acted as though he weren't there. When he returned to the grape harvest in the vineyards, they avoided him. He worked by himself among the almost-bare vines, and when he carried his full basket to the carts, the farmers stared at him in silence and spat on the ground. As soon as he walked away, they whispered behind his back. Johann was too ashamed to go to Maulbronn. Surely Father Antonius would shake his head at a boy who first lost the medicine for his deathly ill mother and then failed to help his little brother and his friend.

Martin remained missing, and the hope of finding him alive dwindled with every passing day.

The fair came to an end, and the jugglers and merchants left Knittlingen. Tonio the magician must have departed earlier—his wagon hadn't been parked outside the Lion for a while now. Hans Harschauber, the innkeeper and one of the few people who still talked to Johann, told him that the itinerant astrologer had indeed left town the morning of the first day of the fair.

Meanwhile, a group of men led by Jörg Gerlach and the prefect continued to search for Martin. They combed the forest with dogs almost as far as the Black Forest and past Bruchsal. They sent messengers to villages and towns near and far, but it was as if the earth had swallowed the boy. All that was found of Martin was a small, crudely carved wooden shoe lying near the clearing.

The worst were the evenings and nights at home. Neither his father nor his brothers, not even the maids, spoke with Johann. His bowl with soup or barley porridge was put in front of him in silence, and he wasn't included in the meal-time prayers. For many hours Johann would lie in his chamber upstairs, staring at Martin's empty bed beside him. What had happened to his little brother? Was he still alive? And if so, how was he doing? Was he sitting locked up in some stable or cage, crying, cursing his older brother who hadn't protected him? Was he lying in chains in the belly of a ship traveling down the Rhine, in the hands of slave traders who treated him like livestock?

Johann also worried about Margarethe. He'd gathered from a few whispered remarks made by the servants that she hadn't spoken since the incident in the woods. She merely lay in her bed in silence, getting spoon-fed, staring at the ceiling with wide eyes. She seemed to have been frightened out of her wits. Johann's heart ached with concern for Margarethe. If only he could see her! But the house of the prefect—the entire prefecture, in fact—remained barred to him. Whenever he approached the entrance, two or three servants appeared and made it clear that he wasn't welcome.

On the eighth day, the prefect visited the Gerlachs' house and spoke with Johann's father behind closed doors. Afterward, Gerlach addressed his son for the first time in a week.

"The prefect wants you to talk to Margarethe," he said frostily. "He reckons you might get through to her, help her get better. And maybe she knows something about Martin. Although I doubt she'll talk to the boy who abandoned her."

Johann was filled with renewed hope. If he could bring Margarethe to speak again, all would end well! She'd describe the men who abducted Martin. They'd search for them across the whole Kraichgau, find them, and break them on the wheel or draw and quarter them. Martin would be brought home safely and Margarethe would love him again, just like she'd told him inside the cave.

He ran over to the prefecture, where the prefect awaited him in the court-yard. In the last few weeks, the once strong, tall man seemed to have aged by years. His hair had turned gray, and deep furrows lined his face.

"She's in the back chamber," he said to Johann, gesturing toward his house. "Try your best, boy. I'm just not sure what else to do. The devil knows what she saw in the forest. It seems to me the dear Lord has turned his back on our family."

Johann walked past Margarethe's father like a whipped dog, crossed the courtyard, and entered the house.

In the chamber, Margarethe lay still on her bed, her eyes wide open. Johann came closer, his heart thumping loudly. But she didn't stir, even when he touched her cautiously. Her skin was as white as chalk, with blue veins showing underneath, and even now, in this sad moment, her beauty mesmerized Johann. He thought about their time together in the cave. That seemed like a lifetime ago. He had fantasized about becoming her husband then, and now she lay in front of him like a corpse.

"Margarethe," he whispered and took her hand. "Can you hear me?"

Her gaze remained blank, her lips unmoving. Only her calm breathing showed that she was still alive.

"Margarethe," Johann continued and knelt beside her. "I . . . I'm so sorry! I should have been there for you, for both of you. Please, talk to me! Just one word, so I know you can hear me. I . . . I love you!"

He squeezed her hand, which was cold and limp, like wet bread. Just when he thought she'd never speak again, her lips began to tremble. The words she breathed were so low that Johann couldn't understand them at first. He had to lean down close to Margarethe's face before he finally understood what she was whispering to him.

It was just two words, and they hit him like a blow to the stomach.

"Go . . . away."

It was the same words she had screamed in the forest when he'd abandoned her—and now they were addressed to him. And then her lips formed a phrase that would forever be etched into Johann's memory.

"Go . . . away . . . You . . . are . . . the . . . devil!"

Johann began to tremble, and everything around him suddenly seemed black and gray. The world was drained of all color. With tears in his eyes, he stood up.

"Goodbye, Margarethe," he whispered. "I will never forget you."

He ran his hand over Margarethe's flaxen hair one last time, then he turned around and walked to the door. Who did she think she saw in him? Or what?

You are the devil . . .

Johann stumbled through the lanes like a ghost, without direction, without aim. His true love—his only love—had cursed him.

~

The following morning, his father called him before breakfast. Like so often in the last few months, Jörg Gerlach was sitting at the kitchen table with a jug of wine, his face red from the alcohol. But unlike other times when he called upon his son, he asked Johann to sit. He stared at his son in silence for a long while before addressing him.

"Your brother Martin still hasn't been found," he said slowly. "And I don't think he will be found. The ravens are probably pecking away at his crooked bones by now."

His father's coldness sent shivers down Johann's spine.

"I want to be honest with you, boy. You're not welcome here any longer. Folks have never thought very highly of you—your tricks, your nosy questions, your fancy ways, acting like you're better than them—but now you've gone too far. Because of you, your brother died in the wilderness and the prefect's daughter is bedridden, more dead than alive." His father looked at him with contempt. "You've brought shame to my family, and I don't want you under my roof any longer."

Johann was dumbstruck. Margarethe had cursed him, and now his father was doing the same. Strangely, his father's words didn't affect him very much; it was as if they couldn't touch him deep down inside. The shock of Margarethe's rejection was too fresh.

"Of course, I can't force you to leave," Gerlach said with a shrug. "A father casting out his son doesn't look proper, even with a mongrel of a son like you. But if you stay, your life will be hell on earth—I promise. No one is going to speak with you, not even your brothers. You'll perform the most menial tasks and take your meals with the dogs outside." He took a sip of wine and stroked his beard. "But I'm not a monster. Upstairs in your room, you'll find a purse with a few coins, a warm coat, and a pair of solid leather shoes. Take it and go with God, or with the devil for all I care. I don't want to see you here tomorrow morning. The people will say you ran away, and everyone will understand." Gerlach made to get up, but when Johann started talking, he sat back down.

"Where does all this hatred come from, Father?" asked Johann calmly.

"Where?" Gerlach gave a laugh. "I think you can answer that yourself."

"I'm not talking about the woods or the fact that I wasn't with Mother when she died. You've always hated me. Am I not right? I've never had a gentle word from you. I was never allowed to sit on your lap. You've never given me as much as a piece of apple for a treat or a spinning top to play with. You even treated little Martin better than me. Why?"

His father said nothing for a while and stared at him from small, bloodshot eyes. Then he cleared his throat. "What the hell. You're leaving anyway, so why shouldn't you know?" He leaned forward and Johann smelled his alcoholic breath.

"Yes, it's true," Jörg Gerlach said quietly. "I never loved you like a son—because you aren't my son."

Johann winced as if he'd been slapped.

"Your mother was the most beautiful woman in town, but by God, people were right, she was a goddamn whore!" spat Gerlach, his eyes flashing with hatred. "I would have given her everything, but I was never enough for her. The whole of Knittlingen wasn't enough for her! She thought she was better than the rest of us, just like you. At home she acted all meek and quiet, but at the inn with the travelers, she laughed and danced and did as she pleased. I could never prove anything, but folks were talking, and I always knew that something was going on. Especially when that young fellow came to town, that . . . that sorcerer!"

"Sorcerer?" Johann felt as if he were in a dream. "What . . . what sorcerer?"

"A pale, black-haired fellow carrying a pack full of magic knickknacks. He was from the west, from beyond the Rhine. Some kind of scholar, traveling student, and juggler." Jörg Gerlach snorted derisively. "Claimed he could read the stars and speak with the dead. He put a spell on your mother, that's what he did! He only looked about twenty years old with his silky black hair, same as yours. But his eyes—I swear it—his eyes were those of an old man. Like the devil's eyes! They met up secretly in the forest, she and he. I'm sure of it. Because afterward she was a different woman, and cold as a fish in bed. Nine months later, you were born, you . . . you bastard!"

Gerlach spat out the last words, spraying saliva all over Johann's face.

"The man had the nerve to come back to town after you were born," Gerlach continued scornfully. "If only he'd taken you with him. But I made sure he left for good. By God, if he hadn't taken to the hills at the last moment, we'd have set that sorcerer alight like a straw puppet." He gave a brief laugh but then turned serious again.

"Since then, people call me a cuckold behind my back. They think I don't notice, but I feel it, every day. Every time I see you I'm reminded of my shame."

Jörg Gerlach rose to his feet. "Now get out of my house! You're not one of us and you never have been! Go and never come back to Knittlingen, so this curse can finally come to an end."

The last Johann saw of his father was his broad back and his bull neck as he stomped out of the kitchen, leaving Johann alone at the table.

Johann remained sitting there for a while. He looked at the devotional corner with the cross and the dried roses; the chicken cages under the bench, where he used to hide as a child; the chest with his mother's dowry; the faded, crooked picture of Saint Christopher that had brought him so much consolation over the years. Then he cast everything off like an old skin. He stood and went upstairs.

His father hadn't lied. On Johann's bed lay a small purse, a coat, and a sturdy-looking pair of shoes. Johann put on the shoes and coat, tied the purse to his belt, and reached for the staff he'd once made for little Martin.

He was about to leave when he remembered the knife under the floorboard. Traveling all by himself—it probably wasn't a bad idea to carry a weapon. And perhaps he could sell the knife. It looked valuable enough. So he bent down, lifted the floorboard, pulled out the knife, and slipped it in his pocket. On his way out, he helped himself to a piece of cheese and half a loaf of bread, placing both in an inside pocket of his coat.

Then he left his home for the last time and went on his way. Johann didn't yet know that this way would lead him to the highest of highs and lowest of lows.

Into the whole world and beyond.

It was still early in the morning, and the lanes and alleyways were empty. A light, cold drizzle set in, blowing against Johann's face. Many Knittlingers would still be working in the vineyards today, bringing in the last few sweet grapes. It was the final day of the harvest, and tonight, everyone would be celebrating. Without Johann, though—from now on, he was an outcast.

Strangely enough, Johann didn't feel sad. On the contrary: with every step he took toward the upper city gate, his spirits rose. He had a small purse full of coins, and he was clever and deft—surely some farmer would employ him as a laborer. And then he'd see. But first he needed to put as many miles as possible between himself and Knittlingen, not least to help him get over Martin, Margarethe, and everything else that had happened there.

He walked through the open city gate without seeing a guard. The old, wide imperial road stretched out before him, leading out into the world. The road led northwest on one side and to the southeast on the other. To the north lay Bretten, then the Rhine, Speyer, and Cologne; the southern route led via Maulbronn to the Württemberg lands, then Ulm, Mindelheim, and eventually Innsbruck, where the king resided occasionally. Johann had heard there were mountains there covered in snow all year round, and beyond them lay prosperous Venice, and somewhere beyond Venice came Rome, the eternal city.

He stopped in the middle of the road, unsure of which way to turn. He had a vague feeling that his future depended on the decision he made now. After standing around indecisively for a few moments, he pulled a stained coin out of his purse. Heads for south, tails for north. He tossed the coin high up in the air, caught it, and placed it carefully on the back of his hand.

It showed heads.

South.

Johann sighed. That meant he'd have to walk past the Maulbronn monastery and Gallows Hill. Evidently, fate wanted to remind him of his shame one last time. He grasped his staff tightly and started out without turning around to look at his hometown again. He walked along the bare fields and the vineyards, heading into the rain with grim determination. When he came past the execution site, he spat over his shoulder to ward off bad luck. This was where all his misery had started; from now on, he thought, his future would be brighter.

Soon the Maulbronn monastery appeared behind the fog to his left. Johann felt a pang of regret. How he had longed to find employment as the librarian's assistant here and delve deeper into the world of books and knowledge! For a brief moment he considered paying Father Antonius one last visit, but his shame was too great. If he returned at all, he'd do it as a celebrated scholar!

Johann imagined what it would be like to visit Father Antonius—old and gray by then—many years from now, bringing a whole wagon full of books and medicines as a gift. All of Knittlingen would regret the way they had treated their most famous son. His horrible stepfather would be dead and Margarethe well again. They would marry, and even little Martin would return from his captivity, laden with riches.

Johann was so wrapped up in his thoughts that he didn't even notice the monastery disappearing behind the trees. He had walked past it without realizing—which meant he'd walked farther than ever before in his life. Until then, Maulbronn had been the end of his small world. Now he'd taken the first step into the unknown.

A new, much bigger world lay ahead of him.

The first few nights of his journey Johann spent in barns, freezing. His happy daydreams had burst with the first hailstorm. He'd also learned that no farmer needed a sixteen-year-old laborer this time of year. The harvest was in and the vines empty. The people of the Kraichgau were sitting at home in their warm kitchens, mending their baskets, fixing leaking tubs and broken crates, or looking after their wine in the cellar. If he was lucky, Johann received a stale chunk of bread when he knocked on doors; if he wasn't, the farmer set his dogs on him.

The road seemed to wind endlessly through flat valleys filled with meadows and fields. Gentle slopes rose on both sides, covered with beech trees and oaks. Since ancient times the track connecting the eastern and the western ends of the German empire had run along here, between the Rhine flats and the lands east of the Neckar River. It was a lovely area during the summer, but now, in early November, autumn storms howled down from the mountains, and the rain whipped the last remaining leaves off the trees, leaving them bare and bending in the wind, like skeletons writhing in a dance of death.

Johann's spirits dwindled by the day, and grief filled his whole heart. The silence that often surrounded him reminded him that he was alone in the world. He had no one. His mother was dead, and his father wasn't his father but a nasty man who'd cast him out. He didn't know his real father—probably some traveling juggler who had courted his mother. All he had left as the stranger's son were the raven-black hair and the curse of being a bastard.

During his lonely nights, Johann sometimes pulled out the knife the magician had given him. He whittled small figures from rotten wood by the wayside and pretended they were his mother, Martin, or Margarethe. Often they'd turn out ugly or they broke, and he threw them away.

The handful of travelers going the other way, on horseback or with carts, were wrapped in heavy coats and wore their hoods pulled down low. They barely gave him as much as a nod in greeting, and soon the next rain shower swallowed them up. Johann's clothes were saturated and no longer dried out. He shivered with cold, his shoes were wet, and the drenched coat pulled on him like chains.

At night he was tortured by dreams of Margarethe and Martin standing above him with accusatory faces.

You frighten us, Johann! They called out and pointed their fingers at him. *You are the devil! The devil!*

Johann still didn't know what had happened that evening in Schillingswald Forest and whom Margarethe had seen. It must have been bad enough for her to lose her mind. Had she seen who or what had taken Martin? Johann guessed he would never find out. All of that was behind him now, and before him unfurled the never-ending road.

Though he'd hoped to save his money for harder times, Johann was soon forced to spend some on food. Every night he counted his coins carefully. There were mainly stained kreuzers and tinged copper pennies, with only three silver pennies among them. His stepfather had remained a miser to the last. Johann rubbed the coins as if they were made of pure gold, stacked them up in little towers, and calculated. If he kept spending at this rate, he'd be out of money within a few weeks. He thought about selling the engraved knife, but he didn't do it. Even though it had come from the magician, it seemed to be part of the world he had lost. Selling it seemed like selling a piece of himself. So he kept it and suffered from hunger.

Johann knew that if he carried on this way, sooner or later, he'd die on the side of the road like a stray dog. Unless he started earning money. If not by working as a laborer, then perhaps by doing something else.

And he had an idea just what he might do.

A wide river appeared in front of him—the Neckar, he gathered. This river also passed through Heidelberg, the city where he would have loved to study one day. Now, in late fall, the river shimmered metallic gray. It looked very cold and very deep, and there was no bridge he could see. Johann had to give away another one of his precious coins to an old ferryman, who eyed Johann the whole way across the river as though he was considering robbing him and tossing him into the water. Johann's tiny fortune seemed to run through his fingers like melting wax.

In the next village, a few miles on, he gathered all his courage and decided to try his luck.

He was still traveling on the imperial road, and so there was a post station here—an inn with a stable for the horses of messengers and travelers. Johann took a deep breath and entered the small, dark inn. It was late afternoon and raining outside, so the taproom was full. All kinds of travelers had sought shelter at the inn. In the flickering light of the open fire, Johann saw a burly merchant wearing a fur coat and a beret, two itinerant Franciscan monks, and several peddlers, whose tall packs were leaning against the wall behind them. Someone else seemed to sit farther back, but Johann couldn't quite make him out in the dim light. A handful of farmers were also sitting at the tables, enjoying the quiet period following the harvest with a few mugs of wine. They laughed and drank and paused only briefly when Johann came in and headed for one of the empty tables at the rear. But instead of taking a seat, he suddenly jumped onto the table and clapped his hands.

Now there was no going back.

"My esteemed audience!" he declared loudly, just like he'd seen jugglers in Knittlingen do. "Watch and be amazed, because I can multiply your money! Forget your worries and fears, because from today, you'll be swimming in coins!"

The people murmured, some of them laughing, some of them jeering. But Johann had achieved what he wanted. He had their full attention.

With a theatrical gesture, he reached into his pants pocket and pulled out one coin. He held it up, transferred it to his other hand, and placed it in his purse. He did the same with a second and a third coin. The first spectators began to mutter.

"He's moving the coins from his pocket to his purse," one of them grumbled. "What's so special about that?"

Johann raised an eyebrow and pretended to be shocked. "Oh, you're saying I should take the coins from somewhere else? Not from my pocket but . . . from the air, perhaps?" He took another kreuzer and dropped it in his purse. But this time, a new coin appeared in his hand as if by magic, then another and another. Each time, Johann took the coin and placed it in his leather purse, which he held up triumphantly once it was full.

"You see!" he shouted. "The pouch is full! A friendly spirit of the air handed me the coins."

The people laughed and clapped their hands. It was a cheap trick Johann had learned from an itinerant juggler in Knittlingen, but here, in a small village, it worked well.

"Now let's see if I find coins on you, too." Grinning, Johann jumped off the table and walked over to the fat merchant. Johann puffed his cheeks and gestured toward the burly man, who eyed him suspiciously. "This moneybags strikes me as a good place to start. May I?"

He leaned over the merchant and pulled a coin from his nose, and then another one out of his mouth. When he leaned down to the man's broad backside and coins jingled in his hand shortly thereafter, the people hooted with laughter.

"Dear Lord!" exclaimed Johann. "The man shits coins! I want a donkey like him in my stable."

The inn guests held their bellies with laughter while the merchant just sat there with a sour face.

But then the man broke out in a grin and extended his hand demandingly. "What a pretty little trick," he said. "And now give me back my money, boy."

Johann stopped short. "What money?"

"The money you pulled out of my backside. It's mine—you stole it from me, didn't you?" He turned to the people sitting at the tables around him and gestured at a leather pouch by his side. "The lad cleaned me out! This bag was full of coins before, and now it's empty."

Johann's smile froze. He couldn't believe what was happening here. The bag had been empty from the start. The merchant was trying to cheat him out of his money.

"So give me back my money!" demanded the fat man. "It was funny at first, but I swear to you, if you don't hand over my coins right now, you're a thief. And thieves get hanged."

"Give him the money!" shouted some of the other people. "Thief! Thief! Or we'll hang you from the linden tree!"

"But . . ." Johann tried to explain. "I promise you . . ."

"Hang him now!" cried one of the peddlers, a bearded knife-sharpener in rags, his belt heavy with grindstones and knives. "Before he steals our money, too. The boy is nothing but a common thief!"

Some of the farmers had sprung to their feet and held up their fists angrily, and the peddler reached for one of his knives. The angry shouts grew louder and louder.

"Hang him, hang him!"

Johann's hand went to the small knife in his pocket. But what would he achieve with that? He looked around in panic. The way to the door was blocked by the crowd, but there was a narrow window covered with parchment to his right. He ran toward the window and jumped through it headfirst. The parchment ripped and he landed hard in a pile of foul-smelling dung. He could hear angry shouts behind him. He briefly considered running out onto the road, but then he thought the merchant would most likely have a horse in the stable. If he ran, they would catch him faster than he could say the Lord's Prayer—and soon after he'd be dangling from the nearest tree. So he changed his plan. Hunched over, he ran around the building and toward the stable. While the people from the inn poured onto the road, he slipped through the stable door and hid in the straw.

It was warm and dark in the stable. A horse snorted somewhere, but other than that, all remained calm. The shouting outside grew quieter; a door was shut. It seemed the people had abandoned the search and returned to the taproom.

Johann waited a while longer, then he got up cautiously. He was about to open the stable door to go outside when he felt a knife against his throat.

"I had a feeling you might be hiding out here," hissed a voice right behind him. Johann saw from the corner of his eye that it was one of the itinerant Franciscans from the inn. A man of God threatening him with a knife—would this nightmare never end?

"Lovely trick you performed in there," said the monk in a growling voice. Johann could smell brandy and stale sweat. "I'm guessing your purse was full to begin with. And now I'd like to have that purse. Hand it over or I'll slit your throat like a lamb!"

"Please," begged Johann. "It's all the money I have!"

The monk laughed behind him. "Then you should take better care of it, boy. Now give it here!"

Johann thought about the knife in the pocket of his jerkin. He could feel it through the fabric. But if he reached for it, the fellow would most likely cut him open without batting an eyelid. Trembling, Johann reached for the pouch on his belt—when he realized it was still lying on the table in the taproom. He'd forgotten to take the purse in his haste!

"I don't have the money anymore," he said anxiously.

"What tricks are you playing now, damn it! Just you wait, kid, I told you I'd—"

Suddenly the man gave a loud groan. The knife fell from his hand and he sagged to the ground, gurgling. Johann spun around; standing behind the monk was a figure like a huge raven silently spreading its wings. Johann couldn't believe his eyes.

It was Tonio.

"Look at that, the oh-so-lucky boy from Knittlingen," said Tonio with a grin, calmly wiping his bloodied dagger on a bundle of straw. To his horror, Johann saw that his rescuer had slit the monk's throat. The wound gaped like a second, grinning mouth with blood spurting from it. The monk wheezed and jerked while the life drained from his body. One last tremble went through his body, and then he lay still.

"Quite a peculiar juice is blood," Tonio continued as he polished his knife, in a tone as if he were talking about the weather. "As much as you wipe and clean, something always remains. If you have five men with clean daggers and you want to find the murderer, just wait and see which blade the flies choose. They smell the blood even if we can't see it anymore. Interesting, don't you think?"

The magician looked just like Johann remembered him. Tall and haggard, with a narrow face and eyes as black as charcoal. Only he didn't look as pale today—his cheeks had a rosy glow, and his lips were red and full. Tonio placed the dagger back in his belt. Then he adjusted his felt hat and studied Johann. "So we meet again. Shouldn't you be at home with your family?"

Johann remembered the dark figure at the back of the inn. Tonio must have sat there earlier and watched him. Evidently he, too, was traveling along the imperial road.

"I . . . I no longer have a family," Johann replied and, still in shock, continued to stare at the dead monk and the growing puddle of blood on the ground. Tonio raised an eyebrow.

"If you're worried because he's an honorable man of the church," he said, "he isn't. Or rather, he wasn't. He was a scoundrel, a tramp, and a thief, like most people here." He shook his head in disapproval. "Didn't I give you a knife? Why don't you use it? You really ought to be more careful—the imperial road is full of scum. You can consider yourself lucky that I was here."

"Th . . . thanks," Johann whispered. He felt terribly faint all of a sudden. Everything went black before his eyes, and he braced himself against a beam.

"It looks like I helped you out once again," the magician said. He grabbed Johann by the arm and pulled him farther into the stable. Now Johann saw the familiar wagon and horse.

"Climb in the back," Tonio commanded with a low, sharp voice. "Before they come to check the stable."

Trembling, Johann climbed into the wagon. It was dark inside and he couldn't make out much, but it seemed to be lined with chests, and bunches of dried herbs hung from the canvas ceiling. The smell was sweet and sickly. The magician flicked the reins, and the wagon went rumbling out the open gate into the pouring rain.

"This time, you owe me more than a small favor," Tonio said over his shoulder as they drove out of the village in the dim light of dusk. "And I think I know just how you can repay your debt."

They rode in silence for the next few minutes. Johann expected the angry mob to pursue them at any moment, or the fat merchant on his horse. But nothing happened. Johann was shivering with cold; his already damp clothes had become soaked again when he'd escaped through the rain. He still couldn't believe what had just happened. He'd almost been killed and he'd lost all his money! Even the staff he'd carved for Martin once upon a time—his last reminder of his brother—was left behind at the inn.

But the worst part was the memory of the casual ease with which Tonio had slit the monk's throat, like a butcher killing a calf. Then he remembered with horror that the false Franciscan had been about to stab him to death for a pouch of rusty coins. How stupid he had been to think he could travel all alone, without a companion, a writ of protection, or a horse! He'd almost paid with his life for his stupidity.

The wagon squeaked and bumped along. Through a slit in the canvas, Johann could make out Tonio as a dark outline. Evening had turned to night, and the rain gradually eased off.

Once Johann's eyes had adjusted to the dark, he could make out more details inside the wagon. There was a lowered section in the middle that was covered with brushwood; he guessed that was where Tonio slept. What Johann had thought were chests turned out to be bench seats with storage space underneath.

The cage holding the two crows and the raven dangled from the ceiling among the herbs. The large, rusty cage swayed back and forth to the rhythm of the wheels, the raven watching Johann out of almost human eyes. The crows shuffled nervously from side to side on their perches, as if they sensed danger. For the first time Johann could study the birds more closely. The raven frightened him the most. It seemed to be quite old, with some feathers missing and a beak that was scuffed and jagged at the edges. There was something sly in its gaze.

Suddenly, the cart stopped. The canvas at the front was pushed aside like a curtain, and Tonio's head appeared in the opening. He gave Johann a sharp look.

"You're cold," he noted. "If you're not careful, you'll get a fever and die on me. Then I can forget about my payment." The magician tossed an old, musty-smelling horse blanket to Johann. "Wrap yourself up in that and then come out and help me with the fire. Go on!"

They were parked a little way off to the side of the road in a grove of dripping fir trees. Shivering all over, Johann searched for any firewood that wasn't quite as wet as the rest. When he returned to Tonio, the magician had already started a small fire with some twigs. Next to him stood a basket with eggs, a fat lump of bacon, and bread. The magician hung a pot above the fire and added water and various herbs from a pouch. Soon a fragrant, almost biting smell rose from the pot. Tonio took it down, poured its contents into a cup, and handed that to Johann.

"Drink," he ordered.

Johann obeyed. The brew tasted bitter, but it helped to dispel the cold. Tonio watched him in silence. When Johann had drained the cup, the magician spoke.

"Are you feeling better now?"

Johann nodded.

"Then listen to what I have to say." Tonio leaned forward, his angular, rosy face below the black felt hat glowing in the light of the fire. "I don't want to know what happened in that shitty little hometown of yours, or why you're traveling all by yourself. I don't care. The devil knows why fate has brought us together! I only know one thing: I've helped you out for the second time, and so you should be at my service. Quid pro quo! I saw the trick you performed at the inn. It wasn't bad, but it wasn't special. Any old juggler can do that. Do you know any other tricks?"

"Well, I . . . I know a few card tricks," Johann replied reluctantly. "And there's the shell game, the coin trick, juggling, the traveling sticks, the cursed die, the egg in the blanket—"

"The egg in the blanket?" The magician's bored expression changed, and he straightened up with interest. He reached into the basket behind him and picked up an egg. "Show me what you mean. I don't know that trick, and believe me, I know most."

Johann looked at Tonio with surprise. He'd once watched a drunken Venetian juggler perform the trick at the fair in Knittlingen and asked him to explain it for a skin of wine. Could it be true that Tonio didn't know the trick?

Carefully, Johann placed the egg on the ground and spread the horse blanket over it. Then he stood up and paced around the fire, making conjuring movements with his hands and muttering the spell the Venetian juggler had taught him. Apparently, it was derived from twisting the words of a Latin mass: "Hocus, locus, pocus!"

"Hit the blanket as hard as you can," he said to Tonio. The magician shrugged. Then he raised his hand and struck the blanket.

"Shame about the egg," Tonio muttered. "Now we're down to four. Scant supper for you."

Johann pulled away the blanket triumphantly. The egg was gone.

"Now lift your hat," he instructed Tonio.

The magician did as he was asked. The egg was lying in his graying black hair like in a nest. Tonio grinned and took down the egg. For the first time he seemed genuinely surprised.

"The trick is not bad," he said. "We can use that. But we need to work on the story around it. Always remember, the show is everything. It must be big and colorful. The mass can only be impressed by masses."

"I could have done the same with a chicken if we had one," Johann bragged, trying not to let his relief show. The trick with the egg and the blanket was one of the most difficult he'd learned. He'd practiced it for weeks in a small wooded area near Knittlingen. He hadn't been entirely certain it would work this time. Something told him it was very important that he'd performed the trick without mistake—crucially important.

"Well done." The magician placed the egg on the ground in front of him. "Now listen carefully. I am a traveling astrologer and chiromancer—am called magister, doctor, indeed, but it is getting harder and harder to attract an audience, especially in the cities. There are just too many jugglers and acrobats. That's why I need a trickster."

"A trickster?" Johann gave him a puzzled look.

"*Sacre bleu!* Don't you know anything? I thought you were a juggler." Tonio sighed. "There are different occupations among jugglers." He counted on his fingers. "Musicians, jugglers who actually juggle, goliards, false alchemists, bear tamers, tightrope walkers, and tricksters. They are young, cocky jesters who know the small tricks. Coin tricks, cups and balls—all those things. It will be your task to gain the people's attention. You're short and scrawny, but your voice is strong enough, as I heard at the tavern. Can you play the bagpipe?"

Johann shook his head. He'd never learned an instrument. He thought he wasn't very musical at all.

"You'll learn," said Tonio. "The bagpipe is the loudest instrument and easy to master. Whoever plays it draws the people in like with a magic flute." He grinned. "Even if it doesn't sound quite as beautiful. We'll start tomorrow."

"I . . . I'm supposed to travel with you?" asked Johann slowly.

"You finally got it?" The magician laughed. "By the devil, yes! I saved your life, and now you shall serve me for one year, as a test and without pay. After that time, we'll see. The pact is valid until I dismiss you." Tonio tilted his head to one side and eyed Johann. "You can't go back home, I can see it in your face. And traveling by yourself means certain death. Either you starve or you'll get butchered. So, what do you say? You'll fare well with me. You'll be amazed to learn what life holds in store for you. Shake on it."

The magician held out his hand. Johann thought of the last time he'd shaken Tonio's hand. The tall, haggard man with the felt hat still frightened him immensely. But did he have a choice? He had no money, and Tonio was right: he was doomed on his own. Besides, he felt almost magically drawn to Tonio, and the feeling was old and familiar.

It stemmed from his childhood, when he'd seen the magician for the first time.

He clasped Tonio's hand. The man's grip was viselike, and he held Johann's hand for so long that Johann gave a little cry of pain. It felt like the magician was squeezing the blood from his hand. Tonio smiled, and once again he reminded Johann of a wolf.

"Welcome to life on the road," Tonio said. "Our pact is sealed."

Johann pulled back his throbbing hand. "You said earlier that the year was a test," he said. "What if I don't prove worthy, if I don't live up to your expectations? If I don't pass your test?"

"Well, it's just like with eggs," Tonio replied and reached for the brown speckled egg in front of him. He held it in his fist. "Some withstand the pressure, while others . . ." He clenched his fist. There was a crack, and yellow yolk ran through his fingers and dripped into the flames. "Others crumble under it."

He wiped his hand on the ground as easily as he'd wiped the blood off his dagger earlier. Then he reached into the basket and started to cut the bacon.

"But now let's eat and drink. Oh, and one more thing." The magician held up his knife like a teacher's pointer. "From now on, you call me master. Understood?" He smiled. "And believe me—you will learn much from me."

Act II

Tonio the Sorcerer

5

THE FOLLOWING WEEKS WERE THE MOST EXHAUSTING OF Johann's life. Instead of returning to the road, the two men stayed in the forest. The weather was too awful for travel anyhow. The road had turned into a mud pit with wheel ruts deep as ponds. While the rain and sometimes hailstones as large as pigeon eggs beat against the canvas, Tonio made Johann show him every trick he knew. Usually the magician merely gave a bored wave or corrected Johann with a growl. Tonio was a tough master, not tolerating any sloppiness or the tiniest mistake.

"You call that a trick, damn it?" he snarled and struck Johann with a cane. "I saw the coin in your hand! One more time—and roll up your sleeves, for God's sake. Or do you want them to call you a swindler in the next village and string you up? I won't help you again!"

Johann got beaten on his second and third attempts, too. The same happened when he performed his card tricks—even those he'd thought he could do with his eyes closed. Tired, hungry, and sick from days of being cold and wet, he soon struggled to manage even the simplest tricks.

"Are you trying to insult me?" snarled Tonio. "Watch. This is how you do it."

The magician produced a deck of cards in one hand, let them slide into his other hand with a sound like a drumroll, fanned them, and suddenly held only kings. Then he closed the fan and opened it again, and now they were all queens. "And now you," he ordered.

Johann clumsily dropped the entire deck, and the cane came whistling through the air.

Soon Johann's hands hurt so badly that he couldn't hold cards any longer, and the master demanded he juggle balls out in the rain. Tonio's balls were red, blue, and gold and made of hard ash wood. When Johann dropped one of the balls, Tonio hurled it at him. After countless failed attempts, Johann had a huge bump on his head and felt every single muscle in his body.

"Three balls are nothing!" shouted Tonio. "Every peasant can do three. You must master four at least, if not five!"

In the evening they practiced the shell game. This trick was especially important to Tonio, and they spent the largest amount of time on it. Three walnut shells and a pea were lying on a small box in the wagon. The pea went underneath one of the shells, the three shells were shuffled about, and the intended victim had to guess which shell the pea was hidden underneath. Tonio didn't take his eyes off Johann as he pushed the walnut shells back and forth on the box.

"It's important you let them win at first," the magician said. "They must feel sure of themselves before you milk them. You only strike when there's enough money on the table. Understood?"

Johann was quite good at the shell game, and Tonio soon left him alone about it—though not before reminding him several times to never become complacent. To Johann's surprise, the magician didn't ask to be shown the trick with the egg and the blanket again. It seemed to Johann the master begrudged him a trick he didn't know himself.

Beaten and humiliated, Johann fell asleep beside the fire soon after dark every night, while Tonio read his books, murmuring silent verses as if he was learning entire pages by heart. Johann's sleep was dreamless and deep. For the first time in a long while he didn't even dream of Margarethe and Martin. But early in the morning, the torture continued.

They stayed in the forest for nearly two weeks, until Johann had mastered the most important tricks. When the weather improved, they set off again, following the post road to the southeast.

The following days went roughly the same and were almost always accompanied by rain, from drizzle to torrential downpours and everything in between. They always practiced in the late afternoon until long into the night. During the day they rolled along the imperial road toward Ulm, making camp away from the road and getting up at the crack of dawn. The master slept inside the wagon while Johann had to lie by the fire with a threadbare blanket. Throughout each chilly, wet night he'd frequently wake up shivering. He suffered from a terrible cold, his nose running and his head thumping. But the master showed no mercy.

Johann was allowed to rest only during the brief hours they traveled along the bumpy road.

Every morning, after a bite of bread and a sip of watered-down wine, Johann had to feed the horse and hitch it to the wagon. Then they set off and drove until they arrived at a village or a larger township. If there was a market square, that's where they went; if not, they simply parked on the muddy road near the village church, where they'd soon be surrounded first by children, then by the rest of the villagers.

For the next few hours, Tonio would hold court in his wagon while Johann made a lot of noise. He performed his tricks, juggled the balls, and declared loudly that the world-famous astrologer and chiromancer Tonio del Moravia had come to town, a master of the seven arts and keeper of the seven times seven seals, to read the future of anyone who'd like to know. It was never long before there'd be a line outside the wagon. For a few kreuzers, Tonio would read their palms or cast hasty horoscopes for them. In the meantime, Johann would clean out people's pockets with the shell game. At some point during the afternoon, when the crowd dispersed or someone arrived from the local authority—the bailiff or some of his henchmen—they'd move on, find a new place to camp for the night, and practice. And so they moved along the imperial road.

It was a hard life, but not the worst, and Johann might have grown to like it. He might even have learned to put up with Tonio's beatings and constant criticism without complaint—if it hadn't been for that accursed bagpipe.

Johann loathed the instrument, which reminded him of a stubborn animal. It consisted of a leather pouch crafted from a stinking goatskin and several protruding tubes. Two so-called drone pipes produced different but equally howling notes, while the melody pipe or chanter was like a flute and was played with the fingers. Another small pipe served to blow air into the sack.

No matter how hard Johann tried, whenever he blew into the pipe, all that came out was a pitiful squealing or an awful squawking, causing the master to throw up his hands in despair every time.

"*Mon Dieu*, are you trying to frighten off every soul between here and Cologne?" he'd exclaim. "The only creatures you'll attract with this music are the wolves. Try harder, God damn it! The bagpipe isn't hard to play—anyone can do it."

But try as he might, Johann wasn't getting any better at it. The master made him practice every afternoon, sending him deep into the forest in rain, hail, or sun. Johann knew the master could still hear him from over half a mile away. If he paused for too long, he didn't get any supper. If Tonio decided he'd produced only caterwauling again, he didn't get any supper, either. Whenever the master told him off, the birds in the cage joined in, bickering and cawing as if they were jeering at Johann. Johann wished he could wring the raven's neck, but he was afraid Tonio would then do the same to him.

One evening, when the master told him once more what a pathetic juggler and embarrassment he was, Johann finally lost his temper.

"If my playing is that horrible, why don't you play the bagpipe yourself!" he shouted. "Or better still, get yourself on stage and perform your tricks like you used to. You're bound to impress the audience more than I do!"

"How . . . how dare you, boy." Tonio's face turned red and he looked like he was about to explode, his hand raised to strike. But then he paused and gave a grin. "All in good time," he said. "There are masters and apprentices. If the master performs the tasks of the apprentice, he makes a fool of himself. And if the apprentice tries to imitate the master, bad things happen."

"But I want to learn how to cast horoscopes and read palms!" exclaimed Johann with indignation. "I'm never allowed to watch when you read people's futures."

"Like I said, all in good time." Tonio tossed the bagpipe at him. "What does it say in the book of Ecclesiastes? There's a time to be silent and a time to speak. Now go back into the forest and practice, boy. If I hear the wolves howl, no supper for you."

December brought snow to the land. They'd left the Kraichgau region behind long ago, and Württemberg, too. From time to time, stone markers indicated when they crossed into another county, bishopric, duchy, or knight's estate. On many bridges they had to pay a toll; sometimes a quick horoscope or a cup of wine would suffice. Tonio explained to Johann that the German empire consisted of hundreds of small states.

"Everyone here cares only about themselves," he muttered. "Praise be to my France, where Paris is the hub of everything. But that's what the Germans are like—they don't look farther than the next tavern."

The area they passed through next was called Albigoi or Allgäu, and it was mountainous and inhospitable. The people here spoke with an accent Johann could hardly understand, though it must have been German. They drank a sour brown ale, completely different from the beer at home—although home was nothing more than a fading memory now. Only at night, when the blackness of a starless sky covered him like a musty shroud, would he suddenly feel homesick, and then he'd think of his mother, of Martin, and of Margarethe.

As a distraction, Johann often took the small knife into the forest along with the bagpipe. He still hadn't figured out what the engraving on the handle might stand for.

G d R.

He didn't want to ask Tonio. He was afraid the master would once again ask him why he hadn't used the knife to stab the false monk. In Tonio's eyes, Johann was a coward and a weakling.

It was a throwing knife, and Johann practiced by hurling it at dead tree trunks. At the beginning he was just as clumsy as with the bagpipe, but after a while his throws became stronger and more accurate. Sometimes he imagined faces of people on the tree trunks—Ludwig, his older brothers, or his stepfather. But he found that he grew increasingly angry that way, more aggressive with every throw until sweat ran down his forehead. Panting, he'd put the knife back in his pocket, where it felt cold and heavy.

Icy winds swept across the fallow fields; icicles like daggers hung from the bare trees. To the south, they could make out the steep, snow-covered peaks of the Alps. Johann remembered that Rome and Venice lay somewhere beyond that mountain range. But how did pilgrims manage to get across that wall of rock and ice? So far, the master hadn't given him any clues about their destination, but Johann couldn't imagine they'd cross the mountains during winter.

At least they no longer slept outdoors but at inns and taverns along the imperial road—mostly at one of the many new post stations, which offered a decent amount of comfort. There was a station every twenty miles, where post riders changed horses or handed over their mailbags to the next rider. That way, the riders could travel up to a hundred miles each day—a speed, compared to their lumbering cart, that seemed to Johann like the flight of a bird.

At every inn, the master, acting like a noble lord, always took one of the best rooms, while Johann, as his apprentice, slept with the horse in the stable. But at least it was warm there and he was left in peace. Only the suspicious looks of the raven and the two crows disturbed him. It almost seemed like they were spying on him so they could report to the master later.

Tonio often held court in the taproom, just like he had done in Knittlingen. It never took long for a crowd to gather when the great Tonio del Moravia spread his books and scrolls full of mysterious symbols on the table. The tomes bound in crumbling leather were part of the show, demonstrating what a learned man the master was. Now Johann could finally watch Tonio at work.

There appeared to be different ways of predicting the future. Most of the time the master studied the client's palm, running his finger along the various lines and murmuring mysterious phrases. If it was a young woman, he'd say, "Look at that, your Fate line and Heart line cross right here—a good sign! Next spring you'll be standing at the altar with your dapper bridegroom." If he was reading the hand of an old man, he'd say, "The Life line has many small branches, but it runs deep. You've been blessed with a long, interesting life, thank the Lord!"

This was what the master called the art of chiromancy. Tonio never foretold harsh blows or death. Mostly it was rich harvests, an imminent wedding, or unexpected wealth that would befall his clients.

For those willing to pay a little extra, Tonio would read their destiny from a glass of water or the flickering flames of the open fire. Those mysterious arts were called hydromancy and pyromancy. The master could also read from the clouds, crystals, and playing cards.

Very rarely someone requested a nativity chart. Such customers would invariably be wealthy citizens, like the village bailiff or burgomaster, and one time even an abbot. A pile of money would change hands, and Tonio would ask for the client's day and place of birth and then retreat to his chamber, where he'd work all night. The next morning, he'd emerge from his room looking pale and tired, carrying a length of parchment covered with small writing and symbols. Johann could make out circles and drawings of animals, though he didn't understand them. But the clients always seemed very pleased.

Johann was dying to know what the master was doing in his room, but as much as he begged and pleaded, the horoscopes remained Tonio's secret. Neither did he allow Johann to look at his books. When they were on the road, he kept them locked up in one of the chests under the benches. At the inns, he took them to his room. Johann suspected the books were very old and very valuable.

Tonio steered clear of larger towns and cities, which sometimes meant long detours. When Johann asked the master about it, he shook his head.

"People around here aren't always favorably inclined toward chiromancers and astrologers," he said. "They're a rough, superstitious people. Some think we're sorcerers or necromancers. I don't want to end up burning at the stake— even though it'd be warmer than this goddamned Allgäu in this weather. Damn the cold!"

Toward the middle of December, they were hit by the worst snowstorm Johann had ever seen. Icy grains stung them like needles, the wind tore at their coats, and visibility was so poor that Johann sometimes feared he'd gone blind. Drifts of snow piled up on the road, and several times Johann had to climb off the wagon with a shovel to clear their path. They barely made any progress, and behind every bend was another drift. The storm howled as if it were laughing at the little mortals below.

In the afternoon, the wagon became stuck in a deep rut. It took them over an hour and many failed attempts to pull it back out. The horse whinnied and shook the snow from its mane. The old nag didn't look as though it would last five more miles.

"Damn, if I didn't have you slowing me down, I'd long be across the Alps and in the warm countries of the south," groused Tonio, his voice carried off by the howling wind. "We are traveling much too late in the year. But no, I must explain to you even the simplest coin trick again and again! Thank God I know an inn not far from here where we can spend the winter. Come on, now! Or do you want to freeze your ass off here?"

He jumped back on the box seat and cracked his whip. The horse moved forward reluctantly. The thought of spending the next few weeks beside a cozy fireplace made Johann feel a little warmer already. Finally this journey through snow and ice would come to an end. They would celebrate the birth of Christ with a steaming mug of spiced wine at a tavern. Perhaps he'd even get to sleep in a bed and be granted a look at Tonio's books.

It was long after darkness had fallen before they finally saw the lights of a village through the driving snow. Mountains like black giants rose behind the lights, silent and insurmountable. Tonio urged the horse on, and half an hour later they'd reached the first houses. A large inn with stables and several out-buildings was situated in the village center. The buildings were arranged around a courtyard, forming a small fortress with only one gate for an entrance.

"The Black Eagle," Tonio said with a grin and climbed down from the wagon. His mood had improved drastically during the past hour. "The best inn between Kempten and Innsbruck. I spent a winter here once before. Their rooms are tidy and the straw beds fresh, with hardly any fleas or lice. And the wine and food aren't bad, either. Even a real-life emperor once stopped here on his pilgrimage to Rome."

Johann caught a glance inside through the crown-glass window. He heard music and laughter, and the warm glow of the lamps looked inviting. Shivering, he rubbed his almost-frozen fingers and couldn't wait to warm himself with a cup of hot wine. Tonio knocked at the gate, and soon a voice answered.

"Who wants to enter the Eagle at this late hour? You can't be a post rider, because you didn't blow the horn."

"The honorable master Tonio del Moravia, astrologer and chiromancer, scholar of the seven arts, requests admittance," replied Tonio loudly. "He is on the search for winter quarters and willing to pay good money and offer up his legendary skills!"

They heard a few shouts inside, then hurried footsteps. A bolt was pushed back and an obese, bald man wearing an apron appeared in the gate. He eyed Tonio and Johann from small, piggy eyes, shifting his weight from one foot to the other nervously.

"I'm the innkeeper," he said haltingly. "And I'm afraid I must tell you that you can't stay here—not for the winter, anyhow. You may consider yourselves our guests until the morning."

Tonio's smile froze. "And why is that?"

"Well, how can I put this . . ." The innkeeper kneaded his apron. "I'm afraid you've come too late, honorable master. We're already putting up another astrologer, and two of your kind, um . . . Do you understand? I'm afraid people will start talking."

"Another astrologer?" Tonio's voice had grown as cold as the winter storm still raging outside the gate. "And who is that supposed to be?"

"He calls himself Freudenreich von Hohenlohe, a minstrel and itinerant doctor. He says he's the only true white wizard."

"Freudenreich von Hohenlohe?" Tonio laughed derisively. "I've heard of the fellow. He's a cunning swindler. Robs people of their money and sells them salves made of bear shit."

The innkeeper made a wry face. "My wife bought one of his salves. She had terrible pain in her arms and legs, and now it's gone. And the horoscope he wrote up for me was very positive."

"Nothing but lies!" shouted Tonio at the innkeeper. "Throw him out and take us in!"

"I can't," the man replied desperately. "He paid in advance. Please understand. All I can offer you is a room for one night. You have to move on tomorrow, or I'll be in trouble."

Tonio said nothing for a long while. Johann started to think he'd turn around without another word. But then he finally replied.

"Very well," he said quietly. "We won't encroach on your hospitality for more than one night. But I promise you, no matter what that Freudenreich foretold, it won't come true."

He handed the reins to the trembling innkeeper and walked into the courtyard. Johann followed him dejectedly. He'd been so excited at the prospect of spending the winter here. And now they'd have to leave again the following morning. Where would they go?

Together they entered the inn on the left-hand side of the yard. The warmth hit Johann and almost instantly made him sweat. The room was quite full. Most of the patrons were farmers, listening to a young minstrel playing the fiddle. He looked like he wasn't yet thirty years old, and wore a garish tunic, one side colored differently than the other. Lined up on the table beside him were rows of jars and bottles, several sheets of parchment, and a crystal ball sparkling in the glow of the fire. When Tonio looked over to him, their eyes met. A mocking smile played on the minstrel's lips as he performed a satirical song about the winter in a delicate, high-pitched voice.

"Winter, O winter, you frighten me not. I sit by the stove and my fire burns hot. O winter, keep howling, I show thee no mercy. I'm drinking my beer where it's warm and it's cozy . . ."

The people danced and clapped their hands. No one paid any attention to the tall, haggard man with the felt hat and the snow-covered black-and-red coat, standing in the doorway with his apprentice.

"Well, well, the famous Freudenreich von Hohenlohe," hissed Tonio. "He never was any good at singing—nor at telling the future, for that matter."

"You know him?" asked Johann.

"We've met a few times on the road. The whippersnapper calls himself a wizard, but in reality he's nothing but a quack and a balladmonger, robbing people of their money. And someone like that steals my winter quarters." Tonio's lips were as thin as knife blades when he glared at the minstrel once more. "Freudenreich, what an incredibly stupid and unfitting name! He won't find happiness in these harsh climes, oh no, he won't."

Johann found himself shivering at Tonio's words.

The innkeeper assigned them the last available room—a drafty hole in the attic that looked like it hadn't been cleaned in a long time. The straw in the cushions was old and smelled musty, and Johann saw lice and bedbugs crawling in the light of the tallow candle. Strangely, the master allowed Johann to stay with him this time. He'd brought the birdcage upstairs, too, and the crows and the raven flapped about restlessly in the corner. They seemed to sense their master's anger and tension.

For a long while, Tonio just sat on his bed and stared straight ahead. When Johann cleared his throat, the master raised his hand imperiously. "Be quiet. I need to think," he growled. "Or do you want us to freeze to death? We need winter quarters, and I can't think of any other inn this close to the Alps that'll take in an astrologer and his good-for-nothing apprentice."

Finally, Tonio seemed to reach a decision. He nodded with grim determination.

"I might know a place. It's about thirty miles from here—two to three days' travel in this atrocious weather. If we lower our expectations a little, it'll do just fine." Then he grinned. "Who knows—perhaps it's a stroke of fate. It can't be worse than this stinking hole."

Tonio's mood improved dramatically. He reached for the bottle of wine and the ham and moldy cheese the innkeeper had brought upstairs for them. The magician hadn't wanted to eat in the taproom. He filled two cups and pushed one toward Johann. "Go on, drink, so you'll get warm."

Johann accepted the cup gratefully and took a few sips. Never before had the master offered him wine. The alcohol warmed him up almost instantly, and he felt a lot less miserable. His spirits rose. Cautiously, he glanced at the leather bag holding the books Tonio had brought upstairs with him as usual. The magician noticed the direction of his look and laughed.

"The books won't leave you alone, will they? You're a clever lad, even though you'll never get far with the bagpipe. Who cares! I hate musicians these days. So why don't we study a little?" He winked at Johann. "Let's see how you do."

Tonio reached into the bag and pulled out one of the books. It was a stained, heavy volume, its yellowed pages covered in drawings. The magician opened the book at a page depicting a hand with lines, bumps, and symbols.

"Let us begin with chiromancy," said Tonio. "It belongs to the arts of divination, the third path of white magic. Of all the different ways of foretelling, it is the easiest to learn." He gestured at the various lines in the drawing. "See for yourself. No two hands are the same, just as every man has his own fate. The left hand shows your dispositions, and the right hand your future. Look at the Life line, which separates the ball of your thumb from the remaining fingers. It tells you how strong someone is, whether he can expect illness, and how he gets on in life. Each disruption has a particular meaning—sometimes even death. This is the Head line. It stands for your mind, and the Heart line for emotions. They mostly run parallel, and interruptions here can mean a broken heart, but also an impending marriage."

Johann studied his own hand, for the first time paying attention to the many lines. All together they really did look like a map, like roads in a yet-unknown land.

"And what is this line?" Johann pointed at a fourth line on his right hand, which ran straight down from his middle finger and was broken in many places. Johann had also found it in the drawing, where it was marked with a strange letter.

"Ah, that is a very special line! The Saturn line, or line of Fate. It tells us about our destiny. If you know how to read it, you can see right inside a person!"

Johann cleared his throat. "When I was still a child, you read my hand. You told me I was born on the day of the prophet, and my mother also spoke of that. She said I was chosen by God. What does that mean? Can I read my own hand?"

"You're taking the second step before the first one, boy." The master smiled. "I told you before: all in good time. Let us study the art of chiromancy first. It's important that you find your own way to yourself."

Without elaborating further, Tonio pointed at several circles and lines underneath the fingers. "Look here. This is the Mount of Venus. And that one is the Mount of Luna, which tells us about a person's transcendental talents . . ."

The master explained long and patiently. But he didn't mention the day of the prophet, and Johann soon forgot his question. Too mysterious, too intriguing were the many different aspects of chiromancy. He'd waited so long for the master to show him more than a few cheap tricks—and now he was finally learning one of Tonio's arcane secrets. How many more of those secrets were written in his books? How much more was there to learn?

"I'd like to try it," Johann said timidly when the master finished his explanations. "May I read your hand?"

Tonio seemed to hesitate briefly, then he gave Johann a mocking smile. "My hand can't be read. See for yourself." He held out his right hand, and to his surprise Johann saw that there were hardly any lines on it. There were calluses and a few scars, but no Head line, Heart line, or Life line.

As if someone had wiped the map clean.

Johann frowned. How was this possible? The master's hand was like a blank page. Didn't he say that every person was readable, that everyone had those lines?

Tonio quickly withdrew his hand and grinned. "Don't worry. You'll soon get an opportunity to practice your skills. You shall read someone's hand in the next village—a simple peasant, perhaps." He pushed the book toward Johann. "Now memorize the lines and mounts well. You have until the candle burns out. Then we'll sleep and get out of this filthy hole first thing."

Johann leaned over the book and studied the lines and their names while the master watched him thoughtfully. Sometimes Johann asked a question and Tonio answered curtly. Hours passed. Eventually, the flame started to flicker, gave one last jerk, and died. Darkness descended over the chamber, and Johann closed the book and lay down. It had felt so good to read and learn something new, like he used to do at the monastery. His hunger for knowledge was insatiable, and there was so much the master could teach him. Johann thanked God for sending him to the southeast when he hadn't known which way to turn, so that he ended up meeting Tonio del Moravia.

He woke up once during the night to find the master sitting by his bed, stroking his hand and watching him with piercing black eyes as if looking deep inside him. Johann wanted to sit up, but Tonio held him back.

"Sleep, young Faustus, sleep," he whispered. "We'll know more about each other soon. All in good time."

Johann wanted to get up, wanted to ask the master a hundred questions, so many things he'd just thought of in his dreams. But he was overcome by exhaustion so strong that he sank back onto his cushion and was instantly asleep.

~

Later in the night, the master stood up and walked over to the cage with the crows and the raven. As usual, when their master approached, they beat their wings and squawked—it was hard to tell whether out of fear or excitement. Johann tossed and turned on his bed at the other end of the room, but he didn't wake. Deep in thought, the master pulled a few bits of dried meat from his pouch and tossed them to the birds.

"The boy is truly astounding," he murmured. "Smart and thirsty for knowledge. And those lines . . ." He shook his head. "Maybe our search really is coming to an end. It's possible. The stars can't lie. Or can they? Baphomet, Azazel, Belial—"

The raven pecked at him, and the master quickly pulled his fingers out of the cage.

"Ouch! How dare you, you bastard?"

A few drops of blood fell to the ground and disappeared in the straw. The bird stared at his master expectantly with his small yellow eyes.

"Lousy beast!" hissed Tonio and licked the blood off his finger. "You can't bear the fact that you failed, Baphomet. That he might be the right one. But you had your chance, and it wasn't you. Now shoo!"

Tonio hit the cage. The raven flapped about wildly, attacking the iron bars with his beak.

"*Kraa!*" called the raven, and it sounded almost human. "*Kraa! Kraa!*"

But the master wasn't perturbed. He looked over to Johann, who was twitching in his sleep.

"I think it's a good idea to go to the tower with him," he said pensively. "What do you think? We'll have all the time we need there. And we've got to stock up on our provisions, and I'll be able to hunt there. The meat is rather tough and stale by now."

He put one of the brown lumps between his teeth and started to chew.

"Oh yes, we need fresh provisions."

~

It would be two more days before Johann was allowed to read his first palm.

The next morning, the storm had passed and they left the Black Eagle. They didn't see Freudenreich again, but when they stepped through the gate, the master turned back one more time. His lips formed silent words, and then he leaned down and placed three black pieces of coal in the snow outside the threshold.

"What are you doing?" asked Johann.

"I'm leaving a message for other jugglers and magicians," Tonio replied. He stood up and wiped the soot off his hands. "No winter quarters to be had here. Saves everyone the argument and disappointment."

He climbed onto the box seat and cracked his whip. Johann turned back to look at the inn one last time. Dark clouds were gathering above it, like the fists of an angry god. In front of them, however, the morning sun made the fresh snow sparkle. The storm had turned the trees along the road into sculptures made of ice. The sky was bright blue, and the countryside was covered in a glittering white blanket. The air was clear and fresh, and Johann felt wide awake.

He would have liked to know what place the master had chosen for their winter quarters. But Tonio said nothing. When Johann asked, he only waved his hand. "I think you'll like it. At least it'll be nice and quiet there." He laughed. "As quiet as a grave. None of those superstitious peasant folk will set foot anywhere near the place."

Even though the weather was fine now, it was freezing cold, and they made slow progress. The road led south toward the mountains, and soon they'd reached the first foothills of the Alps. Their way led through rugged hills and past boulders so big that Johann thought giants must have thrown them from the mountains. The handful of cottages at the side of the road all looked battened down, their shutters closed. Smoke rose from the chimneys, but the inhabitants of this inhospitable area didn't seem to have any interest in passing travelers. When they came through the small villages they hardly saw a soul—only occasionally a shadow behind a shutter, a fearful pair of eyes following them.

"Didn't I tell you?" said Tonio. "They think the devil himself rides in this wagon. Now that Saint Thomas Night is near and darkness wins over the day, people are even more superstitious. I hope they'll at least sell us provisions for the winter."

When Johann became too cold, he went into the back of the wagon and wrapped himself up in a woolen blanket. But the cage with the birds hung there, and Johann felt watched. The raven especially seemed to stare at him with loathing.

"*Kraa!*" called the black bird again and again, almost desperately, as if it was trying to tell him something. "*Kraa!*" The monotonous sound rattled Johann's nerves.

And so he never stayed in the wagon for long, despite the cold.

Late in the afternoon of the second day, they came to a large farmstead standing alone in a clearing in the woods. Dogs growled and barked when the wagon came closer to the solid stone house. But the farmer gave them a warm welcome. He was impressed by Tonio's pompous demeanor and his offer of casting a horoscope for the whole next year for a very small sum. The farmer's sheds and pantries were full, and he agreed to sell them flour, bacon, dried meat, onions, and a small keg of wine.

In the evening, they all sat together in the cozy farmhouse kitchen. Children, workers, and maids all sat on the bench seats looking frightened, their eyes glued to the magician. Tonio was telling the farmer about his travels and the latest news. Those stories were often part of the service.

"After I finished my studies at the celebrated University of Krakow, I moved to the warm south, to Castile, where the sun burns so hot that the people are as black as ebony and as hard as kilned clay," he told them while sipping his wine. "Down there is a huge rock called Gibraltar, populated with herds of small, hairy creatures with sharp teeth."

The farmer's family listened with their mouths open as Tonio continued, waving his arms in dramatic gestures. "Then I continued by ship to Crete, the isle of the happy, and on to Constantinople, which was conquered by the accursed heathens a few years thereafter. My travels led me to countries inhabited by animals whose tails grow from their mouths, and horses with necks as tall as trees."

"But weren't you afraid of falling off the edge of the world?" asked the farmer fearfully.

Tonio laughed. "Haven't you heard? The Earth isn't flat—it's a ball! Just this year, in Nuremberg, I saw a map in the shape of a ball that showed all the countries in the world."

"But if the Earth is a ball, then the people at the bottom are upside down," said one of the workers. He scratched his louse-ridden beard. "How's that supposed to work?"

"Well, how do you think, you dimwit?" Tonio shrugged. "They wear shoes with nails at the bottom so that they always stick to the ground." The family nodded and muttered in agreement.

It was quite late by the time the master rose from his seat and stretched. He gave the farmer a nod. "I'm going to retreat now and work on your horoscope," he said and then gestured at Johann. "My apprentice will keep you company. He is skilled in the art of palm reading. Perhaps one or two of you would like to know what life has in store for you." Tonio winked at Johann before climbing the stairs that led up to the quarters the farmer had prepared for his two widely traveled guests.

The family stared at Johann anxiously. For the first time, he could understand what it felt like to be a traveling magician—respected and feared at the same time, an outcast and yet admired. He possessed a knowledge that was inaccessible to simple people. His words—a single look, even—decided the fates of entire villages and towns.

After a few moments, the corpulent farmer's wife shuffled closer to him and held out her trembling hand. "The last harvest was good," she began haltingly, speaking with a throaty accent Johann struggled to understand. "But a lightning strike destroyed our bakehouse just as I was carrying the bucket to the well. Is lightning going to strike me down next time I leave the house in foul weather?"

Johann took her right hand and tried to remember everything the master had told him and what was written in the old book. First he felt the woman's hand to see if it was clammy or dry, and whether there were many calluses and cracks from hard work. He could already draw some conclusions from that. Then he studied the various lines and mounts.

"The lightning that struck your bakehouse was a warning," he said in a low, mysterious voice. "But if you continue to fulfill your duties as good Christians and give shelter to pilgrims and travelers, no harm or storms will come to you. I can't see any serious misfortunes in the coming years."

Indeed, the woman's Life line ran deeply and evenly, and she looked well fed and healthy. Johann told her a few more things about her godly marriage and future blessings. Then a pretty maidservant came and held out her hand shyly.

"Should I stay with this farmer after Candlemas, or should I find somewhere else?" she whispered.

Johann could tell by her frightened eyes and the sour look on the face of the farmer's wife that there was bad blood between the two women. He studied her lines, especially the Heart line, which was broken and splintered. "You better find a new place to work," he replied quietly so the others wouldn't hear. "You'll find happiness somewhere else."

He proceeded similarly with the next two candidates, a worker and another young maid. He looked at their lines, but what he mostly tried to do was find out what their fears and worries were and what they were hoping to hear from him. Johann realized the art of chiromancy was both easier and more complicated than merely applying knowledge from books. It was about really listening to people, and the hand was just an aide.

Finally, the corpulent wife pushed one of her sons toward him. He was a handsome lad of about eight years, whose curious, alert eyes reminded Johann of himself as a boy. As was customary for a son of a well-to-do farmer, his hair was cut above the ears, which made him look more slow witted than he probably was.

"This is Rafael," said the farmer's wife, stroking the boy's hair adoringly. "My youngest and most beloved. The priest reckons he's smart and ought to attend a higher school eventually—perhaps at Innsbruck, even! What do you think, Master?"

Johann smiled. Evidently, the wife thought he was a gentleman or at least a scholar. Sometimes professors and students traveled from town to town, earning money as scribes. Those students were usually university dropouts who thought they were superior, but they actually were the most educated people many of the rural villagers would ever meet.

Johann picked up the boy's hand and studied it closely. His Head line was very strong indeed, but the bright eyes had already told Johann that Rafael wasn't silly. He was about to speak when an odd feeling startled him. It was like a gentle, warm throbbing coming from the boy's hand, as if the lines lit up underneath the skin for a brief moment.

And then he knew. The realization hit him like a blow.

The boy didn't have long to live.

It was nothing more than a dark premonition; the glow beneath the skin had long gone, but Johann sensed it very strongly.

The mother seemed to notice that something was wrong and eyed him suspiciously. "What is it? Is he going to become a farmer after all? No higher school? Speak up!"

"No, no." Johann shook his head. "It's . . . it's nothing." He tried to smile. "The priest is right. Your Rafael is going to become a learned cleric, perhaps even an abbot. The Lord is smiling upon you."

The wife clapped her hands excitedly, then she hugged her youngest son tightly. "You see, I told you, darling. God has great plans for you!"

Johann felt sweat running down his forehead, and his throat was bone dry. He didn't understand what had just happened. This had nothing to do with anything he'd read in the books or heard from the master. He thought of Tonio's words from two days ago.

It's important that you find your own way to yourself.

Was this what the master had meant? Johann hoped fervently that he was simply tired and had imagined the throbbing. He stood up, said a hasty good night, and climbed upstairs. In the chamber, Tonio was sitting at a table, writing on a piece of parchment in the light of a candle. Jerking shadows danced across the walls. The master looked up and eyed Johann expectantly.

"So? Did you read their futures?" he asked.

Johann nodded.

"It's not always pretty, is it? Now you know what it means to walk on the third, dark path." Tonio turned back to his parchment and drew strange-looking figures with his scraping quill. After a while he spoke again, but without looking up.

"When we reach our winter quarters, I will teach you more. More than you like, perhaps. Be patient, my little Faustus."

Johann dropped into his bed and fell asleep almost instantly. His dreams were gloomy and as sticky as spiderwebs enclosing his mind.

6

THEY LEFT EARLY THE FOLLOWING MORNING. THE FARMER had been very pleased with his horoscope—not least because it was written on real, expensive parchment. In return for his services, the famous and honorable Tonio del Moravia had received a smoked leg of ham, a keg of wine, and two small sacks of flour. In addition, they'd purchased nuts, dried fruit, salt, honey, cheese, and salted meat.

As they slowly rolled through the snow-covered alpine foothills at dawn, Johann's thoughts kept returning to the uncanny feeling that had overcome him when he'd read Rafael's palm. Could it be possible that he had foreseen the boy's death? The master hadn't said anything more about his protégé's first experience as a chiromancer, but Johann thought he could feel Tonio's eyes on him. When Johann had turned around to look at the farmstead one last time, Rafael had stood in the window, smiling and waving. Johann had turned away with a shudder, unable to return the wave.

They had left the imperial road the previous day and were traveling west along a narrow path. It became increasingly difficult for the horse to pull the wagon. The track was steep and in some places ran along a sheer drop into the valley below. Once, Johann caught a glimpse of a city by a wide river behind the crests of several hills, with a castle sitting on a peak above the town. But it soon disappeared from view. Snowdrifts blocked their way again and again, and each time Johann had to climb down and clear the track with the shovel. Each drift delayed them for over half an hour. Meanwhile, Tonio sat on the box seat, cursing and cracking his whip impatiently.

"We'll never get there at this pace," he groused. "Do you want to freeze to death so close to the end? Come on, move it—it's snow, not cement!"

But to Johann, every shovelful of snow felt like a shovelful of lead.

In the early afternoon, they left the track near a small village and turned onto an even-narrower path, which was bumpy, covered in tree roots, and only just wide enough for the wagon. It wound through a patch of forest with dark firs and sharp boulders, some of them as tall as trees. The snow was knee deep in places, and while Johann labored with the shovel, clumps of snow and ice rained down on him from the trees, soaking his clothes. Finally, when the wagon was stuck once more and a fallen tree blocked the road ahead, Johann threw the shovel aside angrily.

"Damn it, where is this journey supposed to lead?" he railed. "To hell? There's nothing but rock and ice here!"

The master grinned. "Well, it's a little too cold for hell. The devil doesn't like to freeze. But let me assure you, we're nearly there." Instead of grousing and cracking his whip, the master jumped down from the wagon and helped Johann shovel the snow. Together they were much faster. After another hour, they'd even managed to drag the tree aside. Tonio grabbed the horse by the reins and pulled mercilessly. The old black nag whinnied and shook the ice from its mane, exhausted nearly to death.

When Johann had almost stopped believing they'd ever arrive, the trees suddenly opened up and revealed a hilltop sticking out of the forest, with the tall peaks of the Alps in the background. Atop the hill stood a single stone tower, defiant as a castle, with a derelict stable beside it. The tower looked ancient, its stones polished by countless storms. Several of the battlements had broken off like rotten teeth. Black windows stared at Johann like the eyes of a huge beast. From up here they could see far down into the valley, where gathering clouds warned of the next storm.

To Johann, the tower on the hill seemed like it marked the end of the world.

"We're here." Tonio gestured at the building and wiped the cold sweat from his forehead. "I can tell you now—I wasn't even sure I'd still find the tower. It's been a long time since I was here last." He trudged up the hill while Johann stayed where he was, gaping at the building in front of them. His breath formed little clouds in the icy air. This pile of rocks was supposed to be their winter quarters? He'd expected a hut, or an old mill, perhaps—but this was nothing more than a ruin! Probably an old watchtower that hadn't been used for centuries. How were they supposed to live here until the spring?

Dejected, he followed Tonio up the hill, which was sparsely overgrown with shrubs at the top. The tower, roughly square in shape, was built from solid granite. Johann could tell by the windows that it contained three stories with a platform on top, which might have been roofed in once upon a time. Now the battlements were crumbled and the walls cracked. When Johann came closer he noticed that some of the windows had shutters that didn't look as old as the rest of the tower. And there was a solid wooden door, almost completely buried in snow. Tonio scooped the snow aside with his arms.

"Apparently, the Romans lived in this area a long time ago," he explained as he cleared the entrance. "The Via Claudia Augusta, an old Roman road, leads across the Alps not far from here. Soldiers and their families built this tower as a fortification against hostile tribes on this side of the Alps. There used to be lodges and a small town as well, but at some point the Romans abandoned it all. I'm guessing they were simply overrun—there was great bloodshed. Men, women, and children were crucified, burned alive in huge wicker baskets, or flayed for some forgotten deity." Tonio winked at his pupil. "They say you can still hear their screams in this tower today."

"What a pleasant place to spend the winter." Johann shuddered and helped Tonio clear the snow in front of the door.

"At least it's a place where we'll be left alone," Tonio replied. "Folks believe the tower is cursed. They avoid it, and if we're lucky, not much has changed since my last visit."

Johann noticed only now that a hastily scribbled black pentagram had been drawn on the door. "What's that?" he asked.

"A protection against travelers and other nosy folk," the master said. "Most people turn around and run when they see that symbol. Now all we need is the key." He walked back and forth near the door until his foot hit a stone slab hidden by the snow. "There we go!"

Once he'd kicked the snow off the slab, he pulled out a large, rusty key from underneath, stuck it into the lock, and turned it. The lock creaked loudly, and then Tonio kicked the door until it swung open. He nodded after his first glance inside. "I think we're in luck."

Johann blinked a few times to get his eyes used to the dim light. He could make out some furniture along the walls: a chest, a table, several stools.

Everything was covered in a thick layer of dust, but apart from that, it all seemed to be in good order. A steep set of wooden steps led upstairs.

Old ashes still lay in the fireplace built into the deep wall. It was bitterly cold. Inside, too, pentagrams had been drawn on the walls, in a color that reminded Johann of dried blood. A cup stood on the table, beside a tinged pewter plate holding something tiny and mummified.

"How long ago were you last here?" asked Johann with disgust. "A hundred years ago?"

"Possibly." The master grinned. "Like I said, it's been a while. Let's take a look at the second floor." He climbed up the creaking stairs, and Johann followed. The second floor was also furnished and adorned with pentagrams. It even contained a bed, but the straw inside was rotten.

Once Tonio had looked about for a few moments, he said to Johann, "We're leaving the wagon at the edge of the woods, and the horse goes in the stable. You bring everything into the tower." He pointed down the stairs. "We cook, eat, and study on the first floor. The second floor is yours."

"And the third floor?" asked Johann, noticing the master hadn't checked above them yet.

"That's mine alone, and you've got no business up there." Tonio gave him a stern look. "If I catch you in my room, I'll skin you like a rabbit—just like the barbarians used to do with the Romans. Understood?"

Johann nodded. He walked outside and started to lug the many crates, chests, and sacks up the hill. The master immediately carried the sack of books upstairs.

As Johann cleaned and swept the worst of the dirt and rotten straw from his room and the first floor, he wondered what was hidden in the uppermost chamber.

For the next few days they were busy fixing up the dilapidated tower. They found lengths of timber in the stable to close off the open windows. They found, hidden under the straw from Tonio's last stay, a stash of tools, including a hammer, a saw, and nails. The master turned out to be quite handy as a carpenter, and they made good progress. They reroofed the stable, and Johann cleared out the worst of the trash.

The chimney finally drew properly once Johann had removed several dead birds and mummified rats, and they were able to cook and get some warmth into the old walls. Johann stuffed his bed with fresh straw and covered it with furs. He filled the small chest in his room with his few possessions. He also had a table, where the master permitted him to study selected books. But the third floor remained closed to Johann.

At the end of the day, they'd sit by the open fire—the warmest place in the tower. The cage with the raven and the two crows dangled from the ceiling, the birds eyeing their new home curiously and flapping their wings. Bear and wolf skins served as cushions, and the large table was covered with books, parchment scrolls, bits of cheese rind, and half-empty cups of wine. Tonio had even built a shelf, which was now filled with neat rows of books, like soldiers of knowledge.

Johann soon had to admit that the tower wasn't as inhospitable as he'd first thought. But when the wind whistled through the cracks, howling and moaning, he thought of the tortured Roman souls Tonio had told him about. And sometimes, at night, he heard a soft murmuring and chanting from the master's chamber, together with heavy footsteps pacing the room. It sounded almost as if the master was speaking with another person, as if someone else was in the room with him, someone very large.

Several times Johann thought Tonio was by his bedside, holding his hand like at the Black Eagle Inn.

There is a time for everything, he heard the master's voice say. *A time to be born and a time to die. A time to heal and a time to kill . . .*

But when Johann awoke the next morning, nothing remained but a vague memory, and he told himself that it had been only a dream.

When they sat together by the fire in late afternoon, Johann finally received the long-awaited lessons. At first he learned more about palm reading, and then they turned to the subjects of pyromancy, hydromancy, and aeromancy, which were all elements of the art of divination. Johann took a particular liking to pyromancy. The master threw a handful of salt into the fire and gestured at the dancing flames.

"Learn to read them," he said. "Watch how the flames crackle and lick. You can learn much from the color, too: Are the flames bright red, or blue, or perhaps purple? Do they climb high or are they dying down? Does the smoke rise in a column or is it a cloud of stinging fumes?"

Sometimes, when the sky was clear to the north and the air icy cold, they went outside and studied the clouds, which were getting caught in the mountaintops like sheep wool in a comb. There was much to be learned from them. The master explained to Johann the various shapes of clouds and what kind of weather each one indicated. They watched the flight of a hawk, studying his wide, lofty circles above the forest. At dusk, when the sun disappeared behind the glistening snow and turned it as red as blood, Johann watched the play of colors, mesmerized, while the master explained the different hues of a rainbow.

"Everything has a deeper reason," Tonio said in conclusion, gesturing at the trees, the mountains, and the horizon to the north. "Nothing is without a plan. And when you recognize that plan, the world lies before you like a naked whore."

To Johann's infinite relief, the master no longer asked him to practice the bagpipe. Johann suspected Tonio wanted to spare his own ears. And perhaps he was afraid the noise might attract prying eyes from the nearby village. The accursed instrument stayed in its chest; Johann hoped it would remain there until it rotted. He didn't find much time to practice throwing his knife, either. He was too busy with other things now.

Saint Thomas Night—the longest night of the year—came and went, and soon it was Christmas. In Knittlingen, there was always a Christmas mass followed by a long, cozy evening together, singing and celebrating the birth of Jesus. Johann used to enjoy this day as a child. His mother had been a good singer, and his father—in a generous mood thanks to several cups of mulled wine—used to be a little nicer to him. Johann wondered how Tonio would mark the feast day. But the master didn't look like he was going to celebrate at all on Christmas Eve—he neither prayed nor sang. Instead, he sat in his chair by the fire with a grim look on his face, leafing through an old tome full of tables and drawings. Johann could hear the bells of the village church from over a mile away. He guessed the people were on their way to mass.

Johann cleared his throat and addressed his master. "It's Christmas," he began awkwardly. "You . . . you aren't particularly religious, are you?"

The master frowned and closed his book. "Just because everyone else sings and cries and turns all sentimental about a Jewish urchin doesn't mean I have to join in with such nonsense."

"So you don't believe in anything?" asked Johann, incredulous. He'd never met anybody who spoke like the master. Such talk was a certain road to hell—and to a crackling fire beneath a stake, if anyone heard it.

"Oh yes, I believe." The master grinned. "I believe in higher powers, much more strongly than you can imagine. Most of all, however, I believe in the power of stars. They never lie."

"Then explain them to me," begged Johann. "I've been waiting for so long."

Palm reading and the other manticisms had been interesting, and Johann still didn't fully understand what had happened when he'd sensed Rafael's death. But he'd been eagerly anticipating the day the master would introduce him to the art of astrology. He had a thousand questions, and until now, the master had always evaded them.

Tonio sighed; outside, the bells continued to toll like a cry for help from afar. Eventually, he gave a chuckle. "The hell with it. Maybe today is just the right day to begin the study of astrology. After all, those three old fools also followed a star."

He opened the book he'd been reading and pointed at strange circles covered with drawings and runes.

"The spheres of Ptolemy," Tonio began and traced the individual circles with his long finger. "More than a thousand years ago, this Egyptian divided the heavens into hollow spheres carrying the celestial bodies, which circle around the Earth, producing some kind of lovely music. A load of nonsense, if you ask me—I've never heard any music coming from the stars. But Ptolemy gives us a good basis to work with. In actual fact, astrology is much older still, dating back to the Babylonians, who also used to practice many dark and desirable rites."

"What do all these symbols mean?" asked Johann, leaning closer to the drawing.

"Earth and man are surrounded by celestial bodies." Tonio counted on his fingers. "The sun, the moon, Mercury, Venus, Mars, Jupiter, and Saturn—and each one is attached to a sphere. Those stars and planets are also known as the holy seven. Then follows the sphere of zodiacs, which is divided into twelve signs. Seven and twelve are magical numbers. Do you follow me?"

Johann nodded, and Tonio continued. "Each planet and each sign of the zodiac has an influence on man, on his destiny and his future. There are two kinds of horoscope: the nativity, which is about a person's character, and the progressive horoscope, which tells us something about the outcome of a future event, like a battle or a business decision. This kind of horoscope is much more difficult and therefore more expensive."

Fascinated, Johann studied the drawing and several tables below it. He'd been waiting for this for weeks. How many times had his mother spoken of the stars on the day of his birth and how because of them, he was a lucky child, a Faustus. Now he'd finally learn what all that meant!

"My mother said I was born under the influence of Jupiter," he said quietly. "On April twenty-three in the year of 1478. She always told me to remember the date well, but she never explained why. Can you tell me?"

"It's a strange date indeed. On that day, at your place of birth, the sun and Jupiter stood in the same degree of the same sign. And some of the other celestial bodies formed a, well . . . a very interesting relationship. It's a constellation that occurs only a handful of times in a century."

"When I first met you, you spoke of a day of the prophet," said Johann. "Do you remember?"

"Oh yes, I remember."

Suddenly, the master's eyes became as empty as glass marbles and he gazed into the distance. When he spoke again, his voice was hollow and so quiet that Johann struggled to understand.

"And I stood upon the sand of the sea, and saw a beast rise up out of the sea, having seven heads and ten horns, and upon his horns ten crowns, and upon his heads the name of blasphemy. *Homo Deus est!*"

Johann frowned with confusion. He'd never seen the master like this before. "What did you say?" he asked.

Tonio shook his head and smiled, his eyes normal again. "An old Bible quote, nothing more." He turned the page, and there were more tables with numbers. "Listen, I have a task for you. A Palatinate abbot asked me to write up a simple nativity for him. I haven't gotten around to it yet, and I'd like you to do it. You've got all winter."

"All winter?" Johann looked at him with surprise. "It can't possibly take that long!"

Tonio laughed. "My dear Faustus, you'll soon learn that astrology, along with alchemy, makes up the crown of the arcane arts. The road to mastery is long, stony, and paved with mistakes. And now listen carefully to what I'm telling you about the time of birth and sidereal time. I'll only explain everything once. Understood?"

Johann gradually came to realize that astrology was an extremely complicated field indeed, more difficult than anything he'd studied so far—yes, even more difficult than playing that accursed bagpipe.

In the following days, he studied the signs of the zodiac and their meanings. Each sign in the outermost sphere occupied a space of thirty degrees, of which ten formed a so-called decade. From a person's time of birth and the sidereal time—time reckoned by the movement of the stars rather than the sun—the so-called twelve houses could be calculated. There were ascendants and descendants, and everything had to be determined with the help of complicated formulas. Many nights Johann sat up late working on the chart just to watch the master tear his work to pieces the next morning.

"You're nothing but a jackass," scolded Tonio. "You can't even manage the simplest calculations. From the beginning! If you're not finished by noon, you're not getting any lunch."

Johann thus studied day after day. He thought about his stepfather telling him that his real father, the juggler and traveling scholar, also used to read the stars. Most likely, it had been nothing but hocus-pocus, not true knowledge, although Johann couldn't be certain. He didn't know who his father was. And he'd never find out, since the only person who could tell him was his mother—and she lay dead and buried in the Knittlingen cemetery. Johann's heart ached at the thought, and he decided to stop fretting about his parents. He might no longer have a father or a mother, but he had Tonio.

Sometimes, when the master was satisfied with Johann and the night was crisp and clear, Tonio would take him outside and show him the constellations. Ursa Minor and Major, Aquila, Andromeda with its milky fog. The great Ptolemy had gazed upon them. The stars were eternal. And yet they changed. Constellations traveled, coming and going like ancient companions of Mother Earth.

"Look there: Orion," Tonio said, pointing to a particularly striking constellation. "Canis Minor and Canis Major rise with him in winter. Together with Taurus, Gemini, and Auriga, they form the winter hexagon. In February, the summer constellations begin to return."

"There are so many stars," replied Johann. "And you can't seem to see the end. Is the universe infinite?"

"Remember the heavenly spheres," Tonio said. "There are eight of them."

"And what comes after the eighth sphere?"

Tonio laughed. "If I were a priest, I'd say, 'God only knows.' But I think we don't know because we can't see that far. Most stars can't be seen with the naked eye. But there are . . ." Tonio hesitated. "Possibilities. Your birth constellation, too, is difficult to discern, especially because our narrow-minded way of thinking ends behind the eighth sphere."

"Do you know when it appears next?" asked Johann.

The master smiled mysteriously. "You'll find out soon enough, young Faustus."

Johann was struck by the thought that the very same stars he was gazing at were also sparkling above Knittlingen, and homesickness flared up in him. He remembered how Father Bernhard also used to explain the constellations to him, and how Father Antonius showed him the printing press at Maulbronn and the book of the great Albertus Magnus—the *Speculum Astronomiae*, the mirror of astronomy.

But most of all, he thought of his little brother, Martin, and of Margarethe.

Some nights, when he couldn't go to sleep, his thoughts of Margarethe became so strong that he had to seek relief with his hand. Afterward, he felt ashamed and prayed for Margarethe's health. Perhaps she'd forgotten him by now. For him, too, it would be best to forget her.

But he couldn't.

During the cold days of January, he was often alone in the tower. The master didn't tell him where he was going, but more than once Tonio stayed out overnight. He always locked the trapdoor leading to the upstairs chamber carefully before leaving and reminded Johann what he'd do to his pupil should the young man ever ignore his order.

When the master would return the next morning, he always looked very pleased. A few times he came back with new books—mostly about astronomy and alchemy—and Johann wondered where he got them. Other times, the master carried sealed clay jugs or leather sacks filled with something bulky. The sacks were damp at the bottom, as if whatever was inside was wet. Johann didn't dare ask about it, though, and focused on his books. He got the impression that

Tonio always looked healthier after his nightly expeditions—less pale, some-what rosier and fleshier in the face. He guessed the master went to the village tavern for a good meal and a few drinks while Johann was stuck in the tower with a grumbling stomach, working on the accursed horoscope of some priest. Sometimes, when he looked up from his work, he felt as though the birds in the cage were watching him so they could tell the master all about his doings.

"Goddamned beasts!" shouted Johann once, throwing a piece of firewood at the cage, causing it to swing back and forth wildly. The birds cawed as if they were mocking him, and the raven glared at him with evil eyes.

"Kraa!" croaked the raven. *"Kraa, kraa!"*

Johann held his hands over his ears to shut out the bird's almost-human voice.

When Johann needed a break from the tables and numbers, he went into the forest to chop firewood. He baked delicious-smelling loaves of flatbread over the fire, practiced his magic tricks and throwing his knife, or leafed through books the master had lent him. Johann had always enjoyed reading, and his Latin was getting better all the time. He was a fast reader and remembered most of what he read. When Tonio quizzed him on a book, Johann was nearly always able to give detailed replies. Then the master would lower the book and gaze at Johann pensively.

"It seems to me you're a better scholar than a juggler and musician," he'd say eventually. "Johann Georg Faustus, you're full of surprises."

Indeed, Johann didn't find much time to practice his tricks over the winter; the horoscope the master had entrusted him with kept him busy. After four more weeks, the birth chart of the Palatinate abbot was finally completed. Making one final stroke with his quill, Johann carried it downstairs. As usual, Tonio was sitting at the table with his books.

"Here you go," Johann said defiantly and handed Tonio the scroll. He fully expected the master to tear it up again, but to his enormous surprise, Tonio didn't seem to find a single mistake.

"What a boring fellow he is, this abbot. His stars are gray and insignificant." Tonio laughed. "But the birth chart is all right. Tiny oversights here and there, but generally well done. I didn't expect anything else of you. You've proven in the last few weeks that you're talented—more talented than many other students I've had."

The birds in the cage started to squawk wildly, shuffling back and forth on their shared perch.

"Hush, you beasts," Tonio shouted, turning to them.

Johann breathed a sigh of relief, but the master wagged his finger in warning.

"This was just a simple task, boy. Nothing more than the horoscope of a pale abbot. Don't let it go to your head. There'll be much harder tests for you yet—especially once we turn to alchemy, the jewel in the crown of the arcane arts. But you've done enough for today." He clapped his hands. "We should celebrate your first horoscope. Go down to the village and get us a small keg of wine, bread, and some juicy smoked sausages. What do you say?"

Johann nodded enthusiastically. Until then, the master had always forbidden him to go near the village so they wouldn't arouse suspicion. This would be his first excursion since they'd moved into the tower almost three months ago.

"Wash your face before you go." Tonio winked at him. "And don't mess about with the village girls. You've grown a fair bit in the last few weeks, and you're a handsome chap. Taller and a little stronger. If anyone asks, you're just a traveling tinker's journeyman, understood? We don't want any trouble. And now off with you—I can tell you're itching to go." He handed Johann a few coins. "I don't want the cheapest wine. Woe to you if you come back with swill!"

Johann took the coins with a grin and reached for the coat he had brought from home, which looked rather worse for wear by now and was becoming too short in the sleeves. Then he hurried outside.

The sun was shining and the first birds were singing, welcoming the nearing spring. As Johann ran through the snow, he could feel the stress of the last few weeks fall away from him like a lead weight.

~

The master waited until he could no longer hear Johann before going upstairs to prepare the ritual. The blood he kept in a small barrel was a little congealed, but it would do. Slowly, he stirred the sticky liquid, dipped his finger into it, and sucked it with relish. There was no taste like blood—warm and salty and full of life.

Especially when it was as young as this blood.

He dipped his hand into the barrel, and the liquid dripped onto the floor like paint. Using his fingers, he drew the ancient pattern that had served as a means of communication for thousands of years. He renewed the faded symbol on the floor, and a faint smell of decay spread through the chamber.

He was almost certain.

He hadn't thought it possible at first; he'd studied the ancient maps and watched the skies with the apparatus he'd invented. But the stars didn't lie. The day was close, very close, and it seemed he'd finally found the right one. The chosen one. They had to act now! Or the moment would pass, and no one knew when it would return.

He paced the circle with measured steps like he'd done countless times before, murmuring the ancient words.

"Remember then! Of one make ten, the two let be, make even three, there's wealth for thee . . ."

When the master had finished, he sat down in the middle of the circle, closed his eyes, and waited for a reply.

~

The trees dripped with melting ice, and the path that had been covered with a thick layer of snow just a few days earlier was now sodden with puddles. Johann nimbly jumped across mud and puddles as he headed down the valley, breathing in the fresh air that smelled faintly of the first buds of spring. He felt as though he'd escaped from a prison.

Indeed, spring didn't seem far off. Johann guessed they'd continue their travels soon. Until then, he hadn't thought about where they might be heading. The master had never mentioned anything. Did they even have a destination? Distant Venice, perhaps—the city he'd heard so much about? Or Paris? Rome? During the first few weeks of their travels, Johann had simply been grateful for the roof over his head. Tonio had given him a home, shelter from the hardships of winter. He had promised to stay with the master for one year, and sometimes, when Tonio had worked him too hard, he'd thought about running away sooner. But now he was happy to be the student of a man like him. Tonio could teach him far more than Father Antonius and Father Bernhard together—the whole world stood open to Johann!

But today, he simply wanted to enjoy life. After weeks of loneliness and studying in the tower, Johann looked forward to seeing other people, even if they were just the slow-witted inhabitants of some mountain village.

After about an hour's walk, he reached the road at the bottom of the valley, which ran along a fir-covered foothill of the Alps. In the distance, Johann could make out the snowcapped peaks surrounded by haze. The village lay about half a mile to the east. It was a small backwater with a tiny, decrepit church surrounded by a handful of houses. Next door to the church was the tavern, a low building made from black tree trunks, with dense gray smoke rising from the chimney. A larger trading route led past it.

It was late Sunday morning, and many farmers from the surrounding area had gone to the tavern for a drink or two following mass. Several oxcarts stood by the side of the road, and a group of young maids sat on the edge of a well outside the church. When they caught sight of Johann, they huddled together and whispered. He straightened up and took a playful bow as he walked past them. The girls giggled and squealed and scattered like a flock of hens. Only now did Johann realize how tattered and dirty he looked—with his torn trousers, too-small coat, and matted black hair that had grown long in the last few weeks. He walked over to the well to wash himself. He was surprised when he saw his reflection in the water. His face had become leaner and more angular since fall. Black fuzz had grown around his lips, and his eyes were almost as black and gleaming as those of the master. The weeks in the tower had turned Johann into a serious-looking young man—and, if he interpreted the girls' giggles correctly, a not entirely unattractive young man.

Once he'd removed the worst of the dirt from his clothes and combed his hair with his fingers, he entered the tavern. It was busy, and the air was heavy with stale sweat and spilled beer. Instantly, several pairs of eyes turned to him, and he thought he heard some snide comments. With his head held high, he walked to one of the few empty tables in the corner and sat down while the villagers eyed him suspiciously. Soon the tavern keeper came over.

"What do you want?" asked the man, briskly wiping the dirty, scratched table with a cloth. "If you're here to beg, sit in front of the church."

"A mug of beer, if you please," Johann replied with a smile. "And some provisions for the road. A keg of wine, a handful of sausages, and some bread, please. I'm an itinerant tinker on my way to Innsbruck." He held up one of the coins the master had given him. "And I can pay—in case you're worried."

The tavern keeper tilted his head and stared greedily at the coin, which was made of pure silver. "You'll get your supplies," he said eventually, reaching for the coin. "But you can't sit here. We don't want strangers in the village."

Johann's smile froze. "But why . . . ," he began.

The tavern keeper had already turned away without offering him as much as a beer. Frowning, Johann stayed put. What sort of a place was this? The Knittlingers weren't particularly fond of strangers, either, but they didn't chase them out of town. His good mood vanished.

"Dirty traveling scum," muttered someone nearby. "They're all in league with Beelzebub."

"They should all be hanged before more terrible things happen round here," someone else exclaimed. "There's a foul wind blowing from the mountains."

Intrigued, Johann turned toward the speakers. They were two elderly farmers, one of whom now spat noisily on the ground. "I'm telling you, the devil is on the loose," he grumbled. "He takes our loved ones and burns down the roofs over the heads of those who give him shelter. Have you heard? A magician stayed at the Black Eagle near Kempten over the winter, and now the inn's burned to the ground—and the heretic is over the hills and far away!"

"I don't think the scoundrel lives far from here," the other man whispered, making the sign of the cross. "I heard someone's staying at the old Roman tower—a sorcerer, so help me God! The charcoal burner saw him dance in the forest the other night with his assistant."

Johann winced. Had he heard right? Those farmers were talking about him and the master. Someone must have seen them near the tower and was spreading rumors. Worse, people seemed to have them mixed up with Freudenreich. Johann suddenly noticed that many of the guests were staring at him with hatred. Some even clutched the hilts of their knives; conversations gradually died down.

"Dirty traveling scum," the old farmer hissed once more. "Spawn of the devil!"

Johann was relieved when the tavern keeper returned to his table. The man handed him a heavy burlap sack. "Here's everything you asked for," he growled. "Now get out of here before they cut your throat. I don't want any blood spilled in my tavern!"

Johann took the sack without comment, stood up, and walked to the door. He had barely made it outside when he sensed that he was being followed. Slowly, he turned around. There were three young men, two of them holding gnarly sticks. The third one grasped a knife and approached Johann menacingly.

"What have you done with my little sister?" shouted the young man suddenly, his face contorted with anger. "Did you eat her like a wolf? Are you a werewolf?"

Johann was stiff with fright. "I . . . I'm just a plain tinker," he stammered. "I'm traveling with my master . . . We'd never—"

"You steal our children!" shouted the second man, cutting him off. He swung his cudgel. "Admit it! Our little Elsbeth and all the others. You steal them at night and you eat them!"

"But . . . that's nonsense!" Johann started walking backward. He raised his hands defensively. "We are no—"

A rock struck his head. A boy standing by the well had thrown it. The giggling maids were long gone. Instead, Johann was facing a growing number of angry young men.

"Grab him!" shouted one of them. "We'll beat the truth out of him. And then let's burn him like a Judas puppet so his black soul can't harm us any longer!"

Another stone hit Johann on the head. He turned around and a cudgel came down hard on his back. The pain made him gag.

"Club him to death like a dog!" screamed someone. "Just look at him! With his black hair and evil eyes. He's Satan's henchman! He killed our children!"

"Satan, Satan!" shouted the others.

Johann stumbled and fell, then got back on his feet before more blows struck him. Another rock whirred past his head. He started running down the road as fast as he could, the mob screaming and yelling behind him. The sack over his shoulder felt like it was filled with rocks. He dropped it into the ditch and ran, stones and clumps of ice raining down on him. For a while he still heard steps behind him, but they faded until he couldn't hear them at all. None of the villagers seemed to pursue him any longer, but he kept running as if the devil were after him. Finally, he reached the part of the woods that led up the hill to the tower. He turned off the road, followed the muddy path, and, panting heavily, arrived at the tower.

"Master!" he called out and rapped at the door. "Something . . . something happened! We must leave, now!"

But there was no answer. When Johann opened the door, the room on the other side was empty. The fire had gone out.

There was no sign of the master.

For a while, Johann stood in the middle of the chamber, breathing heavily and listening for any sound. But everything was silent. The books were still lying on the table, next to the abbot's birth chart. Red embers still glowed in the ashes, and the room smelled of smoke and faintly of sulfur. There was also another smell, but Johann couldn't place it.

His heart still racing, Johann thought about how narrowly he'd escaped death. There was no doubt in his mind that the villagers would have stoned or beaten him to death if he hadn't managed to run away.

He particularly remembered one thing they'd said.

You steal our children . . . You steal them at night and you eat them . . .

It would seem that here, too, children had been going missing, just like in Knittlingen all those months ago. In both cases, the master had been staying nearby. Johann thought about how satisfied and fleshy Tonio looked every time he returned from his nightly excursions. He thought about the clay jugs and the wet sacks—especially the wet sacks.

You eat them . . .

Johann shook himself as though waking from an evil nightmare. What a load of nonsense. Tonio del Moravia may have been a gloomy-looking fellow, a conjurer, an astrologer, and a chiromancer, but he was no man-eating monster. He was a wise and stern mentor, a man who could teach him a lot.

You eat them . . .

Johann's eyes turned to the stairs. What in God's name was his master up to in his chamber? Tonio had strictly forbidden him to enter the third floor. But now doubts gnawed at Johann like a thousand tiny rats. He needed to find out what went on upstairs. He'd never stop worrying about it otherwise. He wondered about his chances of getting caught. Tonio had probably gone out for a while, not expecting Johann home before afternoon. He still had time.

Provided the villagers didn't get here first to smoke out the alleged sorcerers.

Quietly, Johann sneaked up to his chamber and farther up the stairs to the trapdoor, which was usually bolted shut. Whenever the master left the house, he locked the bolt with a heavy padlock, and the key was always on his belt. But to Johann's surprise the bolt wasn't even pushed shut. Had the master forgotten to lock it? Or was he asleep upstairs?

Johann listened. On many occasions he had heard Tonio muttering until late at night, heavy footsteps thumping back and forth, and a dragging noise, as if something heavy was being pulled across the chamber floor. But now everything was silent: no footsteps, no muttering, no snoring, not even breathing.

For some reason Johann couldn't explain, he made the sign of the cross. Then he pushed against the trapdoor. It opened with a soft creak. Johann paused, waiting for an angry scream, but nothing happened. So he opened the door completely and climbed the remaining stairs until he stood inside the master's room.

Like in his own chamber, there was a bed and a table covered in books. A pile of clothes sat next to a chest in one corner, the windows were covered in cobwebs moving in the wind, and nothing seemed particularly out of the ordinary.

Except for the floor.

A huge pentagram had been painted on the floor, taking up almost the entire room. At each tip of the five-pointed star stood a burned-out candle, each candle surrounded by a pool of half-cooled wax. Johann knelt down and studied the rust-colored pentagram more closely. The paint was dry and exuded a faintly sweet smell—the same smell Johann had noticed downstairs. Johann sniffed again. It was just how it used to smell at home in Knittlingen when his stepfather butchered a pig to make sausage and ham.

It was the smell of blood.

You eat them . . .

A ladder led up to a square opening in the ceiling. In a daze, Johann climbed the few rungs until his head was outside, overlooking the platform that formed the tower's roof. A cold wind blew into his face. He spotted a strange construction set up on the roof: a large tube about as long as his arm resting on a stand. Johann guessed it must have been in one of the heavy crates he'd had to lift off the wagon and carry up the tower. He couldn't figure out what the apparatus might be. Was that the master's secret? But why wasn't Johann allowed to know about it? And what was the pentagram about?

Johann couldn't resist the temptation. He walked over to the tube; it was made of copper and shaped like a narrow funnel. Each end was covered with a pane of glass, reminding Johann of the eye glasses Father Antonius used to wear occasionally. The monk had told him they helped him to better decipher the tiny writing in books. Could this mysterious construction also be for reading books? Then he'd probably have to look through it.

He reached for the tube with trembling hands and brought his eye down to the skinny end. At first he saw nothing, just blurred blackness. Then he noticed that he could move the tube up and down and left and right. He played around for a bit—and started with fright.

The mountains that had been so far away a moment ago suddenly stood right before him, as if he could touch them with his hand. He clearly saw the snow glistening in the sun, the rugged rocks, and an eagle circling the mountaintops, just as though they were right there in front of him. When he stepped back, everything was far away again. What a wondrous toy this was! Johann thought of the printing press in the Maulbronn monastery. This tube, too, seemed like an invention capable of changing the world. Was it powerful enough to let him see the stars up close? Would it be possible to see beyond the eighth sphere?

More confident now, Johann spun the tube in the other direction, toward the forest. Again, everything was blurry at first, but after a while he could make out details. The village church looked as if it were directly in front of him, then the road, and the path winding its way up through the woods to the tower.

And the master.

Johann screamed and let go of the tube as if he'd burned his fingers. He had seen the master's sinister-looking face and his thin black hair blowing in the wind. Tonio had appeared so close—and he seemed to have looked right into Johann's eyes. Without the tube, Johann saw only a black dot, but it steadily grew larger as the master rushed up the path.

Johann prayed that Tonio hadn't seen him on the platform. He climbed down the ladder as fast as he could, raced through the master's chamber past the pentagram and the pile of clothes, down the stairs into his own room, and finally down to the first floor, where he quickly sat in front of the cold fireplace with a book in his hands, pretending he'd been reading it all along.

Soon enough he heard the master's footsteps outside. The door was pushed open and Tonio entered. He had apparently been walking fast; sweat gleamed on his forehead, and he breathed heavily. He gave Johann a long, hard look with his piercing pitch-black eyes, and the young man suddenly felt certain Tonio had seen him on the platform. Then the master spoke with a sense of urgency.

"We must leave. I spoke with a merchant on the road. He said the village folk believe sorcerers are staying at the tower. Apparently, there was an incident in the village. Pack your things if you don't want to get burned alive! If we're lucky, they won't come until the morning. They're probably too drunk on a Sunday."

He didn't ask what Johann had been up to and why he was already back from the village. Instead, he went upstairs to his chamber, and Johann heard him packing in a hurry.

While Johann gathered his own belongings, he thought about the clothes he'd seen in the master's chamber. He hadn't paid them much attention earlier, but now, thinking about it, he remembered that there had been a lot of clothes. Many more than the master owned. And he could have sworn that they'd looked small.

Like children's clothes.

Upstairs, he could hear Tonio's footsteps, heavy and ominous, like those of a dark sea captain pacing the deck while their ship slowly sank to the bottom of the ocean.

7

THEY DROVE DOWN TO THE ROAD IN SILENCE. AT THE MAS-
ter's command, Johann had hitched the horse to the wagon and loaded their
bags, sacks, and crates. The cage with the birds was back in its old place, dangling
from the ceiling of the wagon.

One last time Johann turned to look at the tower that had been his home
for the last few months, where he had learned so much. Then Tonio cracked
his whip, and the tower was soon out of sight. It wasn't long before they had to
climb down from the wagon and lead the horse. The snow had gone, but the
track was riddled with deep ruts. Tree roots reached out of the ground like fingers of subterranean ghosts and forced them to take many small detours. Twice
they had to cross a small stream swollen with meltwater rushing down the valley.
The master was silent, pulling on the old nag's bridle when it didn't want to walk
through muddy puddles.

Before driving off, they had nailed the windows and door shut and buried
a large crate behind the tower. Johann had managed to see that the crate was
mostly filled with books, but he'd also seen the copper tube. Apparently, Tonio
had disassembled the strange apparatus and hidden it in the crate. After they'd
filled the hole, the master made some strange gestures with his hands and laid
out five white stones in a circle. "In case we ever come back," he growled. "No
one will dare to dig for treasure here. Not if they value their immortal soul."
With soot, he painted a black pentagram on the door and secured it with a
heavy beam.

Finally, after two hours of pushing and pulling, they reached the bottom
of the valley. They turned west, away from the village. After another half hour,

the church bells started chiming wildly, as if there was a fire somewhere or an impending storm.

As if the villagers are gathering for a hunt, Johann thought. *A witch hunt.*

The bells grew fainter until Johann could no longer hear them at all, and the journey passed quietly for a while. Johann sat beside the master on the box seat, like he'd done so many times before the winter. Tonio still hadn't spoken. He ground his teeth grimly, as if imagining eating every one of those slow-witted, superstitious peasants alive.

You eat our children . . .

Johann now had time to reflect on what he'd discovered at the tower. Had he actually seen children's garments in Tonio's chamber? Suddenly he wasn't so sure. It had just been a pile of clothes, after all, and there was probably a rational explanation for the pentagram, too. Johann knew that alchemy worked with symbols and a wide variety of substances, including blood. Most likely, what he'd seen on the floor was pigs' blood—disgusting, yes, but nothing to be afraid of. What if his imagination was running away with him? What if he was being just as narrow minded and hysterical as the villagers? Children had gone missing—it happened all the time, everywhere. And there'd be an explanation for Tonio's nightly excursions, too.

Suddenly, Johann felt bad. Hadn't the master been very kind to him in the last few weeks? Hadn't he taught him much? Johann had been blind for so long, and finally someone showed him the light. And there was so much left to learn. About the strange tube he'd found on the roof of the tower, for example, or the legendary field of alchemy the master had just begun to teach him about. Tonio might not have owned a library as large as the one at Maulbronn Monastery, but he seemed to be something of a walking library himself. Sometimes Johann thought the master's knowledge was ancient and infinite, reaching back to the very first knowledge of man. How much Johann could still learn from him! Johann cleared his throat. Perhaps the time had come to ask where their journey was headed.

"Now that the snow is melting, the road across the Alps should be clear, right?" he asked.

The master nodded but didn't reply, holding on tightly to the reins.

"Are we going to travel across the Alps?" asked Johann in another attempt. "Perhaps to . . . to Venice?"

"Our plans have changed," Tonio replied curtly. "We're heading east, to the Kingdom of Poland."

"But why?" Johann couldn't hide his disappointment. He'd been very much looking forward to Venice and Rome, to the warm lands beyond the Alps. He'd wanted to see the ocean, and now they were headed to a country he'd never even heard of before. "Why Poland?"

Now the master turned his haggard, falcon-like face to look at him, eyeing Johann intently, making him feel like Tonio was reading his every thought.

"Have you never wondered where I gained all my knowledge?" asked Tonio. "Do you think it all fell from the sky like a dead star?"

"You . . . you studied," Johann replied. "In Paris, Heidelberg—"

"Yes, yes," Tonio said impatiently. "I visited many universities, a traveling scholar, always on the search for new knowledge. But you can only learn the dark arts at one particular university—Krakow."

Johann remembered the master mentioning Krakow—in Knittlingen he had introduced himself with those words.

Tonio del Moravia. Krakow magister of the seven arts and keeper of the seven times seven seals.

"Once upon a time there were other universities that taught the arcane arts," Tonio continued while the old horse pulled them along the bumpy road. "But the accursed church banned them, even though those arts are much older than the church. Now there's only Krakow left. There's no other place if you want to learn about the seven times seven seals!"

"What are the seven times seven seals?" asked Johann.

"Be patient, young Faustus." The master grinned. "You'll learn about them soon enough. I've sent out a messenger to announce your arrival at Krakow."

"My arrival?" Johann stared at his teacher with disbelief. "But why—"

"Did you never wonder what I was doing when I stayed out all night?" asked Tonio, cutting him off. "I was waiting for news, week after week! When none arrived, I went out myself this morning and gave a letter to a merchant. Our friends need to know that you're coming. The stars are extremely favorable."

"That *I'm* coming?" Johann's astonishment grew. "But . . . but why should they know about me?"

The master opened his mouth to reply, but then shook his head. "It's too soon. We've been disappointed many times, even though I'm quite certain this time." He smiled. "Wait a little longer, young Faustus. I'm sure we'll run into some friends on the way to Krakow. There are many of us, and our numbers are growing. It can't be long now. Giddyup, you lazy old nag, pull!"

He cracked the whip, and the old horse lifted its head and whinnied, almost as if it were laughing. Then it pulled them steadily eastward toward this legendary Krakow. Johann sat on the box seat, brooding. Now he had some sort of explanation for why the master had been out so many nights, but one mystery had been replaced with another, much bigger one. Johann had thought he was nothing but an apprentice, a plain assistant who helped Tonio del Moravia, the great magician, during his performances in the German empire.

But it seemed the master had bigger plans for him.

The following morning, they reached a larger road busy with merchants and pilgrims. It led south toward the mountains, but Tonio turned the wagon north.

"The old Roman road," he explained. "Once upon a time these roads covered the empire like a finely woven net spanning many hundreds of miles. They were paved so the Roman soldiers could travel fast. Each road was wide enough for two carts to pass each other. Watchtowers and forts guaranteed safety for travelers." He pointed out some overgrown cobblestones, remains of a footpath on the side of the road, and a crooked milestone with withered Roman numerals that stuck out of the mud. "Hundreds of years have gone by since, and not much is left. But the little that remains is still better than anything the German kings and emperors have managed since."

"And this road leads to Krakow?" asked Johann.

Tonio laughed. "Not quite. But it'll get us close. It's a long way to Krakow. We'll be traveling for many weeks—weeks I can use to teach you many things." He looked up at the sky and squinted. "I only hope we'll make it in time."

Indeed, the master used their time on the road and the evenings to teach Johann more about astrology and the basics of alchemy.

"Many believe alchemy is just about finding a way to make gold," he explained. "I, too, was once obsessed by this desire. But alchemy is much more than that. Alchemy, as it was taught by the great Hermes Trismegistus in Egypt and later by the Greeks and Arabs, grants us an insight into that which the world contains in its innermost heart and finer veins. Do you understand what I mean?"

Johann nodded, though he felt like he'd only tasted the tiniest drop of a vast ocean of knowledge.

The master was much nicer to him now than before their time at the tower. They had all but stopped practicing their juggling tricks, and Tonio rarely read palms and no longer compiled horoscopes at taverns. He seemed in a hurry to reach Krakow. On clear nights, the master spent a lot of time gazing at the stars. Something seemed to excite him very much.

"It's happening much faster than I thought," he'd say again and again, almost to himself. "Much faster. Who would have thought, this early in the year. The day is near . . ."

When Johann asked what he meant, Tonio merely shook his head and told him he'd find out in Krakow.

"You can't keep walking around looking like that," Tonio said one day, eyeing Johann critically. "You look like a scarecrow, not like the promising apprentice of an itinerant chiromancer and astrologer."

Johann looked down at himself. It was true: his clothes were dirty and torn and much too small.

"We'll need a new outfit for you," the master continued. "Nothing in the garish patterns of jugglers' clothing, nor the colorful garb of a dandy. It wouldn't suit you—you're a student of the arcane arts now, so we'll need something serious, something plain."

They visited a tailor in the next town, and Johann was fitted with a long black tunic, a warm black coat, and shiny leather boots. On his head, instead of a hat he wore a gugel—a type of fashionable hood that covered head and shoulders and was ideal in bad weather. His new trousers were made of the finest wool and felt nice against his skin. The master grinned.

"You look like an honorable scholar. Folks are going to doff their hats and ask you to write up documents for them."

The countryside they were passing through now looked much like the Kraichgau. Johann learned that this region was called Swabia. Small villages were dotted among the patches of forests and the fields. The snow was melting, and it was nearly time for the first sowing. The wheel of life kept turning. Hungry faces marked by hardship stared at them from the fields. It looked as though Swabian farmers, too, had suffered much in recent years.

Once they passed a group of Dominican monks clad in black, chanting loudly and calling on people to repent their sins. The monks were accompanied by heavily armed mercenaries pulling a cart containing a chest with several padlocks. The chest bore metal fittings and, on the front, a painting of the devil with his fork, torturing souls in purgatory.

"Damned shavelings!" groused Tonio before spitting on the ground. "Don't the farmers pay enough in tithes? Now they have to pay for a place in heaven, and one for the long-dead great-grandfather on top!"

Johann had heard of priests selling indulgences as a means of gaining forgiveness for sins. In the past, the only way to atone for one's sins was through prayer or pilgrimage, but now people could shorten the amount of punishment they'd have to undergo with money. It was even possible to reduce the time long-deceased ancestors had to spend in purgatory—provided one had enough coins for the chest.

"People are as stupid as pigs," Tonio continued as they drove past the chanting train. "And why? Because the church and the high and mighty deny them knowledge. But all that is going to change soon. Oh yes, soon! *Homo Deus est!*"

Johann had heard the last phrase from Tonio before. By now he could not only read Latin, but also speak it reasonably well. Despite understanding those three words, however, he still didn't understand what they were supposed to mean together. The phrase didn't make any sense to him.

Man is God . . .

There were more and more crossings in the road now, and increasing numbers of villages and towns. Trading routes led off in all directions, and every road seemed to be busy. Knights cantered past on their mighty steeds; expensively dressed merchants drove their heavily loaded carts along at a snail's pace. Johann and Tonio heard some travelers talking about King Maximilian holding an imperial diet in Worms. The French had invaded Italy, and the accursed Ottomans threatened the borders of the German empire. Merchants were conducting business with faraway lands that had hitherto existed only in legends. The whole country seemed to be in a state of excitement, as if spring was liberating the entire empire from a long frost.

Five days later, the walls of a city appeared in front of them. Countless towers jutted into the sky, a large cathedral in their center. The greenish-gray ribbon of a large river gleamed in the spring sunshine. Hordes of pilgrims and merchants flocked toward the gates. Johann had never seen such a huge city before.

"Augsburg," said Tonio grimly.

Johann had heard of Augsburg. He'd heard travelers in Knittlingen talk about this city; it was one of the largest in the German empire. They said it was ruled by patricians—powerful families of merchants and councilors who were unbelievably wealthy, owning properties all over the world and lending money to bishops, dukes, and even the emperor himself. It seemed like those men were the new masters of the world—not knights, counts, and barons, like in his mother's days.

After spending the last few nights in the wagon by the roadside, Johann was glad they'd soon be staying at an inn again—and in such an interesting place. But, much to his disappointment, Tonio gave Augsburg a wide berth, and soon Johann lost sight of the city's battlements, towers, and cathedral.

"Augsburg is far too dangerous a place for the likes of us," Tonio said. "The bishop gives short shrift to sorcerers. Not too long ago they boiled an alchemist alive because he claimed he could turn iron into gold."

"Could he?" asked Johann.

"Only very few are privy to that secret. The quack in question definitely wasn't one of them. I'm guessing he couldn't even tell the difference between copper and bronze." The master gave a laugh. "Do you know what boiled human flesh smells like? Just like pork! At the end of the day, we all wallow in the same mudhole."

Johann said nothing. Once again he realized that magic was a dangerous business. Something that counted as a harmless weather spell in one place could mean heresy and death in the next town. White magic like astrology, chiromancy, and some alchemy was allowed, but black magic like necromancy and sorcery wasn't.

Soon enough, he'd experience the difference between the two worlds firsthand.

Their journey took them to the north, toward Franconia. The snow had all melted now, and the hawthorn and fruit trees were full of buds, birds chirping among their branches. The master whistled a tune and seemed to grow more cheerful with every mile. At night, he barely glanced up at the sky anymore. It seemed he had reached a decision.

"I am hopeful we'll soon be meeting our friends," he said. "In the town of Nördlingen, we're going to meet a man who can help us on our journey. I've known him for a very long time. If the message I sent off in the mountains has been delivered, he should already be there."

Johann had long since given up asking Tonio about his mysterious friends. The master didn't volunteer any more information, but Johann hoped he'd learn more in Nördlingen. He was itching to know why his arrival was eagerly anticipated in Krakow. The only explanation he could come up with was that he'd shown, during their time at the tower, that he was a gifted student. He was a fast learner, interested in everything the master told him—be it the power of steam as taught by Hero of Alexandria, which Johann observed each night above their cauldron, or the technical secrets of mechanical clocks like the ones they sometimes saw on town halls or church spires. The master also taught him about the herbs growing by the roadside. Their lessons often started with Tonio spotting something and jumping off the wagon.

"Black hellebore," he said one time, pointing at a pretty white flower by the wayside. "You can extract a poison from this plant strong enough to kill emperors and kings. In very small doses, it can ease insanity. If you ever pick black hellebore, make sure you wash your hands thoroughly—or you won't live long enough to regret your mistake."

Another time, he pointed at the black smoke rising from a charcoal pile in the woods. "Grind the coal from an alder buckthorn and mix it with sulfur and saltpeter. The resulting powder is powerful enough to burst the walls of Constantinople—I saw it with my own eyes!"

Johann, sitting on the box seat, listening to Tonio, realized he was learning much faster than back at school in Knittlingen. Thoughts and ideas flew into his mind as if Tonio had tapped some sort of spring inside him that couldn't be stopped.

After two more days, they reached a curious area. A ridge of hills forming a gigantic ring spread before them. It looked to Johann like a giant had thrown a rock into an ancient ocean. Once again he was struck by the perfection of nature, the symmetry of the natural world, as though it had been built by a clock maker. He thought of the beautiful crystals of snowflakes melting in his hand; the wings of butterflies; and flower petals following the sun all day. When he told Tonio his thoughts, the master laughed.

"God as a clock maker—don't let the church hear you talk like that. They suspect heresy behind every rock these days. But I like the image. It makes God kind of human, doesn't it? *Homo Deus est!*"

Finally, they reached another large town surrounded by a high wall. The master explained that this was Nördlingen, where he hoped to meet his friend. The lanes and squares in the town were busy; a cattle market was in full swing. Pigs squealed and geese with tied wings cackled in their baskets. A calf on its way to the butcher's block stared at Johann with big eyes. A huge newly completed church stood in the town's center, still partially enclosed by scaffolding. The tall tower showed all travelers that Nördlingen considered itself on par with Augsburg.

"You should see this place at Whitsuntide," Tonio said, carefully steering the wagon through the narrow lanes. "The fair is so spectacular that you even forget the stink."

The air did smell strongly of blood and urine. Johann guessed the stench came from the many tanneries along the city stream. Old and young tanners washed skins in the water and hung them in their airy attics to dry.

They headed toward a tavern near the church. The tavern was several stories high, with a large gate in the center that led into a courtyard. To the gate's left and right were pub rooms, and a wide set of stairs led up to guest rooms. Heavy oaken floorboards and gilded decorations made the tavern look almost palatial.

"The Golden Sun Inn," Tonio explained. "Emperors have stayed here, and His Majesty King Maximilian just visited a few years ago. I thought we'd treat ourselves to some nice accommodation."

Following their long, arduous journey and the many nights spent by the roadside, Johann went to bed early. The down quilt and fresh reeds on the floor seemed like heaven on earth. He slept like a log and only woke late in the morning to drumrolls and flourishes.

When he rushed to the window, he saw crowds of people heading toward the western gate. The master awaited him downstairs in the taproom.

"Quick, have some thinned beer and honeyed barley porridge," he commanded, gesturing toward a jug and a bowl on the table. "We don't want to miss the show. We've arrived at just the right time," Tonio said, rubbing his hands. "A stroke of luck! My old friend hasn't arrived yet, but there's another acquaintance I wouldn't mind seeing one last time."

"Who is it?" asked Johann, curious.

"Oh, you'll know him," Tonio said with a smile.

Johann still didn't understand. After a hasty breakfast, he followed Tonio out into the street. They joined the crowd heading out of town. Not far from the city walls, Johann saw a hill that had been cleared of trees and was crowned by a large rock.

The people seemed merry, buying nuts and pastries from itinerant merchants who carried their wares through the crowd on large back frames. Children squealed and ran after the drummers, and everyone seemed bound for the rock on the hill. It looked like an enormous table or altar and was more than five heads high. A pile of wood as tall as a man had been stacked on top, and a ladder led to a stake in the center of the pile. Dark-clad monks were swinging incense burners, and the smoke seemed to Johann like the harbinger of a much larger fire.

He understood now what kind of a show the crowd had come for.

"Everything's ready," the master said with a smile, his eyes appraising the hill in front of them. "All that's missing is our friend."

Johann was waiting with Tonio and all the people of Nördlingen, who were shouting and cheering, when a tumbrel pulled by a mangy donkey came jolting up the road. The hangman stood atop the cart, wearing a red shirt and a mask, and next to him, a man bound with ropes swayed back and forth as if he was drunk. Despite his torn shirt, blood-encrusted face, and arms twisted like those of a broken doll, Johann recognized him immediately: Freudenreich von Hohenlohe, the young minstrel from the Black Eagle Inn.

"They arrested him two months ago," Tonio explained as he joined in the rhythmic clapping of the crowd. A kettledrum provided the beat. "The poor bugger conjured up a calf with two heads and a hailstorm that devastated the fields around Nördlingen. If you ask me, he probably didn't pay his bill at the tavern or screw the landlady hard enough. Folks around here are easily angered. Apparently, good old Freudenreich was stubborn during torture, and that's why it took so long to get him sentenced."

The hangman dragged the trembling minstrel down from the cart. He barely resisted. The hangman's assistants had to carry him for the last few yards because he could no longer walk. It looked as though his legs were broken, along with his arms, which were bent at unusual angles.

Tonio began to sing quietly. It was the same song Freudenreich had performed when they'd seen him at the Black Eagle at the start of winter.

"Winter, O winter, you frighten me not. I sit by the stove and my fire burns hot. O winter, keep howling, I show thee no mercy . . ."

Rough-hewn steps led up the rock to the pyre. The assistants tied Freudenreich to the stake and held a burning torch to the wood. The sticks were dry, and the flames devoured them hungrily. Soon the stake was enshrouded in thick white smoke.

Like a giant incense burner, Johann thought.

The crowd fell silent, tense with expectation, even the children. Then a scream rose out from the smoke, animalistic and shrill. Johann thought about how beautifully the minstrel had once sung. And he thought about the master's words back at the Black Eagle.

He won't find happiness in these harsh climes, oh no, he won't.

Johann shuddered despite the heat of the fire. They had denied the great Tonio del Moravia his winter quarters, and he had taken terrible revenge. First the inn had burned down, and now the minstrel burned, too.

Freudenreich's screams turned into inhuman screeching and finally a wailing that stopped abruptly. Then the smoke turned black. Johann smelled burned flesh, and it smelled like pork. He felt sick.

"Keep howling, I show thee no mercy," Tonio sang once more, clapping his hands.

The execution was over, and after staring at the glowing embers for a while, the crowd began to make its way back to town. Johann was still in a daze, snapping out of it only when Tonio tapped him on the shoulder.

"I like fires," he declared cheerfully. "Even though they remind me of darker times. Once I watched a young maiden I was very fond of burn in France. We were like siblings—that's when it all began." He turned around and didn't look at the smoking pyre again. "And now let's go. If we're lucky, my friend has finally arrived."

~

The master's friend arrived in the evening. Tonio had been awaiting him impatiently at a corner table of the Golden Sun. Johann sat next to him, reading a book. The master had been drinking expensive Rhenish wine for hours but didn't seem to be getting drunk—not even tipsy, although Johann noticed that he looked paler than he had back at the tower.

A broad-shouldered man entered the inn, dressed entirely in black, wearing a long coat and a floppy hat like Tonio. He was so tall that he was forced to stoop as he walked through the door. He carried a long staff, like that of a shepherd, except it looked like a little twig in his huge fingers. He smiled as he walked toward their table, but his smile seemed false, as if someone had painted it onto his pockmarked, bearded face.

"*Mon baron*, it is an honor to see you again after such a long time," greeted the man with a rough voice, bowing low. Like Tonio, he spoke with a French accent, but his was much stronger.

"Don't, Poitou," said Tonio. "Not in front of the boy."

The man scrutinized Johann, who suddenly felt naked.

"That's him, yes? Looks rather unremarkable. Pale as a bookworm."

"I'm a bookworm, too, if that's what you want to call it. When will you learn that appearance doesn't matter, Poitou? On the contrary. You may be big and strong, but your mind doesn't allow you to think further than the next meal."

"Oh yes, I like thinking about the next meal." The giant gave a grin. "You're right, milord. I can eat as much as my horse munching on his barley outside the door. I rode for two days and one night straight to proclaim your arrival and meet you here. There is much to talk about."

"*Parle français,*" said Tonio, waving to the innkeeper to bring them more wine.

The men conversed quietly in French, and Johann pretended to be focused on his book while casting furtive glances at the master and the foreigner. Why had the man named Poitou addressed Tonio as a baron? Was the master a descendant of French nobility? The other man's submissive behavior seemed to suggest as much. Johann didn't like the way they'd spoken about him—like a precious object. What were their plans for him?

He listened intently to the strange-sounding conversation, trying to understand anything at all. The words *diable* and *réunion* were mentioned several times and sounded familiar, but other words sounded harsh and throaty to him, like *garache*, *béliche*, and *bête bigourne*. Johann couldn't make any sense of it, and he sank deep into thought.

Following the gruesome execution in the morning, he and the master had returned to the inn, where Johann told the master he wanted to study. But in truth he'd needed some time to think. He owed the master a lot. Tonio had taught him so much already, and he'd teach him more still.

On the other hand, Johann grew more afraid of Tonio every day. He was repulsed by the glee with which the master had watched the execution—he'd enjoyed it, even. But worse still was the suspicion Johann harbored deep down—that Tonio was somehow responsible for both the execution and the fire at the Black Eagle Inn. Could it be possible? Johann remembered the three pieces of coal Tonio had placed at the Black Eagle's threshold, muttering incantations, and also the bloody pentagram at the tower. Were there symbols and formulas that could conjure up lightning and flames, and even kill someone? Or had everything just been a series of unfortunate coincidences? But the coincidences were piling up, and Johann struggled to believe in them any longer.

As if the master had read his thoughts, he paused in his conversation and looked over at Johann. Like an alert wolf or lynx, he seemed to detect something, but then he smiled.

"Look, the boy studies even now," he said to Poitou in French. "He's truly insatiable."

"Then I'm sure he'll like what we have planned for him," replied Poitou with a laugh.

Johann gave a grin, even though he hadn't understood a word, and then returned to his book. He was scared of the big Frenchman—but not as scared as he was of Tonio.

On top of everything else, earlier he'd discovered that someone had rummaged through Johann's few possessions in their room upstairs while he'd been out. For a brief moment, Johann had suspected the two crows and the raven, who always watched his every movement from their cage. Then he realized how ridiculous the thought was. Nothing was stolen, but nonetheless he decided to wear his little knife on a leather string around his neck from now on, underneath his shirt and jerkin, where Tonio couldn't see it.

But supposing the master actually was a sorcerer—why should he care? Tonio was his teacher, and he'd find none better in this world. What were Father

Antonius's superficial knowledge and Father Bernhard's awkward attempts to study the stars compared to the arcane arts, the ancient knowledge about "that which the world contains in its innermost heart and finer veins," as Tonio had put it not long ago. Johann guessed black magic was a part of it. He felt certain the master would teach him about it someday. Johann's nightmares and twinges of conscience were simply the price he had to pay. Perhaps that was exactly what that strange Latin phrase Tonio always recited was supposed to mean.

Homo Deus est . . .

Perhaps God didn't lead man's way, but everyone was responsible for their own path.

Meanwhile, the innkeeper had brought them platters of roast piglet with slices of deliciously fragrant white bread, and a serving of wild onions and carrots in a steaming herb sauce. The men ate ravenously, pausing the conversation. After eating in silence for a long while, Tonio burped loudly, wiped the juices from his lips with the last bit of bread, and leaned back contentedly.

"I haven't eaten like this since the Battle of Patay, and that was a long time ago," he said. "Just what we needed to strengthen us for what comes next." He turned to Poitou. "Is everything prepared?"

The man nodded. "All is ready, milord. You are expected. Although some of them said we should wait till Krakow."

"We don't have time," snarled Tonio. "The stars are favorable right now. Who knows how long it would take us to get to Krakow. I don't want to risk it. We're doing it here—that's my final word!"

Poitou looked at Johann, who had hardly eaten anything and seemed to be focused on his book again. But he was listening to every word. So were they not going to Krakow at all now? What were those two men going to do with him?

"And you really believe he's the right one?" asked Poitou. "I have an uneasy feeling about this. We could pay the midwife here a visit. A different child, born around the same—"

"It's him," Tonio said so quietly that Johann struggled to understand. "If we go about this the right way, he will change the world. But we must act *now*! If we miss the moment, it won't return anytime soon. You know how long we'd have to wait."

He stood up and signaled to Johann to follow. "Let us go." The master gave him a cheerful wink. "All this might seem strange to you now, young Faustus.

But trust me. You'll soon know more. I arranged for your ordination to take place here, so we don't have to wait until Krakow. We have enough friends around here—by now, we have friends everywhere."

"Ordination?" Johann was confused. "What ordination?"

"You'll find out soon enough. And now come, before the moon disappears behind the hills again."

A short while later, they set off. Tonio had sent Johann up to his room to pack his few belongings. The master's crates and the birdcage had already been taken to the wagon. Night had fallen outside, but a full moon bathed the lanes of Nördlingen in a pale light. Tonio and Poitou sat on the box seat while Johann found a place among the chests and sacks under the canvas. They tied Poitou's exhausted horse to the back of the wagon, where it plodded along leisurely.

They drove toward the closed city gate. The road beyond led back to Augsburg; it was the road they'd come from the day before. Poitou whistled, and the gate opened with a soft squeak. Johann guessed the man had bribed the guards earlier. Outside the gate, they turned right. When they passed where Freudenreich the minstrel had been burned to death that morning, Tonio whispered something to Poitou in French and the man laughed out loud. The air still smelled faintly of smoke and roast meat.

The moon was high in the sky as the wagon rolled past fields and small patches of forest. No one else was on the road at this time of night. It was as quiet as if the whole world were asleep—except for once, when Johann heard wolves howling in the distance.

They turned onto an unmarked, narrow track. Their surroundings became increasingly rough and overgrown. Moss-covered boulders were scattered among the trees, looking as if they'd fallen from the sky in ancient times. Johann thought about the giant throwing the huge rock into an ancient sea. Were these boulders remnants of that rock? Had God been the giant?

The master repeatedly looked up at the sky and the pale stars. Each time, he nodded with satisfaction, as if confirming an observation. After about two hours, Poitou asked Tonio to stop. He gave a whistle that imitated the call of a nightingale. Then he waited, and after a short while, an owl hooted three times. "We have arrived," said Poitou, looking around searchingly. "It's not far from here. I suggest we leave the wagon hidden among the trees over there. And then we walk."

The three birds in the cage flapped their wings excitedly and cawed, as if they sensed that someone was nearby. Tonio gave the cage a shove.

"Be quiet, God damn it!" he barked. "I know you're hungry. Not long now." He turned back to Poitou. "Did you bring what I asked you for?"

Poitou grinned. "It wasn't easy at such short notice." He opened his wide coat and pulled out a clear vial with a cork, containing a liquid the color of swamp. "The black potion. La Meffraye herself brewed it."

"Well done." Tonio climbed down from the wagon and led the horses a little deeper into the forest. Then he waved for Johann to follow him. The three of them sat down on a rock that gleamed pale in the moonlight, as if it had been covered with a white sheet. Poitou handed the vial to Tonio, who raised it toward the moon with both hands.

"The black potion," he announced solemnly. "He who drinks it is close to Pan."

"So be it," Poitou murmured as if praying. "Now and forever."

The master removed the cork from the vial and handed it to Johann. "You must empty it in one go," he commanded. "It doesn't taste particularly good, but it acts fast."

"What . . . what is it?" asked Johann. He still didn't have the faintest idea what the purpose of their excursion might be. "Why should I drink it?"

"My little Faustus," Tonio sighed and placed one hand on his shoulder in a fatherly gesture. "I've always encouraged you to ask questions. Only those who ask will receive an answer. But for once I'm telling you not to. You must cross the threshold naked and unknowing. It's the rule." He smiled and stroked Johann's cheek. "But you can trust me. Once you swallow that drink, your knowledge is going to be infinite. And that is what you want, isn't it, my Faustus? Knowledge at any cost, just like me. This world is waiting for people like you and me—people who will finally lift the veil."

Johann hesitated. He sensed that he was once more standing at a fork in the road, like when he'd set out from Knittlingen. If he took the potion, there was no way back. But did he really have a choice? He'd left everything behind. His mother was dead; he didn't know who his father was. His only brother had vanished, probably eaten by wild animals. And the only girl he'd ever loved had cursed him with words he'd never forget.

Go away. You are the devil.

Tonio gave him a nod. His black eyes seemed to pierce Johann.

"It's time," the master said. "The stars don't wait. Drink."

The liquid felt thick on Johann's tongue; it slowly ran down his throat and into his stomach. It burned like fire and tasted slightly rotten, of sulfur and vomit. Johann coughed and spluttered, and the master grabbed him by the collar.

"It's crucial that you keep the drink down, my boy," he said urgently. "It'll soon be over."

Johann closed his eyes, and the nausea indeed eased. But the feeling of fire in his stomach remained, as if something was eating into his guts. Poitou laughed.

"The first time is the worst. You'll get used to it after a few years. The path to hell is lined with fire—but the ripest fruit awaits you on the other side."

"Shut up, Poitou," hissed Tonio. "Help me get him to the clearing."

He dragged Johann to his feet like a puppet, but the young man shook his head.

"Leave . . . me. I . . . I can walk by myself." With great difficulty, he took a few steps. For some reason he didn't want the master to lead him. No matter what came next, he wanted to walk this path alone.

"As you wish," said Tonio, letting go of him.

The two men walked on either side of Johann as they went deeper into the dense forest of fir trees and gnarled, scattered yews. It was much darker now, but Johann thought he could see better than before, as if the potion had sharpened his senses. A wolf howled somewhere very close to them, and Poitou gave a laugh.

"*Loup-garou,*" he said. "*Tout est prêt.*"

The men started talking in French again, while Johann staggered along like a drunkard. His throat was still on fire, but his legs felt strangely light. He seemed to walk faster and faster, almost flying. He listened to the sounds of the forest and made out dozens of different creatures: the howl of the wolf Poitou had called *loup-garou*, the hooves of a deer on a distant game path, the flapping of a small owl's wings—yes, even the whispering of mice in their little underground caves. The trees seemed to glow with a strange light, their outlines sharp against the black sky. Every branch, every twig seemed unnaturally clear.

"*C'est une bonne nuit pour le diable,*" Poitou was saying. "*La réunion va être une réussite.*"

"*Tais-toi,*" growled Tonio. "*Ne parle pas du diable.*"

Suddenly, something strange happened to Johann. The men were speaking French, and yet he thought he could understand them! Some words, at least, because they were very similar to Latin. Was this the knowledge the master had promised him? Did the potion allow him to understand any tongue in the world, even the oldest? Words flashed through his brain like lightning bolts. *Loup-garou, garache, bête bigourne, Belial, Beelzebub, Satan, Baphomet, béliche, le diable* . . . Johann winced.

Le diable . . .

The beast had many names.

His heart skipped a beat when the realization sank in. The men were speaking of the devil. They were talking about a meeting with the devil, here in the forest. In an instant he saw everything very clearly. The potion allowed him to think faster, and now various memories came together like the pieces of a mosaic. The handshake with Tonio outside the Lion Inn, followed by the death of Margarethe's brother, Ludwig; the missing children in Knittlingen as well as near the old tower; the drawing of the horned creature on the rock; Martin, and Margarethe's screams in Schillingswald Forest that day. It must have been Tonio she'd seen! And it had also been the master she had spoken about in her fever. She hadn't cursed Johann, but Tonio.

Tonio del Moravia. Keeper of the seven times seven seals.

Go away. You are the devil.

Johann's legs, so nimble just a moment ago, suddenly gave way. He tripped on a root and fell, but Tonio caught him as easily as if he were nothing but a leaf in the wind.

"The potion is working," said Tonio. "That's good, very good. Soon the pact will be sealed."

Johann tried to speak, but it felt as if a fat frog were sitting in his mouth. His eyes seemed sticky with a gooey black mass, and his whole body suddenly went numb. His soul tried to flee, but there was no escape, no way out. A wolf howled once more, someone screamed, and a low, dull groan like from a large animal came from somewhere nearby.

"We're nearly there," whispered Tonio.

As Johann's soul frantically searched for a way out—for some kind of escape—Johann heard a familiar sound in the distance, like from another world. He heard beautiful, sparkling laughter ringing out as clear as a bell. For a brief moment, it drowned out all the howling, screaming, and groaning.

It was Margarethe's laughter.

Johann's mouth twitched and saliva ran down his chin while Tonio held him by the collar. Her laughter had always been what he loved most about her. He used to think it wonderfully naive and simple—completely innocent. But in retrospect he felt Margarethe had always laughed at his longing for knowledge, his serious determination, and his need to be someone, to mean something. She had laughed at him like a child who doesn't care about yesterday or tomorrow but only lives in the here and now.

Margarethe was laughing at the devil.

Johann straightened up and shook off Tonio's hand. His tongue still felt heavy.

"Can . . . walk . . . myself . . . ," he managed eventually.

"*Chapeau!*" Poitou gave a cackling laugh. "The boy is tougher than I thought."

Johann walked straight ahead for a few steps, then he veered sharply to the right and ran into the forest. His legs were as soft as molten wax, and he staggered and stumbled, but he didn't fall.

"Stop, little Faustus!" shouted Tonio. "Where are you going? There's only the one road now. The pact is almost sealed."

Johann knew he'd never get away from the master and Poitou. They'd catch him and finish whatever it was they were doing with him. Still he ran on, until he saw the outline of a large boulder in front of him. Johann's eyesight was still blurred, and the rock seemed to grow and shrink at the same time. He staggered around the boulder and dropped to his knees.

Then he stuck a finger down his throat and vomited.

Stinking black bile dripped onto the ground and disappeared among the pebbles and rotting leaves. He scrambled to his feet and stepped out from behind the boulder, where Poitou spotted him immediately.

"I've got him, milord!" he called out, breathing heavily. "He's here. He didn't get far."

"Then bring him to me, God damn it!" shouted Tonio. "Let's get it over and done with."

Now that the potion was no longer in his body, Johann felt a little better. But the drug had already begun to take effect. Everything seemed like a dream. Poitou lifted him up like a bundle of kindling and carried him through the forest. The screaming and moaning grew louder, and Johann made out a faint glow beneath the trees ahead. Soon they reached a clearing with a large bonfire in its center. Ancient, dead oak trees stood in a ring around the opening, their naked branches reaching for him like the fingers of a witch. Johann squinted. There was something hanging in the branches, something that squirmed and whimpered. A thick black liquid dripped to the ground like blood. But every time Johann tried to take a closer look, his eyes watered.

Someone leaned over Johann, and he could smell soil and sweat.

"He is yours, Meffraye," Tonio said, his voice sounding far away.

Hands pulled and tugged at Johann, undressing him. He didn't resist. He felt a mighty erection grow, and then everything felt moist and warm. A chorale of female voices began to sing around him as a voluminous creature he couldn't make out properly with his watery eyes lowered herself upon him.

"O Ostara, hear us," chanted the chorale. "O Belial, hear us!"

There was a smacking sound. The odor of soil was overwhelming now; Johann could smell fresh humus, grown and perished in the everlasting circle of life. Large, heavy breasts appeared in front of his face, and he reached for them, still feeling like he was in a dream. Someone groaned with pleasure, and he gave himself up to the rhythm, to the up and down, like waves in a sea of blood. The groans grew louder, eventually turning into cries, and Johann realized it was his own voice. He was crying out with pleasure and lust. He thought he could also hear Poitou and Tonio cry out and laugh in the distance. The cawing of the raven and the two crows sounded like the laughter of the insane.

The crimson waves grew higher and higher, and Johann sailed on their crests. More hands tugged at him, and suddenly everything around him was naked skin tasting of soil and blood. He grasped a handful of long, matted hair like that of an animal—black curls, and blonde, brown, and red. Countless naked arms, legs, full breasts, and soft buttocks rubbed against him. Tongues licked him everywhere, and he licked, too, tasting salt and also something fishy, like from the depths of the ocean. As the chorale rose and ebbed around him, Johann let himself flow in the wild whirlpool of bodies. Voices whispered in his ear, urged him on, cried and exulted and moaned, together pushing toward the imminent climax.

Then his semen spilled and the moaning stopped abruptly.

Johann fell into a deep black hole.

When he came to, he could see clearly again: the huge, dying fire, and surrounding it, wrapped in blankets, sleeping men and women, exhausted from their shared ritual. Above them, small, lifeless bodies hanging in the branches like burned-out lanterns. Everywhere around him was silence and death. The potion's effect had let up, and reality hit Johann like a bucket of cold water. He scrambled to his feet and ran—stark naked—into the woods. Twigs and thorns tore at his skin, and a cold wind whistled through the trees, but he felt none of it. He ran away like prey running for its life.

Suddenly, an angry scream rang out behind him, followed by the familiar, demanding voice.

The voice of the master.

"Come back, Faustus!" he yelled. "Come back! I command you!"

Ignoring the voice, Johann ran on.

"Stop! Don't do this to me! Don't do this to *you!*"

Something in his voice made Johann slow down. It sounded like he was begging him, pleading with him.

"Come back, Faustus! I can teach you so much more. The world could lie at your feet—at our feet. You have the power to set the world on fire! *Homo Deus est!* Faustus, I'm begging you."

Johann paused for a moment, but then he ran on. He leaped over bushes and fallen tree trunks, crossed streams and ditches, stumbling and falling but getting back up every time, pressing on without looking back. The voice behind him grew more and more plaintive and eventually began to scream furiously.

Johann was still running when the voice fell silent.

Tonio del Moravia, the magician, keeper of the seven times seven seals, had vanished from Johann's life.

Act III

The Train of Jugglers

8

THE EFFECT OF THE POTION DIDN'T FULLY WEAR OFF UNTIL daylight broke. Until then, Johann ran through the forest like a restless wolf, naked and filthy. Whenever his strength failed him and he needed to rest, he'd find a dip in the ground or a rotten, fungi-covered tree trunk to hide behind. But his fear of Tonio and the horror he was running away from was greater than his exhaustion.

Johann kept running as if the devil was after him.

Every now and then he thought he was being pursued by a flock of black shadows attacking him like bats. He screamed and lashed out at them even though he knew they weren't real. He could hear whispering voices; the roar of a great, angry animal; and the soft crying of children. The crying was the worst, because then he again saw the small, lifeless bodies hanging in the trees, and the blood dripping down from them.

Finally Johann's steps slowed. He staggered and then fell flat on his face. He managed to cover himself with twigs and rotting leaves before sleep overpowered him.

When he woke, the sun was high in the sky.

Johann blinked a few times, then shot up as if waking from a long bad dream. He was cold—colder than he'd ever been. His toes and fingers were blue, and his limbs ached, shivering so badly that he struggled to gain control of his movements. Only now did he notice that he still wore the knife around his neck. It was all he had left.

While he slowly rose from his bed among the leaves, images of the previous night returned. He had a pounding headache and struggled to tell the difference between real and imagined memories. He hadn't been able to think straight since Tonio and Poitou had given him the black potion. Father Antonius had told Johann about such drinks. They contained henbane, devil's trumpet, deadly nightshade, and other intoxicants that gave the user the impression of soaring high in the air or brought on hallucinations like lewd, buxom women.

Drink too much of it, though, and you'd go straight to hell.

Father Antonius once told Johann that older boys and girls from remote villages sometimes used those plants to cook up a brew that helped them escape the prisons of their drab lives for a short while. And witches concocted similar potions to mate with the devil. They smeared their broomsticks with the potions for the so-called witches' sabbath and soared up into the thunderclouds. Back then, those stories had seemed like old wives' tales to Johann.

But now he wasn't so sure.

If he wasn't mistaken, Tonio and Poitou had invoked some kind of evil creature in the clearing—perhaps even the devil himself. Evidently they were Satanists, followers of Lucifer who practiced horrific rituals. Had all the women who had kissed, licked, and mounted him really existed? And the large, soft creature that had lowered herself on him?

Had it been a witch? Or something much worse?

Johann looked down at himself. His private parts were sticky, and there were leaves all through his pubic hair. Then he thought of the bloody, whimpering bundles in the trees, and a wave of nausea overcame him.

He broke down and vomited, gasping. He had nothing left but green bile. Nonetheless, he felt a little better afterward. He looked around, his teeth chattering. If he didn't want to freeze to death, he needed to find clothes. Tall fir trees stood all around him, blocking out the sunlight almost completely. He had no idea where he was or what direction he ought to take. He decided to follow a narrow game path, so at least he didn't have to battle the thorny undergrowth.

Trembling and keeping low like a frightened deer, Johann made his way through the forest. He was still terrified of Tonio finding him. The master wasn't someone who gave up in a hurry. Johann started to notice dozens of small wounds on his body. At first he thought they were scratches from running through the trees, but when he looked more closely, he saw that the marks seemed to have been made by long fingernails. Some of the cuts formed symbols he couldn't read.

What in God's name happened last night?

A terrible suspicion sprouted in his mind. What if Tonio hadn't invoked the devil, but if instead . . . The thought was so awful that Johann didn't even want to think it through.

What if Tonio is the devil himself?

Johann remembered that he'd heard Margarethe's laughter through his delirium. Margarethe had saved him—she had opened his eyes. If he hadn't thrown up the potion in the last moment, he'd never have been able to run away from Tonio. Perhaps he'd be hanging in the branches of a dead oak by now, gutted like those poor little creatures; Johann still didn't know whether they had been real or a figment of his imagination.

Johann hoped—prayed—that he'd only imagined them. But then he remembered all the missing children. He thought of Martin, his little brother.

Small, whimpering bundles . . .

He forced the thought aside and banished it to a deep, dark place.

After another hour of aimless wandering, he spotted a column of smoke rising up above the firs about an arrow's shot away. Cautiously, he headed toward it and soon reached the edge of a clearing with a solid two-story log cabin. The clearing was covered in charred tree stumps, and the ground in between them had also been burned. A little way off, a charcoal pile smoldered steadily, filling the air with biting smoke.

Ducking behind a dew-covered blackberry bush, Johann watched the clearing for a while for any signs of life. He could hear the blows of an axe in the distance and guessed that the charcoal burner was out chopping wood somewhere in the forest. The relatively large house suggested he had a family.

Johann sneaked over to the house as quietly as he could. It was built of hefty logs, and the windows were as small as arrow slits. The door stood ajar. Johann nudged it open carefully and found a tidy room within. It was warm inside, and a large bowl of barley porridge stood in the middle of the table—probably breakfast leftovers. Johann devoured it like a famished wolf. Using both hands, he shoveled the sticky mass out of the bowl and into his mouth. When he had cleaned out the bowl, he licked his fingers. He stopped short when he heard creaking footsteps on the boards above him.

There was someone upstairs. He didn't have much time.

He frantically looked around and spotted a chest next to the stove. His heart leaped with joy when he opened the lid. Inside the chest were clay bowls, wooden spoons, a tarnished copper candlestick holder, and—most importantly—clean linen shirts and leggings, like farmers wore in the fields. There was even a pair of wooden clogs. Johann quickly gathered up an armful of the clothes. He was about to run outside when he spotted a bowl of milk in the corner that someone must have left for the cat. He was still so hungry that he knelt down, held the bowl to his lips, and slurped up the milk like an animal.

In that very moment, the door to the next room opened and an older woman wearing an apron and a bonnet gaped at him. There were more people in the house than he'd thought. The woman turned pale and then pointed at the kneeling, naked Johann with a trembling finger, screaming loudly.

"A wolf-man!" she screamed. "God help us! There's a wolf-man in our house!"

Johann dropped the bowl and it shattered on the floor. Holding on tightly to the clothes and the shoes, he ran out of the house while behind him the woman continued to shriek, calling upon all fourteen holy helpers to save them. Much to Johann's horror, the charcoal burner emerged from the forest. His bearded face was black with soot, making his eyes gleam very white. He was holding his axe like a weapon and came running toward Johann between the charred stumps.

"Stop, whatever you are! Stop, beast!" shouted the man.

Swinging his axe, the man cut across the clearing and blocked Johann's way. Johann managed to dodge the axe at the last moment, hearing it whooshing past his ear. He staggered and almost fell but caught himself and rushed toward the forest edge. He could hear the charcoal burner closing in on him.

"Martha, get the workers!" the man shouted. "We must catch the beast. I won't let it get away! Hans, this way!"

From the corner of his eye, Johann saw a younger man with an axe run toward him from the right. The strong-looking lad was about to cut off his escape route. Johann desperately hurled himself shoulder-first at the worker. There was a loud crack, and a sharp pain shot down Johann's arm. The young man cried out and fell to the ground. Johann still clung to the bundle of clothes as if it were a treasure. He got back on his feet and ran into the forest. Soon the fir trees swallowed him up.

"Go back to the hell you came from, you demon!" yelled the charcoal burner. "May God strike you down with a bolt of lightning!"

The shouting gradually eased and eventually stopped altogether, but Johann kept running until he came to a narrow track. After a little while, the trees opened up and Johann saw a larger road that led out of the forest and through fallow black fields.

Johann washed himself as well as he could in a ditch by the wayside before putting on the shirt, leggings, and wooden shoes. Then he stepped out into the road. The sun was high in the sky—Johann guessed it was around noon. He was gasping with exhaustion, and he was shivering—not just with a chill that seemed reluctant to leave his body, but also because he was terrified that the charcoal burner and his workers might appear from behind the next bend. His shoulder hurt like hell. He was too weak to run now, let alone defend himself. But at least he looked like a human again.

Which way should he turn? He had nothing left but the clothes he was wearing, and even those were stolen.

Quo vadis, Faustus?

The choice was made easier when a squeaking horse-drawn cart appeared from the right. At first Johann thought it was the master's wagon, and he was about to jump into the ditch, but then he saw it was just a cart driven by a portly old man—a wealthy farmer or a merchant, he guessed. The man was wearing a fur vest and a warm, woolen coat that was clasped together at the front with a silver pin. Upon seeing the shivering boy in the thin shirt that was much too big for him, and whose face was covered with nasty scratches, the man gave him a look of pity.

"Where are you headed, lad?" he asked, pulling a stalk of straw from between his few remaining teeth. "You don't look like you'll get very far."

Johann hesitated. Then he named the first city that came to his mind. It was the city he would have liked to visit a few days ago, but Tonio had steered clear of it—another reason that it seemed like a good choice. Hopefully, he'd be safe from Tonio and Poitou there. There was a good chance they were still searching for him.

"Augsburg," he said.

The old man grinned. "You're in luck, boy. That's just where I'm taking my wine." He gestured at the load of barrels behind himself. "Jump on up. But don't you dare sample my wine—or I'll drown you in it like a rat!"

And so Johann went to Augsburg—the biggest, loudest, and wealthiest city he'd ever seen.

They had reached the imperial city in two days, arriving around noon.

Like the last time, Johann couldn't get enough of gazing at the countless rooftops and towers rising up behind the battlements of the city wall. Tallest of all was the grand cathedral tower. By comparison, Knittlingen's Saint Leonhard's Church looked like a dirty stable.

"Close your mouth before the flies crawl in, sleepyhead," said the old man with a laugh. "This is golden Augsburg—the wealthiest city in the world. That's what the late, great Pope Pius II called it, and, as God is my witness, it has only grown wealthier since."

The corpulent old man turned out to be a stroke of luck for Johann. He was a wine merchant from Würzburg whose only grandson had been taken by fever a few months prior. Apparently, Johann reminded the man of his beloved boy, who'd died far too young. Therefore, the merchant had bought Johann a bowlful of steaming stew on both nights of their journey, helping to dispel the cold from Johann's limbs. The rest of the time, Johann had slept between the barrels on the wagon like a log. His shoulder still hurt, and the many scratches on his skin were still healing, but he felt strong enough to continue his journey on his own now.

Only where this journey was supposed to lead, Johann didn't know.

He had decided not to think about that terrible night near Nördlingen. God only knew what sort of heathen ritual Tonio and Poitou had been trying to achieve there. Ancient ceremonies that used to serve some nameless god and that the church hadn't entirely managed to exterminate. Tonio called himself a magician, so what did Johann expect? The whole thing had been nothing but cheap hocus-pocus, just like the pentagrams, the black potion, and all the rest. Something unspeakably evil had happened that night. No magic tricks, nothing that had actually invoked the devil—and yet it had been something devilish for which Tonio would someday burn in the deepest depths of hell.

There was a great hustle and bustle outside the gates of Augsburg. Johann and the merchant circled around the city and eventually entered it through the Red Gate, a massive fortification on the Via Claudia Augusta, which led south toward the Alps. The wine merchant had told Johann that Augsburg had been founded by a Roman emperor—and not just any emperor, but the famous

Emperor Augustus, who had lived at the time of the savior. Johann reverently gazed at the worn cobblestones in the streets, imagining Roman soldiers marching across them long ago.

From the Red Gate they came to a busy avenue that was so wide that there were even houses in its center. The street, which led all the way to the cathedral, was lined with huge patrician palaces several stories high and adorned with colorful frescoes. The two men passed wealthy patricians wearing velvet tunics and fur-lined coats, women clad in colorful scarves and the finest fustian, and one man who wore a cap laced with gold thread instead of a hat.

The wine merchant winked at Johann. "Did you see that vain peacock? That was young Jakob Fugger. They say his family will soon be the most powerful family of Augsburg. Since Maximilian is the new king, Fugger has been doing business with him and lending him money. Ha, to think that Jakob's grandfather started life as a simple weaver from the country! That's what it's like nowadays—nothing is certain anymore, and anyone can become someone." He gestured toward an ostentatious building in the middle of the street. "All the high-class ladies and gentlemen—the Fuggers, the Welsers, the Gossembrots, and the Rehlingers—are meeting for the *Geschlechtertanz* here tonight—a fancy dance. Apparently, the youngest Rehlinger girl is getting hitched. It'll be a big night of politics. And that always goes best when the throat is well oiled." He gave a merry laugh. "And that's where I come in. Five barrels of the finest Franconian wine! There's none better far and wide, believe me."

They drove a little farther and reached a long square surrounded by barns and more patrician houses. A huge crowd of people pushed past market stalls and makeshift tables. Behind the stalls and tables, dozens of barrels of every size stood stacked in piles, chalk marks designating each barrel's origin and owner. Merchants walked up and down in front of their stalls, hawking their wares and handing out small jugs for sampling. The cobblestones were red and slippery with spilled wine.

The stench reminded Johann of the Trottenkelter press at Knittlingen, and the image of Ludwig's brutally disfigured body appeared in his mind's eye. He chased away the thought as quickly as he could. Knittlingen, Margarethe, Ludwig, Martin, Tonio—all of that was in the past. The future lay in front of him, even if he didn't yet know where it led.

"Looks like the wine market opened earlier than usual today," the old man growled, looking around anxiously. "Fingers crossed that we aren't too late. Hey, Albertus, old friend! Here I am!"

He jumped down from the box seat and was soon deep in conversation with a grumpy-looking bald-headed man. It wasn't long before a heavy purse changed owners. The wine merchant returned to Johann with a wide grin.

"Albertus has been awaiting me desperately. He supplies the dance hall. Apparently, the Rhenish wine is so sour this year that they have to sweeten it with honey. Two of the barrels he was sold can only be used as vinegar. Albertus thanked God and all the saints when I told him I had five barrels of good wine left—at a price, of course." He opened the purse and tossed Johann a coin. "Here, for you. You brought me luck. And now off with you before I get too softhearted." He frowned. "The devil knows what you've been through. You screamed in your sleep last night as if all seven hounds of hell were after you. I wish you good luck for wherever you're going next."

He gave Johann one last pat on the shoulder, and then he turned away to help the other man unload the barrels.

"Thank you," Johann called after him. "And God bless you!" But the old man seemed not to hear him.

Clutching the coin tightly in his hand, Johann drifted with the crowd until he'd left the wine market behind. Another square with stalls followed—the fish market, judging by the smell, and some of the wares didn't seem to be the freshest. A tall tower rose up behind the fish market, and Johann headed toward it. He walked around the tower and found a mangy bear locked up behind an iron grate. The beast was lying in a corner, looking tired, its dull fur matted with scabs and dried blood. Every now and then children would prod it with a stick until the bear growled and swiped at them angrily before lying back down. The once-proud animal reminded Johann of himself. Tired, hurt, no way out . . .

Thoughtfully, he studied the coin in his hand. It was an old Augsburg penny, so smooth from handling that the image of Emperor Friedrich was barely recognizable. Well, the coin would buy him a warm supper and one night at a flea-infested inn—and then what?

Dejected, he moved on. He felt even more pathetic amid all the splendor of this wealthy place. Perhaps it hadn't been such a good idea to come to Augsburg, the golden city, after all. What was he doing here, surrounded by rich, confidence-oozing burghers? He reached another square and thought the huge building at its far end must be the city hall; it wasn't far from the cathedral. A crowd had formed outside the building. At first Johann thought it was another type of market, but then he heard a loud, cheerful voice and stopped.

"Not three, not four, no, *five* balls are going to be juggled by our very own Emilio! Only the most talented jugglers can accomplish this feat. Watch and be amazed!"

Johann smiled. He thought about the time he and Tonio traveled from village to village as jugglers. It seemed like an eternity ago, though only a few months had passed since then. He made his way through the spectators and soon caught sight of two wagons with colorful canvases. Between them, blue and red ribbons roped off an area where a juggler was throwing leather balls into the air, accompanied by a man on the fiddle. Both wore the typical colorful garb of a juggler: yellow and red for one, the other one clad in green and blue.

The juggler—Emilio, evidently—didn't look much older than Johann, while the fiddle player was probably past thirty. He had fiery red hair and a raw face with a huge beak of a nose. He played faster and faster while the boy threw the balls higher and higher. Small bells attached to the juggler's clothes jingled to the beat of the music. His curly brown hair and his handsome, dark face suggested he came from southern lands.

"And now, it is my pleasure to introduce to you the beautiful Princess Salome from the Orient! Once upon a time she turned the head of John the Baptist," announced the fiddler loudly. "Watch and be amazed! But beware, dear husbands—it's going to be hard to remain faithful to your wives at the sight of the princess."

A young woman emerged from behind one of the wagons, and a murmur went through the crowd. Her jet-black hair reached down to her hips. Her skin was dark—almost as dark as a Moor's. A fire burned in her eyes, and her mouth was hidden behind a veil. She was dressed in colorful silk scarves that she twirled all around herself as the fiddler played an exotic-sounding tune. She moved her hips suggestively as she danced, causing some of the spectators to sigh out loud.

A hulk of a man who was just as dark skinned appeared behind her. He wore tight leggings, and nothing but a leather vest covered his chest, revealing his bulging muscles. He stared straight ahead with dark eyes, his strong arms crossed in front of him. The giant's head was as bald as an egg.

"Mustafa the Strong, an Ottoman eunuch, is always at Salome's side, watching over her," the fiddler declared. "Beware of him! He can rip out entire trees with his arms and bend iron rods. He will demonstrate his skills shortly. But now, behold the Princess Salome!"

On cue, the foreign-looking girl pulled from under her dress several wooden skittles painted gold. She began throwing them to Emilio, one after the other. For each skittle, Emilio threw one ball to her. The woman continued to dance while she managed to keep the balls and skittles in the air like pearls on a string. The crowd exploded in raucous applause. The male spectators couldn't stop gaping. With her low-cut outfit and wide hips, Salome did indeed look like a princess from the Far East. Her flowing black hair was stunning. Women never wore their hair down in public—only dancers and other dishonorable folk went out without a bonnet. Salome, however, wore her hair as proudly as precious jewelry.

The fiddler played one last quick run that ended on a high-pitched, mournful note—and suddenly the balls disappeared, swallowed up by Salome's flowing garments. The juggler caught the skittles, and together they bowed to the fierce applause of the people of Augsburg.

Johann grinned. The show wasn't bad, even if he'd seen better in Knittlingen. Some jugglers performed their tricks with closed eyes or while balancing on a rope; others ate fire or swallowed entire swords. But this girl was as beautiful as the dawn, and the red-haired fiddler played like the devil. Together with the rest of the audience, Johann felt transported to a different, faraway country.

The fiddle player, who appeared to be the leader of the troupe, raised his hands and asked for silence. "We've arrived at our next highlight!" he shouted. "From the hot plains of Jerusalem, we've been joined by a man whose reputation precedes him like the roar of a lion. He once lived as a hermit in the desert and is so wise that sultans and emperors sought his advice. Bow your heads to the widely traveled Magister Archibaldus!"

The cloth covering the door to one of the wagons was pushed aside, and out came a skinny old man with wild gray hair. His almost-white beard reached to his navel. He was wearing a slightly threadbare red frock and held a plain wooden staff, which he used to help him climb down the few steps from the wagon. He tried his best to appear dignified, but he clearly struggled to stay on his feet, swaying from side to side. Countless tiny veins crisscrossed his beefy nose.

"Magister Archibaldus has been fasting for nearly fifty years and consumes nothing but water," the fiddler explained.

"And wine!" shouted one of the spectators, and the people around him laughed.

The red-haired man put on a stern look. "Don't mock him. The venerable master is privy to the secret of the philosopher's stone—do you want to see it or continue to crack jokes?"

The crowd cheered and clapped. Meanwhile, Archibaldus had walked to the middle of the arena, where the strong Mustafa had prepared a copper bowl that looked like a large mortar. The beautiful Salome and Emilio the juggler appeared with flasks and jars.

"Hear, worthy people of Augsburg! I succeeded where Albertus Magnus and Avicenna failed," said Archibaldus with a rasping voice, raising his staff into the air like a monstrance. "I studied the forbidden art of alchemy for many years, and now finally I have found the philosopher's stone. A tincture that has the power to turn any kind of material into gold. Even"—he paused for effect—"even this plain wooden staff from a yew tree."

The audience murmured appreciatively, and Archibaldus turned to Salome.

"Well, then, my beautiful assistant, prepare the magical tincture." He struggled to suppress a hiccup. Then he pointed at the various flasks, one after another, as Salome poured a few drops of each into the bowl.

"The blood of a unicorn," Archibaldus counted. "The tears of a person in love, three ounces of liquid lead, the juice of a whole orange picked in the garden of Eden—"

"No wine—because he drank it all up!" shouted the same joker as before, but the audience ignored him this time. Spellbound, they stared at the bowl while Archibaldus continued with a heavy tongue.

"Dragon saliva from distant India, as well as ground pepper, nutmeg, and cloves—but only a pinch of each!"

With the tips of her fingers, Salome sprinkled a little powder into the bowl before stepping aside with a bow. Then Archibaldus dipped his staff into the bowl, and blue smoke began rising out of it, enshrouding the alchemist like a saint. For a few moments, he was barely visible.

"By the seven times seven magical formulas of Hermes," the old man muttered while moving his stick around in the smoke. "Dust to dust, ashes to ashes, and . . . wood to gold!"

He stepped out of the smoke and held up his staff. A murmur of amazement went through the crowd.

The tip of the staff gleamed golden.

"It is done!" declared Archibaldus, bowing low and staggering a little. The crowd cheered, and a few people tried to grab the stick, but Mustafa the Strong took one step forward and they stopped.

"Magister Archibaldus must rest now," the redhead said loudly, casting a stern look at the old man. "Following the show, you are invited to his wagon to gaze upon some relics the wise man has brought with him from the East. Among others, hay from the crib at Bethlehem and a feather from the wings of Gabriel the archangel. Only one kreuzer per visit." He gave a wide grin. "And for those of you who think they can't afford it, come and win yourself some money. It's child's play!" He snapped his fingers and Mustafa brought a table, which looked like a wooden toy in his big hands. When the fiddler produced three nutshells from his pocket and placed them on the table, Johann knew immediately what was happening.

"Believe me, it has never been easier to make a quick buck," the red-haired man said. "All you need is a fast pair of eyes and your wits." He held up a pea. "I'm going to hide this pea under one of the shells now, and then I'll move the shells around. If you can point to the shell that the pea is hiding under, you get back double the money you put in. Who wants to give it a shot?"

A few curious onlookers came and tried their luck. The first two put in one kreuzer each and guessed correctly. The fiddler handed them their winnings, seeming disgruntled. The participants became braver and put in more money, but increasingly, the fiddler won.

Johann grinned. He'd practiced this trick so many times that he could do it with his eyes closed. The knack was in managing to make the pea disappear in one's hand while lifting one nutshell and transferring it to another without anyone noticing. Every second or third customer needed to win so the audience wouldn't grow suspicious. Occasionally jugglers even paid people to pretend they'd happened to pass by and wanted to play.

Suddenly Johann knew how he could make a little money.

He waited until it grew quieter around the table. Then he approached the fiddler, holding up his coin shyly. The man smiled.

"Ah, someone wants to try his luck. Well, then, my boy." Slowly, he moved the shells from side to side. "Place your coin where you think the pea is hiding."

Johann guessed right, which didn't surprise him. The man wanted him to feel safe.

"Now you have two pennies," said the fiddler with a sigh. "And I have none. Do you want to try again?"

Johann nodded eagerly and the musician started moving the shells around again. This time Johann saw how the man hid the pea in the palm of his hand and then placed it beneath another shell. He was good at it, but not good enough. Without hesitating, Johann placed his coins in front of the right shell, and the fiddler's smile froze.

"Right again. Well done." The redhead waved to Salome. "Be so kind and fetch two more pennies from our savings. A promise is a promise." He gave Johann a challenging look. "Another round?"

"Why not? What do I have to lose?" Johann grinned and placed four coins on the table. "I only started with one penny."

This time the man moved the shells so fast that Johann's eyes could barely follow. But Johann picked the right shell again. The small crowd of onlookers laughed as the fiddler pushed eight pennies across the table with a doleful expression.

"You're good," he hissed from between clenched teeth, watching Johann closely. "You know the game, don't you?"

"I want to play again," Johann said, ignoring the man's comment and dropping his coins onto the table with a jingle. "For all or nothing."

"I think we've had enough for one day," the fiddler said. "Folks still want to see the relics, after all, and Magister Archibaldus—"

"If the boy wants to play, he should play," said a broad-shouldered laborer standing next to Johann. "A promise is a promise. You said so yourself."

Others in the crowd joined in, and the fiddler waved dismissively. "All right, why not? Every winning streak must come to an end."

The shells flew across the table at a speed that made the spectators gasp with amazement. Johann saw that the fiddler kept the pea in his hand.

"Which shell?" asked the man harshly.

Johann shook his head. "I can't say."

The fiddler grinned and reached for the coins. "Ha, you can't say, which means—"

"I can't say because the pea isn't under any of the shells."

"What are you saying?" The man pretended to be outraged. "Just look for yourself, numbskull."

Before the man could touch one of the shells, Johann quickly turned over all three.

The pea wasn't under any of them. A cry of outrage went through the crowd.

"Um, the pea must have rolled off the table," the fiddler said vaguely and leaned down. "It must be here somewhere . . ."

"Cheat!" shouted the man next to Johann. Other spectators joined in. "Cheat! Dishonorable fraudsters! Hang them!"

The table with the nutshells was pushed over, and the first few stones were thrown. The fiddler, Salome, and Emilio the juggler took cover behind a wagon while Mustafa struck one of the assailants. From the corner of his eye, Johann saw several Augsburg city guards run over from the city hall. He bent down and quickly gathered up any coins he could find, and then he strolled off at a leisurely pace. The guards rushed past him with raised halberds. No one cared about the boy in simple peasant clothes.

As Johann walked past the city hall, he could hear cries of pain and the sound of splintering wood behind him. Someone blew a horn. He left the main street and turned onto a smaller lane, and the noise ebbed off.

He counted his winnings with trembling fingers. He'd managed to pick up nine Augsburg pennies—not a bad day's work, even though he felt sorry for the jugglers. The red-haired fiddler had done nothing Johann himself hadn't been doing a few months ago. Johann hoped the outraged people of Augsburg wouldn't hurt the jugglers too badly and the guards wouldn't lock them up.

With the coins in his hand, he prowled through the narrow lanes, wondering how much wine and roast chicken one could buy for a fistful of pennies in the wealthiest city on earth.

A few hours later, Johann came staggering out of a tavern in the hope of sobering up a little in the fresh air. He soon realized that wasn't going to happen quickly.

To celebrate his winnings, he had decided on one of the better taverns near the cathedral. He struggled to remember what had happened after. At first the tavern keeper didn't want to serve the gaunt young boy who clearly came from the country. But when Johann showed him his silver pennies, the man suddenly turned friendly and brought him roast venison with cranberry sauce, white bread baked from the finest flour, and a heavy deep-red wine that, according to the keeper, came from France. Wherever it came from, it was damned strong and just as expensive.

After the third jug of wine and a dessert made from egg yolk and honey, Johann was five pennies poorer. He gave two more to a busty, almost-toothless prostitute who disappeared quickly. In a generous mood fueled by alcohol, he gave the eighth penny to a homeless musician who was hanging around outside the tavern. Johann vaguely remembered that he'd performed card tricks at the tavern—hadn't that tattered beggar played some music to his tricks on his old lute? Whatever the case, now his money was almost all gone, and all he had left was the one coin the wine merchant had given him.

Only just won, already gone, Johann thought in his drunken stupor.

He weaved along the dark lane without knowing where he was headed. He needed a cheap place to stay for the night, but one penny wouldn't get him far in a city like Augsburg. Or should he just sleep out of doors? Chances were some scoundrel would slit his throat while he was asleep. Strangely, Johann wasn't frightened by the thought. What reason was there for him to still be in this world? Everyone he'd ever loved was gone. Mother, Margarethe, his little brother. And his teacher, who had shown him the workings of the world, had turned out to be a profoundly evil man and a heretic. He thought about what Tonio had said to Poitou about him at the Golden Sun Inn.

If we go about this the right way, he will change the world . . .

What a joke! He must have heard wrong. He was a nothing, a nobody.

Grief and self-pity overwhelmed Johann. Tears streamed down his face, and he wanted to die. He felt awfully sick from all the wine and the sweet dessert. He braced himself against the wall of a house and took a deep breath, when suddenly someone slipped a sack over his head from behind.

"Hrmh—" was all he managed before everything turned black.

The attack had come as a complete surprise—he hadn't heard anyone approach. Johann thrashed about widely, but the sack only grew tighter. A rope closed in around his neck, and Johann thought he was being throttled, but then someone lifted him up like a piece of furniture and tossed him over their shoulder. Johann cussed and screamed, and his abductor knocked Johann's head against the wall so hard he thought his skull was going to burst.

Someone growled angrily, like a bear. Johann gathered it was a warning and kept quiet. He tried to figure out what the fellow wanted from him. Was he going to throw him into one of the canals running through the city and leave him to drown? But if he wanted to kill Johann, that would be unnecessary. The man carrying him was strong enough to squash him like a bug.

Johann was bounced through Augsburg like a sack of flour on the man's shoulder. He smelled dust and musty grain but couldn't see a thing. Finally the man's steps slowed. His mysterious abductor lifted him up and threw him onto the hard ground. Johann gasped with pain when he landed on his sore shoulder.

"Open the sack, Mustafa," said a voice he'd heard before.

Johann heard a ripping sound, and then he was blinded by the light of the moon. He blinked repeatedly and waited for his eyes to adjust. It seemed he was lying in a dirty back alley amid piles of foul-smelling garbage. Two wagons he'd seen before stood nearby. Their canvases were torn, the front wheel of one of the wagons was broken, the box seats were damaged, and one of the shafts was shattered.

And standing in front of Johann was the redheaded fiddler.

He wore a dirty bandage around his head, and his right eye was swollen shut. He studied Johann with pinched lips, as Johann, trembling with fear and cold, looked about himself. The muscular body of Mustafa towered behind him, and Salome and Emilio emerged from the shadows of the yard.

"So we meet again," snarled the fiddler, still wearing his yellow-and-red costume. He spoke with a slight lisp, and Johann saw in the pale light that he was missing a tooth. "Soon you'll realize that it was a mistake to mess with Peter Nachtigall. No one makes a fool out of me—no one! Understood?"

"*Madonna*, calm down, Peter," said Emilio in a foreign-sounding southern accent. The little bells on his costume gave a jingle. "No one is helped if you skin the boy alive, eat him up, and spit out his bones. We need him to give us back our money and pay his debts."

"Debts?" said Johann hoarsely, feeling stone-cold sober now. He rubbed his throbbing forehead and slowly got to his feet. "What . . . what debts?"

"Are you kidding me?" shouted Peter. "You . . . you . . ." He lowered his voice. "Our wagons have been trashed—not to mention my face. We can consider ourselves lucky that the guards didn't lock us up and we're allowed to stay in this stinking yard for the night. We must leave Augsburg in the morning because we've been banned from performing here. And all that just because one little good-for-nothing thought he'd pull one over on us!"

"That's not quite right," Johann said quietly. "You were trying to pull one over on me."

"You dirty little smart-ass . . ." Peter Nachtigall raised one hand, ready to strike, but stopped short when Salome laughed out loud behind him. Her voice sounded husky and quite low for her delicate stature.

"He's right, Peter. I told you in Würzburg that the shell game is too dangerous. People see through it—though usually not as quickly as this clever boy." She eyed Johann closely and not without sympathy. He guessed she was about ten years older than him, although it was hard to tell. "I wouldn't be surprised if you turned out to be a juggler yourself. Are you?"

Johann hesitated briefly, then nodded.

"Ha! So you were sent to have us chased out of town," Peter growled. "Who do you work for? Steffen Lautenschläger? Or Karl Froschmaul and his gang? Speak up before I cut out your tongue!"

"For . . . for no one," Johann replied. "I'm on my own. I traveled with an astrologer for a while, but we . . . we went our separate ways."

"With an astrologer?" Salome gave him a wink. "I hope he wasn't an old drunkard like our venerable Magister Archibaldus. I swear, if *you* hadn't blown up our show today, he would have ruined the next. He drinks like a fish and then passes out." She gestured behind herself. "Hear him snore?"

Indeed, Johann heard a wheezy rattling from one of the wagons, followed by a loud fart and more snoring.

"We should cut the old boozer loose, damn it," grumbled Emilio. "His gold trick is ridiculous, and if we're not careful, he'll fall into his own bowl sooner or later."

"You know very well why he's with us," Peter said. "So shut up." He turned to Johann with a challenging look. "Now back to you, boy. Give me back my coins!"

"I . . . I don't have them anymore," Johann replied sheepishly. "I spent all but one at a tavern."

"At the White Lamb, we know." Salome nodded. "You acted like a little lord and splurged on a night out. But your card tricks weren't too bad, apparently."

Johann's jaw dropped. "How do you . . . ?"

"*Maledetto*, we've been looking for you since this afternoon," Emilio exclaimed. "When one of the Augsburg harlots told us there was a young man in peasant's clothes with too much money at the White Lamb, we sent Mustafa."

The giant nodded and cracked his knuckles.

"Search him!" commanded Peter.

Mustafa grabbed Johann, shook him like a wet coat, and patted down his pockets. He pulled out the last coin and handed it to Peter Nachtigall.

"Damn, he wasn't lying," Peter said and tossed the penny onto the dirty ground. "And how are we supposed to fix the wagon now?"

"One of the wagons still goes," said Salome soothingly and picked up the coin. "We can sell the broken one and the old horse and still have enough room for all our gear. The old nag would never have made it across the Alps anyway."

Johann's heart started beating faster. "Across the Alps, did you say? Where are you going?"

"Where do you think?" Emilio gave a shrug. "To the warm lands beyond the mountains. That's where I come from, and I speak the language. Jugglers are always welcome in the cities of Lombardy. Everything is much brighter and friendlier over there, and the people are so wealthy that there's always enough for the likes of us. And we'll have winter quarters in Venice that Archibaldus—"

"That's enough!" barked Peter. "I'm still not convinced that this guy isn't a spy for another troupe. So you better shut it." He pointed at Johann. "And you better run along now, before I tell Mustafa to beat you to a pulp."

"I . . . I could come with you," Johann blurted suddenly. The words had simply slipped out. Ever since he could remember, he'd dreamed of seeing Venice. He had almost traveled across the Alps with Tonio; perhaps this was his last chance.

"Come with us?" Peter raised his eyebrows, then he gave a laugh. "And why should we take a weed like you to Italy with us?"

"I . . . I could pay back what I owe you."

"And how are you going to do that?"

"Jesus, Peter, don't act more stupid than you are," said Salome. "He's a juggler, remember? Clearly, he's one of those little tricksters like Lukas used to be." She gave Johann an encouraging smile. "What can you do, boy?"

Johann swallowed hard. His head felt like thick honey, and his right shoulder ached. Whenever he looked up, he felt dizzy. And yet he knew this was his only chance.

"Does anyone have an egg and a hat?" he asked.

He performed his trick with the egg and the blanket, a few coin and card tricks, the seven Dalmatian knots, the broken stick, and the snake of Giza, whereby a length of rope was brought to life. He briefly considered juggling but decided against it. The troupe already had a juggler; what they needed was a magician, and a good one—who could do more than card tricks.

When Johann was finished, he bowed and awaited their judgment. Cold sweat was running down his forehead, and he thought he might faint.

The jugglers were sitting in a half circle in front of him, eyeing him thoughtfully.

"Not bad," said Peter Nachtigall grumpily. "Almost as good as Lukas—but only almost."

"I think he's better," said Salome, gazing at Johann with a look he couldn't read. "He's charming, and, well . . . not too bad looking. And he can talk. People will like him—the girls, especially."

"The trick with the egg is good," said Emilio. "I've never seen it before. And we can work with the coin tricks. I think he might be a good addition."

"You're not serious about taking him along, are you?" groused Peter. He pointed at his missing tooth. "I've got him to thank for this! And one of our wagons is wrecked!"

"Come on, we've had blowups before," said Salome. "If he hadn't called you out on the shell game, someone else would have." She ran her fingers through her long black hair. "He'll pay back his debt. Coin for coin. Isn't that right?"

Johann nodded, and Salome turned to Mustafa, who hadn't said a word the whole time. "What do you think?"

Mustafa gave Johann a long look. Then he made a few strange signs with his hands.

"What's he saying?" asked Peter.

"He's saying there's some dark secret surrounding the boy," Salome replied. "But he doesn't think he's a spy for another troupe." She gave a grin. "And Mustafa likes the trick with the egg, too."

Peter Nachtigall sighed and raised both hands as if surrendering. "All right. We'll give him a chance." He looked sharply at Johann. "But I promise you one thing, boy: I'm keeping an eye on you. And I'll find out about your dark secret."

9

THEY LEFT AUGSBURG THE FOLLOWING MORNING, USING the same gate through which Johann had entered the city the day before. He turned to cast one last glance at the famous golden city with its towers, patrician palaces, and mighty cathedral. But he no longer felt awe. After just one night, Johann's enthusiasm had given way to the conviction that there was as much poverty and misery in the empire's wealthiest city as anywhere else. Only very few were benefiting from the new times the wine merchant had spoken of, while the rest went hungry and struggled to get their children through the next winter or the next drought.

Feeling much better than the night before, Johann walked beside the only slightly damaged wagon drawn by a skinny gray horse. Emilio had managed to sell the second, broken wagon and the old nag to the Augsburg knacker. They hadn't gotten much, but it would be enough to have the other wagon fixed up in the next town. And they'd bought some food for their journey.

The road followed the Lech River, which was already busy this time of year. The troupe passed rafts laden with wine, oil, and bales of fabric, which were wrapped in a waxed layer to protect them from water. Watching all the action coming downstream, Johann tried to imagine how difficult it must have been to cart all those wares across the mountains. Now he'd be making the same journey, only in the opposite direction.

Peter Nachtigall sat on the box seat with the reins in his hand and stared straight ahead. His eye looked even worse than the day before, and he still wore the bandage around his skull. Johann guessed it would take some time before the troupe's leader would say more than a few words to him. Peter still didn't seem fully convinced that this serious-looking smart aleck was a good addition to his troupe. But at least Emilio and Salome were on Johann's side. He wasn't so sure about Mustafa—the hulking man hadn't uttered a single word so far. Johann suspected he was mute.

Salome, Emilio, and Mustafa also walked alongside the wagon. The group headed south at a leisurely pace, straight toward the Alps. When Johann discerned the mountains as a white ribbon on the horizon, he walked a little faster. Finally he had a destination. He would see Venice, the best-known city in the world! All he knew about Venice so far were the stories his mother had told him. Apparently, the city was built on islands in the sea and crossed by countless canals. The roofs of the houses gleamed like pure gold, and every day, ships arrived carrying spices and the strangest goods from Africa and India. Hundreds of Christian pilgrims started their journeys to Jerusalem in Venice. For the first time in days, Johann managed to forget Tonio and the gruesome experience in the woods.

Salome was walking a few steps ahead of him. Suddenly she climbed a small tree by the wayside, as nimble as a cat, sat on a branch, and winked at him. Johann looked away with embarrassment. He wasn't sure what the exotic beauty, with her long black hair and voluptuous curves, thought of him. He guessed Salome to be in her late twenties, and if he interpreted Emilio's looks and gestures correctly, the two of them were an item. But he wasn't certain. He decided to be careful, in any case. The last thing he needed right now was more trouble.

Johann could hear soft, flat singing from inside the wagon. It was Magister Archibaldus, who had slept late and now seemed to liven up. So far, Johann had only seen him drunk or asleep.

"Hey, boy!" Peter Nachtigall whistled and nodded at Johann. "Do me a favor and check on the old drunkard in the back, will you? I've got a feeling he's on the wine again. I want to give a show at Landsberg tonight and need him sober."

Johann nodded, glad that Peter had given him a task. He jumped on the back of the wagon, pushed aside the canvas, and climbed in. He was immediately enveloped by a cloud of alcohol fumes and the smell of old man. The wagon was loaded heavily with chests and sacks. In one corner, Archibaldus was leaning over an open chest and seemed to be searching for something, humming softly to himself. Johann awkwardly cleared his throat, and Archibaldus slammed shut the lid with a start.

"Um, I was just making sure the straw of Bethlehem was still there," the old man gabbled. "I was afraid we'd left it behind in the rush." His hair looked as wild as the day before, but his beard was noticeably shorter. Johann realized the straggly, Methuselah-like growth had been a fake.

"If I'm not mistaken, that's the chest with the supplies," Johann said, gesturing at the chest. "The one with the relics is over there."

"Of course, you're right, boy!" Archibaldus slapped one hand against his forehead. "I'm getting old and forgetful." He squinted and looked more closely at Johann. "You're the new fellow, aren't you? Well, at least you're older than Lukas." He winked at him. "And smarter, from what I hear."

"Who is Lukas?" asked Johann. He'd heard the name the day before but hadn't asked about him.

"The question should be, Who *was* Lukas?" replied Archibaldus dryly. "One of the wagon wheels got the poor lad as we were rolling down a hill near Leipzig. His leg broke like a twig. I put a splint on it and treated it with a salve, but fever took him in less than a fortnight. He was only fifteen years young." The old man suppressed a burp. "Shame about the boy. He was a good juggler. Knew a lot of tricks."

"I'm sorry," said Johann.

Archibaldus waved his hand dismissively. "That's just life. We come and we go, and no one knows when his time will be up. I never thought the dear Lord would grant me this many years. Almost seventy now." He gave a grin. "I was a dapper lad when I was your age. And I had a smart mouth on me. A traveling scholar who never turned away a girl, no matter how ugly." He laughed loudly.

"Did you study?" asked Johann. He knew students often traveled from university to university, sometimes succumbing to drink and idleness and ending up as jugglers. Itinerant clergymen known as goliards also frequently joined the performing troupes.

"Oh yes, I come from a good family. Although you wouldn't think so, looking at me now."

Archibaldus had taken a seat on a bench along the side of the wagon, and now Johann joined him. The man's clothing smelled of rancid fat, and his hair was full of nits.

Archibaldus shook his head as he continued. "My father was a wealthy merchant from Hamburg. The Stovenbrannts were once among the most powerful families there. I was the third-born son and supposed to study philosophy and medicine, and law, and ah! Theology, too." He sighed deeply. "Let us speak of other things. I hear you're a good trickster. Who taught you?"

"A . . . widely traveled man. Tonio del Moravia."

Archibaldus frowned. "Tonio del Moravia? I feel like I've heard the name before. Hmm . . ." He paused. "A juggler, you say?"

"A chiromancer and astrologer," said Johann, disliking the intent look Archibaldus was giving him.

"And did he teach you any of the arcane arts?" asked the old man.

"Just bits and pieces." Johann suddenly felt very uncomfortable. Maybe it had been a mistake to mention Tonio's name. Quickly, he changed the subject. "Are you a real alchemist?"

Archibaldus looked surprised. "What makes you think that?"

"Well, the golden tip on your staff . . ."

"Oh, that." The old man laughed. "It's just a little gold leaf. If you smear a little mud on it, you can't see it. The rest is hocus-pocus."

Johann grinned. *"Hoc est enim corpus meum . . ."*

"So you speak Latin. A learned trickster. Wonders never cease!" Archibaldus gave Johann a mischievous wink. "Or is that the only phrase you know?"

"Lingua latina sermo patrius meus est," replied Johann in fluent Latin. *"Deorum antiquorum modo colloqui amo. Homo Deus est."* The last sentence had just slipped out—and Tonio's favorite phrase had a strange effect on Archibaldus: the man flinched as if Johann had struck him.

He gave Johann a long, hard look. "How do you know these words?"

Johann shrugged, rattled by Archibaldus's gaze. "I guess I heard them somewhere." He quickly changed the topic. "Emilio mentioned yesterday that it was thanks to you that the troupe has winter quarters in Venice. Is that true?"

"Hmm," said the old man hesitantly. "It's true. And it's the only damn reason they're letting me come. I know I'm a lousy alchemist and relic peddler these days. The straw from the crib of Bethlehem is moldy, and Archangel Gabriel's wing feather is as tousled as if the cat had got him."

Johann smiled, glad for the change of subject. Relic peddlers traveled the country with more-or-less-genuine relics, displaying them for money. He'd once heard that there were enough pieces of "the true cross" to build an entire city.

Partly to blame was the fact that items were sometimes declared relics when they'd merely touched a relic.

Archibaldus gave an almost-toothless grin. "But I still have a few connections in trading circles because of my family name. Among others, in the German trading post in Venice. That's where we stay for the winter, in exchange for a bit of juggling and music." He snickered. "I've got a letter of recommendation from Hamburg, from very high places. It's my retirement security, so to speak. And—"

"Hey, you two!" shouted Peter from up front. "Are you draining our wine together now? Come here, Johann, I need you to push. There's a hill up ahead, and this horse won't manage on its own."

Johann was about to get up when Archibaldus clutched him by the sleeve.

"Those Latin words you said before," he said quietly. "You know: *homo Deus est.* I don't care where you got them from, but keep them to yourself from now on. You don't want the wrong ears to hear them. Do you understand?"

Johann nodded, even though he wasn't sure he understood. Was the old man trying to frighten him? He turned away and climbed out of the wagon. Long after Johann had left, Archibaldus's eyes remained on the slit in the canvas. Then the old scholar sighed deeply and continued his search for the keg of wine.

With the slightly damaged wagon, their progress went slower than expected, and they ended up spending the night beside the river. Cold fog rose up from the water at sunset. Johann shivered but tried not to let it show. As the new one in the troupe, he sat a little apart from the rest while eating his stew. Salome gave him a few strange smiles.

Following their sparse supper, Peter played his fiddle for a while, and Johann thought once more that he was an excellent musician. Most musicians he knew from Knittlingen were drunken drifters who could barely keep a rhythm. But Peter was bowing his instrument like an angel, closing his eyes and losing himself in the music. Johann envied his apparent ability to shut out all his worries and fears for a while. He himself couldn't do it, and so he slept poorly once more, dreaming of Tonio and small, squirming bodies in a clearing somewhere in the woods near Nördlingen. Several times he was woken by sighs and moans, but it was only Emilio and Salome, enjoying themselves not far from him under a thin fur blanket.

They finally reached Landsberg in the late morning of the following day. Johann was supposed to perform his first show there.

Like Augsburg, this town also lay by the gentle River Lech. A castle sat upon a steep hill in the east, tall defensive walls telling of the city's power and wealth. Peter had been here many times before, and it wasn't long before they were granted permission to perform on the market square.

Along with dozens of other travelers, they crossed the river on a wide wooden bridge with a weir on one side. The salt road led through Landsberg—it was an important trading route on which precious salt was carted from Reichenhall via Munich to Lake Constance. A salt store and road tolls ensured that the people of Landsberg got their share of the daily salt transport.

As soon as their wagon rolled into the market square, the first curious onlookers began to gather. Children flocked around the troupe; old men and women muttered prayers and made the sign of the cross but couldn't help gawking at the jugglers' colorful costumes. Johann knew from his time with Tonio that people were grateful for any distraction. There wasn't much entertainment outside of church fairs and the occasional execution, particularly in smaller towns and villages. One or two convivial hours, a bit of laughter and amazement—jugglers took people on a journey to a land far away from the misery and monotony of their daily lives.

There was a fountain in the center of the square unlike any Johann had seen before. Water spouted into the air several yards high, resembling lances glinting in the light of the sun. Behind the fountain lay the three-story city hall with its tall, crenellated facade and stair turret and many windows. Johann thought about the old well outside the Knittlingen town hall and the moat with its murky waters. The closer they got to the Alps, the wealthier the towns and cities seemed to be.

"Nervous?" asked Peter mockingly. Johann was still gaping at the fountain. "Don't soil your pants—Salome won't want to wash them for you." He laughed and handed Johann some items of clothing. "Put these on. They were a little too big for Lukas, so they should be just right for you."

Johann pulled on a pair of bright-green leggings and a red jerkin with a hood as long as his arm. Colorful pieces of fabric had been sewn onto the jerkin, and it had several slits with yellow cloth showing underneath. It was warm and elaborately made, even if he looked like a fool in it. To his horror, Johann noticed that the right trouser leg had been poorly patched up and was speckled with dried blood.

"It's a good jerkin," said Peter, noticing Johann's look. "Poor Lukas was given it as a gift from a Saxon nobleman who liked his tricks. Just before his death. We cleaned it as well as we could." He gave a grin. "You're not fussy, are you?"

Johann said nothing as he fastened the jerkin.

Their show on the market square was a great success. Emilio juggled, Salome danced with her veils, and Mustafa bent iron rods like willow branches. Even Magister Archibaldus appeared to be relatively sober, and the crowd bought his alchemist story and clapped wildly at the sight of his gilded staff.

Peter's playing was so heartrendingly beautiful that people's eyes welled up with tears. Johann thought he understood now where Peter's name came from—*Nachtigall* meant "nightingale." He wasn't just a gifted musician but also an astounding singer. His voice was loud and clear both when he sang and when he spoke, and his announcements between acts made people laugh and gasp with amazement. Peter was without a doubt a born leader, even if his speech suffered slightly from the new gap in his teeth.

Johann thought his own performance hadn't been too bad, either. The audience loved the trick with the egg; this time, he'd asked a slow-witted butcher's apprentice on stage to pose for him. When Johann lifted the boy's hat and people saw the egg, they roared with laughter. His card and coin tricks worked well, too, especially with Salome acting as his assistant. She handed him the cards and patted him down to prove that he didn't have any additional cards hidden on his body, touching him in places that weren't strictly necessary for the act.

Johann noticed that the young female spectators eyed him differently than had the girls he'd seen a few months ago. He had grown taller and had filled out a little. His hair was black and luscious, and his teeth gleamed white, thanks to a cleansing recipe from his mother using mint and mallow root. Still, he felt rather ridiculous in the slit jerkin and the long gugel hood.

Added to the proceeds from the sale of the broken wagon, the money they made was enough for accommodation at a decent inn near the church and a bowl of hot meat stew for each of them. And the innkeeper promised to have their battered wagon fixed the following day.

They stayed in Landsberg for two more days, giving three shows a day. At first Johann's performance had been a bit rusty, but with each show the tricks came a little more easily. Still, Peter remained cold toward him. Johann feared the man would never forgive him the gap in his teeth.

In the hours before and between shows, Johann practiced juggling with Emilio and learned that the young juggler was deft with a throwing knife. Johann pulled out his own knife and hurled it at a wagon wheel, where the blade came to a trembling halt in the hub of the wheel. He'd had plenty of practice during his time with Tonio, especially when his hatred of all those narrow-minded Knittlingers had become unbearable. Emilio nodded appreciatively.

"If you get a little better, we might be able to turn it into an act," he said with a grin. "With Salome, perhaps. But we better practice without live targets first—I don't want you to make a hole in my pretty girl's dress."

On the second night, Johann needed to empty his bladder long before sunrise. He got up as quietly as he could. He shared a chamber with Archibaldus, who was snoring beside him. As usual, the magister had stayed up drinking until late and reeked like an old barrel of wine. Johann thought even the fleas in the beds must find him disgusting. He sneaked downstairs on tiptoes and walked into the yard behind the inn to the wooden outhouse. When he was finished, he lingered in the yard for a while, gazing at the waning moon. It had been only a week since he'd fled from Tonio beneath the same moon. It seemed to him like a different, long-gone life.

Then he felt a hand on his shoulder.

Johann spun around and saw the fine features of Salome's face. She looked even more exotic in the dark, with her oval face the color of burned clay, high cheekbones, and bushy eyebrows. Her hair was tousled, and she wrapped herself up in a blanket that didn't hide her curves. Her full lips twisted into a mocking smile.

"Are you howling at the moon, my little wolf?"

Johann shook his head. "I'm thinking of something I'd rather forget."

"Aren't we all?" She gave a hoarse laugh, sounding almost like a man. "Archibaldus would like to forget that he's just an old drunk and not an itinerant scholar from a wealthy house. Emilio wants to forget what the mercenaries did to his parents in Lombardy. Peter wants to forget that his time as a great showman is over."

"He really plays like the—"

"Like the devil, I know." Salome grinned. "How appropriate! The church considers jugglers as lures of the devil and dancing as their mass." She swayed her hips suggestively. "And especially dishonorable jugglers' wenches like me. Well, can you feel the lure of the wench? Can you feel it?"

"Peter could play his music at the courts of noblemen," Johann said without responding to Salome. "But instead he travels from town to town with your troupe—why?"

Salome gave him a wink. "Once again it was an accursed wench dragging the man to his demise. As far as I know, Peter is the youngest son of a Franconian knight. He loved a girl—a simple barber's daughter, apparently—and left his family for her. But the lass died young, and not even his music could save her. He's been roaming the empire with a broken heart ever since." She shrugged. "At least that's what he says when he's drunk. And then he's pretty hard to understand. Sometimes, when he's in a really bad state, he talks about some pact that stole the girl from him."

"I understand Peter too well," said Johann glumly.

"Because you, too, loved a girl?" She came closer. "Did you?"

"And what about you?" asked Johann quickly. "Are you also trying to forget something?"

"Every day I forget what happened the night before."

She opened the tattered blanket, revealing her immaculate naked body, with her fuzzy black triangle and full breasts bathed in pale moonlight. He couldn't move. She brusquely pulled him against her and kissed him hard and passionately, her tongue burrowing into his mouth like an angry viper. Johann felt her hand on his crotch, and there was nothing he could do to stop his penis from growing.

"I like your eyes, my little wolf," she breathed. "They're as dark and deep as ponds in the forest. There's something gleaming under the surface I don't understand. Can you explain?"

"What . . . what about Emilio?" he asked, breathing heavily.

"Who is Emilio?" She gave a giggle. "I'm free, little wolf. I belong to no one—not even to a god."

She had pushed him against the rim of a barrel. Johann feverishly grabbed her buttocks and lifted her onto him. Her hips moved slowly and rhythmically, her eyes closed and her delirious face turned toward the crescent moon. They made love in silence except for their gasping breath, wrapped tightly around each other as if they were wrestling. Then Salome gave a soft cry, and her whole body tensed before growing limp. Johann inhaled the scent of her salty sweat. Even though it was cold, he felt as hot as he had that day in the field with Margarethe.

After a few moments she let go of him and wrapped the blanket back around her. She was smiling.

"We should go back before the others wake up. Peter wants to leave early." She ran her thumb over the black fluff growing on Johann's chin. "My cute little wolf," she whispered. "We'll taste each other again." Then she turned around and quickly walked back inside the inn.

Johann stayed in the yard for a long time, spellbound, as in a dream.

Johann could not sleep. He tossed and turned in his bed, thinking about Salome. It had been the first time he'd truly had sex with a woman. Back in the cave in Schillingswald Forest, he and Margarethe hadn't gone the whole way, and whatever happened that night near Nördlingen—he didn't want to think about. When Johann closed his eyes, he thought he could still smell Salome's sweat and the scent of her sex. So that was the great magic everyone talked about. And he had to admit: he was bewitched. Still, how could he ever look Emilio in the eye again without blushing? Would Salome tell him what had happened?

But when they finally sat together in the gray twilight of the taproom downstairs, eating their barley porridge and drinking their thinned beer, Salome didn't even look at Johann. She seemed cool and distant. She never even gave him a smile but bantered with Emilio all the more. Johann was deeply confused at first, but then he thought he understood. If she and Emilio were a couple, the other man couldn't know about his mistress's excursion. Johann thought about Emilio's knife and how quickly men started brawls about women.

Worried and tired, Johann leaned over his bowl and tried to forget about Salome. But he couldn't. What had happened between them had been amazing. Something stirred inside him every time he thought about it. He tried to eat his porridge quickly and hurried outside to brush the horse.

They left Landsberg in the light of the rising sun, following the Lech River until they came to a crossroad near a town called Schongau. Two years before, a fire had devastated the entire town, and not all the houses had been rebuilt yet.

A performance among the ruins didn't seem practical, so they decided to rest outside the town walls.

Johann filled a bucket with water for the horse from a cold, clear stream that was lined with ice crystals. The mountains were much closer now, and he thought he could smell the snow even though it was already the beginning of April. When he returned, Peter and Archibaldus were in the middle of a loud argument, but for once it didn't seem to be about the old man's drinking.

"I'll say it one more time: it's nonsense taking the upper route," Archibaldus was saying, still reasonably sober at lunchtime. "It's longer and more dangerous. I know what I'm talking about—I've traveled through the Finstermünz Gorge before. It's still deepest winter there in April! There'll be avalanches, and storms can break out at any moment. The Eisacktal Valley, by Bozen, on the other hand—"

"Is just as dangerous, if not more so," Peter retorted. "Even though the toll keepers are trying to tell us otherwise—I don't fall for their tricks." His eyes narrowed and he crossed his arms on his chest. "Believe me, old man, I spoke with several merchants about this, just last night in Landsberg, when you were already under the table. The lower route is flooded with meltwater in many places and blocked by landslides. And the locals demand horrendous tolls for the detours. We can't afford those. The upper route may be longer, but it's safer and—most importantly—cheaper. I've traveled it twice myself."

"But the gorge—" tried Archibaldus again.

"That's my final word," snarled Peter, cutting him off. "I'm the leader of this troupe, and I don't let anyone tell me what to do, especially not an old drunkard who last traveled that road in the time of Methuselah."

Grumbling, Archibaldus retreated back inside the wagon.

Johann put the bucket down in front of the horse and gazed at the Alps. They suddenly seemed a lot more menacing. Evidently, there were several different routes across this tall, impregnable-looking wall of mountains, and none of them was absolutely safe. As the sun drifted toward the western horizon, it painted the mountains in a red light, making them look like they were on fire.

That night, as they were sleeping around the wagon, Johann heard Salome's soft cries. Emilio giggled, then groaned loudly. Johann thought of how Salome had cried out for him just the night before, and the thought drove him wild.

He pulled his hood over his ears and held them shut, but he could still hear the moans and lustful sighs of the lovers.

The next evening, the travelers finally reached the foot of the mountains. A newly built castle rose up beside a monastery right where the Lech River came roaring down from the mountains. Below the castle lay the town of Füssen, which Johann had heard of. It was the starting point of the Lech's navigable section; beyond lay nothing but mountainous wilderness. The king himself had visited Füssen on his way from Innsbruck to Augsburg. The tall townhouses were surrounded by a thick wall. Many merchants and pilgrims chose to stay here at the start of their journeys to Italy.

Peter thoughtfully studied the fluffy clouds above, which covered the evening sky like spilled milk.

"The weather's turning," Peter muttered. "Damn it. Pray to God it'll last for a while longer."

After a lengthy search they found an affordable tavern near the town's granary. Over wine, bacon, and eggs, Peter blathered about Füssen's excellent lute makers and a number of new songs he intended to perform in Venice. He said nothing more about the upper route they were going to take the following day, or about the changing weather. Archibaldus sulked in the corner, emptying cup after cup until he finally passed out at the table.

"He's going to drink himself to his grave," said Emilio.

"Let's hope that won't happen before Venice," Peter replied grumpily. "He's the key to our winter quarters. Now let's get to bed—tomorrow is going to be a long day. And don't forget to pray to Saint Peter to chase away the clouds."

Peter didn't play his fiddle that night, and the others also went to bed early. In the middle of the night, Johann got up and sneaked over to the chamber where Salome and Emilio slept. He paused for a while outside their door, listening to the calm breathing of the sleeping people inside. Then he called himself a fool and went back to bed.

But he still couldn't sleep.

The next morning, the sky was overcast and there was a light drizzle as cold as snow. Johann thought about how beautiful the last few days had been—and now it seemed winter wanted to wield its power one more time. Peter scrutinized the mountains, which were enveloped in a gray haze. Clouds stuck to their peaks like poisonous mushrooms. The leader of their troupe spoke with other travelers, and they decided to wait until the weather improved.

They stayed at Füssen for three more days. The mood and the wine worsened, but the weather remained unchanged. It seemed like the snow and hail were lurking in the mountains—waiting for the travelers to start their journey. On the morning of the fourth day, Peter woke the others with loud knocking and ordered them to pack up.

"No one said it was going to be easy," he growled. "Now let's go before we all freeze to death in this place." Archibaldus was about to respond, but Peter silenced him with one stern look.

They joined a group of merchants from Augsburg who also had decided to attempt the crossing. They carried linen, wool, and furs, and they were accompanied by several pilgrims, whose brown woolen coats, wide-brimmed hats, and staffs were a familiar sight on the roads. The pilgrims' number had grown steadily since Augsburg. They were headed for Rome or Venice and the Holy Land, sang and prayed continuously, and weren't intimidated by wind and rain. Johann envied the pilgrims' trust in God, their perpetual smiles and camaraderie. He wondered if he couldn't be a pilgrim, too. But search as he might, he couldn't find the voice of God inside him. He felt perhaps Tonio's black potion had tainted and sealed him from the inside.

The jugglers didn't have to pay for the protection the train of merchants afforded them—but they promised to brighten the cold mountain evenings with music and dance. Peter was glad they didn't have to travel alone, because the French under King Charles VIII had been fighting the Italian cities since the year before. Florence, Rome, and Naples had already fallen, and no one could tell how far north the fighting was going to reach. People were telling tales of horrific slaughters, even in the Vinschgau and Tyrol areas.

"At the imperial diet in Worms, the upper classes demanded an everlasting public peace from the emperor so that the knights can't keep thieving and murdering as they please," said Archibaldus, sitting in the wagon with Peter. "They even want to found an imperial court of judgment and a council that controls the king." He gave a laugh. "And all the while the noble lords can't even keep the lousy French out of Italy. This empire is a joke!"

"The situation is much too serious for a joke," grumbled Peter. "Now shut your trap, old man. I'm getting sick of your grousing."

Slowly, like a fat centipede, the caravan of about thirty people and a dozen wagons moved toward the mountain ranges, which formed a natural gateway near Füssen. The narrow, rocky gorge through which the Lech River rushed right behind the city made Johann shudder. It felt like they were crossing an invisible boundary. Behind him lay the lovely fields and rolling hills of the Allgäu region, and in front of him was the inhospitable world of mountains, with its raging rivers, avalanches, and landslides—and, somewhere to the south, far beyond the horizon, the legendary Venice.

The river was their steady companion for the next two days, growing ever narrower and wilder. Wide valleys stretched between the mountains, which seemed to get taller with every mile. The path climbed gently uphill, but so far they'd had no trouble with the wagons and pack animals.

The area they now traveled through belonged to the county of Tyrol; it was heavily wooded and sparsely populated. Johann thought about his winter with Tonio, spent not far from here. He even thought he recognized some peaks. A shiver ran down his spine.

Is he still looking for me? he wondered.

Sometimes he thought he could still feel Tonio's hand squeezing his as they'd sealed their pact. Peter had also spoken to Salome of an unholy pact. Johann wondered with whom the fiddle player might have made a deal. Another powerful man who'd promised him the world and brought him nothing but misfortune? Johann wiped his hand on his trousers as if it was dirty, but the memory of Tonio stuck to him like a greasy coating. He remembered Tonio's words to him as his apprentice.

The pact is valid until I dismiss you.

In conversation with the merchants and pilgrims, Johann learned that not many travelers chose the upper route these days. Most took the shorter lower route, which led to Venice via Innsbruck and a pass called Brenner. Apparently, it took a horseman only ten days from Augsburg on that road, although by wagon it took much longer, of course. The Romans had established both routes a long time ago, and they were still the main passageways across the Alps. But the lower route currently suffered from severe flooding. Looking up at the cloudy sky, however, Johann feared the upper route wasn't much safer.

The path led them higher and higher. They eventually left the Lech behind near a castle called Ehrenberg, which sat enthroned above them like the nest of an eagle. The road became muddy and rough. Potholes as large and deep as ponds slowed their progress. Archibaldus was forced to climb down from the wagon and walk. Sometimes they had to push, but they still fared better than the merchants, who regularly became stuck in the mud with their heavily laden wagons. On some days, they made only a few miles. Mustafa pulled and pushed like an ox, his muscles moving under his skin like fat snakes. Despite the cold, he still wore only his leather vest, and he still hadn't uttered a word.

"Not long now and we'll need additional draft animals," said Emilio, panting as they heaved the wagon across the next pothole. The rain poured down relentlessly, turning the road into a field of mud. "That'll be expensive. Let's pray we won't get caught in a landslide."

Archibaldus nodded underneath the brim of his hat. "Yes, yes, like I said," he replied, grumbling. "And this is only the first pass. But no one wants to listen to an experienced old traveler."

At one point the road had been washed away for over a quarter of a mile. The detour cost them two extra days. Everything around them was gray and shrouded in fog; only rarely did they catch glimpses of jagged peaks stretching to the horizon.

Salome didn't visit Johann during any of the following nights, either. The weather worsened. Thick snowflakes began to fall from the sky, and a few times it hailed. They still hadn't reached the highest point of their journey. Green lakes sparkled between the rocks; chamois and ibex leaped along narrow tracks impassable to humans. Eagles circled high above them like messengers from another world.

"They look as if they're just waiting for one of us to freeze so they can peck out the liver," said Emilio, shivering in his thin juggler's garb. Now Johann was grateful for his brightly colored jerkin with the ridiculous hood—at least it kept him warm.

They couldn't afford the expensive mountain taverns, tempting as they were with their warm rooms and hot mulled wine. Just like the pilgrims, they slept in flea-infested, drafty hostels where monks served watery gruel. When there was no hostel, they slept underneath the wagon, tortured by wind, hail, and Archibaldus's snoring and farting, which drove Johann to the brink of insanity.

But worse still was the fact that Salome ignored him completely.

Had she only been toying with him? Sometimes, while Johann trudged through the snow and fog, she walked ahead of him like an apparition from another world. He could make out her curves even under her warm coat; her swaying walk, the way she tossed back her hair, and how she shook the snow off her shoulders caused him to think of nothing but her naked body. He became quiet and withdrawn. He felt Peter's hard looks on him from time to time—the troupe's leader had noticed his changed mood. Johann held back in the evenings when the other jugglers entertained the travelers, contributing to the shows only when Peter asked him explicitly. He practiced with the knife in silence, throwing it at tree trunks again and again. Sometimes he imagined Tonio's grinning face in the bark, and other times it was Emilio, his mouth open in a lustful moan.

By now they were following the Inn River, wider than the Lech. They'd been crossing the Alps for nearly two weeks, and the mountains weren't coming to an end—on the contrary, they seemed to rise up higher than ever. The river roared and twisted in its bed between cliffs as high as cathedral towers. At the narrowest point, when Johann thought the path must have ended, a fortification jutted out from the rock face on the opposite bank like a wart on the nose of a giant. A wooden bridge led across the raging river, and in its middle stood a fortified tower with a bretèche, the water foaming up at the tower's base. A wall with a walkway ran along the rock face, although Johann struggled to make out details of the river's far bank through the rain and the sleet.

"Fort Finstermünz," said Archibaldus glumly. "From here, the path winds its way up to the Reschen Pass. Last year a bunch of wagons fell into the river not far from here." He gave a dry laugh. "Of course, our dear Peter Nachtigall didn't tell you that part of the story—nor about the massacres at the hands of Swiss mercenaries nearby."

In the bridge tower they were received by a group of surly Tyrolean soldiers dressed in tattered clothes and rusty armor, whose job it was to collect the toll. Some wagon hands were also stationed there, ready to offer services like additional draft animals for the pass. They spoke in a language that sounded strangely old, like an ancient precursor to Latin.

"See how low the gate is?" Archibaldus asked Johann, gesturing toward the dark passage in the tower. "Those bastards built it that way on purpose. If a wagon can't fit through it, smaller wheels must be fitted. The guards charge three kreuzers for the service—per wheel, that is. And on the other side, when the wheels get changed back, they charge as much again. Damn Tyrolean thieves! They'll never change."

The water below them gurgled, and the bridge quivered and swayed slightly as the wagons drove across it one by one. A few of them indeed had to change their wheels, and oxen and strong draft horses were hitched in front of the merchants' own animals on the other bank to help pull their wagons up the pass. The jugglers waited for their turn to cross. Emilio made to wave over one of the wagon hands, but Peter stopped him.

"We don't need those cutthroats," he said with a growl.

"But our wagon—" began Emilio.

"Isn't nearly as heavy as those of the merchants. We'll get up the pass just fine." Peter grinned. "And we've got Mustafa, remember?"

"If you say so." Emilio didn't seem convinced. He looked over to Archibaldus, who was watching the clouds.

"It looks rather dark in the west," said the old man. "If we don't take extra draft animals, we should at least wait until tomorrow for the weather to settle."

"And pay a fortune for accommodation at the fort?" Peter waved dismissively. "That's precisely what those thieves want us to do. We're leaving now. Everything going well, we'll be up the pass in just a few hours."

"Everything going well," muttered Archibaldus. But he had given up trying to oppose Peter.

It wouldn't be the last time his warnings were ignored.

Disaster struck about halfway up the pass.

It had started to rain heavily again, and swollen brown streams flooded across the path in regular intervals, rushing down into the gorge and making progress difficult. Peter and Salome were up in front with the horse, while Emilio, Johann, and Mustafa pushed from behind; Archibaldus followed with his staff. By the time Peter's cry of warning rang out, it was too late.

There was a low rumble, and then an avalanche of snow and debris came sliding down the mountain and into the caravan. The noise was tremendous, as if the entire mountain were exploding. All around them people screamed, horses neighed, and wood splintered as the avalanche poured across the narrow track. Johann watched in horror as the wagon in front of them, heavily laden with bales and crates, was pushed toward the edge by an enormous force. The driver tried to jump off his seat, but then the wagon plunged into the depths. The man's piercing scream was cut off abruptly when he hit the raging brown floodwaters of the Inn.

A smaller arm of the landslide struck the troupe's wagon at the rear. Emilio, Johann, and Mustafa managed to jump aside at the last moment. The wagon's back axle hovered dangerously above the abyss, the wheels spinning in the air.

"Over here!" shouted Peter. "Help me!"

The horse, trapped in its harness, whinnied in fear and reared up while Peter desperately hung on to the reins. But as much as he pulled on the leather straps, he couldn't manage to soothe the panicked horse. Inch by inch the wagon slid over the edge while Johann just stood there, unable to move. He watched as Mustafa rushed to the horse, grabbed the reins, and yanked them down hard. The horse regained its footing, and Mustafa and Peter dragged it away from the cliff step by step.

At that moment, a second landslide hit the travelers.

Like the first one, it consisted of mud, rocks, and brown lumps of snow and ice, and it came rushing down the mountainside like a huge tongue, swallowing everything in its way with a hungry and awe-inspiring force. Another wagon not far from the jugglers plunged into the gorge, but this time, the avalanche came to a halt just before the troupe's wagon.

Johann was standing with his back against the rock wall when he heard a high-pitched scream. Through the veil of rain he spotted Salome clinging desperately to a splintered tree trunk. She had sought shelter a little farther up the path and had been sucked off her feet by the second avalanche. Her legs were already over the edge, and the trunk steadily pushed her down, moved by a mound of mud and debris. Archibaldus and Emilio were closest to her. The young juggler was about to rush to Salome's aid when another shower of small stones came down the mountainside. Emilio stopped dead in his tracks, his face twisted in a grimace of fear. Then he turned around and sought shelter underneath a ledge.

Johann woke from his daze. He stormed across the mud and debris, fell to his knees, and reached down to Salome, who was struggling to cling to the tree trunk.

"Take my hand!" he shouted, his voice almost completely drowned out by the rain. "Quickly! Take it!"

For a brief moment she looked at him almost defiantly, her lips pinched, her eyes fearless—then she grasped his hand.

Johann immediately felt her weight. He pulled as hard as he could while his feet slipped on the muddy ground. He could feel himself sliding closer to the abyss. Desperately, he dug his toes into the ground and kept pulling, his hands clasped around Salome's as if they were one. With an angry cry he reared up, fell backward, and caught her body in his arms. Her clothes were soaked with water and mud, and she was panting heavily. He could smell her sweat. For a while they remained there, lying on the ground without moving, while all around them people were screaming, praying, and crying for help.

Eventually, Salome sat up and then tried to stand on her shaking legs.

"Thank you," she said softly. "Not everyone would have done that for me."

Visibly shaken, but with her head held high, she walked over to the others. They were standing around the wagon, exhausted but happy to be alive. Archibaldus looked deathly pale leaning against one of the wagon wheels, but none of the jugglers seemed injured.

When Johann stood up from the dirt, he noticed Emilio staring at him with a strange expression.

He couldn't tell whether it was hatred or relief.

It took more than three hours before the path was cleared sufficiently for the caravan to continue its journey. The Augsburg merchants had lost two wagons and three wagon hands. Two pilgrims had been killed by falling debris. Most of the travelers had suffered scrapes and bruises, and one young pilgrim bore a nasty head wound. Johann thought to himself that not even their boundless love of God had saved the pious men. Today the Almighty had been angry, not merciful.

Three more wagons were too damaged to continue on and needed to be pulled back to Fort Finstermünz for repairs. Many of the costly bales of cloth were torn and filthy—a harsh blow for the merchants.

"I knew this journey wouldn't end well," muttered Archibaldus again and again as they made their way up the steep mountain pass in the fading daylight. "I knew it."

He avoided looking Peter in the eye. The troupe's leader had checked and fastened their gear in silence, making sure his new fiddle was unharmed. No one dared to address him—not even Salome, who was fine apart from a few minor scratches.

Finally, long after sunset, they reached the village of Nauders, which lay close to the top of the pass. Utterly exhausted, they sought out the local hostel, where a handful of gout-ridden monks took care of the injured. The rain had finally stopped, and the survivors lay down to rest. Some of the pilgrims sang a hymn, which sounded hollow and desolate among these frigid walls. The dead would be buried in the morning.

Shivering with cold and exhaustion, Johann was lying wrapped in a damp woolen blanket. He'd never felt more tired in his life, and yet he struggled to fall asleep. He closed his eyes and was listening to the prayers of the pilgrims when he felt a hand on his cheek.

It was Salome.

"Come," she whispered.

He got up and quietly followed her past the sleeping travelers, through the gate, out into the fields, until the hostel lay far behind them. A dark castle watched over the plateau, and snow stretched before them like a sea of black pitch.

"Our bed," whispered Salome.

She pulled him down into the snow, and they loved each other passionately, as if it would be the last time. The wind pushed the clouds aside and the snow sparkled in the moonlight. Johann didn't feel the cold, and his exhaustion had vanished as if by magic. Salome was showing him a world he'd never known before. Her hands clawed his back and he cried out, because some of his wounds from that unfortunate night near Nördlingen hadn't fully healed yet.

"What's that?" she asked and ran her fingers over the bumpy scabs. She gave him a wink. "Another woman? Should I be worried, little wolf?"

"Sometimes I ask myself the same thing," Johann murmured. He stroked a long scar that ran right across Salome's back. "And what about this one? What secret are you carrying around with you?"

Salome smiled, but her eyes looked sad. "We all have our little secrets, don't we?"

He grabbed her again and made love to her in silence with an aggression that was new and a little frightening to him. Salome groaned and cried out—he couldn't tell whether with pleasure or pain.

When they sneaked back to the hostel a while later, she gave him one last kiss.

"Thank you," she breathed and disappeared inside the wagon.

Johann wasn't sure whether she was thanking him for saving her life in the gorge or for their lovemaking in the snow.

He slipped through the gate and entered the dark, foul-smelling hall. He was about to wrap himself back up in his blanket when he noticed Emilio watching him.

"I guess you think that just because you saved her life she'll be forever at your feet," said the young juggler. "Forget it. That woman can't be owned—you'll learn soon enough."

"I don't want to own her," Johann replied.

"I first met her more than three years ago, when she arrived at the port in Genoa with Mustafa," Emilio continued as if Johann hadn't spoken. "Did you know the two of them are brother and sister? She said they came from Alexandria, where they used to be slaves of a wealthy Syrian merchant. She was his plaything and he raped her several times a day, torturing her with whips, chains, and other instruments. One time, Mustafa tried to defend her, and the merchant had his tongue cut out. The devil knows how those two managed to escape." Emilio gave a sad smile. "Believe me, Salome's had many pets like you. I was her companion for a while, now it's you, and soon enough it'll be someone else. She needs us men to help her forget. We're just her toys."

"I'm tired," said Johann. "I want to sleep now."

"Don't worry, I'm not trying to fight for her. I'm merely warning you. She can eat a man up—that's what she did to me." Emilio hesitated. "Earlier, in the gorge—I was trying to save myself," he said pensively. "Of course I was scared of falling to my death, but more than that, I was afraid of her dragging me down further into her abyss. Good night, Johann."

Emilio turned away and said no more. After a few moments, Johann pulled the damp blanket up to his chin and closed his eyes, aching from the long, hard day. He was filled by a quiet happiness, despite Emilio's words of warning.

His last thought before he fell asleep was that today was April 23—his seventeenth birthday. He'd heard some of the pilgrims mentioning Saint George's Day that morning. In all the excitement in the gorge, he'd almost forgotten the day that used to be so important to his mother. He smiled wistfully.

He was seventeen years old and a man.

10

THE WEATHER IMPROVED THE FOLLOWING MORNING.
Clouds and fog dispersed as they buried the dead at the small hostel cemetery.
They set off when the bells rang the noon hour, and soon after, they reached the
top of the pass. Johann looked down at valleys and lush meadows grazed by fat
cows. The grass was knee high and glinted with the rain of the previous evening.
Colorful meadow flowers and herbs were speckled among the green. But the
mountains weren't finished yet—snowcapped ranges stretched in every direction.

"The Vinschgau," said Peter with a sweeping gesture. "It's a fertile valley with
lots of cattle and grassland. Beyond it is the Etschtal Valley, which leads us to
Meran and eventually Bozen."

"Will these mountains never end?" asked Johann.

Peter laughed. "Not until we reach the Val Padana, and that's still a fair way
off. The great Po River runs through its plains and makes it Italy's granary. The
people there are wealthy and grateful for any diversion. That's where we want to
try our luck before spending the winter in Venice."

Despite the harrowing events of the previous day, Peter seemed rested and
almost cheerful. "Thank you for saving Salome yesterday," he said to Johann,
patting his shoulder. "I didn't think you had it in you. Looks like there's more
to you than I thought."

Johann shook his hand, pleased the troupe's leader finally seemed to have
accepted him. Peter's snarly remarks in the last few weeks had begun to bother
him.

The road was no longer extremely steep; it led gently downhill, past lakes,
meadows, and farmers with scythes doffing their hats. Johann noticed that the
houses and churches looked different here than on the other side of the pass. The

language of the people living here was barely understandable. Peter explained that the inhabitants of this area belonged to an old people who'd mixed with the Romans a long time ago. Here, in the remote mountain valley, its ancient culture had been preserved.

As predicted by Emilio, Salome was much nicer to Johann now. She gave him furtive smiles, squeezed his hand, or brushed against his codpiece when she thought no one was looking. They made love every night of their journey through the Vinschgau and Etschtal Valleys, finding outlying barns and other secluded places. Salome proved to be a good teacher. She knew countless games and positions, and Johann tried not to think about what Emilio had said about her past. He didn't want to be reminded of the source of Salome's knowledge. Much to his relief, Emilio kept his word and didn't try to compete for her. The young juggler seemed relieved.

Every night, they put on a show for their fellow travelers and for the villages they passed through. Each time Johann made an egg appear beneath the hat of a farmer or wagon driver, or made coins disappear and reappear, the spectators laughed and cheered. The warm receptions encouraged Johann to put great effort into each performance.

One evening, after yet another successful show, Peter asked Johann to join him by the fire.

"Magister Archibaldus told me you used to travel with an astrologer and chiromancer. Is that true?"

Johann nodded reluctantly. He wasn't sure what Peter was getting at.

"Does that mean you know how to cast horoscopes?" asked Peter. "Mine, for example?"

"Horoscopes are time consuming," Johann replied. "I'd have to make calculations and check tables I don't have. And I'd need to know the exact date and place of your birth."

"I know the place." Peter's expression turned dark. "Even though I don't like thinking about it. Too many unhappy memories. I don't know the date of my birth, but it must have been the summer the Ottomans conquered Constantinople, in the year of our Lord 1453."

Johann counted back and realized that Peter was over forty years old. He'd always thought the man with the lively eyes and fiery red hair was younger than that. But then Johann realized something else: Tonio del Moravia had also spoken of Constantinople once—of a Constantinople he'd visited *before* the Ottomans had conquered the city. That would have been almost fifty years ago. Could that be right? After all, Tonio hadn't seemed like an old man, but more like someone in his late forties or early fifties. Johann shuddered.

How old was the magician?

"If you can't cast a horoscope for me, at least read my palm," said Peter, tearing Johann from his thoughts. He held out his hand with a laugh. "There's no way every twist and turn of my life can fit on one hand—you'll probably have to continue up my arm."

Johann started to reach for Peter's hand but then paused. He hadn't read a palm since his experience at the Allgäu farmstead. He still didn't understand how and why he'd foreseen the boy's death.

"Go on," Peter said and gave an encouraging wink. "Or I'll have to assume that you're nothing but a fraud."

Johann was glad Peter had finally accepted him, and he didn't want to offend the troupe leader. So he took the hand and bent over it. Peter's fingers were long and slender—not surprising, since he was a talented fiddle player. The Mount of Luna was very pronounced on the outside edge of his palm, which also suggested musicality. The Life line running right across the ball of the hand was furrowed and showed lots of small branches.

Johann was about to start talking when he flinched. He was overcome by the same strange feeling he'd sensed at the farmstead that time: a soft, warm pulsating, as if the lines lit up for the briefest instant. Fear shot through him, and he dropped Peter's hand as if it were on fire. He knew immediately what the pulsating meant.

He had foreseen Peter's imminent death.

"What is it?" asked Peter, who noticed that Johann had turned white as chalk. "Something bad? You're trembling."

"No, it's nothing." Johann shook his head. "Just a fever I must have caught in the last few cold nights."

"Yes, and I know just what kind of fever." Peter grinned. "Salome is one hell of a woman. Don't think I don't see what's going on. I can't blame you!" He laughed and gave Johann a pat on the shoulder. "But be careful Emilio doesn't slit your throat at night. Those southerners can be rather jealous."

Johann gave a strained smile. "We already worked it out like men."

"Like men? Hear, hear! That's good." Peter nodded. "So, then, what do you see in my hand, great chiromancer?"

Johann cleared his throat. Then he told Peter about complex Life lines, interestingly curved Head lines, and a promising future as the leader of his troupe. He hinted at something dark in the man's past, according to the pieces of gossip he'd heard from the other members of the troupe. He tried his best, and Peter was impressed. When Johann had finished, the fiddler frowned.

"I think you understand me better than my dear mother used to, God rest her soul," he said. "I applaud you. We really ought to make this part of our show—for money, of course. What do you say?"

"Let me think about it," Johann replied weakly. He quickly got up and walked away, feeling sick to his stomach.

"I must have a word with Salome," Peter shouted after him. "I'll lose my best juggler if she continues to wear you out like this!"

Johann felt like he was in a bad dream as he staggered past the pilgrims and other travelers who sat around the fire, laughing and drinking. He still had a vivid image of Peter's glowing hand in his mind.

And he prayed that it truly was a fever playing tricks on him, and nothing else.

The farther down the wide valley they went, the warmer it got. Johann noticed that the air smelled different on this side of the Alps. The mild breeze carried the scent of flowers, grass, and, very faintly, something salty. They were still traveling between mountain ranges, but the peaks weren't as high and rugged. Johann also discovered plants and trees he'd never seen before. The sky was blue, and apart from the occasional shower, the weather remained fair.

For the first time since his escape from Tonio, Johann felt lighthearted. He tried to forget what he'd seen in Peter's palm. The man seemed healthy and happy, and Johann came to the conclusion that he'd only imagined the throbbing in Peter's hand. After all, he didn't even know whether the boy from the farmstead had died in the end.

Only rarely and late at night did he think of Margarethe, his young brother Martin, and the eerie gathering in the forest near Nördlingen. His nightly rendezvous with Salome helped him forget his gloomy thoughts. She always came up with new games; occasionally they involved binding her wrists with ropes or blindfolding him. Johann always went along without resisting, and he didn't ask why Salome allowed him to orgasm inside her. He assumed she was unable to bear children or took certain remedies to prevent a pregnancy.

Each night, it was as if he were in a state of intoxication that only ended just before dawn. Accordingly, he was exhausted during the day, but he tried not to let it affect his performances. The applause of the crowd gave him the strength he needed. However, he grew more sullen and moody by the day. The arrogance he'd shown even as a child increasingly came out as violent fits of temper. If something went wrong during a show, he would vent his anger on Emilio and the others. And when he lay with Salome, their play was often like a battle where he was the conqueror.

In the evenings and between performances he continued to practice with his knife, throwing the blade with a force and accuracy that caused Emilio to shake his head. Since their nighttime conversation up on the pass, the two young men had become something like friends, even though Salome still stood between them like an invisible shadow.

"It's amazing how skilled you've grown with the knife in just a few weeks," said Emilio. "You're gifted. But try not to throw with so much force—it's scary to watch." He gave a laugh. "It looks like you're trying to kill someone with every throw."

Maybe I am, Johann thought and hurled the blade at a tree, where it lodged dead in the center of a knothole, the blade quivering.

The following day, they included knife throwing in their show. The audience groaned with fear as Johann threw knife after knife at Salome, who was tied to a board. Every time, the blade landed only a finger's breadth away from her face or her chest. It seemed to Johann that Salome was enjoying the mortal danger. She never so much as blinked and always gazed at him with an encouraging smile. He, too, enjoyed the thrill of the game, the gauging of the boundaries—life and death separated only by a thin, invisible line. He felt almost delirious when he threw the knives, one after the other, driven by an inexplicable fury. But he never performed with the knife Tonio had given him, although he couldn't say why. Maybe it was the absurd thought that it would somehow, magically, find its way to Salome's heart. Johann still didn't know what the strange initials on it stood for.

Another week later they came to a lake that seemed to Johann as large as an ocean. They traveled along its eastern shore until they reached the city of Verona. Johann had never seen anyplace like it. Roman palaces and ruins stood among the tall, imposing patrician villas like witnesses from a long-gone era. There was a huge, crumbling arena that people were using as a quarry. Once upon a time, heretics had been burned in its center; now the old arena was sometimes used for plays. The Italians, Johann realized, loved pomp and all things bright and cheerful much more than the dolorous Germans did. The country reminded him of an elderly, drunken harlot who had applied a little too much makeup but still radiated plenty of charisma.

Peter asked him repeatedly whether he was ready to read people's palms, and each time, Johann made up excuses. Here at Verona, Peter tried again.

"The Veronese are wealthy and superstitious. We could make a pile of money with palm reading." Peter gave Johann a pleading look. "Come on! It's just a bit of hocus-pocus. What's so hard about it?"

But Johann remained stubborn. Archibaldus gave him a thoughtful look. Following their evening performance on the Piazza delle Erbe, which had been used as a market and meeting square since Roman times, the old man sought him out. Together they sat on the bank of the River Etsch, which flowed underneath a huge stone bridge. On the opposite bank, the arena rose up among houses. A small fire at their feet dispelled the chill of the night. Archibaldus took a long sip from a wineskin and burped.

"Did you know that they used to set lions on Christians in arenas like this in Roman times?" he said. "How strange the course of this world is. First the Christians are persecuted and burned as heretics, and then they go and burn heretics themselves. Cathars, Waldensians, sorcerers . . ." He gave Johann a sideways look. "Was your mentor one of those sorcerers?"

"He is an astrologer and chiromancer," replied Johann hesitantly, unsure of Archibaldus's question. "He only dabbles in the kind of white magic that's permitted by the church." Johann had no intention of discussing Tonio's other side with the old magister—the dark, evil side Johann had only really seen at the end.

The old man cleared his throat and scratched his louse-ridden head. "Seems to me you're no friend of chiromancy," he said. "How come? Don't you trust the skills of your former master?"

Johann gave a shrug. "Peter's right. There's a lot of hocus-pocus to it."

"Is that so?" Archibaldus raised an eyebrow. His voice sounded steady and serious now, not at all like that of a drunkard. "Perhaps that's true for some chiromancers. But I've also heard there are a few who can actually foresee a person's fate—even his death." He looked intently at Johann, who gave an embarrassed laugh.

"Oh, I don't know—"

"I've watched you the last few days and weeks, Johann," said Archibaldus, cutting him off. "I've been in this world for a while now, and I think I know a fair bit about people. You're not just a juggler. You're damned clever—the cleverest lad I've ever met. You could become a great scholar—or a fool who mocks the world. There's something dark inside you that I can't read, and the darkness is growing. Something inside you is searching, looking for answers, foraging in depths we mortals aren't supposed to explore. You're changing, Johann, and I'm afraid for you. Those words . . ."

"I . . . I don't know what you're talking about."

"That Latin phrase you used a few weeks ago," Archibaldus said. "I can't stop thinking about it. Remember? *Homo Deus est.* How do you know those words?"

"My . . . my mentor mentioned them once. Why do you ask?"

"Tonio del Moravia. That was his name, wasn't it?" Archibaldus nodded pensively. "An interesting name for an itinerant white magician. I'll find out where I've heard that name before. Man is God . . . Hmm. They like to use those words to identify themselves."

"Who? What do you mean?" asked Johann. But Archibaldus said nothing. The logs crackled in the fire, and Johann thought of the burning minstrel in Nördlingen. He could almost hear his screams—just like the screams of all those Christians chased to death by beasts of prey in the arena of Verona once upon a time.

Archibaldus looked up to the cloudless night sky and the sparkling stars. He gestured upward. "The honorable Bertold of Regensburg, a learned Franciscan and assistant of Albertus Magnus, once said that heaven consisted of ten heavenly choirs, but one of them rebelled against God and became the flock of the devil. According to Bertold, the Earth is also divided into ten groups, one of which is devoted to the devil."

"And who is that group supposed to be?" asked Johann.

Archibaldus smiled. "Haven't you figured it out? It's the jugglers, travel-ing magicians, and charlatans. Bertold even gave them names of devils. Azazel, Baphomet, Beelzebub, Mephistopheles . . ." He took another sip of wine and burped loudly.

"Damn good wine they make, those Italians. But they should leave the brewing of beer to the Germans." Archibaldus rose to his feet, and Johann saw how exhausted the old man looked. His face was gray and gaunt, covered with a web of red veins and wrinkles. "Those daily shows take it out of me," he said. "I'm very tired. Too tired to drink, even. I must be getting old. Good night, Johann. And stay away from sorcerers."

He nodded at Johann and walked over to the troupe's camp.

That night, Johann made love to Salome so hard that she screamed out loud with pleasure and pain.

With May, summer came to this bright country, which was so different from the cold German lands that had been Johann's home. He thought the light seemed more intense here, making the villages and towns they passed through appear much friendlier than the gloomy backwaters in the Allgäu or in Franconia. It was much warmer, too, and finally he understood why German jugglers preferred to spend winter here.

They arrived at the Val Padana, the valley of the Po River, where endless fields of grain stretched along the banks of the wide, lazy waterway. On their journey through the cities of Lombardy, Johann saw ancient Roman ruins, but also magnificent palaces and stone churches financed by citizens who were conscious of their power and wealth. Northern Italy was ruled by patricians—members of influential dynasties who accumulated their riches through trade, interest, and a good deal of artfulness. The old nobility and faith in the church had been gradually replaced by an all-powerful, unstoppable force: money. Money didn't care about rank or title.

Occasionally, Johann could feel Archibaldus's eyes on him, but they never again spoke about Johann's former master or that which the old man had called the darkness inside him. Johann learned to better control his temper, although anger continued to fester within him. At night, when everyone was asleep and he lay beside Salome, he wondered if it had been Tonio who'd awakened the darkness in him. Or had it always been there and was only becoming more pronounced now that he was growing into a man?

Emilio told him that northern Italy actually still belonged to the German empire, but it had been many years since a German emperor had managed to assert his claim in the region. Decades had gone by since a German ruler last marched an army across the Alps. Over the years, many city-states had evolved; some of the most powerful included Venice, Milan, Florence, and Geneva. In between, countless small fiefdoms remained that were still loosely connected to the empire—and that always welcomed German jugglers and paid well for their performances.

Together the troupe had decided to travel through Lombardy and farther south over the summer. In fall, they'd head for Venice and the trading post where Archibaldus held sway. They knew their journey wasn't without danger. The land they were moving through had been at war since the year before, although at this stage, the fighting took place elsewhere. The French king, Charles VIII, had conquered Naples and Rome in an attempt to gain a foothold in wealthy Italy. Rising up against him was the so-called Holy League, led by the pope and the Venetians. The battle lines were shifting back and forth, and the jugglers heard rumors about groups of marauding mercenaries who terrorized remote parts of the country, even up here in the north. Apparently, Charles VIII was on his way to Lombardy with more than five thousand men to defeat the Holy League for good.

"Damn those Frenchmen!" groused Peter, cracking his whip. "King Charles is an ugly gnome who sends his soldiers anywhere he suspects there's money. The devil take the lot of them!"

Little did he know that his curse would soon come true for many French soldiers—but also for himself.

On a hot, dry day in July, the two opposing armies met in combat near the city of Parma. The battle was short and devastating. Thousands of French soldiers bled to death in the dusty fields of Fornovo, and Charles VIII was forced to retreat from Italy.

Many of his mercenaries stayed behind, however, leaving a bloody trail of torched villages, murdered farmers, and raped women in their wake.

The troupe had given several successful shows at Mantua—a city favorably inclined toward Germans and ruled by the powerful Gonzaga dynasty. Now they wanted to continue on their way, crossing the Apennine Mountains toward Florence and Siena.

The Apennines were a karstic, densely wooded mountain range, and the troupe rarely passed other travelers. The road wound its way across hills that were covered with thick, nearly impregnable brush. The sun beat down mercilessly from a cloudless sky, and the only sound came from the cicadas, singing their monotonous lullaby. Salome had retreated into the wagon, and Mustafa brought her some water. Johann longed to be alone in the wagon with her. But she'd been cold toward him for days now. Things between them usually went like this: at night she loved him and dug her fingernails into his sweat-covered back, and during the day she completely ignored him. Johann had no idea why. *She'll drive me insane,* he thought. Each climax seemed to drain him a little more, as if she sucked the blood from his veins—and yet he couldn't keep his hands off her.

While they passed through a shady ravine one afternoon, Johann heard a conspicuous whirring noise. In the next moment, a crossbow bolt struck the side of the wagon, quickly followed by a second. Johann and Peter dived headfirst off the box seat and, together with Archibaldus and Emilio, sought shelter behind the wagon. They could hear shouts in a foreign language—French, Johann thought. Moments later, half a dozen mercenaries in colorful slashed trousers and rusty cuirasses emerged from the bushes. Two of them were armed with crossbows, while the rest slowly walked toward the troupe with drawn swords. Johann could tell by the look in the soldiers' eyes that they'd show no mercy.

"La fille," growled the front-most mercenary, a tall, bearded man with a poorly healed scar on his face. *"Donne-moi la fille!"* He gestured toward Salome, who was peering out from behind the wagon canvas. Two of the men slowly stepped toward Emilio and Archibaldus, raising their swords with smirks on their faces. Clearly, they didn't expect much of a fight.

Johann frantically tried to figure out what to do. Defend Salome and die? He had no weapons other than Tonio's knife. Peter owned a rusty short sword, and Emilio and Mustafa were tough opponents in a pub brawl, but they didn't stand a chance against half a dozen trained French mercenaries. Should he try to run away? He shot a glance at the thorny bushes by the wayside. They were just a few steps from him, but even a few steps was too far with a crossbow pointed at you. And he couldn't abandon Salome.

Meanwhile, two of the mercenaries had dragged the screaming Salome out of the wagon. She thrashed about wildly, but to no avail. The men were already tearing off her clothes, laughing as they groped her naked breasts. The rest of the troupe was herded together like a flock of chickens waiting to be slaughtered.

Salome was lying on the road with her legs spread apart, held down by two struggling soldiers. One of the mercenaries opened his fly, knelt down, and gave his comrades a triumphant look.

"C'est moi le premier," he said, rubbing his hard penis. *"Et ensuite—"*

A rumble went through the wagon as if a volcano were erupting inside. The next moment, Mustafa lunged down from the box seat, holding one of the chains he used during his performances. He roared as he swung the chain wildly above his head. It was the first sound Johann had ever heard from the dark giant. His roar sounded like that of an angry bear. The chain hissed like a snake and struck the face of the soldier kneeling in front of Salome, turning it into a bloody mess. Screaming with pain, the man fell to his side, his trousers slipping down to his knees. Mustafa swung the chain and it wrapped itself around the neck of the next man. The soldier turned red in the face, then Mustafa jerked the chain and there was a cracking sound. The man's legs gave way and he fell to the ground with a broken neck.

Everything had happened so fast that none of the remaining four soldiers had had time to react. But now they came to their senses.

"En garde!" shouted the leader, running toward Mustafa, who was standing with his back to the soldier.

When the man ran past, Johann threw his knife.

He did it with the exact same movement he'd practiced time and time again over the last few days and weeks, his face twisted into a grimace of determination and hatred. When the blade left his fingers, he felt an enormous sense of relief, as if something inside him let go. For the briefest moment, the face of the mercenary leader turned into Tonio's grinning visage.

Then the knife entered the soldier's left eye with a smacking noise. The man kept running for another yard or two, as if he hadn't noticed his own death, and then he collapsed like a puppet whose strings had been cut.

Mustafa turned around and gave Johann a nod as the giant bent down to pick up the dead man's sword. A crossbow bolt struck Mustafa's left upper arm, but he didn't even seem to react. He hurled himself at the next opponent with a dull cry. The man raised his weapon, gasping with fear, but Mustafa shoved the blade aside as if it were a twig and buried his own sword in the crook of the soldier's neck. A fountain of blood spurted from the wound and onto the dusty road.

The two remaining men didn't linger for long when they saw their comrades lying dead in the dirt. They threw down their crossbow and sword and turned to run. But Mustafa wasn't finished. He went after the men, grabbed the slower one by the collar, and yanked him back like a rag doll. Then he pummeled the mercenary's face with his fists until it was nothing but bloody pulp. When Mustafa finally let go of him, the man groaned, gave one last twitch, and died. The last mercenary got away through the bushes.

The man whose face Mustafa had demolished with the chain was still screaming. *"Mon visage, mon visage!"* he moaned over and over, rolling around on the ground. *"Je suis aveugle, je ne vois rien! O Vierge Sainte!"*

Mustafa walked over to him and slit his throat with one swift movement.

A heavy silence descended over the ravine. Blowflies found the dead bodies and landed in the gaping wounds. Among the corpses sat Salome, her dress torn, almost naked, staring straight ahead. She was trembling, but she held her head high like a proud queen of death. Eventually she stood up, leaned over the man with the slit throat, and spat in his bloodied face.

Mustafa pulled the bolt from his upper arm as if removing a splinter, and then he gently wrapped a blanket around his sister's shoulders. Johann thought about what Emilio had told him a few weeks ago. Apparently Mustafa had tried to defend Salome in faraway Alexandria, whereupon their master had cut out his tongue. No wonder Mustafa wasn't going to stand by and watch while someone tried to rape his sister again. He'd rather die—or kill.

Peter was the first to speak after a long silence. "That . . . that was damned close," he said. "Thanks, Mustafa."

Mustafa didn't deign to look at him but continued to care for Salome. Johann walked over to the body of the lead mercenary and pulled his knife from the man's eye. The blade was sticky and bloody, and the man's other eye seemed to stare at him reproachfully. It was the first time Johann had killed somebody. It had been so easy.

And if he was being honest with himself, he'd even enjoyed it.

The desire for vengeance and retribution had flowed through his veins like sweet poison, just like the time in Knittlingen when he'd met Tonio and wished for the death of Margarethe's brother. He remembered Tonio's words.

Hatred can be very healing, purging the soul like fire.

Tonio had been right. Hatred was as sweet and delicious as freshly baked honey cake. The anger that had been stewing inside Johann for so long was wiped away, and all that remained was a pleasant emptiness.

"We should get away from here," Archibaldus said warningly and brushed the dust off his frock. He was trembling, in dire need of a swig of wine. "One of them got away. We don't know if he went to fetch reinforcements."

"You're right, old pisshead," replied Peter. "Let's get going." His eyes turned to Mustafa again. Then he grinned. "I swear, that was the quickest fight I've seen in my life! You truly are—" Suddenly Peter grimaced with pain and he clutched his hands to his stomach.

"What is it?" asked Emilio. "Are you hurt?"

Peter shook his head with clenched teeth. "It's . . . nothing. Probably just an upset stomach. It's been paining me for a few days now. Perhaps the water from one of the wells I've been drinking from was foul." He gave a strained laugh and gestured at the corpses around them. "By Christ, I could be lying there getting eaten by flies, so I'm sure I can put up with a bit of stomach pain. Let's go before more of those French bastards turn up."

Peter climbed onto the box seat with much difficulty, and Johann noticed that he continued to hold his side. Johann was overcome by an uneasy feeling and wondered whether Peter had really just drunk a bit of foul water.

During the following days and weeks, they crossed the Apennines and headed south toward Florence and Siena, avoiding the smaller roads whenever possible. Most French soldiers had left the country, but the troupe didn't want to risk running into any who had stuck around. They couldn't always rely on Mustafa.

Thankfully, the crossbow bolt hadn't penetrated Mustafa's arm deeply, and the wound healed fast. Peter's stomach pains, on the other hand, persisted. Sometimes they would go away for two or three days just to return all the worse.

Peter grew visibly skinny, and his face became drawn and pale. He barely ate. But he still played fiddle during their performances; in fact, he played even more heartrendingly beautifully than before—as if his life came pouring out of him with his melodies.

"What kind of a terrible disease is it?" Johann asked Archibaldus at a tavern one evening. They had just given a show in a large, magnificent town called Pisa with an oddly tilted bell tower on its market square. The old man wiped the drops of wine from his beard before replying to Johann.

"I can't tell you for certain, but I'm afraid it's something serious. It could be a growth in his stomach that is eating him up from the inside. The Greeks call it cancer, because apparently the growth looks somewhat like a crab."

"Does that mean he's going to die?" asked Johann haltingly. He'd grown fond of Peter in the last few months, admiring the man's vivacity and leadership, but most of all his musical talent, which was unparalleled and otherworldly. But—if Johann was entirely honest—it wasn't Peter's probable death that scared him the most, but the fact that he had foreseen it in Peter's palm. He remembered what Archibaldus had said a few weeks ago about chiromancers.

I've also heard there are a few who can actually foresee a person's fate—even his death.

Johann turned pale at the thought. Could it be that Tonio had taught him such an ominous skill without his noticing?

"I think Peter knows that he won't be with us for much longer." Archibaldus sighed. "No one can say how much longer exactly. But I fear he won't be going to Venice with us."

"But . . . but Peter is our leader!" said Johann stubbornly. "What's going to happen to us?"

He had become fixated on Venice as their destination. Perhaps it had something to do with the stories his mother used to tell him about the city. Johann hoped that after so much traveling, his life would settle down a little in Venice, at least for a while. He didn't know what would come afterward.

"What's going to happen to us?" Archibaldus gave a dry laugh. "It would be worse for you if *I* drank myself to death before the autumn. Remember, it is my invitation alone that will open the gates of the Fondaco dei Tedeschi to us. With Peter, we merely lose a fiddle player—a damn good one, though." He shook his head. "It's almost as if the devil himself taught him to play! I'd love to help him, but my knowledge of healing isn't great enough. I guess I studied the wrong subject."

"Where did you study?" asked Johann.

"At one of the oldest and most venerable universities in the empire: Heidelberg."

"Heidelberg?" Johann's heart beat faster. "That's not far from where I come from. It's always been my dream to study there."

"Well, it's a beautiful city that tends to lead a young man to feast and drink more than study," Archibaldus replied with a grin. "My father, the great Karl Stovenbrannt, said I ought to at least gain my baccalaureus there. I was talented and thirsty for knowledge, and so I even gained the degree of magister. Then I went on trips to our trading posts at Bergen, Bruges, London, and also to Italy. And that's where I experienced the *dolce vita* and was forever lost to my father and the trade." He gave Johann an inquisitive look. "How come you're not at the university? You're as clever as you are learned, and you are ambitious, even though you try your best to hide it from everyone else. I've told you before: you could be a great scholar."

"The man who raised me would rather have set fire to his own house than allow me to go to the university," Johann replied bitterly. "He thought I was a good-for-nothing."

Archibaldus laughed. "I still don't know who you really are, Johann, but you're certainly no good-for-nothing. If you wish, I could teach you a few bits and pieces on our journey to Venice and throughout the winter. About the *artes liberales*, at least."

"The *artes liberales*?" Johann frowned. Evidently, he still had much to learn. "What's that?"

"The liberal arts are the prerequisite for any higher education. The three lower ones, also known as the trivium, are grammar, rhetoric, and dialectic. Then follow the four upper arts, called the quadrivium. They include arithmetic, geometry, music, and astronomy." Archibaldus looked at him sharply. "Although I think you've learned enough of the latter from your former teacher. Those arts are very old. Long taught by the Greeks and Romans, they are the foundation of all sciences."

"And you . . . you'd really instruct me in all those arts?" Johann stared at him with an open mouth. He suddenly realized how desperately he longed for knowledge; he craved it like one craves water after wandering the desert for weeks. He craved it even more than Salome's breasts and the warmth between her legs. "But how could I possibly pay you back?"

"By telling me who you really are, Johann." He raised one hand. "Don't worry—not right away. Perhaps I'll learn more about you in the course of our lessons." He took a long sip before continuing. "And perhaps I'll even find out more about your former mentor."

During the following months, they moved through the heat of upper Italy and performed in many towns and cities. For Johann, it was a time of both pain and fulfillment. Archibaldus remained true to his word and instructed him in the liberal arts. Johann's anger abated, replaced by his thirst for knowledge. Perhaps his inner rage had something to do with a frustration at the lack of mental stimuli. He felt at peace while he discussed grammar, arithmetic, and dialectic with Archibaldus. At the same time it pained him to watch Peter crumble, even though the redhead put on a brave face and continued to play his fiddle and make the announcements between their individual acts. Emilio especially tried to raise the subject of his illness with Peter every now and then, but the man cut him off every time.

"I'm going to keep playing the fiddle for as long as the dear Lord—or whoever else—lets me play," Peter would reply gruffly. "Each one of us is only given a certain amount of time on this earth. It's pointless to grieve before my time's up. Now go practice your act, you lazybones. You dropped two balls during the last show!"

In Genoa, Archibaldus bought expensive poppy juice from a pharmacy for Peter, who took it mixed with brandy. At least it helped him to bear the pain. During the evenings, Peter would often sit by the campfire, staring into the flames and muttering to himself.

"Now he's finally come to fetch me," he said quietly. "Damn, was it really worth it? If I could only turn back time—I would gladly have paid the price for her! For her, not for this cursed fiddle."

No one knew what Peter meant by those strange words. Johann didn't have much time to ponder them, because Salome didn't give him a break. They made love so passionately under the starry skies that Johann wished the sun would never rise again. Sleeping with Salome was like a drug that helped him forget everything else—his mother, his years in Knittlingen, little Martin, Tonio, the black potion, and even Margarethe.

But as hard as they loved each other at night, Salome was no companion to him during the day. Just the opposite: she was cold and unapproachable. One day, when she and Johann followed the wagon at a little distance and Salome—as usual—said nothing and focused on picking rosemary and sage by the wayside, he grabbed her by the arm and forced her to look at him.

"Damn it, Salome, what are you playing at?" he said angrily. "Don't toy with me—I'm not a puppet. If you don't love me, just tell me to my face. But then let's stop with those games at night!"

"Games?" Salome gave a thin smile. "Is that what you really want, my little wolf? To stop doing that?"

Johann didn't answer, because he knew she was right. He needed Salome as badly as Peter needed his poppy juice. He'd never be able to leave her, no matter how poorly she treated him during the day.

"But . . . but why are you acting like this?" he asked. "I honestly have no idea what to think. You're so different at night from how you are during the day. Don't you love me, Salome?"

She looked at him for a long time before replying in a quiet voice.

"I loved for the last time when I was fifteen years old. He was a boy from Armenia, handsome like you, smart, and always had a big smile on his face. When they dragged me and Mustafa onto the ship, he tried to block their way. They cut his throat and threw him into the water like a dead rat. I watched the sharks tear his beautiful body into pieces. That was the second-to-last time I cried. The last time was when they cut out Mustafa's tongue." Her lips were thin lines, her eyes as cold as ice.

"I won't let them hurt me again. Ever! Now let go of me before I cut off your best piece. It would be a shame, no question, but I'd do it anyway."

A small knife suddenly flashed in her hand, and Johann let go. She didn't come to him for four nights. When she slipped underneath his blanket during the fifth night, they didn't utter a word. The pain when her fingernails dug into his skin was sweet and made him howl like a wolf. Johann carried red streaks on his back for many days. And Emilio studied him with a quiet smile.

"She's eating you up," he mocked. "I warned you, Johann. She devours men."

His hours with Archibaldus helped take his mind off Salome. The two men often rode in the back of the wagon on their trips between villages and towns. Archibaldus had organized a slab of slate and a piece of chalk for Johann, as well as an abacus to learn arithmetic. Of the seven liberal arts, Johann particularly enjoyed rhetoric. He and Archibaldus spent hours practicing the sequence of thesis and antithesis, whereby Archibaldus thoroughly enjoyed refuting Johann's arguments.

"Socrates likened philosophers to midwives," Archibaldus said with a smile when Johann found himself outwitted once more. "They are merely helping to deliver someone's thoughts, but the initial spark has to come from within yourself."

Johann groaned. "So much knowledge. It's a crying shame that there isn't a place where all that knowledge is stored and accessible to everyone, not just to a select few. Each monastery only hoards books for their own benefit, or you have to attend university and pay a pile of money."

Archibaldus slowly shook his head. "Times are changing. There is a public library in my hometown of Hamburg now. It's huge, and anyone can enter and browse through the books as they please."

"I want to go there one day," Johann replied. "And to Heidelberg, Prague, and Vienna—to all the great universities of the empire."

Archibaldus was now drinking much less than he used to, going to bed only moderately drunk in the evenings. The lessons with Johann seemed to have rejuvenated him. He kept trying to find out more about Johann's former teacher and master, but the young man gave almost nothing away about Tonio. On the one hand, because Johann hardly knew much about the man himself, and on the other, because he had the strange feeling that Tonio would be able to hear them if they talked about him—as if he came to life just by being spoken about. Or as if Tonio's raven and crows were circling somewhere high above them, reporting to their master.

September came, then October. There were increasingly more rainy days now, and the mild, warm weather gave way to a dull grayness that seemed to win over the sun a little bit more every day. Storms rumbled along the coast, and sea fog crept into the land from the ocean. Still, it was much warmer than the October days Johann remembered from Knittlingen. Whenever they passed slopes planted in vines heavy with grapes, he wistfully thought about the harvests back home, about the German songs and the laughter of the pretty Knittlingen girls.

When October turned to November, they decided it was time to start heading for Venice. They had been in the mighty city-state for a while now. Venice's properties stretched along the entire northeast shore of Italy and also included colonies on the shores of the Adriatic Sea and on large islands like Crete. But they hadn't come near the city itself so far.

It had been Peter's greatest wish to see the most glamorous city in the world, known as La Serenissima, or "the most serene," one last time. But he'd spent the last two weeks lying in the back of the wagon, staring at the ceiling. His daily doses of poppy juice had steadily increased. Peter's fiddle hung from a hook on the wall, gently swaying from side to side when they were on the road; he hadn't played it for a while now.

Their last performance on the mainland was in a town called Treviso, only twenty miles from Venice. That night, Johann was woken by groans coming from the wagon. Someone was calling his name.

It was Peter.

Carefully, Johann peeled himself out of the blanket, trying not to wake Salome, and climbed into the wagon. Peter had managed to light a tallow candle, and Johann could see his haggard face. The formerly proud, strong-minded fiddle player looked like death himself. When his mouth twisted into a sad smile, Johann thought he was looking at a skull. The red hair stuck to his forehead like wet straw.

"The . . . the end has come," Peter said with wheezing breath. "I can feel it."

"Shall I fetch the others?" Johann squeezed Peter's hand, which seemed to consist of nothing but skin and bones.

Peter shook his head tiredly. "I don't want them to see me like this. I . . . only wanted to speak with you."

"With me? But why—"

Peter raised a hand, cutting Johann off. "Please, Johann, tell me . . . ," said the sick man, pausing with exhaustion. "Back when we crossed the pass and you read my palm . . . something frightened you. It . . . it was because you foresaw my death, didn't you? Am I right?"

Johann hesitated briefly, but then he nodded. Why should he lie to a dying man?

Peter nodded. "I . . . I thought so. Accursed magicians and chiromancers!" He made a sound that Johann didn't immediately recognize as a laugh. "I never trusted you, lad. You've got something about you, something dark, restless. As if . . . as if the devil himself touched you."

Johann said nothing and Peter continued, his voice taking on a dreamy tone. He stared up at the ceiling as if he could see his life replay before his eyes.

"I knew a girl once. She was as beautiful as the sun, but she came from a lowly home, while my family was of noble blood, and so I wasn't permitted to marry her. We ran away together. We made a living as jugglers. It was the best time of my life." Peter smiled. "People liked it when I played the fiddle, even though I wasn't very good yet. But then . . ." He wheezed and gasped for breath. "Then she fell ill. Very ill. I had to watch her fade away before my eyes. I swore I'd do anything to save her. And . . . and someone asked me, 'Anything? Would you even give me three fingers of your right hand?' I . . . I said I would, but then I didn't give him the fingers—even though I'd promised. A fiddler needs his fingers like a fish needs gills to breathe! Do you understand, Johann? Do you understand me? And so she died, and I . . ." He paused. "I played better and better. The devil knows why." He gave another laugh. "By God, I *know* he knows! And now he's coming to take his part of the bargain."

Johann was still holding Peter's hand—the hand of the red-haired fiddler who played heavenly melodies so beautifully that they had the power to break hearts. Peter's story was confused—the last stammered words of a dying man, not making a lot of sense. But they filled Johann with a sense of dread. Suddenly Peter grasped Johann's hand so hard that Johann winced.

"Pray for me, Johann Faustus," the fiddler begged. "Pray for me, for a poor sinner who loved playing the fiddle more than he loved his girl. Pray for me! And burn . . . my . . . fiddle."

Peter's hand squeezed Johann's one last time, then life left his body with one final wheezing breath. His eyes turned glassy, and he fell back onto the bed. A nameless terror filled his gaze, as if he'd seen something horrible in the last moment of his life. Johann couldn't bear the sight and closed Peter's eyes. Then he lifted the violin from its hook and climbed outside, where the moon cast its pale light through the clouds. He walked over to the fire and threw the fiddle into the flames, which crackled hungrily as they ate their way through the wood with blue tongues. None of the others woke up.

Johann wanted to pray for Peter, but he realized that he didn't really know how. The last time he'd prayed was such a long time ago—by his mother's grave. The words fell from his mouth like dry crumbs of dirt.

"Our father in heaven, hallowed be thy name . . ."

Johann hastily made the sign of the cross before going to wake the others to tell them that Peter Nachtigall, the red-haired devil of a fiddler, leader of their small troupe of jugglers, had passed away.

And he wondered how Peter had known his nickname—the name his mother used to call him.

Faustus, the lucky one.

But it was too late to ask him.

11

THEY BURIED PETER NACHTIGALL NEXT TO THE CEMETERY of the small Treviso church. As a dishonorable juggler, he couldn't be buried within the cemetery walls, but at least the priest said a quick prayer for his soul and there was a wooden cross with his name on it. As Johann studied the crudely carved inscription on the cross, he thought about how far from Peter's home the fiddler had been put to rest, as a stranger. Johann wondered if he'd share this same fate one day.

Once the priest had left, the troupe stood around the grave in silence for a while. There was a light drizzle in the air and the hollow sound of a death knell. Eventually, Emilio spoke.

"What do we do now?" he asked the others.

"What do you think?" replied Johann. "We go to Venice. That's what Peter would have wanted."

"But we need a new leader," said Emilio.

"Indeed we do." Johann gave them a challenging look. "And that's going to be me. It was Peter's dying wish. He asked me to burn his fiddle and lead his troupe from now on."

The latter was a blatant lie, but Johann had long felt a desire to change the face of the troupe. Some of their acts were outdated, and for the last few months, Peter had treated him as a full-fledged member of the troupe and promised him a great future as a showman. Something inside Johann told him that it was time to step up.

"You?" Emilio gave a thin smile. "How old are you? Seventeen?"

"Which makes me not much younger than you," replied Johann. "You may be a good acrobat, but your speeches are dry and boring. The leader should be articulate. And you have no idea about business. I know arithmetic and how to negotiate."

"I may not be the best at delivering speeches." Emilio crossed his arms on his chest and returned Johann's defiant stare. "But you don't stand a chance in Venice, because you don't speak the language. Unlike me."

"Then you can translate for him," Archibaldus said. "I also think Johann would make a good leader. He is clever and won't let anyone pull one over on him—or us. And he certainly knows how to talk."

In the past few weeks, the sicker Peter had gotten, the more often Johann had taken over the announcements during their shows. He was good at catching people's attention with his loud voice and witty speeches, and he knew how to use just the right amount of persuasion—the mark of a good juggler. Their audience numbers had grown steadily since Johann had begun helming the shows; even Archibaldus's tattered relics had been making money again, with numerous believers paying to touch them.

"What do you think?" Emilio asked Salome, who had been watching in silence with her brother. "Do you also think our young Johann is the best for the job?" He pulled a mocking face. "You know him best of all of us."

Salome gave a little smile. "Let's give him a chance," she said. "He's pretty to look at and he's funny—the women will love him. And your speeches, Emilio, are truly as uplifting as a eulogy."

When Mustafa nodded in agreement, Emilio sighed and gave up. "All right, then. I don't feel like grappling with city officials about show permits, anyway. As long as we share fairly. I will continue to juggle, but I'll also play the wheel-fiddle like I used to—and I get a pay raise." He gave a shrug. "We need music, at least until we find someone else." He cast a dark glance at Johann. "Pity you burned the fiddle. We could've gotten good money for it."

"It was Peter's last wish, remember?" said Johann. He clapped his hands. "Now let's sell our horse and wagon. We have no use for either of them in Venice. And come springtime, I'm sure we'll find something better than that old nag."

He turned to leave, and to his secret relief, the others followed.

The city of Venice welcomed them with fog and rain.

They had boarded a barge at Mestre with all their crates and bags, and, along with numerous pilgrims, they'd set off toward the sea. The river ended in a brackish, foggy lagoon where a lonesome tower rose out of the mist.

"The Torre di Marghera," said Archibaldus, who had been to Venice as a young man. The old drunkard donned his best clothes for their arrival at the trading post, making him look almost dignified, the red nose and the matted hair aside. "The tower was the first structure the Venetians erected outside their city. And since then, they've conquered half the world."

Gradually, an entire city emerged through the dull, foggy haze. It seemed to hover above the water. Johann made out a maze of houses, palaces, churches, and bridges leading across many small canals. Fishing boats and larger ships were moored just outside the city, and a wider canal led right through town. More and more sounds came through the thick mist: the slapping of oars, the cries of the market women, the chiming of church bells. The saline smell of the water mingled with the scents of the city, and wafts of smoke, food, and filth surrounded them.

The barge was full to the last spot, and the low railing was almost level with the water. Despite the danger of falling overboard, the passengers pushed to the front to get a better view of the magnificent palaces lining the waterfront. Each building had its own dock with colorfully painted posts. Wide arches led into inner courtyards, and elaborately designed balconies adorned the upper stories.

Johann, too, was standing at the front of the boat. Black gondolas slid past him like swift fish. The gondoliers, standing at the rear, steered their boats into the smaller canals using long poles. Their passengers were ladies clad in satin and damask embroidered with gold and men wearing wide berets adorned with pearls and other trinkets. This city was so magnificent that by comparison, thought Johann, Augsburg seemed to live in an earlier era.

"Apparently, all this used to be lots of small islands," said Archibaldus, gesturing at the foggy waters in front of them, where Johann could make out several larger islands. "Over time, they grew together. The houses and even the lanes are resting on thousands of logs. But almost everything takes place on the water here."

The large canal took a bend, and then they saw a steep wooden bridge with two cranes in the middle. Both banks of the canal were bustling with people, and the lanes were full of market stalls. Just as they were heading toward the bridge, a loud horn sounded. The barge with the jugglers and pilgrims slid to one side, and Johann watched as the cranes pulled up the center piece of the bridge. A large galley with masts as tall as trees sailed past them. Waves caused the barge to sway from side to side, and some of the pilgrims cried out in fear. The galley passed through the bridge and the center piece was lowered again.

"I think it's better if we get off here," said Archibaldus, who was surprisingly sober. "God knows what other ships want to pass through the Rialto Bridge. The Fondaco dei Tedeschi isn't far from here."

Some of the pilgrims had also decided to disembark. The troupe gathered their belongings, and Mustafa carried the two heavy crates with the relics. Loaded like mules, they followed Archibaldus through a tangle of lanes and alleyways. It took Johann a few moments before he realized what was so strange about this city: there were hardly any wagons or oxcarts. Everything was transported via the canals. The lanes were so narrow that the troupe struggled to make any progress among all the pedestrians, shouting peddlers, beggars, and colorfully clad patricians. Johann noticed that the buildings' main entranceways always lay on the side of the water and included a small dock or pier, whereas the doors leading into the lanes were small and plain, more like servants' entrances. Archibaldus was right: life did take place on the water here, not on the land.

After a while they came to a building several stories high, with noise and shouting coming from inside. Johann could make out bits of German. An open gate led to a courtyard where many tables had been set up. Bales and crates were stacked up in front of the arcades surrounding the courtyard, and men wearing the bright garb of wealthy merchants walked around. Abaci and inkwells stood on the tables; pale-faced scribes sat hunched over documents bearing seals or entered numbers into lists.

Archibaldus grinned and pointed toward the courtyard. "The Fondaco dei Tedeschi. No other trading post in Venice is as busy as this one. The Germans are veritable penny-pinchers—especially the Swabians." He rubbed his hands. "Now let's go and see if the name Stovenbrannt still counts for anything in this city. Follow me."

He was about to walk into the courtyard when two broad-shouldered men wearing the typical jerkins and slit trousers of German soldiers blocked his way.

"No begging in here, old man," barked one of them in German. *"Capisci? Qui non si mendica!"*

"Dear gentlemen, I'm not here to beg but to speak with the German representative," replied Archibaldus as gracefully as possible, brushing a strand of tangled gray hair from his face. "Please tell him Archibaldus Stovenbrannt has returned after many years."

"Stovenbrannt?" The fatter of the two guards scratched his head. "Never heard of that name."

"Better not say that to the German representative," Archibaldus said sternly. "The Stovenbrannts used to sell nearly as much cloth in this town as those nouveau riche Welsers and Fuggers. Now off you go—we're expected."

The guard hesitated, clearly wondering whether he was looking at a drunk, confused old man or an influential merchant who could get him in a lot of trouble. Finally, he reached a decision.

"Wait here," he muttered.

He walked over to the arcades while the other guard continued to watch the colorful troupe in silence. After a short while, an obese man of around fifty wearing a beret and a fur-lined coat walked toward them. In his hand he carried his staff of office, which designated him as the German merchants' representative in Venice. When he saw the jugglers at the gate, his face darkened.

"You dragged me out of a business meeting for these jokers?" he snarled at the guard. "Throw them out and—"

"My dear Rieverschmitt," said Archibaldus, spreading his arms with a smile. "Don't you recognize old Archibaldus?"

The merchant frowned. "I can't say I—"

"Archibaldus Stovenbrannt. Remember?" Archibaldus pulled out his crumpled document and handed it to Rieverschmitt. "Perhaps this'll jog your memory."

The merchant skimmed through the brief letter, and his face broke into a strained smile. "Look at that, Hans Stovenbrannt's uncle. I do remember now, though it's been a long time. I was a young man then, and you were visiting your nephew in Hamburg. You . . ." He paused. "You studied for many years, they say."

Archibaldus gave a shrug. "No need to beat around the bush. I decided on a different career from the rest of my family. What you're reading there is a letter of recommendation for me and this exceptional troupe of jugglers I'm traveling with." He gestured at Johann and the others behind him. "You do need jugglers over the winter, don't you? The days are gray and boring, and if you want to close a lucrative deal, you first want to get your business partner in the right mood."

"It's true, we could do with a few jugglers, but . . ." Rieverschmitt eyed Johann and the rest of the troupe. He didn't seem particularly impressed. "Two young boys—juggling acts, I take it—and a huge Moor. And who's at the back?"

Until then, Salome had hidden her face behind a veil. Now she lowered it and took a step forward. The merchant gave a whistle and licked his lips. "By God, does this beauty have a price? I know a wealthy Venetian patrician who'd—"

Mustafa stepped forward and glowered at Rieverschmitt as if the man had just blasphemed against God and all the saints at once. The merchant sensed he'd made a mistake. "Well, I only thought—"

"Great, then we're all agreed," Johann said and positioned himself next to Archibaldus. "What about accommodation?"

"Um, well, you can't stay here at the Fondaco—not as jugglers," Rieverschmitt replied, his eyes still glued to Salome. "But many Germans stay at the Flute Inn. It's not far from here. Just tell them Rieverschmitt sent you."

"The Flute?" Salome smiled and gazed deep into Rieverschmitt's eyes. "I like to play the flute, signore. A fitting place for jugglers. I'm sure we'll get free meals and lodging there, right?"

"We . . . we can talk about that," said Rieverschmitt, squirming. "Best you move into your rooms first, and then come back and show me what you can do."

"We will," said Johann confidently. "You won't be disappointed, Master Rieverschmitt. Johann Faustus's Fabulous Troupe is the best troupe of jugglers you'll find in the entire German empire."

Johann Faustus's Fabulous Troupe . . .

Johann repeated in his mind the name he'd just come up with. It seemed to strike the right note, because Rieverschmitt grinned.

"Faustus, the lucky one? Well, we can always use a bit of luck at the count-inghouse. I'm expecting you back in an hour for your first show."

As promised, they performed at the Fondaco later that afternoon. Rieverschmitt seemed happy enough, but Johann got the impression that the trade represen-tative was mainly interested in Salome. She danced her seductive veil dance to a queer melody played by Emilio on his wheel-fiddle. Mustafa tore a massive chain apart and flexed his muscles, and Johann performed magic tricks, causing the merchants watching to gasp and laugh. Archibaldus appeared to be of the opinion that he'd fulfilled his part of the day's work by talking to Rieverschmitt, and he retreated beneath the arcades with a jug of wine. The others found him passed out behind some bales of cloth later. Johann wasn't particularly upset that Archibaldus hadn't been part of this important performance.

Johann agreed to Rieverschmitt's request that over the winter they give two small performances a day—one in the morning and one in the afternoon—to keep the German traders entertained. They received free board and lodging at the Flute Inn, and Johann even managed to negotiate a small sum the Fondaco would pay them each week. It wasn't much, but enough to make their winter much more pleasurable than if they'd had to spend it north of the Alps, where it was probably snowing by now.

But even in Venice, November was cool. A thick fog covered the city, and the troupe's clothes were always damp, no matter how many times they dried them before the fire. Johann roamed through the lanes, shivering, watching the black gondolas as they appeared from the mist and vanished again. In Saint Mark's Square, the large piazza, stood the biggest, most magnificent church Johann had ever seen. It was dominated by five domes that gave the building a fairy-tale quality—like a castle from the stories his mother used to tell him. A huge tower stood in front of the structure, and right next to it was the Palazzo Ducale, where the Venetian doge ruled over the republic.

Archibaldus had explained to Johann that Venice was ruled by a powerful council of patricians led by the doge. The patricians acted like small kings. They never strutted through the city without at least a page boy by their side, if not also a Moor serving as their slave. The high and mighty kept those poor people as if they were pets.

Even more than in Augsburg, pomp and misery, wealth and poverty lived side by side here. Ladies with hair bleached with lemon juice, wearing expensive silks and high platform shoes, tottered past gaunt, hungry street urchins and condemned men who were tortured publicly beneath the arcades of the doge's palace. There was an entire street dedicated to the manufacture of extremely precious mirrors, while a few streets down people were dying in the gutter.

Exploring the city helped Johann clear his head and gave him time to think. After just a few days, the troupe had accepted him as their new leader, along with their new name. No one asked where the Latin word *faustus* came from. In Venice, they acted more as court jesters than as jugglers performing set shows;

they'd exhibit a magic trick here and do a bit of juggling over there. On good days, they even sold a few bottles of the overpriced theriac Archibaldus brewed from cheap liquor and herbs. The magister touted it as an astonishing miracle tincture and didn't mind trying it out on himself. But the relics stayed in their chests; the troupe didn't want to risk getting in trouble with the Venetian authorities. Venice boasted plenty of relics of its own in its many churches.

Everything was going as well as it could, and yet Johann felt restless. Venice had been his goal, the star he'd followed ever since leaving Tonio. But now he realized that this city was just another station in his colorful life. And he didn't know how to handle Salome. He felt jealousy creeping up in him whenever men gaped at her as she swayed her hips to Emilio's music.

"I don't think you have to dance quite so salaciously," he told Salome one evening, following their show at the Fondaco. "One day some drunk will drag you behind the cloth bales."

"Maybe I want to be dragged behind the bales," Salome replied coldly. "Always remember: you don't own me, little wolf."

To take his mind off Salome, Johann continued his lessons with Archibaldus. He worked hard, getting up before sunrise to practice arithmetic or check the grammar in his writings. When Archibaldus quizzed him at lunchtime, the old man would sometimes pause and gaze at him thoughtfully.

"You're quick, Johann," he'd say, stroking his louse-ridden beard. "Almost frightfully quick. The devil knows how you do it."

Johann grinned. "I'm only at the start. Do you happen to know Greek?"

Archibaldus groaned. "A little. But I need a fresh jug of wine for that. Be so kind and fetch one, will you?"

The Fondaco grew quiet in December. The alpine passes were blocked by snow and ice, and no more German traders arrived in Venice. Instead, Rieverschmitt frequently received Venetian guests who were interested in German linen, salt, beeswax, silver, and amber. Often they'd feast together late into the night on wine, dried fish, and roast meat. The Venetians at their food with three-pronged forks—an item that was still considered a tool of the devil north of the Alps. Johann thought it was quite practical for keeping one's hands clean.

One particularly cold afternoon, when fires were lit in iron baskets throughout the Fondaco, Rieverschmitt pulled Johann aside.

"We're expecting very important visitors this evening," he said. "Several gentlemen from the *signoria* are coming tonight. I want you to put on your best show. It is crucial the councilors are well entertained."

"The signoria?" Johann frowned. "What's that supposed to be?"

Rieverschmitt laughed. "You might as well ask who is the king of the Germans! The signoria is the elite council, the most powerful panel in Venice. The doge is elected from their ranks, and they decide the city's politics. Those councilors are more powerful than many dukes and monarchs. And they are shrewd businessmen." He grinned. "This evening could mean a lot of money for the Fondaco."

Johann nodded. "You can count on us. Johann Faustus's renowned fabulous troupe of jugglers will put on a spectacular show for the mighty gentlemen."

Shortly after dusk, Emilio and Johann juggled burning torches on the quay as the Venetians arrived in their gondolas. Afterward, Salome danced her veil dance and let Mustafa toss her high into the air. Together they balanced on thin ropes suspended above the courtyard and performed cartwheels, and Mustafa swallowed three burning torches thrown to him by Emilio—a feat they'd learned only since their arrival in Venice. Johann had left Archibaldus at the inn with a jug of wine. He didn't want to risk the old man spoiling their show in a drunken stupor.

Like so many times before, one of the highlights was Johann's trick with the egg. He'd selected one of the Venetian councilors for the purpose, a pale older gentleman in a black coat. The man wore dark eye glasses that stayed on his nose with the aid of wires that hooked around the ears, giving him the appearance of a large insect or a snake. Johann had heard of such vision aids but never seen any before, which was probably why his attention had fallen on the tall signore.

The egg appeared in an inside pocket of the old man's coat, and the audience clapped as the man extracted it with the tips of his index finger and thumb. The pale patrician seemed surprised for a moment, but then he gave a mocking smile. He pulled out a sharp dagger, pierced a hole in the egg, and sucked it empty. Johann was reminded of a hissing black snake.

After the show, while Johann sat a little off to the side, enjoying a hot cup of mulled wine, the man approached him. Johann quickly put the cup aside and bowed low. He hoped the patrician wouldn't punish Johann for making a fool of him in front of all the others. But the man was smiling. He sported a pointed beard and bushy black eyebrows, and his face looked as white as if he'd painted it with chalk.

"Not a bad trick, young man," said the Venetian. He spoke quietly; his voice was a little hoarse. His German had a soft, exotic accent that seemed strangely familiar to Johann, somehow. "How did you know I like eggs?"

Johann grinned. Evidently, the man bore him no ill will. "You forget I'm a magician," he said with a wink. "And most people like eggs, don't they? Eggs are highly symbolic and play a role in many Christian customs."

"You're right, of course." The man gave a quiet laugh. Johann had the feeling that behind the eye glasses the patrician studied him with great interest. "Eggs contain life in its purest form. When we eat them, we eat life—we practically drink it in. A lovely thought, I believe."

The patrician gave a thin smile, and Johann thought once more that he looked like an old snake. "You seem to know a lot for a simple juggler," the man said after a few moments. "Or are you perhaps a traveling scholar? A monastery student who ran away from his abbot?" He smiled again. "Or from someone else, perhaps?"

"I . . . I have studied a little," replied Johann, proud that the man thought he was a student. "And I speak a little Latin and Greek."

"Indeed?" The patrician adjusted his glasses and eyed Johann intently. *"Quemadmodum omnium rerum, sic litterarum quoque intemperantia laboramus,"* he said.

"Non vitae sed scholae discimus," replied Johann, happy because he'd understood the man's test. It was a famous quotation by Seneca, which Archibaldus had taught him not long ago. *"Si tibi libet colloqui in hoc modo: homo Deus est,"* he added.

The last phrase had come out before he knew he was saying it. Johann remembered that Archibaldus had advised him not to utter it in public. And indeed, the patrician raised an eyebrow and tilted his head to one side. Johann suddenly felt he was being scrutinized, like a mouse sitting petrified before a snake.

"How do you know this phrase?" asked the man. "Man is God. Don't you know that the church forbids such talk?"

"Oh, I . . . I didn't realize . . . ," stammered Johann. He cursed himself for failing to keep his mouth shut. At least now he knew why Archibaldus had warned him: it seemed those words were proof of heresy. There were bound to be severe inquisitors in Venice following up every account of blasphemy. "I . . . I must have heard it somewhere," he said, trying to get himself out of the situation.

The man smiled coolly. "Don't worry, I won't tell on you. I like your wit and your cleverness. You crave knowledge, don't you?"

Johann nodded, relieved the conversation was taking a different turn.

"I live in a very old house in the Sestiere San Marco," continued the patrician. "My family owns one of the biggest libraries of Italy. Would you like to see it someday? I would be glad to welcome you there."

"Thank you, but that's . . . that's too generous." Johann blushed. "I'm just a simple juggler who—"

"Nonsense." The man waved dismissively. "I can tell that there's more to you than magic tricks with eggs." The man smiled. "Although you're trying hard to hide your true self underneath that ridiculous costume. I wasn't so fortunate as to be blessed with a studious son. If it helps, consider my wish a command. I will send you an invitation."

"An invitation? Who from?"

"Expect a letter from Signore Barbarese." For a brief moment, Johann thought he could see the man's eyes light up behind the dark glasses. He licked his thin lips, like he'd done earlier when he sucked out the egg. "You will like my library, I'm sure of it. *Arrivederci.*"

He turned and disappeared into the fog beneath the arcades like a large old reptile gliding into the water.

Late that night, Johann lay in bed thinking about the strange Signore Barbarese and his invitation. What were the Venetian's intentions? Johann had heard stories of men who liked to keep pretty boys as catamites. Was that the reason for the invitation? It wasn't just since Salome that Johann had become aware of the fact that he was a handsome young man; in their travels he had noticed several older men looking at him in a certain way.

The thought of Barbarese's long, spidery fingers stroking his skin made Johann feel sick; he found the Venetian creepy with his weird glasses and black clothes, which smelled as musty as if he'd risen straight from a grave. But Johann knew he couldn't refuse. Barbarese was a member of the signoria, the most powerful council in the city. If Johann didn't follow his order, they'd probably arrest him, lock him in some dingy hole, and leave him to rot.

The entire following day, Johann was distracted. During their morning performance he botched the easiest tricks, and Emilio studied him with a frown.

"What's the matter with you today?" he asked during a break. "I would say you're hungover, but I didn't see you drinking last night."

"I slept poorly," Johann grumbled. "That's all."

He decided against telling the others about the invitation. It was just between him and Barbarese; he didn't want to drag anyone else into it and potentially get them in trouble.

So he waited the whole day and the next, but no letter arrived. When there was still no word from Barbarese on the third day, Johann decided there wouldn't be a message. Perhaps the patrician had only been messing with him, or it simply wasn't important to him and he'd forgotten all about it. Johann felt relieved and returned his focus to the shows and rehearsals. He also continued his studies with Archibaldus, but the old man was nearly at his wit's end.

"I've got nothing left to teach you, lad," said the magister. "Your Latin is better than mine now, and I only know enough Greek to teach you a few dirty poems by Sappho."

"Then tell me more about arithmetic and geometry," said Johann.

"All right." Archibaldus sighed and started drawing lines on a piece of paper. "I will teach you Euclid's theorem. Watch this . . ."

An hour later, Johann was poring over formulas and prime numbers in his chamber at the inn. Archibaldus had left him with some exercises, and Johann was so engrossed in his work that he didn't hear the knocking at first. He started with fright when the sound grew louder.

"Yes?" he called out impatiently and pushed his papers aside.

It was one of the footboys Venetian patricians liked to use as messengers. When the boy handed Johann a sealed letter, Johann knew immediately who had sent it. The coat of arms showed a roaring lion and a Latin motto, as was typical for noble families.

Aude sapere.

"Dare to know," Johann whispered. He broke the seal and read the letter. The handwriting was old fashioned and written in dark-red ink, the color of blood. Signore Barbarese asked him to wait at the quay of the Fondaco dei

Tedeschi at nine o'clock that evening. The letter didn't say what would happen after.

Johann gave the boy a small coin and sent him away. Then he gathered his study materials and left a message with the innkeeper for Salome, saying that he had some errands to run after dark.

Johann had asked the innkeeper at the Flute for a lantern to help him find his way through the lanes. It was pitch black outside and, as usual, foggy. Not a single star could be seen through the clouds. Unlike the rich citizens who were still out and about, he couldn't afford an armed bodyguard. He relied entirely on his wits and the knife he always carried. Venice at night was a dangerous place—not only because of scoundrels but also because any wrong step on the slippery stones could send a man straight into the water. Alleyways often ended abruptly by a canal, the waters cold and black. Venice was a devilish labyrinth; most of the lanes had no names, and the best way to navigate through the city was by using the churches as points of reference along with the *campi*—old meeting places, of which each of the former islands had one.

Wearing his warm hooded jerkin, Johann hurried past several taverns with lights burning behind their windows. Then the voices, music, and laughter grew fainter and eventually ceased altogether. All Johann could hear now was the gurgling of the water as it gently splashed against the slimy walls of the canals.

Luckily, it wasn't far from the inn to the Fondaco. The guards knew Johann by now and let him pass once he explained why he was there. He hurried across the deserted courtyard, past crates and bales, and onto the quay. During the day, boats came and went constantly, and the German merchants argued over the best docking spots. Now it was as quiet as a graveyard.

A solitary black gondola bobbed on the water by the quay, illuminated dimly by a golden lantern in the bow. A gondolier clad in black was standing at the stern, his face covered against the cold and partially hidden by a wide-brimmed hat. He gave Johann a wave.

"Dimmi, èquesta la gondola del Signore Barbarese?" asked Johann in broken Italian. He'd tried to learn some of the language over the last few weeks. His voice sounded strangely thin in the fog, as if the darkness was swallowing it up.

The gondolier nodded silently, and Johann climbed into the boat. There was only one bench seat in the middle, covered with red velvet. Everything else was painted a dull black, even the oar. They set off the moment Johann sat. The gondola glided through the oily water and past the many palaces whose black silhouettes blocked out the sky.

It started to drizzle; icy drops of water ran down Johann's face as the gondola silently moved through the night. The gondolier didn't say a word, and the only sound came from the occasional slapping of the oar. A few times they passed other boats going in the opposite direction that, like theirs, carried a lantern at their bow. They were small dots of light in the fog, like stars in a sea of darkness.

A few hundred paces before the doge's palace, they left the Canal Grande and turned into a small side channel that led to a stately three-story building. It was richly decorated with mosaics and frescoes in a strange style, as if from a time before Christianity. Only one window high up was illuminated. The poles in the water bore the roaring lion that Johann already knew; a stone pier and a gate formed the entrance to the first floor. The gondola docked; the gondolier remained silent.

Johann rose and climbed out. He walked up a few slippery steps and reached an inner courtyard. A deathly silence lay over the place, and Johann was confused. This was supposed to be the palace of a Venetian councilman—where were the guards and the servants? The walls were crumbling, the frescoes looked faded; the corners were covered in cobwebs and the floor with dust. Had the gondolier taken him to the wrong house? Or could this be a trap, for whatever reason?

Johann was about to turn back to the quay when he noticed a servant in golden livery standing in a small alcove. He was a tall Moor and reminded Johann of Mustafa—probably because he was just as silent. He'd been standing still as a statue, but then he lifted a candelabra with white wax candles and walked ahead of Johann. A wide set of stairs with worn marble steps led to the upper stories. Johann reluctantly walked past lugubrious portraits of men who all shared a certain resemblance with Signore Barbarese. Between the portraits hung paintings of landscapes and Bible scenes; to his growing wonder, Johann noticed that some of the paintings had been hung upside down, while others were covered with black cloth. This house was becoming stranger by the minute.

Signore Barbarese was waiting for him in the corridor of the house's top floor. He wore a black jerkin that looked as old as the furnishings. It had a high collar and was cut very low on the chest. His leggings were so tight that his legs looked like those of a giant spider. He also wore the glasses, even though the hallway was dimly lit. When Johann approached the Venetian, the man spread his arms as if Johann were a long-lost son.

"How good of you to come," said Barbarese, dismissing the servant with a lordly gesture. "Forgive me for keeping you waiting, but I was, um . . . busy. But now you're here." He gestured toward the expensive damask wall hangings and portraits in the corridor. A chandelier cast the paintings in an eerie, flickering light. "So many beautiful pictures," said Barbarese enthusiastically. "They were painted by Gentile Bellini, a good friend of mine. Have you heard of him?"

Johann shook his head.

"What a shame—he's a true master in his field. Although a while ago, an artist named Dürer visited Venice, and I like his work, too. Apparently he comes from Nuremberg." Barbarese sighed. "It's a shame hardly anyone gets to admire my paintings. My wife died young and we weren't granted any children. Yes . . . I'm afraid the long line of Barbarese ends with me." He raised a thin finger that looked oddly animallike in the twilight of the candles, like a claw or a feeler.

"Our line can be traced back all the way to the first refugees who found a new home on these islands almost a thousand years ago—on the island of Torcello, to be precise. That's where mighty Venice was born. My ancestors came from Rome, where some Barbareses even became senators. But I'm digressing." Barbarese smiled, and Johann noticed how pale he was, as if there wasn't a drop of blood flowing through the signore's veins. But the poor light in the corridor probably didn't help. "I promised you a library," said Barbarese. "Well, here it is."

He pushed open a two-winged door, and Johann saw a large room with bookshelves from floor to ceiling. There were hundreds of books, parchment scrolls, and other documents. Johann stood rooted to the spot with amazement. He had never seen so many books at once before—not even in the Maulbronn monastery!

When Barbarese saw the expression on Johann's face, he gave a quiet laugh. "I knew you'd like it. To be honest, I've only read a fraction of these books myself. My eyes are getting worse all the time, and not even the glasses can change that. Allegedly, there are documents among those scrolls that survived the great fire of Alexandria. Some books are copies of the works of Greek scholars, and there's even a handful of Arabic translations. Books have always been the passion of my family. And this newfangled book printing is just astonishing.

Written works are going to be more accessible and cheaper in the future." He made a sweeping gesture around the room. "Make yourself at home, my boy."

"Do . . . do you mean I'm allowed to read all those books?" asked Johann, stunned.

Barbarese laughed again, and it sounded a little like the hissing of an adder. "I don't think you'll quite manage to get through all of them. But you're welcome to study here and borrow some books, too. I'm looking forward to discussing the contents with you."

Still feeling like he was in a trance, Johann nodded. Then he slowly walked toward the shelves. The books were bound in old cracked leather. There were piles of parchment scrolls and tattered documents covered in Latin handwriting. Johann shyly started to pull a few books from the shelf. He leafed through a heavy tome entitled *Opus Majus*, written by someone named Roger Bacon. Then he replaced it and chose another work, *Poetics* by Aristotle, whom Father Antonius and Father Bernhard had told him about.

"Feel free to make use of the table and chair. There is ink and a quill if you want to take notes," said Barbarese. "Over there you'll find wine, cheese, and bread in case you're hungry. I'm going to leave you for a while now—and then we can discuss what you've read, if you like. My gondolier will take you back to the Fondaco at dawn. All right?"

Johann nodded, but his thoughts were with the wealth of books surrounding him. He sat down at the table and started to read.

"Enjoy," said Signore Barbarese.

Then he closed the door and left Johann on his own.

At first Johann felt like he was sitting at a table filled with so many different delicacies that he didn't know which one to sample first. He leafed through crackling pages of parchment, gently brushed his fingers over bindings, admired the colorful letters, and deciphered Latin and Greek titles just to return them to the shelf and hastily pick another volume. Some of the books were as large and heavy as cobblestones, while others were small and easy to handle, with pages made from the finest vellum. Most of them were handwritten, copied by monks who'd lived a long time ago. Johann found beautiful illustrations on some pages; the elaborately adorned first letters of chapters were true masterpieces. Johann inhaled the smell of ancient dust, glue, and lye.

After a while he started looking through the books more slowly, and he became absorbed by writings about the tides of the seas, explanations of the function of optical lenses, and illustrations of the open human body. One of the images even showed an embryo in its mother's womb. Whenever he found something particularly intriguing, he jotted down notes. Some of the books were locked with heavy padlocks, and Johann wondered what could be so bad that people weren't allowed to read it. They bore titles like *Dialectica* and *Periphyseon*. Others seemed to be about Jewish cabalism or the Cathars, a Christian sect whose treatise bore the title *Liber de Duobus Principiis*—the book of two principles. One of the locked books was by Albertus Magnus, the man whose praises Father Antonius had sung at Maulbronn so long ago. It was entitled *De Secretis Mulierum*; Johann assumed it explored the secrets of the fairer sex.

As promised, Signore Barbarese returned after a few hours. Johann hadn't touched the wine or the food; he'd been too engrossed in the books. They spoke about some of the works Johann had read, and Barbarese asked questions or made suggestions that gave Johann food for thought.

Shortly before dawn, the black gondola carried Johann back to the trading post, where he slept for an hour or two before Salome shook him awake.

"Where have you been?" she asked sulkily. "Your bed was empty and I was cold."

Johann rubbed his eyes. Despite the lack of sleep, he felt strangely refreshed and rested. "You've got your secrets and I've got mine." He placed his finger on her lips. "That was the deal, wasn't it? 'You don't own me.' Your words."

Salome studied him pensively for a while. Then she smiled. "Let's see if that hussy left anything for me," she said and grasped him between the legs.

They made love hard and fast, and Johann enjoyed the fact that Salome thought he had a lover.

Not one, but hundreds, he thought as she straddled him. *Every one of those books is like a virgin waiting to be discovered.*

~

The gondola was there for him each of the following nights. At Signore Barbarese's house, the host welcomed him politely and led him to the library. He was always dressed in his old-fashioned garb and never once took off his glasses. After a few hours of studying in solitude, they would engage in lengthy conversations, during which Johann learned more than he'd learned with Archibaldus in a month. The topic of discussion frequently was man and his position in regard to God and the church.

"The scholasticism as it is taught by the church assumes there are invariable facts—irrevocable truths—that must not be questioned," explained Barbarese. "Everything is laid down in the old scriptures. There is no room for creative thought, except perhaps in the way God's words are interpreted. But if you're not careful, you're a heretic—even though humans are perfectly capable of observing the world around us and drawing conclusions. We ourselves can dissect the world to find out what's in its innermost heart and finer veins, see all its energies and seeds. Many scholars have chosen this path by now and have turned their backs on the church. Times are changing, Johann. I own notes by a certain Leonardo da Vinci—a very clever man who works with geometry, mechanics, human anatomy, and many other subjects. His genius is like that of a creator, a god."

"But man can't be God," replied Johann. "Behind everything, even behind us, there must be something else—a higher power of some kind, God. What sort of a world would this be if it was based on coincidence, on chaos?"

Barbarese smiled. "Well, it would be a very human world, wouldn't it?"

During the day, Johann was increasingly sleep deprived, especially since Salome pushed him harder than ever. She was jealous of his imaginary new lover, and she desired him and demanded him with a passion that left Johann hollow and spent. He was frequently unfocused during their shows now, and his temper returned, especially because the troupe was beginning to make new mistakes. Their routine had become a daily grind, and the plentiful wine and good food were taking their toll. Johann, too, blundered in ways he wouldn't have a few weeks ago.

"You look more dead than alive," said Emilio one day after a show in which Johann had nearly hit Salome with a knife. "Are you ill? Do you need some rest?"

Johann shook his head grimly. "You worry about your own problems," he said gruffly. "And throw the balls to me better next time, or I'll start looking for a new juggler."

Emilio stared at him in silence, and Johann felt bad about his remark. He wasn't getting enough sleep, and that made him irritable, though his mind was awake as never before. He couldn't stop thinking about Barbarese's books—not when he was at the Fondaco or in his chamber, and not even during his time with Salome.

At least he had stopped studying with Archibaldus. The old man didn't seem to mind, believing there was nothing more he could teach Johann anyhow. But he worried about Johann.

"Something's up with you, boy. I can tell," said the old man.

"What do you mean?" Johann gave a shrug. "I'm growing up and making up my own mind about things."

"A Venetian ducat for your thoughts," murmured Archibaldus.

Johann often borrowed books from Barbarese's library now so that he could continue his studies at the inn. He was always careful to hide them under the bed so Salome and the others wouldn't see them. He didn't feel like justifying himself for being distracted. The books were his secret, his treasure, his hoard that he was protecting like a dragon.

The weeks went by, and Johann became increasingly uncommunicative and brooding. He spent Christmas alone in his chamber with his books, telling Salome that he was bed-bound with a fever. He snarled at the others during rehearsal. If something didn't work right away, he practically exploded. The only time he felt happy was during his nightly conversations with Barbarese. They still discussed God and man, but also inventions and man's latest discoveries. But they never spoke about the books with the padlocks.

It was almost February when Johann gathered his courage and asked Barbarese about those mysterious volumes. The signore smiled as if he'd been expecting the question.

"Those books contain knowledge that isn't for everybody," he said after a few moments. "Some readers might feel, well . . . overwhelmed by their contents."

"Why?" asked Johann.

"Because they question the world as we know it. No, they rattle its very foundations. Our view of the world relies on a God at its helm. But what if . . ." Barbarese paused. "What if that God doesn't exist? What if man is his own master? If he can take charge of everything? Even life and death! Man would be the architect of his own fortune."

"That would be heresy," said Johann.

The idea of there being no God was preposterous. Johann felt a black abyss opening up beneath him at the mere thought of it. Everything he knew and held dear—the whole world around him—was built on the fact that God existed. God was the beginning and the end. He made trees grow and flowers blossom; He granted good harvests and brought fertile rain and mild winters. And He alone decided when a man's time on earth was at an end. A world without God seemed impossible.

"Well, now you know why those books are locked," Barbarese replied. "Some books can kill the weak, but they can open up new worlds to the strong."

"I want to read those books," said Johann stubbornly.

Barbarese eyed him thoughtfully. "Are you sure?" Then he gave a laugh. "To hell with it! I can tell you've made up your mind. All right, then. I trust you won't hand me over to the church." He pulled a large key ring from a pocket and went over to the shelves. "I think we'll start with Leonardo da Vinci. I met him in Milan a few years ago. He had written thousands of pages of notes and drawings. When I asked him if I could have some, he didn't even look up from his work. He's a genius! A painter and inventor who represents nature as it actually is and doesn't just copy the way the church likes it." The signore smiled. "The notes are a little chaotic, but they give you a good idea of what the man is capable of. I had them bound and chose one of the artist's drawings for the cover." Barbarese picked a key and opened a book bound in black leather; on its front was an image of a naked man standing at once in a circle and a square with outstretched arms and legs. Barbarese handed the book to Johann with an almost reverent gesture. "Read it and let me know what you think. But you must promise not to take it back to your inn. The book's contents are too dangerous."

Johann promised, and Barbarese left the library. The book was like a bucketful of cold water in the face. Johann had never seen anything like it. The illustrations were the most fascinating part. With astonishing intricacy, the man had drawn war machines, boats propelled by paddle wheels, flying apparatuses, and suits that apparently enabled a person to breathe under water. Cut-open bodies displayed life so clearly that Johann thought all the sinews, bones, and organs looked like they were part of a large clock. The notes were difficult to read, especially because large sections had been written back-to-front like some kind of secret code. Still, Johann soaked up much of it like a dry sponge.

When Barbarese returned a few hours later, Johann was still spellbound.

"I'm glad you like it," said Barbarese. "I knew you were ready for it."

"He writes a lot about machines," said Johann. "But all these anatomical sketches suggest man himself is also a kind of apparatus that can be repaired. And somewhere Leonardo da Vinci writes that one day, man might be in a position to decide over life and death himself—do you think that's really possible?"

He thought about Margarethe and young Martin, and of his mother, who had died of a disease Father Antonius wanted to treat with moldy cheese. He thought about all the victims of the Black Death, which people blamed on some sort of vapors coming from the ground or on original sin—so much speculation and so many dated beliefs without any research or proof. The notes in front of him could achieve so much if they were developed in the right way!

Barbarese gave him a long, thoughtful look from behind his glasses. "To conquer death would be the crown of human achievement," he replied eventually. "If anyone can do it at all, it would take years—decades—of dedicated studying. But yes, I think it's possible."

"I want to learn it."

Barbarese laughed softly. "One thing at a time, my young adept. One thing at a time."

Over the next few weeks, Johann studied Leonardo da Vinci's notes and other books, like Roger Bacon's *Opus Majus*, in which the author turned against traditional scholasticism. Johann read that it was the people's fear of authority and their dependence on popular opinion that prevented them from thinking independently. In his *Epistola de Secretis Operibus Artis et Naturae,* Bacon prophesied that one day there would be machines that enabled humans to fly like birds. Anything was possible!

The books with the padlocks discussed science and machines, but also forbidden philosophy and magic. Increasingly Barbarese picked out volumes for Johann that weren't just about the sciences but also about magic—white as well as black. And it was no silly hocus-pocus like Johann had first practiced with Tonio del Moravia, but a secret, esoteric field of study that asked questions no one had ever asked before. There were no boundaries in that world, and nothing was forbidden.

"If we want to understand the universe as a whole, we must leave no stone unturned," said the signore. "There can't be any taboos—it's the only way for man to achieve godly wisdom. *Homo Deus est.*"

And for the first time Johann thought he truly understood what that sentence meant.

~

That night, while Johann continued to peruse da Vinci's and Bacon's works and tried his hand at a few sketches of his own, Signore Barbarese went into his secret chamber. A steep ladder led to the attic, where a well-concealed door led into Barbarese's demesne: a tiny room full of books whose contents were so frightening and revolutionary that the signore didn't dare keep them in the library.

In one corner stood a wardrobe full of wigs, fake beards, and costumes, just like in the travel chest of a juggler.

Dangling from a beam of the roof was a cage with two crows and a raven.

"I think he's ready now," said the master, sitting at a small table in front of a silver-framed Venetian mirror. He took off his glasses and wig and wiped the soot from his eyebrows. "What do you think, Baphomet, Azazel, and Belial?"

The birds screeched, cawed, and flapped their wings. The master silenced them with a wave of his hand. He carefully peeled away the beard from his lips and studied his pale reflection in the mirror. He had always been good at disguising himself.

"You can't force them," he said as he wiped away the white makeup. "Never. It's the law. They must come of their own free will. That's how it always has been. Sometimes it just takes a little longer."

Humming a tune, he took a piece of paper from a drawer in the table and started to write a long letter. When he was done, he folded and rolled it up until it was as small as the finger of a child; he sealed it with wax as red as blood. Then the master opened the cage and took out the raven. At first the animal wanted to peck at him, but then it flapped its wings with fear.

"*Kraa!*" cried the raven, sounding whimpering, childlike. "*Kraa, kraa!*"

"Good boy, Baphomet," said the master. "Always remember your reward. Only those who obey me will receive salvation."

The master pushed the tiny paper scroll through a ring on the raven's right claw. He double-checked that it was secured properly, then he nodded and walked over to the window with the raven.

The master pushed the shutters open wide. Pale moonlight fell into the small room and illuminated the chalky, expressionless face with its still slightly sooty eyebrows.

"Tell them that he's ready," said the master. "The arrival is near."

He threw the raven out into the night like a black snowball, and the bird spread his wings and headed north, toward the mountains.

12

JOHANN GREW INCREASINGLY WITHDRAWN, AND THE OTHers hardly ever saw him. As far as they knew, he left his chamber only for the shows. Contrary to his promise to Signore Barbarese, he had taken some of the forbidden books with him to the inn, including some works on sorcery. It had been easier than he'd thought—Barbarese had left them unlocked on the table in the library. Johann simply hid them beneath the other books he was borrowing. It was almost like Barbarese had wanted Johann to take them.

Thus passed January and February, and with March came the birds. There was chirping all through the city, and people no longer wore long, warm coats. Spring put a smile on everyone's face, and even the perpetual fog withdrew. When the days started to get warmer, the jugglers began to ask how much longer they'd stay in Venice. Johann's replies were always evasive. He didn't want to leave this city, least of all Barbarese's library, where he felt like his eyes were being opened afresh every day. He hadn't thought of Margarethe, his mother, or little Martin in a long time; he kept his dark memories locked up deep inside.

One afternoon in March, Johann was so engrossed in his reading that he didn't hear the knock on the door. When he started up, it was already too late. Archibaldus had entered his room.

"I wanted to check on you, lad," he said. "The others are worried about you and—"

He broke off when he saw the books on the bed. "Where did you get those?"

"None of your business," snarled Johann, gathering up the books. He shoved them under the bed, but Archibaldus had already deciphered one of the titles.

"*The Sworn Book of Honorius*?" Archibaldus turned pale. "Who gave you that?"

"I told you it's none of your business!" shouted Johann feverishly.

"My boy, you don't know what you're doing." Archibaldus raised one hand in a placating gesture. "Whoever gave you this book dabbles in things that are too dangerous for a young student, no matter how talented."

"Perhaps they are too dangerous for an old drunkard," Johann jeered. "But not for me. Now please leave. I want to study."

Archibaldus gave him a serious look. "I always knew there was something dark inside you, Johann," he said eventually. "It went into hiding for a while, but now it seems to have returned. Please don't let it take over—I'm begging you! It would destroy you and maybe even those you love. You're clever and keen to learn, and you could become someone great—or someone very dangerous." He hesitated. "I've got a suggestion for you. You said it was your greatest dream to study at Heidelberg University. I could ensure your dream comes true."

Johann blinked with irritation. "And how are you going to do that?"

"I still have a little influence. And I know the right people. What do you say: you leave those books alone, and in return I'll get you a spot at Heidelberg." Archibaldus held out his hand. "Agreed?"

"I . . . I'll think about it," Johann said and spurned the old man's hand. "But now I'd really like you to leave."

"May God protect you," said Archibaldus. "I fear something deeply evil is trying to grab ahold of you."

Johann woke from his fixation on the books only once.

One day toward the end of March, Rieverschmitt came rushing up to him in a state of excitement.

"We need you for a bigger show tonight. The first German merchants have arrived at Venice. It was a long winter and there's still snow on the passes, so not much comes through. There is a huge demand for their wares. The Venetians want to butter them up, so please think of something special."

Johann nodded distractedly. His thoughts were on other matters. Barbarese's books robbed him of his sleep. But he knew he couldn't disappoint Rieverschmitt if he didn't want to jeopardize his stay in Venice. There were so many books left to read. It pained him to think that he wouldn't be able to visit Barbarese that night.

"You can always rely on Johann Faustus's Fabulous Troupe," he said and gave a strained smile.

A few weeks ago, Johann had taken some Venetian jugglers under contract for larger shows. One pleasant result was that it put pressure on Emilio. Johann thought the young juggler had become a little too complacent in the last few months and no longer practiced enough. And he was always badgering Johann with the question of when they'd leave Venice. But so far, Johann had managed to convince him to stay.

Even though he barely slept, Johann had his troupe under control and even managed to negotiate a higher wage with Rieverschmitt. The jugglers had become a fixture at the Fondaco. If they wanted to, they could stay for the whole year—maybe even forever, as Johann secretly hoped. He continued to spend the nights at Signore Barbarese's, although the previous night, he'd had the feeling he was being followed there. A gondola appeared to follow his at some distance, but he hadn't been able to make out any details in the evening fog.

The German merchants started to arrive at the trading post around sunset. There were more than a dozen of them, their heavily loaded vessels lying low in the water. The train of merchants included numerous footmen and even some mercenaries who had helped them to safely get their wares across the Alps. When the servants carried the crates and bales into the storehouses, Johann saw the finest Augsburg cloth, amber, furs, and chests full of silver. The risky journey had undoubtedly paid off for the merchants; they'd get an excellent price for their goods.

The troupe received the merchants with music and juggling at the quay. The tables set up in the courtyard were bending under the weight of the food. Three of the hired Venetian jugglers beat drums and played the lute while Salome danced seductively.

Their show later on was a huge success. Germans and Venetians applauded and tossed coins at them; several men lay drunkenly under the table or vomited in a quiet corner. Archibaldus snored with his head on the table, his tousled beard hanging in a puddle of wine. Johann hadn't used him for their shows in a long time. He'd avoided the old man since their argument at the inn but noticed that Archibaldus eyed him with suspicion whenever he wasn't too drunk.

Before the show and the feasting, the German merchants had closed their deals and earned a fortune. Even Rieverschmitt's face glowed red with alcohol and excitement. Visibly drunk, he waved Johann over to him late in the evening.

"Didn't you say once that you are from the Kraichgau region?" he asked with a heavy tongue. "From Knittlingen?"

Johann nodded. "Why do you ask?"

Rieverschmitt grinned and gestured at an equally drunk merchant beside him, who was struggling to sit up straight. "This gentleman here comes from a neighboring town, from Bretten. I thought perhaps you know him. His name's Klaus Reuter."

Johann was shocked. He felt a wave of homesickness at the thought of meeting someone from home here in faraway Venice. But at the same time, he was afraid the man might know him. He had made a good name for himself here at the trading post. Rieverschmitt thought Johann was much older than he actually was, and Johann had told him he was the third son of a wealthy cloth-making family. Johann nervously studied the drunk merchant, but he'd never seen the corpulent man with the saggy cheeks and the piggy eyes sunk deeply into his doughy face. Still, he knew the Reuters were a respected merchant family in Bretten and had produced many burgomasters. They also traded with the Maulbronn monastery and in Knittlingen. Did this man know his stepfather?

Johann forced himself to smile. "How nice to see someone from home. How are things in the Kraichgau?"

The man burped loudly. "Well, the Swabians are getting pushier all the time," he said with a broad Kraichgau accent. "Last year, Württemberg was made a duchy by the king and doesn't know where to put all its power. People are talking about war."

"What about Knittlingen?" asked Johann shyly, his heart beating faster. Could it be possible that Klaus Reuter knew Margarethe? Her father was the prefect, after all. "How is business going there?"

Reuter gave a shrug. "I stayed at the Lion for the first night of our trip. That was back in fall. The wine is awfully sour this year." He grinned and took a large swig from a goblet made of blue Venetian glass that sparkled in the light of the torches. "Nothing compared to this excellent grape juice."

Johann cleared his throat and made another attempt. "I knew the prefect a little. My father used to do business with him. You don't happen to know how he's doing?"

"The Knittlingen prefect?" Reuter laughed. "I can't say he's doing too well. He wanted to marry his daughter off to a Bretten merchant's son—a good match. Young Schmeltzle may not be the most handsome lad, but the family's got money. What can I say? The girl lost her mind."

"Is . . . is that right?" Johann struggled to keep the quiver from his voice. "How come?"

"No idea." Reuter wiped some drops of wine from his fleshy lips. "That was almost two years ago now. She stopped talking and just lay in bed like a cold fish." He burped again. "The wedding didn't happen, not least because she'd allegedly lain with another man—some young smart aleck. Her father gave her to another man, a vintner from Heidelberg. He was the only one who didn't ask questions and didn't mind the small dowry."

"So Margarethe lives in Heidelberg?" asked Johann quietly, more to himself.

The merchant seemed to wake from his stupor. "Margarethe, huh?" The piggy eyes scrutinized Johann closely. "How do you know her name, boy?"

"Um, didn't I mention that our fathers occasionally had dealings with each other?" replied Johann, standing up hastily. "It was nice talking with you, Master Reuter. Give my regards to the Kraichgau when you return."

Before the man could say anything else, Johann turned away. He gave Rieverschmitt one last nod and rushed out into the Venetian night. He needed to be alone now, alone with his thoughts. As the fog wet his face with dew, Johann repeated one name over and over.

"Margarethe, Margarethe, Margarethe . . ."

His greatest love, his only love, had entered his life again.

In the following days, Johann struggled to focus on his studies. Every time he bent over the books at Barbarese's library, he thought he could hear Margarethe's laughter. The signore noticed that he was distracted.

"What is it, my boy?" he asked with a frown. "I was under the impression that you were seriously interested in my collection. But now you're unfocused and keep staring out the window." Barbarese eyed him suspiciously from behind his glasses. "Has someone talked to you? Has anyone found out about our nightly meetings? Speak up!"

Johann shook his head. "I'm just tired, that's all. I think I need a little rest."

"Well, if that's the case," Barbarese said, smiling and placing an ice-cold hand on Johann's shoulder, "take a few days off. I will tell my gondolier to pick you up again next Friday. Enjoy your time off and take a good look around Venice. It's the most beautiful and most curious city in the world. But you must promise me one thing." He raised a finger and spoke slowly and intently. "You speak with no one about this library and the books inside it, understood? The consequences could be"—he hesitated—"incalculable. For you, too."

Johann nodded, glad to be dismissed. Everything had become a little too much for him in the last few days. He needed some quiet time and some distance—especially from Signore Barbarese and the books that seemed to drain him.

During the following days he only went to the Fondaco for their shows, spending the rest of the time walking the lanes of Venice. But as much as he admired all the palaces, churches, and canals, he couldn't find peace. He hadn't been able to stop thinking about Margarethe since the German merchant had told him about her. How was she doing? Was she speaking again? He was filled with a deep longing that pushed aside all other thoughts.

On the afternoon of the third day, Johann sensed that he was being followed. His pursuer didn't try very hard to hide his intentions, or perhaps he wasn't very good at it. Like a shadow, he kept ducking into gaps between houses or alcoves, always trailing twenty or thirty paces behind Johann. When the figure followed Johann into a narrow alleyway, Johann hid behind an old barrel. When he heard the quiet footsteps approach, he jumped out with his knife raised. He was about to put the blade to his pursuer's throat when he stepped back with surprise.

"Archibaldus!" exclaimed Johann. "What . . . what are you doing here? What's this about?"

Magister Archibaldus held up his palms. "Forgive me, but I saw no other way to talk to you in private."

"So you follow me halfway across Venice?" asked Johann. "You could have seen me in my room."

"It's not safe there." Archibaldus looked about himself. "And neither is it here. Come with me!"

Before Johann had time to protest, Archibaldus had dragged him into an even smaller alleyway. Washing hung on lines between the close walls of the houses; some hungry cats were fighting underneath a bridge. The air smelled of rotten fish and stagnant brackish water. They entered a small church that lay at the edge of a campus and was empty at this time of the day, apart from two elderly women in the front pew. The late-afternoon light fell through the narrow windows and onto an altar decorated with dried roses. It was as cold as winter inside the church.

"What's all this about?" asked Johann again. "Have you had too much to drink again, Archibaldus? Admit it!"

The magister gave a desperate laugh. "Oh, I wish I had! Then the truth would be easier to bear. But no, I'm stone-cold sober. Well, almost . . ." He lowered his voice. "I know now who you're visiting every night, Johann. And you ought to know the truth about him."

"So it was you who followed me the other night?"

"Salome asked me to. She . . . she thought you were with some harlot or another, and she was jealous. But I've long been suspecting something else. Your temper, the way you've become withdrawn, and then those books you had in your chamber. *The Sworn Book of Honorius* and those other books of spells—"

"What are you getting at?" snapped Johann. He wanted to get out of this cold place as fast as possible.

"I made some inquiries about your host, Johann." Archibaldus was speaking close to Johann's ear, and he reeked of alcohol. Evidently, he wasn't quite as sober as he'd said.

"Your Signore Barbarese, as he calls himself, is known to move in certain circles," whispered Archibaldus. "Oh yes, he's rich and powerful! So powerful that no one dares to touch him, no matter how much they whisper behind his back."

Johann couldn't help but smile. "And what do they whisper? That he eats snakes? Admittedly, he does look like an adder, but—"

"Signore Barbarese is a Satanist."

"A what?" Johann stared at Archibaldus with his mouth open.

"You know exactly what I'm talking about," hissed Archibaldus. "Barbarese is a devil worshipper. His family has been practicing the cult for centuries, probably since pre-Christian times. Nothing could ever be proven. But they say he's involved in horrific ceremonies, nightly rituals with human sacrifices. Sometimes he's gone for long periods of time—for years, even. But when he returns to Venice, he . . . he . . ." Archibaldus faltered.

"He what?" asked Johann.

"Well, he seems strangely rejuvenated. There are people who say he must be ancient. Not even the oldest men in Venice remember Barbarese ever being a child."

"But that's nonsense!" replied Johann. "Ghost stories spread by jealous competitors. And devil-worshipping ceremonies . . ." He gave a laugh. "If that were true, I'd know about them, wouldn't I? As you know, I've been at Signore Barbarese's house nearly every night. We talk about literature. I can't see anything satanic about that. And I've never seen him draw pentagrams on the floor of his house." He tried to sound mocking but failed. He couldn't help thinking of the meeting in the woods with Tonio and Poitou. They, too, had been followers of some kind of satanic order.

And they had sacrificed humans.

Johann thought about the squirming bodies in the trees. He'd managed to suppress that memory for so long, and now it came back with a vengeance. He shuddered, and this time it had nothing to do with the cold in the church.

"So? Have you considered my proposal?"

Archibaldus's question tore Johann from his thoughts. "What do you mean?" he asked. "What proposal?"

"You stay away from Barbarese and his books, and I get you into Heidelberg University."

Archibaldus fished a wine-stained folded document from under his coat and held it out to Johann with a trembling hand.

"This is a letter of recommendation to a friend who got somewhere with his studies—unlike me. His name is Jodocus Gallus, and he teaches as a magister of the liberal arts at Heidelberg. He's even made it to rector. The letter bears the seal of my family." Archibaldus gave a sad smile. "Lucky I haven't pawned my signet ring for a bottle of brandy yet. It came in handy for once. When we're finished in Venice, go to Heidelberg and give Jodocus my regards. You will get far with the right teacher, Johann!"

"Thank you." Feeling a little embarrassed, Johann accepted the sealed paper.

Archibaldus turned deadly serious again. "There's something else I must tell you. It's about your former mentor, Tonio del Moravia. I finally know where I've heard the name before. It sounds incredible, but—"

Archibaldus broke off when someone entered the chapel. The figure remained in the dim twilight and moved into one of the dark side aisles, where it stood in silence. The person might have been someone who'd come to pray, or the priest preparing for the next mass, or a harmless pilgrim . . .

Or someone who followed us here, thought Johann.

He shook himself. Now he was becoming as paranoid as drunken Archibaldus.

"We can't talk here," whispered Archibaldus. "I want to make a few last checks before I can be absolutely certain, anyhow. The truth would be . . ." He broke off as if afraid of his own words. "I want you to come to Torcello tomorrow morning," Archibaldus whispered. "It's a small island in the Venetian lagoon. They say the first Roman refugees settled there. Perhaps that's why they chose the place, or perhaps they've always been there."

"What do you mean, *they?*" asked Johann.

"On Torcello, follow the old canal to the Ponte del Diavolo, the devil's bridge. From there, go to the old basilica. All will be explained there. I'll be waiting for you. And now go with God."

Archibaldus squeezed Johann's hand, stood up, and hurried toward the entrance. The door opened with a squeak, and the old man disappeared into the dusk. A cool draft blew in from the door and swept the rose petals from the altar.

When Johann looked back to the dark side aisle, the figure from earlier had vanished.

13

MAGISTER ARCHIBALDUS DIDN'T COME TO THE FONDACO
for the evening show, nor was he at the inn when the others returned. But no
one seemed particularly worried.

"He probably just had one too many again, and now he's sleeping it off in
some alleyway," said Emilio with a shrug. "Let's pray he didn't fall and drown
in one of the canals."

Johann said nothing. He'd spent the last few hours contemplating what the
old man had told him about Signore Barbarese and how he'd mentioned Tonio,
too. Was there a connection between the two men? He thought about Barbarese's
old house, about the upside-down paintings and the many books about sorcery.
Tonio would have enjoyed those books.

The knowledge Johann had drunk in at Barbarese's library was enormous,
as vast as the ocean, and behind every thought, every idea, lurked another flash
of inspiration.

And another abyss.

Johann's thoughts returned to Margarethe. She had been afraid of Tonio
the magician as a child. And, he guessed, she'd be afraid of the Johann of today,
too: the grim, taciturn fellow who was consumed by books and who sought his
salvation in books of spells and sorcery. Suddenly, Johann saw himself through
Margarethe's eyes and realized how much he'd changed. Were the books to
blame? Was Signore Barbarese actually a devil worshipper?

Johann knew he'd have to speak to Archibaldus again to find out with
certainty—provided the old man wasn't dead drunk and already regretting his
remarks from earlier.

"I'm going to look for Archibaldus tomorrow," he told the others. "He must be somewhere."

"Stay with me for tonight at least, and don't go running to your whore," said Salome, running her hand through his shaggy black hair.

He slept poorly that night, dreaming repeatedly of Margarethe. She staggered toward him with outstretched arms, her face covered in blood. But when he tried to approach her, she shrank back. Her face turned into that of Salome and then that of his mother.

Go away, go away, she breathed. *You . . . are . . . the . . . devil . . .*

Early in the morning, Johann awoke bathed in sweat. He turned to the sleeping Salome and kissed her gently on the cheek. Then he set off for the island of Torcello, as Archibaldus had instructed him.

He asked his way to a quiet quay in the city's east with the help of gestures and his broken Italian. Several fishing boats moored here, and apparently they also went to the smaller islands of the lagoon. For a few coins, an older fisherman with a weather-beaten face agreed to take Johann to Torcello.

While the small boat slowly sailed through the lagoon's still waters, Johann gazed at the many islands in front of them. Some were tiny, nothing more than a few rocks, while others held villages with churches and monasteries. He'd heard that the Venetians sent their sick and their lunatics to the islands, as well as seamen and travelers suspected of having contracted the plague. Other islands served as walls of defense, and others again were used to grow crops or pasture livestock. On one of the largest islands, the Venetians manufactured their world-famous glass. They guarded their secret painstakingly, and there were harsh penalties in store for any treason.

Torcello was a rather plain, swampy island whose shoreline was overgrown with impenetrable reeds. The only spot to moor was at a weathered pier, and beside it, an old canal that had almost completely filled up with silt led inland.

The fisherman had talked about Torcello during the entire crossing. From the little Johann understood, he gathered that the island was indeed the oldest settlement in the lagoon, much older than Venice. Thousands of people used to live here, but then something terrible happened. Johann wasn't sure if he'd understood correctly, but apparently Torcello had been punished by God. The people had left the island, and now only a few peasants with their sheep and cows lived there. The old fisherman had shaken his head and repeated one word several times.

Maledetta.

Johann gathered that he meant the island was cursed.

What in God's name might Archibaldus want to show him here? Maybe the old boozer had truly had too much to drink.

Johann climbed out of the wobbly boat onto the pier. The fisherman made the sign of the cross, turned his sail into the wind, and took off. Johann had asked him to return at sundown. He only hoped the superstitious old man would keep his promise—otherwise he'd be stuck there.

A towpath led along the muddy, algae-covered canal inland. Hundreds of mosquitoes buzzed around Johann and turned every step into torture. They rose in huge swarms from the salty marshes that stretched on both banks of the canal. Every now and then a solitary cow stared at Johann as he passed by, but he saw no other living soul. Ruins covered in thorny brambles showed how many people used to live on the island. Why had they all left Torcello? Had God sent a flood to punish them for their sins? And what sins could they be?

After a while he came to a low stone bridge that led across the canal. He assumed it was the Ponte del Diavolo, the devil's bridge. The old fisherman hadn't been able to tell him why it was called that—or perhaps Johann hadn't understood.

Johann could see, rising up between the trees not far from the bridge, a bell tower and the roofs of a smaller church and a taller, three-aisled basilica. Johann still hadn't seen another person. He passed by some derelict houses and finally reached the two churches that were connected by an arcade walkway. They were situated at the edge of a square that probably used to be the center of town. A few ruinous buildings surrounded the square, and the bell tower stood behind them. The square itself was overgrown with bushes, and in the middle of it stood a large chair made of stone, like a throne used in ancient heathen ceremonies. This must have been a bustling place once, with markets and court trials. Now the only sound came from the buzzing of the mosquitoes.

A sudden noise made Johann spin around. An old man was getting to his feet amid the ruins with the help of a cane. He must have been resting among the rocks.

"Buongiorno!" called Johann. But the man didn't reply. He just stood there and stared at Johann.

"Sto cercando un uomo," Johann tried again. *"Si chiama Magister Archibaldus. Lo conoscete?"*

Still the man said nothing. A flock of pigeons rose up from the ruins behind him, and then the silence returned.

Johann gave up. He entered the smaller church, whose bare stone walls inside looked naked. There was no sign of anyone. He took the walkway toward the basilica, his solitary footsteps echoing loudly.

The basilica's double doors were closed, and when Johann opened one, a heavy red curtain blocked his view. It smelled musty, as if it had been hanging there for centuries. Johann pushed it aside and gazed into the large space in front of him. Tall, narrow windows allowed some light to fall upon golden mosaics so magnificent that Johann shuddered. They showed the Virgin Mary with her child and the twelve apostles. The apse was separated from the rest of the church with columns and a splendidly decorated choir screen. High up above the screen, a sad-eyed savior looked down at Johann.

There was no sign of Magister Archibaldus.

"Archibaldus?" called Johann, his voice echoing through the huge space. "Are you here?"

The sound of dripping came from somewhere, as if it was raining and the roof had a leak.

Drip . . . drip . . . drip . . .

Johann called out once more, but there was no reply. He decided to give up. Archibaldus wasn't there. The old man had probably had too much to drink the day before and told Johann some old wives' tale. Or was he waiting somewhere else on the island? But there wasn't anything else here apart from swamp, mosquitoes, and the overgrown square. Johann feverishly tried to figure out what to do next. Clearly, his trip to the island had been for nothing. But the worst part was that the fisherman wouldn't return until sundown. He was stuck here until then.

Drip . . . drip . . . drip . . .

The steady dripping unnerved Johann. His anger at that drunken old codger grew with every second. What had Archibaldus been playing at, sending him here? Damn it, if he really had anything to tell Johann, he could have done so in Venice and not on this mosquito-infested, godforsaken island! Hopefully he'd find another fisherman to take him back to the city. Or—

Drip . . .

That goddamned dripping! It sounded like it came from somewhere behind him. What could it be? Annoyed, Johann turned around—and froze.

Since he'd set foot in the basilica, he'd looked only to the front, to the altar. The entire back wall was covered by a huge mosaic that reached right up to the high ceiling. It showed the Last Judgment. At the top, people awaited their fate before God. From a Christ medallion in the center, a glowing stream of fire fed the flames of hell below. Angels forced the unhappy souls into damnation with their lances; snakes crept out of the eye sockets of dozens of skulls, and heads of kings were roasting in the eternal fire. To the left of the door, enthroned on a seat with a dragon's head, was Hades, the lord of the underworld, and in his lap sat the Antichrist himself. He was displayed as a handsome young man wearing a toga, and his eyes seemed to stare straight at Johann, as if waiting for a reply.

And hanging beneath the Antichrist was Magister Archibaldus.

Like a mockery of the crucifixion scene, the old man had been nailed to the wall with heavy nails, his face frozen in a grimace of horror. Blood was dripping from the hole in his left hand, which hung down loosely at his side.

Drip . . . drip . . . drip . . .

For a long while Johann could do nothing but stand there and stare at the gruesomely staged scene. The culprit or culprits must have crucified Archibaldus alive, because it looked as though he'd managed to free his left hand before he died. Using his own blood, Archibaldus had written three words on the wall with his finger. They were badly smudged and barely legible, but Johann thought they spelled a French name.

Gilles . . . de . . . Rais.

"Gilles de Rais," whispered Johann, and something crept up the back of his neck as if the sound of the name alone sent waves of fear and terror through his body. "What in God's name . . ."

Speaking the name of the Lord in front of the crucified old man suddenly seemed wrong. He broke off and felt a wave of nausea wash over him; his legs almost gave way. He flashed one last look at Archibaldus's twisted face and ran out of the basilica, along the arcade walkway, through the smaller church, and finally outside.

The old man was standing directly outside the door.

Johann almost ran right into him. He screamed and jumped back. The old man grinned, baring his almost-toothless gums.

"Il diavolo," he mumbled. *"Benvenuto nella casa del diavolo."* Then he chortled softly.

Johann pushed the grinning old man aside and ran across the square toward the muddy canal. He needed to get away from here, no matter how! He ran along the canal without looking back. Almost blind from sweat and persecuted by a swarm of mosquitoes, he rushed past the devil's bridge and toward the shore, which was somewhere behind the crippled trees and the crumbling ruins. Finally he caught sight of the rotting pier. The words of the old man echoed through his head.

Benvenuto nella casa del diavolo.

Welcome to the house of the devil.

Far out in the gray waters of the lagoon he could see fishing boats, but they were too far away to hear him. There must be some way to get off this—

A solitary low bell sounded.

Johann spun around in panic. The sound had definitely come from the campanile by the two churches. Had that crazy old man rung the bell?

Another chime rang out.

In the distance, right about where the square in front of the churches lay, Johann saw a small cloud of dust rise into the air. Something was brewing there.

Something was coming closer.

A third stroke of the bell.

Without thinking about it, Johann started racing along the shore like a hunted animal. The bell was just ringing out for the fourth time when he spotted a small rowing boat covered with rotten leaves amid the reeds. A fisherman must have hidden it there, maybe one of the few people who still lived on the island. Maybe even the man from earlier. The boat was flat and looked rather rotten, with several inches of bilgewater within it. But at least there were oars. Panting, Johann pushed the boat out into the water and jumped inside. The vessel rocked dangerously, but it didn't sink and didn't take on more water. As the bells continued to toll, Johann rowed as if the devil himself was after him. His heart raced. He only slowed down a little when the shore was nothing but a thin brown stripe. He tried to catch his breath.

He scanned the distant shoreline one last time—and started with fright once more.

Someone appeared to be standing on the pier. Johann blinked several times, but he was too far away to make out any details. Still, he thought the figure wasn't the old man from before, but someone else.

It was a man, and he waved as if asking Johann to come back.

Johann knew this was impossible. What he was seeing was merely a figment of his panicked imagination. But far, far away and at the same time deep down inside him, a voice called out again and again, asking him to return to Torcello, the island of the devil.

It was the voice of Tonio del Moravia.

It took Johann a good three hours to make it back to the Flute Inn. He rowed over to the isle of Burano, from which a larger fishing boat carried him to Venice. When the fishermen gave the young man with the chalky-white face and the flickering eyes a closer look, they decided not to ask where he had come from. There was something sinister about the black-haired youth, something as ominous as the scent of pestilence, and the men were relieved when they dropped him off at the quay in Venice.

During the silent crossing, Johann had come to a decision: he would leave Venice that very day. He had no idea what had happened on Torcello or why Archibaldus had to die in such a cruel way, but evidently it had something to do with Signore Barbarese and the man's library. Archibaldus had tried to warn Johann and paid with his life—but not without leaving him one last clue. A name.

Gilles de Rais.

Johann had never heard the name before, but he sensed that he was in grave danger. Those who had crucified Archibaldus wouldn't hesitate to kill him, too. The magister had been right: Signore Barbarese really was a devil worshipper, or at least had something to do with those circles. There was no other explanation for the cynical execution at the church. Barbarese must have been afraid that Archibaldus would betray his secret. And so he'd punished the poor old man in a gruesome manner. But what was it that Archibaldus had wanted to show Johann on Torcello? What secret lay on the swampy island?

On his way back to the inn, Johann kept looking over his shoulder in the narrow lanes. His enemies could be anywhere. But try as he might, he couldn't spot any pursuers. Out of breath, he rushed up the stairs to his chamber and immediately began stuffing clothes into his travel bag. When he was about to pack his knife away, he paused with fright. For the first time in a long while he noticed the initials engraved in the handle.

G d R.

"Gilles de Rais," whispered Johann.

Could it be possible? Had this knife belonged to the man whose name Archibaldus had written on the church wall in his blood?

A sound caused him to spin around. It was Salome entering his chamber. She took only a moment to grasp what Johann was doing.

"You're leaving?" she asked, crossing her arms on her chest. "Without a word of farewell? Without telling us where you're going and why?"

Johann slipped the knife back into his pocket and continued to pack. "Trust me, Salome, it's for the best. All I'm going to bring you is misfortune—all I'm bringing anyone is misfortune!" He laughed with despair. "And I don't even know myself yet where I'm going. I've been running for so long. I think it doesn't matter where I go—they'll find me."

"They?" Salome frowned. "Who's going to find you?"

Johann didn't reply and continued to stuff things into his bag. Salome watched him in silence for a while, and then she said, "I told you once that you don't own me, Johann, and that's true. But still, I feel something with you that I've never felt with any other man."

"And what is that?"

"Jealousy. If that's the beginning of love, I'm glad it's coming to an early end." Salome gave a bitter smile. "You don't fool me, Johann. You've met another girl and you're going away with her. You haven't been with me for weeks. Even when you entered me and made me moan with lust, you were somewhere else. You were with her the whole time. And now you're leaving with her."

"Jesus Christ, I'm not going with anyone . . . ," began Johann, but then he stopped. Perhaps it was better if Salome believed it was another woman. It would help Emilio and Mustafa understand his sudden departure, too. He had never fully belonged to them, had always remained an outsider, just like in his old life.

A stranger among men.

"Did you find Archibaldus?" asked Salome abruptly.

Johann hesitated for a moment, then nodded. He didn't want his friends to find out about Archibaldus's brutal death. Whoever had done that would kill anyone who knew too much—or sacrifice them.

Twitching bodies in the trees . . .

"He . . . he told me he was tired of life with a troupe," he lied. "Apparently the German merchants offered to take him back to Hamburg with them. He still has a few living relatives there who are willing to put him up for the remainder of his days. He took a boat to the mainland first thing this morning."

"Well, his relatives better make sure they order enough wine." Salome smiled. "It's probably for the best—both for him and for you. Neither of you are jugglers. You never have been and never will be."

Johann nodded and tied up his bag.

Who am I? he wondered.

"And where are the two of you going now?" asked Salome.

"The two of us?" Johann was puzzled for a moment, then he remembered. "Oh, we'll figure something out," he replied, trying to sound lighthearted. "Just like Peter Nachtigall and his beloved back then. Remember? He loved a girl he wasn't allowed to marry. They ran away together and . . ."

He trailed off.

"What is it?" asked Salome.

Johann looked up. It was so blindingly obvious. Why hadn't he thought of it sooner?

He loved a girl . . .

Margarethe had saved him twice already. Once during the eerie ceremony in the forest near Nördlingen, and for the second time here in Venice, at Signore Barbarese's library. Both times her laughter had led him back to the right path.

He prayed she'd do it for him a third time.

Margarethe alone could show him where to go.

"We're going to Heidelberg," said Johann with a strong voice. His hand felt for the letter Archibaldus had given him the day before. He'd almost forgotten about it in all the excitement. Now it might really be of help.

"I know someone there I must go see. It's important—a matter of life and death."

"Is that so? Life and death?" Salome walked up to him and stroked his cheek. "Then go, my little wolf. I will never forget you." She winked at him. "Or one particular body part of yours, at least."

Johann leaned down to give her one last kiss, but she turned away.

"Goodbye, Salome," he whispered.

Then he shouldered his bag and walked down the stairs and out into the dusk. It took a pile of money and all his skills of persuasion to find a ferryman willing to take him to Mestre on the mainland at this time of the evening.

As the boat glided through the night like a blade, the lights of Venice sparkled behind him.

"Margarethe," said Johann softly, pushing Archibaldus's letter deep into the pocket of his jerkin, where he also kept his knife. "I'm coming, Margarethe. I'm coming to find you. Everything is going to change."

His words sounded like a magical spell more powerful than any other spell in any other book in any other library anywhere in the world.

Act IV

The Student and the Girl

heir brows. They seemed proud and aloof to Johann, who looked down at his wn dirty clothes with embarrassment. All of a sudden he felt completely out of lace, like a stupid peasant at the court of a king. It took all his courage to ask ne of the students about the name Archibaldus had given him.

"You want to see Rector Jodocus Gallus?" The student didn't look much der than sixteen, but he eyed the taller Johann with a mix of mocking and ntempt. "If you've come to beg the old man for a penny, let me tell you that e honorable doctors don't earn nearly enough to feed scroungers like you. u're better off going to the Augustinians—they'll give you a bowl of gruel."

Johann clenched his fists but forced himself to stay calm. "I haven't come to g but to deliver a letter to Doctor Gallus," he replied coolly.

The student gave a shrug. "Try at the *schola artistarum* next to the monas- y. I think old Gallus might be holding a lecture." He raised a finger. "But you ter not disturb the class—or you'll be in deep trouble!"

Johann turned away without another word. After searching for a while, he lly found a smaller single-story building close to the Augustinian monastery. oked new, like many other houses in this part of town, with whitewashed s and expensive crown-glass windows. Johann could hear monotonous Latin tals through the open windows. He looked inside and saw a long room d with about two dozen students sitting on wooden benches. Some were taking notes, but most of them looked as though they needed to sleep ast night's feasting. Their heads kept slumping forward in regular intervals, eupon their neighbors would giggle and elbow them. Standing by a lectern e front of the room was an older, stern-looking man, wearing a gown and g about arithmetic. A blackboard on the wall behind him was covered in ly scribbled formulas and calculations. Johann knew many of the terms, e listened intently, holding his ear as close to the window as he could. It een a long time since he'd last exercised his mind. He drank in every word man dying of thirst.

o his disappointment, the lecture was soon over and the students pushed way outside. Johann gathered from their relieved expressions and scraps of rsations that they'd meet again for their next bender in just a few hours. hann waited a few moments before entering the room. The man at the n was packing his papers into a leather satchel. He was almost completely nd very thin; his gown hung loosely on him like clothes on a scarecrow.

14

JOHANN ARRIVED IN HEIDELBERG ON A SUNNY DAY IN JUNE in the year of the Lord 1496.

His coat was dusty and full of holes, his jerkin and shirt had been patched up half a dozen times, and his toes stuck out from gaps in his shoes. With pinched lips and grim determination in his eyes, he clutched his crudely carved staff as he walked toward the large wooden bridge spanning the Neckar River. On the other side stood the city gate, the houses and churches, and an imposing castle on a hill.

Many times during the last few months when Johann thought he couldn't go on, he had invoked two images in his mind: the moment when his eyes would first behold Heidelberg, and Margarethe's look of surprise when she recognized him and embraced him joyously. Those daydreams had carried him through the boiling heat of the Po Valley and Lombardy, across the Brenner Pass, and through the many counties, duchies, and principalities beyond. He had fallen ill on the pass, struck down by a strong fever that kept him bedridden for several weeks. Kindhearted pilgrims had found him unconscious and bathed in sweat by the wayside and carried him to a hostel. In his fever dreams Johann had seen Magister Archibaldus time and time again, nailed to a cross and always mutter- ing the same words.

You're guilty . . .

Yes, he had loaded an enormous guilt upon himself. Archibaldus had been murdered because of something he'd wanted to tell Johann, because the old man had wanted to help him. He'd wanted to protect Johann from something unspeakably evil—and from the darkness that slumbered within Johann like a small animal and that broke out from time to time.

As Johann gradually and very slowly recovered—a gentle old monk spoon-feeding him soup three times daily, like a small child—he often thought about the name Archibaldus had written on the church wall at Torcello with his own blood.

Gilles de Rais.

Johann still didn't know what that name meant. He studied the initials on his knife repeatedly but still couldn't figure it out. Perhaps it was just coincidence that the name bore the same initials as his knife—although Johann didn't really believe in coincidence anymore.

He'd matured in the last few months like a good, earthy wine in the barrel. He was eighteen years old now, with wiry muscles tough as hemp ropes. He'd cut his curly black hair and beard with a knife the day before, making him look almost like a monk. His face had become haggard and angular, his eyes gleamed dark and mysteriously, and there had been more than a few maidservants and daughters of innkeepers who had made sheep's eyes at him along the way. He had ignored them all, as if he really were a monk. He was urged on by his love for Margarethe and the hope that everything would be different from now on. Sometimes he thought of Salome, and of Emilio, Mustafa, and poor Peter. He had enjoyed his time with the jugglers, but that journey hadn't shown him where his path was leading, what his goal was supposed to be.

Perhaps he was finally looking at his goal.

With long strides he paced across the bridge that now, around noon, was busy with peddlers carrying their willow packs and farmers steering their oxcarts toward town. Armored horsemen vociferously demanded room, and a troop of grim-looking mercenaries with slit shirtsleeves and polished cuirasses marched past Johann.

These were the days leading up to Saint John's Eve, the feast when the longest day of the year was celebrated across the Palatinate with burning wheels of straw and hill fires. Finally summer had arrived—although it wouldn't be long before fall and winter would replace the lengthy, warm days again.

Johann watched laughing children running across the bridge and holding sticks decorated with colorful ribbons, painted eggshells, or sweet yeast pretzels. Johann could hear music coming from the city and smelled delicious wafts of fried food. He realized he'd eaten nothing but a stale piece of bread that day. His

savings from Venice were almost completely gone, and he'd been holdin[g] his last few coins for his arrival in Heidelberg.

The week before, his journey had led him very close to Knittlingen[.] been filled with a silent longing, but most of all he'd felt pain. He had n[ot] to return to the city of his childhood. Why would he go where everyo[ne] him? And those he had loved were either dead or no longer there. If h[e] going to return to Knittlingen, he wanted to do so with his head hel[d] a magister or doctor, even.

Johann's hand went to the pocket where he still kept the letter A[rchibaldus] had given him. He'd touched it so many times that the paper was thi[n] ing at the edges. He prayed that this document would indeed help h[im] the university. Archibaldus had gotten them into the Fondaco dei Te[deschi] all, so perhaps the Stovenbrannt name still bore some weight.

Johann had been to Heidelberg once before, as a small child w[ith] father, and he remembered the bridge and the new castle that sat e[] the opposite slope beneath an older fortress. Wedged between the foothills of the Odenwald Mountains lay the city, which had grown over the last decades.

On the market square, Johann bought one of those sweet pre[] the children carrying, from a baker who had set up his stall be[] umns of the large red sandstone Church of the Holy Spirit. He in expensive clothing and admired the pretty gables of the house[s] along the paved main streets. This city didn't stink half as badly he'd passed through.

Johann stopped and cast a reverent gaze at the electoral ca[stle] was no Augsburg and certainly no Venice, but it was where Ph[ilip] ruled; as count palatine, he was one of the most powerful rule[rs] One of his ancestors had been the king, and another relative, Ruprecht I, had founded Heidelberg University more than a hu[ndred] It had always been Johann's dream to study here, and he cou[ld] that it might actually become reality.

The lanes around the market square were bustling, and Joh[ann] to the university buildings. They lay on both sides of a street n[ear] the Holy Spirit in the city center. A group of students clad i[n] gowns were just emerging from a chapel, wearing their ber[ets]

14

JOHANN ARRIVED IN HEIDELBERG ON A SUNNY DAY IN JUNE in the year of the Lord 1496.

His coat was dusty and full of holes, his jerkin and shirt had been patched up half a dozen times, and his toes stuck out from gaps in his shoes. With pinched lips and grim determination in his eyes, he clutched his crudely carved staff as he walked toward the large wooden bridge spanning the Neckar River. On the other side stood the city gate, the houses and churches, and an imposing castle on a hill.

Many times during the last few months when Johann thought he couldn't go on, he had invoked two images in his mind: the moment when his eyes would first behold Heidelberg, and Margarethe's look of surprise when she recognized him and embraced him joyously. Those daydreams had carried him through the boiling heat of the Po Valley and Lombardy, across the Brenner Pass, and through the many counties, duchies, and principalities beyond. He had fallen ill on the pass, struck down by a strong fever that kept him bedridden for several weeks. Kindhearted pilgrims had found him unconscious and bathed in sweat by the wayside and carried him to a hostel. In his fever dreams Johann had seen Magister Archibaldus time and time again, nailed to a cross and always muttering the same words.

You're guilty . . .

Yes, he had loaded an enormous guilt upon himself. Archibaldus had been murdered because of something he'd wanted to tell Johann, because the old man had wanted to help him. He'd wanted to protect Johann from something unspeakably evil—and from the darkness that slumbered within Johann like a small animal and that broke out from time to time.

As Johann gradually and very slowly recovered—a gentle old monk spoon-feeding him soup three times daily, like a small child—he often thought about the name Archibaldus had written on the church wall at Torcello with his own blood.

Gilles de Rais.

Johann still didn't know what that name meant. He studied the initials on his knife repeatedly but still couldn't figure it out. Perhaps it was just coincidence that the name bore the same initials as his knife—although Johann didn't really believe in coincidence anymore.

He'd matured in the last few months like a good, earthy wine in the barrel. He was eighteen years old now, with wiry muscles tough as hemp ropes. He'd cut his curly black hair and beard with a knife the day before, making him look almost like a monk. His face had become haggard and angular, his eyes gleamed dark and mysteriously, and there had been more than a few maidservants and daughters of innkeepers who had made sheep's eyes at him along the way. He had ignored them all, as if he really were a monk. He was urged on by his love for Margarethe and the hope that everything would be different from now on. Sometimes he thought of Salome, and of Emilio, Mustafa, and poor Peter. He had enjoyed his time with the jugglers, but that journey hadn't shown him where his path was leading, what his goal was supposed to be.

Perhaps he was finally looking at his goal.

With long strides he paced across the bridge that now, around noon, was busy with peddlers carrying their willow packs and farmers steering their oxcarts toward town. Armored horsemen vociferously demanded room, and a troop of grim-looking mercenaries with slit shirtsleeves and polished cuirasses marched past Johann.

These were the days leading up to Saint John's Eve, the feast when the longest day of the year was celebrated across the Palatinate with burning wheels of straw and hill fires. Finally summer had arrived—although it wouldn't be long before fall and winter would replace the lengthy, warm days again.

Johann watched laughing children running across the bridge and holding sticks decorated with colorful ribbons, painted eggshells, or sweet yeast pretzels. Johann could hear music coming from the city and smelled delicious wafts of fried food. He realized he'd eaten nothing but a stale piece of bread that day. His savings from Venice were almost completely gone, and he'd been holding on to his last few coins for his arrival in Heidelberg.

The week before, his journey had led him very close to Knittlingen. He had been filled with a silent longing, but most of all he'd felt pain. He had no reason to return to the city of his childhood. Why would he go where everyone hated him? And those he had loved were either dead or no longer there. If he was ever going to return to Knittlingen, he wanted to do so with his head held high, as a magister or doctor, even.

Johann's hand went to the pocket where he still kept the letter Archibaldus had given him. He'd touched it so many times that the paper was thin and tearing at the edges. He prayed that this document would indeed help him get into the university. Archibaldus had gotten them into the Fondaco dei Tedeschi, after all, so perhaps the Stovenbrannt name still bore some weight.

Johann had been to Heidelberg once before, as a small child with his step-father, and he remembered the bridge and the new castle that sat enthroned on the opposite slope beneath an older fortress. Wedged between the river and the foothills of the Odenwald Mountains lay the city, which had grown dramatically over the last decades.

On the market square, Johann bought one of those sweet pretzels he'd seen the children carrying, from a baker who had set up his stall beneath the columns of the large red sandstone Church of the Holy Spirit. He saw burghers in expensive clothing and admired the pretty gables of the houses as he walked along the paved main streets. This city didn't stink half as badly as other towns he'd passed through.

Johann stopped and cast a reverent gaze at the electoral castle. Heidelberg was no Augsburg and certainly no Venice, but it was where Philip the Upright ruled; as count palatine, he was one of the most powerful rulers in the empire. One of his ancestors had been the king, and another relative, Count Palatine Ruprecht I, had founded Heidelberg University more than a hundred years ago. It had always been Johann's dream to study here, and he could hardly believe that it might actually become reality.

The lanes around the market square were bustling, and Johann asked his way to the university buildings. They lay on both sides of a street near the Church of the Holy Spirit in the city center. A group of students clad in the typical black gowns were just emerging from a chapel, wearing their berets rakishly low on their brows. They seemed proud and aloof to Johann, who looked down at his own dirty clothes with embarrassment. All of a sudden he felt completely out of place, like a stupid peasant at the court of a king. It took all his courage to ask one of the students about the name Archibaldus had given him.

"You want to see Rector Jodocus Gallus?" The student didn't look much older than sixteen, but he eyed the taller Johann with a mix of mocking and contempt. "If you've come to beg the old man for a penny, let me tell you that the honorable doctors don't earn nearly enough to feed scroungers like you. You're better off going to the Augustinians—they'll give you a bowl of gruel."

Johann clenched his fists but forced himself to stay calm. "I haven't come to beg but to deliver a letter to Doctor Gallus," he replied coolly.

The student gave a shrug. "Try at the *schola artistarum* next to the monastery. I think old Gallus might be holding a lecture." He raised a finger. "But you better not disturb the class—or you'll be in deep trouble!"

Johann turned away without another word. After searching for a while, he finally found a smaller single-story building close to the Augustinian monastery. It looked new, like many other houses in this part of town, with whitewashed walls and expensive crown-glass windows. Johann could hear monotonous Latin recitals through the open windows. He looked inside and saw a long room filled with about two dozen students sitting on wooden benches. Some were busy taking notes, but most of them looked as though they needed to sleep off last night's feasting. Their heads kept slumping forward in regular intervals, whereupon their neighbors would giggle and elbow them. Standing by a lectern at the front of the room was an older, stern-looking man, wearing a gown and talking about arithmetic. A blackboard on the wall behind him was covered in hastily scribbled formulas and calculations. Johann knew many of the terms, and he listened intently, holding his ear as close to the window as he could. It had been a long time since he'd last exercised his mind. He drank in every word like a man dying of thirst.

To his disappointment, the lecture was soon over and the students pushed their way outside. Johann gathered from their relieved expressions and scraps of conversations that they'd meet again for their next bender in just a few hours.

Johann waited a few moments before entering the room. The man at the lectern was packing his papers into a leather satchel. He was almost completely bald and very thin; his gown hung loosely on him like clothes on a scarecrow.